PRAISE FOR
AWAKENING THE MYSTIC

"*Awakening the Mystic* is a wonderful, inspiring story of how yoga can change one's life. The main character and I share more than 1.13 as our birthday, we also share the belief in the power of meditation—that anything is possible when we drop into stillness and return there as needed. We are that stillness. That stillness is our true essence. This story is so compelling in its telling. I recommend it to anyone who needs to be inspired that love is the greatest power on Earth."

—LILIAS FOLAN, the First Lady of Yoga, host of *Lilias!* on PBS
from 1970 to 1999, author of *Lilias! Yoga Gets Better with Age*

"Read this book and get a cosmic jumpstart for transformation in your spiritual life. This is a story of hope, love, truth, mystical teachings, and an evolutionary spark for humanity. This is no ordinary book. It is a road map for revolutionary mysticism, filled with profound teachings from the yoga tradition, astrology, meditation, and about accessing superconscious states of being. Rob Dorgan has hit the mark in his extraordinary novel, *Awakening the Mystic*, and weaves the teachings with a riveting story that opens the heart, expands the mind, and invokes the power of grace into the whole of life. Imaginative, transformative, and radically alive, this book will awaken the mystic in you!"

—SIANNA SHERMAN, international yoga teacher,
founder of Rasa Yoga Collective, Mythic Yoga Flow®
and RITUAL, a 13-Moon Mystery School

"From the very first page, *Awakening the Mystic* envelops you in a world where the lines between reality and the divine blur in the most enchanting ways. The journey Rob invites us on is one of introspection, healing, and profound discovery. Through the book's intertwining of fiction and memoir, it offers a beacon of hope and wisdom for those yearning to understand the deeper mysteries of life and love. An absolute must-read for anyone seeking to unlock the secrets of the universe within themselves."

—RICHARD C. MILLER, PhD, founder of iRest Institute, author of *Yoga Nidra: The iRest Meditative Practice for Deep Relaxation and Healing*

"*Awakening The Mystic* is a multifaceted jewel of a love story. It reminds me of the luminous threads that weave us together in beauty and the sacred adventures that await us when we trust in the divine mystery and follow the path of the heart. This miraculous story is medicine for the magical soul in all of us."

—MEREDITH HOGAN, shamanic healer, singer-songwriter and vocalist with Goodbye Gemini, founder of the Beauty Way Collective, owner of Embra Wellness Studios, Yogini, spiritual guide

"Mystical, ethereal, and humane, *Awakening the Mystic* is imbued with the metaphysical elements of yoga. Fans of the Yoga Sutras attributed to Patanjali—and everyone that seeks to understand their true nature more clearly—will love this novel as it traverses the deepest questions of life, love, and the nature of reality."

—ANDREA FERRETTI, host of *Yogaland* podcast

"Wow! I was instantly pulled into this journey about facing and conquering our fears with love and compassion. *Awakening the Mystic* is an inspiring and fascinating journey of self-discovery. The twists, turns, poetic prose, ancient manuscripts, time travel—I laughed. I cried. But most importantly, it left me with hope for our species and our planet. Read it!"

—PAUL S. BOYNTON, author of *Begin with Yes* and
Be Amazing, motivational speaker, social media guru

A NOVEL OF COSMIC LOVE AND HEALING

AWAKENING
THE
MYSTIC

ROB DORGAN

RIVER GROVE
BOOKS

This book is a work of fiction. Names, characters, businesses, organizations, places, events, and incidents are either a product of the author's imagination or are used fictitiously. Any resemblance to actual persons, living or dead, events, or locales is entirely coincidental.

Published by River Grove Books
Austin, TX
www.rivergrovebooks.com

Rumi quotes from the book *Rumi: The Beloved Is You* by Shahram Shiva are used with the permission of Rumi Network, www.Rumi.net.

Distributed by River Grove Books

Design and composition by Greenleaf Book Group
Cover design by Greenleaf Book Group
Cover images used under license from
©Adobestock.com

Publisher's Cataloging-in-Publication data is available.

Print ISBN: 978-1-63299-899-6

eBook ISBN: 978-1-63299-900-9

First Edition

AUTHOR'S NOTE

As you begin this journey . . .

. . . What if we could tap the power of the mind to heal ourselves and others?

. . . What if we realized reality is far more than what is tangible, touchable, and provable?

. . . What if we looked upon all Beings as God—the Divine?

. . . What if we could tap into the power of the divine feminine to heal the planet?

. . . What if we all recognized the beautiful Mystery of Life?

. . . What if we realized all our relationships are mirrors of the Divine Love we seek?

. . . What if love never dies?

. . . What if we are living in a time of Revolutionary Mysticism?

This is a work of fiction with intertwined elements of a memoir. It is instilled with hope for the future of humankind as we move through the unknown.

As you read,

and live,

and breathe,

stay open to possibilities.

1

A NEW JOURNEY

" *I want to find inner peace.*"

At age nine, that was the first line I penned in my journal. It was a clue to the lifelong intensity that still resides inside me.

My parents had recently divorced, and my mother had become the sole support for my brother, Dave, and me. Working as a waitress, she was gone many nights until midnight. Dave, who was ten years older, had recently moved out at nineteen to explore, grow, and find his way. Alone in the house much of the time, I sat behind an overstuffed chair in the living room waiting . . . for someone. While I was waiting for my mom to step through the front door, I was also anticipating someone or something far more etheric. I had no words for the otherworldly expectation as I huddled alone in my hiding space, but this time of deep introspection at such an early age put me in touch with a vivid world that existed behind my closed eyes.

The three-story, six-room shotgun house built in the 1890s had been in my family for four generations. It was located in a densely populated neighborhood in Newport, Kentucky, just across the Ohio River from Cincinnati. The houses were so close to each other that even as a kid, I could stand between any two and stretch my arms out and touch both.

From the third floor of the house, I could see the bridges and the impressive skyscrapers of the big city. My urban neighborhood was a racial and religiously mixed hybrid.

Growing up Catholic, I'd always loved the elaborate ritual of Mass, with the soft light of the candles, the wafting scent of frankincense, and the melodic rhythm of chanting. Yet, even as a kid, I felt something was missing from the religion of my ancestors. With the blessing of my mom, I explored the different religions of my neighborhood friends—from attending Protestant vacation Bible school to partaking in seder meals to joining in rollicking services where the congregation was saved and spoke in tongues. Yet none answered my questions about life, death, love, meaning, and longing that had been ruminating in my young being ever since I could remember.

So, I tried to make Catholicism work for me, but even after attending Catholic schools all the way through college, I was left without answers.

I was engaged to my best friend, Lisa, in my early twenties when I realized I was gay. I truly loved Lisa, but while in college, my deeply buried desires emerged. I sought the advice of the campus chaplain, who had also been my theology teacher. Sitting across the desk from him, I hoped he would give me guidance.

I began, "Father, I recently discovered that . . . well, I suppose it's more that I admitted to myself . . . that I'm attracted to both men and women." It felt good to be honest. "But after some deeper self-inquiry, I find I'm more attracted to men. I think a serious, loving relationship with a man is what will make me truly happy."

The chaplain nodded. "Well, Ren, the good news is you *can* be gay and Catholic," he said.

I let out a sigh. "So . . . what's the bad news?"

"You have to be chaste, celibate."

"Father, being celibate is like a prison sentence."

"The church says that sex between people of the same gender is a sin and immoral."

"What about the same-sex relationships referenced in Greece and Rome?" I asked.

He shrugged his shoulders. As far as he was concerned, the matter was closed.

I would have rather been slapped than deal with the abandonment I felt as I left his office.

How could I be affiliated with a doctrine that said how I loved was wrong? That day, I came out to myself and said goodbye in my heart to a religious philosophy that was intensely ingrained in my DNA.

For a few very long years, I kept up the facade of being Catholic, heterosexual, and happy. I felt I had no choice. I graduated from undergrad and accepted a full-ride fellowship to work on a master's degree in history at the University of Cincinnati. I dove into my studies as a diversion from reality. Then, deep grief entered my life when my older brother Dave and his wife were in a fatal, tragic car accident. Their nine-year-old son, Josh, wanted to live with me. *Me!* As I mourned the loss of my brother and his wife, my questioning self kept me up at night. Should I marry Lisa and give my young nephew, whom I loved so much, a stable home? Would that be fair to Lisa? I was already "going through the motions" at this point in our relationship. What about *my inner peace*? To say I was desperate for answers was an understatement.

Then, one day, a fellow graduate student, Thad, told me about a part-time physics professor who was also a practicing astrologer. Thad had recently gone to the man for a reading.

"Astrology?" I said with a laugh. "That seems so out there."

"Oh, come on, Mr. History," Thad said. "You know this stuff—from the time of the Babylonians up to the Scientific Revolution, astrology and astronomy were sister sciences. Kepler, Copernicus, Galileo, and even Newton were astrologers as well as astronomers . . . at least until the Catholic Church threatened them with excommunication."

"Yeah, at least until then," I muttered.

"Look, this guy gave me some real insights into myself," Thad said. "It's helped me so much. You should give it a try."

"I don't know," I said.

"Newton once said to Edmond Halley when he denigrated astrology, '*Sir Halley, I have studied the matter, you have not.*'" Thad gave me a Cheshire cat smile. "I dare you," he said.

Never one to turn down a dare, and with nothing to lose and lots of questions swirling inside me, I called the part-time professor and astrologer. He asked for the date, time, and place of my birth, and we set an appointment.

The astrologer's office was in the back room of a New Age bookstore just off UC's campus. The man looked like a dark-haired Einstein, with wild curly hair and out-of-control, bushy eyebrows. We sat at an antique, claw-foot table in a room well-lit by natural light from a bank of floor-to-ceiling windows.

"Ren, with the birth information you supplied, this is your natal chart," the astrologer said, intently focused on the colorful circle filled with lines and symbols on the page between us. "To begin, you have a lot going on, but let's start with your ruling planet, Saturn."

"Oh, okay," I said with a grin. "Saturn sounds important. What does it mean?"

"He is the father of the zodiac. He rules discipline, structure, and manifestation through hard work. All things that I see are important to you." He squinted at the chart.

"Well, sure, structure and discipline are important, but—"

"Here!" He pointed to an image of a small circle with a cross at the bottom.

"Isn't that the symbol for the feminine?" I asked.

"Yes, it represents Venus and yours is in Pisces, which is in an exalted position, always seeking love and compassion. Saturn and Venus are working to teach you some interesting lessons about combining discipline and love. It's a major part of your journey to higher consciousness."

I nodded as my heart began to beat harder with an unexplainable recognition of his words.

"To be more specific, Saturn is in charge of your four planets in Capricorn, which is called a stellium, while Venus oversees your grand trine in the emotional element of water *and* calls the shots in your T-square, creating issues with women and nurturing."

He paused and looked up from the chart and his notes.

"Wow, it sounds like there's a lot of conflicting energies going on:

structure, love, discipline, compassion, father energy, nurturing," I said almost as a question.

He sat back in his desk chair and smiled.

"Think of yourself as the Capricorn mountain goat steadily climbing the steep rocky road of success, structuring everything along the way," he said. "Saturn, the father of structure and discipline, wants you to get things done, while Venus, the energy of love, is trying to teach you about compassion and Oneness. They are not comfortable companions as He wants to strive and climb, and She wants to relax and let everything unfold. All these energies combined in your chart add to your overall nervousness, self-doubt, and angst about life."

By the end of the reading, I was convinced that this man I had never met had not only nailed my nervous inner nature but he'd also adeptly described my existential inner struggle between a need for structured discipline and a transcendental experience of unconditional love.

As I stepped across the threshold of his office to leave that day, I turned to him and asked, "Any advice for me?"

"Find a way to combine the energies of Venus and Saturn in your life to offset your innate nervous disposition. Try something like yoga that uses discipline to facilitate deep levels of relaxation. As you learn to let go, you'll be better able to hear your Venus in Pisces–ruled heart. The trick is to use Saturn's discipline constructively. Otherwise, he will wring the life out of *your* life. I also suggest you explore astrology. Discipline and compassion are the perfect mix for studying it. You have both traits *and* deep questions, Ren. Learn how to unlock the secrets of the Universe. They are all inside you."

"Thank you," I meekly mustered as tears welled up. This stranger had planted some powerful seeds. Encouraged by memories of calmness watching Lilias Folan's *Lilias, Yoga and You* on TV as a kid, I began searching for local yoga classes in Cincinnati. Much to my chagrin, this wasn't an easy find in the early eighties. But a few days later, while studying off campus at the Highland Coffee House, I spied a flier with tear-off phone number tabs:

Interested in Hatha Yoga?

And with that, I was off to my first yoga series with a woman who taught small groups in the upstairs loft space of her 150-year-old stone carriage house. The yogini had a unique mystique. She wore dangling feather earrings and a loose, gauzy peasant shirt over her black leotard. I was intrigued. Like Lilias, she had a huge heart that spoke directly to mine.

That first day in the carriage house, as our teacher told us to breathe and led us in *oms*, my mind bombarded me with thoughts like, "This is dumb," "What are you doing here?" But in my heart, I felt myself relax and breathe deeper than I ever had! Was this a glimmer of inner peace I had been seeking since I was a child? Lying on the floor that morning, I finally felt . . . hopeful.

Each week in class, we centered on breathing and rounds of oms. Then we did poses. Toward the end of each class, she adjusted our bodies into *savasana*, or resting corpse pose, and read poetic verses from what I now know are the *Upanishads*. I found them inspiring.

By the end of that year, I'd taken what would become a permanent leave of absence from my PhD program and had decided to tell Lisa the truth. It wasn't an easy discussion, but we ultimately went our separate ways as friends. And after much thought, I said no to my nephew's request to live with me. As much as I adored Josh, I certainly wasn't in a place to raise a kid. I was still raising myself! I became a steady student of yoga and found a mentor for my dive into astrology.

I left my old life and started anew.

And then I met Sean. The moment we set eyes on each other, I knew there was something different about him. I somehow recognized him from a different time, a different place, a different skin, a different robe . . . perhaps a different lifetime. We'd needed to meet again, and here we were.

Our current United Soul journey began with a chance introduction from our mutual friend, Carol. She was the bartender at the restaurant where I had started waiting tables after departing from school. Sean lived upstairs. That fateful evening, Sean walked into the restaurant carrying a colorful bouquet.

Carol and I were talking at the bar as Sean presented the flowers to Carol.

"What's the occasion?" Carol asked, looking slightly bewildered.

"It's Saturday," Sean said. "You wanna hang out after work tonight?"

"Aw, you just made my night. And, yes, let's get together. Oh, this is Ren. He just started."

Sean turned to look at me, and his piercing blue eyes took my breath away. "Hi, Ren," he said.

Something happened to me then—that first time he said my name, and I saw his sapphire eyes.

Was it fate? Coincidence? I call it synchronicity—looking at the divine plan with hindsight and seeing how things lined up and offered you opportunities.

We first hung out as friends and had great conversations about life, love, and our hopes and dreams for the future. We had a lot in common, but we also appreciated our many differences. He seemed so unencumbered by all the stuff I was lugging around.

"I grew up fairly agnostic," Sean explained one evening.

"That is so cool," I said. "I don't think I know anyone who grew up without *some* kind of religious background."

"I mean, we celebrated Christmas and Easter with my cousins," Sean said, "but it was more about getting together, having dinner, presents, and egg hunts. There wasn't any talk of what it was really about. We didn't go to church as a family. The few times I went to church with friends, it all seemed like superstition and BS."

I laughed. "I wish I'd had that clarity early on. It would've saved me from a lot of guilt and a lot of heartache."

He smiled. "Don't get me wrong; I might be too analytical to simply believe in some otherworldly being, but I'm still searching for answers. I may just need some proof!"

"What's your sign?" I asked.

"Virgo. Why?"

"Well, there you go!" I said with a grin. "In their search for perfection, Virgos like to dissect everything. That can be useful when you're processing and synthesizing mental information, but it can also be a block when the frontier being explored is your inner terrain, where you ultimately must trust something other than the mind."

"I see," Sean said with a cute little mischievous grin. "You know, I'm drawn to you like a moth to a flame. I just hope I don't get burned."

Now, we both smiled.

Even before we moved in together, I knew Sean was the soul I had dreamed about as a child, hiding and waiting, alone behind the overstuffed chair in my childhood home. Now, instead of hiding, I could find solace in his arms when I was fearful. I soon recognized that I could be me—with all my self-doubt, my insecurities, and my emotional ups and downs. He understood my searching nature and my need to find meaning in life. I could cry when inner peace seemed so far away.

I knew our love was ancient. We were meant to help each other evolve on this mysterious path of human consciousness. We knew in our hearts that we were United Souls, the true essence of what it means to be US in capital letters. The collective is the ultimate US, but within this macrocosm, there are souls that work in tandem to stretch and mold each other: Soul Mates, Twin Selves, Twin Souls.

Over the next three decades, Sean and I matured personally and as a couple. There wasn't much we didn't know about the other. Our relationship was completely entwined. Sean accepted my gnawing, insatiable need to feel loved and understood, stemming from a lonely childhood and having Saturn, the ultimate taskmaster of the zodiac, as my ruling planet.

I knew Sean's fears, worries, and Virgo insecurities about not being good enough or perfect. We shared "the wallet" and "the phone"—yes, between us, we only had one of each. Some of our friends thought of this as over-the-top or the ultimate in co-dependency, but we maintained our separate daily lives. Sean and I preferred to think of it as a synchronicity of our souls.

We also shared a profound need to understand the mysteries of the Universe. Through our constant studies of the sister arts of astrology and yoga, we searched for the signposts that helped us understand the maps and synchronicity that guided us.

As we settled into our fifties, we also settled into our lives as yoga teachers, meditation practitioners, and massage therapists. Yes, we did it all, offering holistic healing not only to ourselves but also to our students and clients. I loved that our uncomplicated existence provided me with lots of time to study, meditate, and explore the meaning of life through my practices. I felt quite fortunate.

In the spring of my fifty-eighth year on the planet, I once again began collaborating with my friend Kate in co-facilitating a yearlong yoga teacher training program at her supernal studio in Hyde Park, a half-hour drive from home. This was my sixth partnership with her. I always said yes to her because these teaching opportunities fed my soul. Each time, these trainings would bring together like-minded seekers, hungry to find more meaning in life, as well as increase my motivation to brush up on yoga philosophy and study new meditation techniques. Kate and I were known for taking our students on a deep yogic dive of self-discovery. For me, it was one way to be of service to many. It was a beautiful web of connection.

I volunteered to teach the class about *Patanjali's Yoga Sutras*, a text that is the basis for every entry-level yoga teacher training program. The Sutras are divided into four sections or Padas. Pada One, Two, and Four describe what can be obtained from a consistent yoga practice, which practices to execute, and instructions on how to do them. I found that it was Pada Three that would intrigue, put off, or confuse most students. It describes what, in Sanskrit, is called the *siddhis*, or abilities you develop when practicing yoga with clear intention.

I'd read the Sutras numerous times, but in preparation for this training, I made it my mission to dive even deeper, wanting to come from a place of personal experience and understanding. After setting a daily intention to understand this 2,500-year-old manuscript on my deepest inner level, I began studying for hours on end.

At one point, a few weeks before the training began, Sean called me into our front room, home library, with a serious look on his face. We sat across from each other in two brown leather chairs that sat in front of the fireplace.

"Even though I study and practice too," Sean began, "I am amazed at how long you can sit in meditation and how deep you go. Now you know I've never been jealous, but your yoga practices are like another person I share you with." He bit his lip and looked to the floor before continuing. "Meditation has become your mistress."

Rarely speechless, I was in that moment. My silence spoke volumes. I reached for and lifted his chin so our eyes could meet.

"Something is different," I finally admitted. "But it doesn't have to be a choice between you and yoga, Sean. My love for you is part of my practice. Our deep love is what yoga is all about."

Sean nodded. "You know I've always supported you in your spiritual quest. Even when you had those wild dreams or visitations or whatever they were . . . of that council. Remember, during your first Saturn Return? I didn't question it. But I don't want anything to come between us—ever."

"Always!" I said.

"Forever!" he said back, now with a slight smile.

Then, in a matter of days, came the unexplainable moment when something came to life right before my eyes: shattered-altered-expanded me.

I was forever changed.

2

THE DAY BEFORE

Sean was right about the change in my practices. The last few months had been pregnant with an energy of inner transformation. Since I'd begun my exploration of Pada Three, I went deep instantly when I sat for meditation. With no effort or sense of time, I would slide behind the veil of thoughts that usually crowded my mind to a place of peace. My physical body had an ethereal buoyancy. A slight vibration moved through me, and my head was gently tugged to the heavens by a luminescent cord of light. There was another difference, too: I had always been a prolific dreamer, but now they were in full color, with vivid details.

The night Sean had expressed his concerns about my all-consuming practices, I was sitting on the edge of the bed before lying down for the night, and Sean was propped up on his side, reading a book. I placed my hands into *Abhaya mudra*, the yogic gesture of fearlessness. With my left hand over my heart and my right arm bent at the elbow with my palm facing out, I recited, "Universe, which encompasses all spiritual archetypes, both female and male, please guide Sean and me to a path of greater service. May the love we cultivate between us swirl out from our hearts to the world. *Swaha!*"

"So be it, my love," Sean said with a smile. "Are you going to meditate?"

"No, bud, it's time for my journey into the inner darkness of the unconscious. Sweet dreams. See you in the morning."

"Always." He to me.

"Forever." Me to him.

As my head rested on the pillow, "*Love*" crossed my lips in a whisper.

Instantly, I was in a dreamworld swirling with a discordant mixture of images and sensations. Then the dream shifted . . .

I was flying over Times Square, not in a plane or a glider, but of my own accord. There were the familiar lights, traffic-filled streets, and thousands of people, but unlike anything I had ever experienced in New York City, everyone was still and focused on the jumbotron at the end of Times Square.

Strangely, I saw the screen was black. From my perch high above the huge crowd, I could sense the mass of people breathing in unison. Then, as if choreographed, everyone brought their hands into Abhaya mudra— just as I had before falling asleep. Then, I heard their many voices:

"*I am not afraid of my life or what is in my heart.*"

New York City paused in silent reverence. What had caused this?

Then, thin silver threads of light began to rise from the crown of each person's head. As I hovered above, the streams of light came toward me, but not the me that was floating above them. Where were they heading? Where else could I be? Then, my hovering self glided slowly over several tall buildings until I came to rest blocks away, high above Rockefeller Center. My heart center warmed as I watched the threads of light pass into the familiar figure below that I knew was me but was somehow separate from my current observing awareness. I had become electrically charged.

Inside this visionary experience, my eyes closed, and euphoria washed over me. As my eyes reopened, the scene changed, and I was being escorted down a long corridor by a beautiful, brown-skinned male angel with four-foot wings attached to his six-foot frame, wearing a white flowing robe. He ushered me into a room with two barber chairs and lots of lights and mirrors.

"Hi, I'm Kelly," said a woman who was now standing in front of me, applying makeup to my face.

"Why am I here?" I asked.

"Why?" she asked, her eyebrows rising sharply. "Because you're about to go on television, and it's my job to make sure you look good, sweetheart. And I really like your tattoo," she said, pointing to my forearm.

"Tattoo?" I asked as I looked to see **ABHINIVESHA**, printed in half-inch, bold, black letters, stretching the length of my right forearm.

"Isn't that Sanskrit for 'clinging to life'?" she asked.

"It's the word for the fear of death," I said.

In a flash, I was on an outdoor stage in front of thousands of people at Rockefeller Center. I was seated directly across from Katie Couric, speaking about the power of love. The crowd cheered and applauded.

Then, Katie asked a question, but before I could answer, her eyes widened with fear as her head darted between production staff, yelling directions to get off the stage. Chaos ensued as everyone began running. At that moment, a shrouded figure in black appeared before me and dropped a veil at my feet. Then, I heard a loud *pop*, which threw me back into the quiet, hovering first above Rockefeller Center and then Times Square. Once again, I watched as the people holding Abhaya mudra stared at the black screen of the jumbotron.

Suddenly, I was propelled upward. I moved faster and faster, losing sight of the crowd, the city, the Earth, and the stars, finding myself in total blackness. Unable to see anything, I had become only an essence of myself, surrounded by a hum. *Is this Aum, the sound of the Universe?*

Then, all thought disappeared. What was left?

Peace, bliss, euphoria, Ananda, love, kindness, compassion . . . and a comforting blackness.

My eyes opened. It was the next morning. I was staring at the sky-colored ceiling of our bedroom. Sean was already up and making his way to the stairs.

"I'll see you in the kitchen," he said.

"I need a couple of minutes," I said. "I had a really weird dream, and I want to write down the details before they fade." Sitting up, I reached for my dream journal.

"Take your time, Reno," Sean said with a nod. "I'll get things started."

I smiled. I loved it when he called me Reno.

After a few minutes, I made my way downstairs, where Sean had lit candles on our kitchen altar. The scent of Nag Champa incense and freshly brewed coffee wafted through the air. I took a seat at the breakfast table, journal in hand.

"How did you sleep?" Sean asked, placing a cup in front of me and kissing me on the head.

"Okay, but that dream was both peaceful and disturbing," I said.

"You were really restless," Sean said as he took his seat across from me.

"I'm not surprised. Wait till you read this," I said as I opened my journal and slid it over to him.

As I sipped my coffee, he read. "Wow," he said when he'd finished. "What do you make of it?"

"I don't know. It was real but at the same time . . . not. I mean, Times Square, Katie Couric?"

"It's just a dream, bud," Sean said, clearly picking up on the worry in my voice. He reached across the table and squeezed my hand. "The unconscious clears itself out in the wildest ways. Remember the one I had a couple of weeks ago? The one where I was giving swimming lessons to a bunch of ducks?"

"I do," I said, laughing. "But . . . I have an odd sense about this one. It's almost as if it's a premonition."

"Hmmm," he said, releasing my hand and leaning back in his chair. "If you end up flying over New York like Superman, there are going to be headlines." He stood, came over to my side of the table, wrapped his arm around my shoulder, and pulled me into him. "Hey, shrug it off, Mr. Worrywart. Focus on your class today. Are you ready for that group of aspiring yogis?"

I smiled. "I am. We're going to start our dive into Patanjali's Yoga Sutras this weekend."

"All four Padas, or are you skipping the enigmatic Pada Three?"

"Nope. Their homework was to read all four sections. We're delving into the whole thing today. We're also going to work with Abhaya mudra and the *Gayatri* mantra. You have to meet this group. They're keeping Kate and me on our toes."

After our morning ritual of meditation and breakfast, I headed out to class. On my drive along Columbia Parkway toward the yoga studio, pieces of the dream kept flashing in my mind. Even after all these years of meditation, old habits of worry and fear still showed up for me. *That's why I keep practicing.*

As I pulled off the Parkway and headed up the hill, the last stretch to the studio, the strangest thought emerged in my psyche. *How do you tell the difference between an old, negative thought pattern and your intuition?*

3

THE CLASSROOM

Any remaining angst I had about the previous night's dream faded when I began class. The morning sun filtered in through a bank of tall windows to my right, illuminating a large, colorful mandala of the seven chakras painted on the wall behind me. The light also gave an angelic glow to the thirteen women, ranging in age from twenty-two to sixty, sitting on the floor cross-legged, forming a semi-circle in front of me.

"Come to your meditation posture," I instructed. "Let's join our voices in three oms and one round of the Gayatri mantra to invite the sacred into our learning space."

The sound we created was ethereal. I was transported to a place deep inside my heart. I took a deep breath to bring myself back to the classroom.

"I love that version of the Gayatri," said Janet, a fit blond in her fifties. "How can you possibly go wrong invoking the light of the divine feminine to stimulate your intellect and infuse you with true knowledge?" I loved listening to her lilting British accent.

"I agree from the depths of my very soul," I said with a grin. "The world needs more of the feminine to help us heal from all the aggression and hate that's out there."

"But Ren," Janet said, "there have been a few times this month when I've chanted the Gayatri that I've felt a bit . . . disconnected from my body but connected to . . . I don't know what. It feels daft. Is that normal?"

"Our practices are so individual; it's hard to say what's normal. But I'm also having unexplainable experiences with the Gayatri. I wake up reciting it and find myself chanting it spontaneously in my *asana* practice. Maybe we're tapping into the divine through it," I said with a wink.

"Well, love, I can relax knowing you're having a similar go-round with it."

Everyone laughed.

"Let's get to your homework." I turned to the large whiteboard I had propped up next to the chakra mandala and wrote across the top, "Patanjali's Yoga Sutras."

"Why study the Sutras?" I asked, turning to face the class.

Maureen, a longtime student of mine in her late forties, raised her hand. "It's a manual for yoga teachers, so it outlines specific practices and the results you can expect."

"Yes, it's a teacher's manual," I said, "perfect for a teacher training program. What does Patanjali say about the practices?"

I pointed to Karen, a corporate executive in her early sixties, who had told me she was studying yoga to balance her left-brain propensities.

"He says the practices help organize our senses, emotions, and thoughts so we can quiet what he calls 'the fluctuations of the mind,'" Karen said. "When we quiet the mind, we experience deep inner transformations, helping us realize we're all connected by a shared inner god-force, *and* any concept of being separate from one another is all in our mind and not in our heart or soul."

"Brava," I said. "The Sutras are a road map to finding that shared inner god-force, known as our divine consciousness. We can't do it from here." I pointed to my temple. "It must be uncovered from here." I placed my hands on my heart. "Uncovering this divine consciousness we hold inside brings us to the 196 verses of the Sutras, divided into four chapters, known as Padas. Who can give me a line or two about Pada One called *Samadhi*?"

"*Samadhi* translates to 'bliss,'" said Anna, the youngest of the group.

"Pada One outlines the bliss we'll experience if we do the practices laid out in Pada Two. Patanjali describes the outcome before he describes the process. I feel he's trying to lure the student in. It worked on me."

"Excellent, glad to hear you're hooked on the Sutras," I said, with a slight grin and a nod. "Cheri, tell us about the alluring bliss of Pada One."

"Patanjali says there's a bright luminosity awaiting us behind all the mental chatter of our mind," said Cheri, a retired philosophy professor in her late fifties, who was always willing to share her knowledge. "He says most of us are so attached to what the mental mind tells us that we never develop the ability to hear the heart."

"What's the problem with that?" I asked.

"The mental mind, which is our ego, creates a smokescreen, making us believe we're islands and that reality is *only* what we perceive with our outer senses, like our physical needs and our day-to-day existence. We forget the true focus of our life, which Patanjali says is our soul's journey to the bliss of Oneness and connection with each other."

"Excellent!" I said, surveying the intensely engaged group. "Remember, the crux of yoga is we're *all* connected, and rediscovering that connection is bliss. Forgetting we're *all* spiritual beings having a human experience allows anger, fear, and hatred to take control of us."

I turned back to the whiteboard and wrote, "Pada One: The bliss of connection through experiencing Oneness through the heart."

"What about Pada Two?"

"Let me take a shot at this," said Becca, a high school guidance counselor in her early thirties. "It's the only section that really makes sense to me." She raised both eyebrows and shrugged.

We all chuckled.

"The floor is yours," I said.

"Pada Two is called *Sadhana*, meaning 'practice.' It's the down-and-dirty how-to section on calming the mind, which I'm starting to understand is the path to bliss, which Anna and Cheri described."

"You're on it," I said. "We work the practices to find yogic bliss."

Under Pada Two on the whiteboard, I wrote: "The Practices."

"What's the most well-known part of Pada Two?" I asked. Several hands went up. "Sophie."

"The eight-limbed path to self-realization," she said. Her bright, radiant smile stretched from ear to ear.

"Can you name the first five limbs?"

Using her fingers to enumerate them, she said, "The *yamas*, and *niyamas*, which are the ethical foundations to living a meaningful life, *asana*—which are the postures, *pratyahara*—withdraw from the senses, and *pranayama*—breath control."

I nodded as I turned back to the whiteboard and wrote, "*Dharana, Dhyana, Samadhi.*"

"What are these?" I pointed to the board with my marker.

"They're the last three limbs," said Maureen. "Working the first five helps us learn to focus—*Dharana*, which brings deeper levels of concentration—*Dhyana*, which leads to meditation—*Samadhi*. That's the path to finding the luminosity and bliss of Pada One."

"You're on a roll, Maureen. Do you remember what the combined practice of *Dharana*, *Dhyana*, and *Samadhi* is called?"

"*Samyama!*" she answered, raising her right arm overhead in triumph.

Everyone applauded. I loved the support these women gave to each other. It was a beautiful example of what was possible in our world.

"Perfect!" I said. "Who besides Maureen can tell us about the five mental obstacles we all face on our soul's journey to bliss?"

"The kleshas," Jeri said, wiggling back and forth in her seat. "In English, they're ignorance, ego, attachment, aversion, and fear."

"Good! The Sanskrit words are . . ." I turned and wrote them on the board as I said them aloud. "*Avidya, Asmita, Raga, Dvesha,* and *Abhinivesha. Abhinivesha* is fear, but the fear of what? And why do you think it's listed last?"

"It's the fear of death, being separated from our bodies," Jeri said. "I think it's last because *Abhinivesha* brings us face-to-face with all the other kleshas, and we get the opportunity to see if our practices of the eight-limbed path have transformed our ultimate fear—death."

The image of ABHINIVESHA tattooed on my right forearm in last night's dream flashed through my mind. In it, I heard Kelly ask, *"Isn't that Sanskrit for clinging to life?"* Goosebumps covered my skin.

"Ren?" Jeri asked.

"Yes . . . I mean, exactly," I said, shaking my head to bring me out of my trance, "at the end of our physical journey, we get to see if we truly believe, as the Sutras teach, that our essence is eternal and more than what we feel, hear, and taste."

I took a deep breath.

"Let's jump to Pada Four," I said, turning to the whiteboard. "What's this?" I asked, writing the word "*Kaivalya.*"

Anna raised her hand.

"In Pada Four, Patanjali describes *Kaivalya* as the ultimate state of *Samadhi,*" she said, "where we're liberated from fear and break the cycle of birth, death, and rebirth."

"Yes. So, to summarize," I said, walking the length of the semi-circle, "Pada One, Two, and Four describe the bliss a yogi obtains with dedicated practice. The bliss is recognizing they are a spark of the creator force. This spark has the strength to face the challenges of the kleshas. Ultimately, the yogi finds the world behind their closed eyes is just as real *and* important as what they see with their eyes open. Now, let's all stand up and—"

"Wait, wait, wait!" Erin said. Her dark, curly, shoulder-length hair bounced as her hand jetted to the ceiling. "Don't you dare skip the super-power section!"

Everyone laughed.

"I promise I'm not skipping Pada Three, Erin, just taking a break from sitting so I can teach you a new mantra and mudra." I smiled. "Stand tall with your feet hip-distance apart and even out your weight between left and right. Relax your shoulders and the muscles of your face. Take some deep breaths, and with each exhale, let go of any tension you feel in your body."

The group was soon breathing as one entity.

"Now, bring your left hand to your heart. Bend your right elbow and turn your right palm to face forward. This is *Abhaya mudra*—the hand gesture of fearlessness. Let's add the mantra, 'I am not afraid of my life or what is in my heart.'"

As we chanted, last night's dream once again crept into my awareness. I saw the crowd in Times Square, holding the mudra and reciting the mantra.

"We use the tools of mantra and mudra to bring the lessons of yoga into our spiritual heart center, the *Hridaya*. Breathe deep and take the mantra inside," I said.

As we silently chanted, I sensed an energy like a warm blanket of love permeate the room and surround the group.

"Beautiful," I said, savoring the connection of love we'd created. "Please take a seat."

"So, Ren, let's get to it." Erin's eyes were wide open. "Do you think the superpowers described in Pada Three are real?"

"Okay, let's move into Pada Three, *Vibhuti*," I said, glancing around and smiling at the group.

"I'm sorry to be so impetuous," Erin said. "But Pada Three's like an outline for a Netflix series, and it's coming from a 2,500-year-old yoga book. Really, Ren, what do you think?"

"I'm not sure about superpowers," I said, "but I *do* know the practices have changed *me* in powerful ways. I'm happier. I have less judgment about other people, myself, and life in general," I said, making eye contact with each of them. "I'm better able to look at life through the Tantric lens that there is no black and white, good or bad, and *all* of that combined helps me deal with the challenges of the kleshas. That's pretty miraculous stuff for a guy who's stalked by his Capricorn shadow of fear and self-doubt."

"That's a great way to think of it," said Tiffany, the highly skeptical voice in the group, "*but* every translation of Pada Three that I've read says if you practice with diligence and consistency, the innate luminosity we've been discussing can make a direct connection with the intuition of your higher mind, which then communicates with your spiritual heart that *then* makes what was thought to be impossible in the physical world—possible."

"I know it's confusing," I said. "My partner, Sean, calls Pada Three an enigma. Personally, I like to think Patanjali is speaking metaphorically, *but* if any of you master the art of turning invisible before our next class, please give us all fair warning." I smiled, hoping to move on, but Tiffany's hand shot up. I'd known her probing, Scorpion-like nature would not let this go.

"Ren!" Tiffany said. "I'd like to think it's a metaphor too, but Pada Three states that the practice of yoga-*samyama* can lead to levitation, walking on water, becoming invisible, entering someone else's body, supernatural powers of touch, mastery over the foundations of birth and death, knowing the day and exact time of your—"

"I know," I said, "it's a long list."

"My point," she said, staring at me with dark, hypnotic eyes, "is that list is *not* metaphoric. What's your take on that?"

There was a heavy silence.

"I'm skeptical, just like you," I said to Tiffany and then looked to the rest of the group, "but because of that skepticism and knowing the mind can create walls to truth, I've been working intensely with the practices of the Sutras to see what effect they'd have. I feel as if I'm experiencing deeper levels of compassion bubbling up inside me. I don't know. My life is filling up with . . . a mystical essence."

A comfortable silence descended, and a soothing energy wove through the group, uniting *us* in a timeless, meditative void for several moments.

"Wow," Tiffany finally said, shaking her head. "I think we *all* just experienced a mystical essence." She took a deep breath. "So, Ren, let's just say the *siddhis were* real—which one would you pick as your superpower?"

"I'd heal the sick all day long," I said, surprised at my words. "I mean, I think I would . . . but who really knows? And remember, Pada Three warns that ultimately, these *supernatural abilities* . . ." I paused and took a deep breath. ". . . will derail the yogi from their true path of self-discovery and love. Can't you see the kleshas, especially ego, going on steroids once you tap into the *siddhis*?"

Everyone laughed. The levity felt good.

"Any questions before we bring today's session to a close?" I asked.

"How do we integrate all this into our practice?" Erin asked, shaking her head. "It's still confusing."

"Please," I said, placing my hand on my heart. "Don't let it confuse you. Just let it go. Work with the practices and observe your life. Remember, yoga is meant to be experienced, so explore for yourself, and at some point, if Pada Three wants your attention, it will make itself known. In the meantime, practice, practice, practice."

I looked around at their loving faces.

"Okay," I said, taking a deep breath. "We've covered a lot of ground and stirred up a lot of mental energy. Let's finish up with a meditation. Sit up tall. Bring your hands into Abhaya mudra. Let's join our voices in the lyrical version of the Gayatri, the alluring 3,000-year-old mantra, which is also the name of the divine mother."

Aum Bhur, Bhuvah, Swaha
Tat Savitur Varenyam
Bhargo Devasya Dheemahi
Dhiyo Yonaha Prachodayat

Chanting with these luminescent beings, I found myself once again immersed in the euphoric bliss I felt as I hovered in last night's dream. I savored it in my soul.

Scan to experience the Gayatri Mantra.

4

DREAMS OF REALITY

"How did class go?" Sean asked as I walked in the door.

"This class is sharp. We had an amazing conversation about tantra, the kleshas, and the Sutras," I said as I put my bookbag on the kitchen table.

"That's fantastic! Any skeptics when you discussed Pada Three?"

"Not one!" I said, stifling a smile.

"What?" He turned from the sink to look at me. "Not one . . . ?"

"I'm kidding. Of course, they were all skeptical, especially Tiffany."

"I knew they would be. And how did you address that?" he asked, wiping his hands on the royal blue chef's apron he wore as he prepared dinner.

"I pointed out personal shifts I'm experiencing that I consider miraculous and told them not to get distracted, to keep practicing and observe what happens for themselves."

"That sounds like a politician's dance around the question to me. Let's be real. Do you really think that with enough practice, a person can do what is listed in that part of the Sutras? I don't. I never have—"

"I know you don't, bud. But don't you feel our practices have shifted us in some mystical ways?"

"What do you mean?"

"You know the adage, 'familiarity breeds contempt'?"

"Yep." He looked perplexed.

"That's not happening. In thirty years, there could be a lot of contempt, but instead, there's a deep compassion growing. Don't you feel it?"

"I do. But—"

"I believe compassion is growing because of the practices we do. We close our eyes and sit in silence every day to increase our reverence for life and to realize the connectedness between everything and everyone. When I open *my* eyes, I see the Universe in you. You know when we say, *I'm feeling it*? That feeling is the connection of love I'm talking about. That's proof enough for me that there is magic in yoga and the world. In that space, I believe anything can happen."

"But that's way different from walking on water."

"Is it? It's the power of dedication and love coming together to manifest deep transformation."

"Man! Why do I find your naivety so alluring?" Sean grinned.

"I see you're chalking up my beliefs to being naive." I chuckled. "I'll admit your practical nature keeps me grounded, and I am thankful for that." I brought my hands into prayer position and gave a slight bow.

"And you, my love, give me hope, which keeps me questioning my own 'doubting Thomas' nature," he said.

"Hope's a good thing," I said, staring into his iridescent blue eyes.

"I'm feeling it right now," he said, gazing back.

"Me too," I said.

"To that, I have no doubt," he said as a huge smile lit his face. "Now come on, dinner's ready."

After savoring a delicious veggie stir-fry, we took the love buzz we created to our converted attic bedroom on the third floor. The skylights installed on each side of the slanted ceiling allowed us to see the massive maple tree that covered much of our roof. It was *our* magic treehouse.

"I'd like to go over some of the materials for tomorrow's class," I said as we climbed into bed, "but I'm exhausted." I closed my eyes for what I thought would be a moment, but in no time, my psyche passed from conscious to unconscious to dreaming.

As my inner awareness kicked in, I knew exactly where I was. I was standing in my childhood parish church, Corpus Christi.

I looked down the main aisle at its familiar seven-story vaulted ceiling, the six enormous stained-glass windows lining the nave, and a monstrous crucifix hanging above the main altar. It was all very majestic.

As a kid, I had always been drawn to the back of the church near the spiral staircase leading to the choir loft. Back in that cove lived lifelike replicas of St. Veronica, St. Mary Magdalene, St. Clare of Assisi, and St. Teresa of Avila.

Standing there, in my adult body, I realized I was reliving the days I'd volunteered as an altar boy for the 6:00 a.m. weekday Masses. By the time I was nine, I had a key to the church, and I would get up well before the sun, walk the four blocks from my house, and then slip inside to visit with the saints. Each sculpture was set with a kneeling pad and a votive stand so you could say a prayer and light a candle. For me, they were the guardians of Corpus Christi, all aglow in the light of the flickering flames. St. Veronica, dressed in black flowing robes and a veil that cascaded down to her feet, was my favorite.

In grade school religion class, we were told how Veronica pushed her way through a screaming, jeering crowd to offer compassion to a fellow human in need. She handed Jesus her veil. He held it to his face to wipe his brow and then gave it back, leaving the imprint of his face on the shroud forever.

As a child, I prostrated myself in front of her and felt myself relax. I did not feel the need to hide or be afraid. I felt safe in the candlelit church surrounded by these guardians.

Now, in this dream, I walked closer to St. Veronica, moved to my knees, then lay flat on my belly in yogic pranam, a gesture of surrender. This scene was familiar and eerily comforting. As I lay there, I heard a voice. I looked up. The statue of Veronica, now animated, was speaking to me.

"We all need compassion," St. Veronica said to me. "Learn to first give it to yourself, then you will be able to give it to and receive it from others.

You are beginning to open to the energy of higher love that is inherent in the collective but is buried deep. Buried deep with Her."

I was mesmerized and speechless.

She continued.

"I was drawn by a force greater than fear to face the crowds. I had no choice but to offer compassion where it was needed. If I did it, so can you."

At her pause, I pulled myself to my knees as I kept my gaze on her enchanting, fully human features—her eyes were golden-brown and her skin the color of ripe chestnuts.

"Face the coming crowds that represent the doubt, fear, and anger all humans harbor. Alchemize them with the discipline you know so well from Him and the belief in connection that is bubbling up in you from Her. Together, these two will give you the courage to bring compassion out in the open as a human alternative to hate. Continue to remind all who have ears that *all* of life is necessary."

Her left hand moved to the area of her heart, and she reached out toward me with her right as she continued.

"All suffering comes from how you perceive your life. Decide, Ren, to make your life a balance of discipline and love—not one or the other. Everything you experience is necessary. Even death, the ultimate human fear, has its place. It brings the sharp beauty of sadness and grief so you might know great joy and the heights of ecstasy.

"I know you are confused. That is part of the process of awakening the mystic." Her golden eyes continued to look directly at me. "Why am I coming to you now? Because it is time. Find the buried diamond of love in your heart by wiping away the blood and sweat that hide it from your sight. Once clear of illusion, the diamond radiates love. Love is the bond. Love is the silver cord, you see. It is a silver thread of love that binds you all together. Remember to trust your visions. Your visions are not seen by your soul or spirit but by the purified mind of yoga that lives between them," she said, turning slightly to her right to glance at the inanimate statue of Mary Magdalene.

"Place your trust in what we represent. We are the legion of feminine archetypes ready to be heard again. We are the compassion you find opening within yourself, and we are the discipline of your practices. We are both She and He.

"Continue to follow the path of *samyama*-yoga from *Dharana* to *Dhyana* to *Samadhi*. Apply the effort, do the actions, and bring yourself to a stable and tranquil state of being for the coming journey. Let us all light a candle of love for the world and illuminate the darkness surrounding so many," she paused. Then, with a hint of a smile, she added,

"*Tatra sthitau yatnah abhyasā.*"

With that, her human features were once again frozen in plaster.

I woke surprisingly calm, even after an encounter with a talking statue. I sat up in bed and then decided to go to my journal to write down the dream.

It was still dark outside, so I lit a few candles in the library and climbed into one of the deep-seated brown leather chairs. I thought of the nine-year-old me. We now had a shared experience. If St. Veronica had spoken to me then, I wonder how I would have reacted.

"Hey, you okay?"

I looked up to see Sean standing in the doorway.

"5:00 a.m. is early, even for you." He looked so beautiful in the candlelight. His energetic presence was far larger than his five-foot-nine-inch, slender physical stature.

"I had a dream of a statue of St. Veronica reciting the Yoga Sutras. I want to write it down while it's fresh."

"Just another ordinary dream," he said with a smile. "How interesting—a Catholic saint speaking about yoga. Maybe she was a yogi."

"I've read theories that certain sects of that time were studying and practicing with esoteric teachings. They're said to be the authors of the deleted *Gnostic Gospels*. Actually, I think Veronica quoted the Gospel of Mary Magdalene. And she talked about love connecting us as silver threads of light, balancing discipline with compassion, and something about an upcoming journey."

"Hmm . . . that's two dreams in a matter of days with silver threads of light."

"I know. I'm so confused."

"Well, let's not get whacked out. It was just a dream, my love."

"Was it?" I asked. "Times Square and now talking statues . . ."

Sean walked over, placed his hand on my shoulder, and gave it a light squeeze. "How about I get the coffee started, and then we sit for our meditation? I know you have to get out of here early for class."

"Thank you," I said as he left the library.

I took a deep breath and closed my eyes in the wonderful silence of the early morning hours, just before dawn. It is a sacred time when the veil between light and dark is thin. In the twilight, mysteries reveal themselves. I opened my eyes and picked up my journal, expecting to recount the dream, but instead, the first thing I wrote across the top of a page was:

Tatra sthitau yatnah abhyasā

I knew it was a Sutra but which one? I reached across to the bookshelf nearest me, pulled out my Yoga Sutra notebook, and found it:

1:13 Practice (*abhyāsa*) means choosing, applying the effort (*yatnah*), and doing those actions that bring a stable and tranquil state (*sthitau*).

In my notebook, I had highlighted it and drawn five stars next to it. In the margin, I wrote: *This can lead to the inner peace I have been seeking all my life. It can lead us all to a sense of peace through being steady and disciplined. I am ruled by Saturn, the master of discipline. That part should come easily. At least, I hope.*

I leaned back and took a deep breath. *What am I missing?* Why was Veronica, who says she represents a legion of female archetypes, showing up in my dreams, speaking Sanskrit, and quoting Sutra 1:13?

Was there something more about her than a story of an unexplainable image on a veil?

I reached for my laptop on the coffee table and typed "St. Veronica" into a search. Within a few sentences, I knew!

In my journal, under the Sutra, I wrote:

Veronica
Reciting Sutra 1:13
My underscore of the Sutra in my notebook 1:13

My birthday 1–13
Veronica's feast day 1–13!!!
Coincidence? No!

This is getting weirdly interesting. Okay, Veronica, I am paying attention.

5

FOREVER CHANGED

After meditation and breakfast, I gathered my notes and books, kissed Sean on the forehead, and headed out to class. As I drove to my training session along Columbia Parkway, traffic was light. This beautiful urban roadway, perched on the hillside, meanders along with the curves of the Ohio River. The early morning sky was ablaze with shades of pink, orange, and red as the sun's rays danced exquisitely on the water. The Queen City was waking up.

I was in a place of reverence as I opened myself to the beauty of Mother Nature and chanted the *Gayatri* mantra. This ancient mantra, whose name means "she who protects the singer," flowed from me without pause.

Within seconds, that Sunday turned into anything but ordinary.

A boy. A bike. The intersection. A traffic light. My car propelling him fifty-plus feet. The *thump*. His young body hitting the Parkway's pavement.

I had no feeling of being scared, no feeling of "what have I done," but rather a deep recognition of being fully present in the moment. There was no guilt or regret, only a deep feeling of connection. I felt a thin thread of light joining our heart energies together, he and I.

I got out of the car and walked slowly toward his body on the ground, the thread pulling us closer. My left hand moved to my heart center, and my right hand lifted, palm out. I could sense vague noise and chaos as people ran about; some were crying. Sirens wailed in the distance.

As I was magnetically pulled to the boy, those around him cleared a path. Although I was conscious of my movements, I was not the one in control. The Gayatri mantra continued to flow through me silently and effortlessly. I was not moving. I was being moved. My heart was orchestrating both my movements and my breath.

I went to my knees, close to his lifeless body.

My left hand remained on my heart center; my right hand went to his heart. As I touched him, a quiet calmness descended. I became aware of more thin threads of silver light coming from every direction: in front, behind, above, and below. They came from everywhere, even the trees and the plants, all of which streamed to the boy.

A deep breath filled my whole body. My eyes closed. There was no separation. There was no skin and bones, no form, only the sensation of thin threads of pure light energy joining the two of us as one.

After placing my hand on him, I felt as if my next breath was a breath of the Universe, a breath he *and* I somehow shared.

Another breath and another breath, and then I felt our chests expand simultaneously. We were in sync with the *prana*, the life force of the Universe.

I heard an audible inhalation from him, a slight whimper, and the whispered words:

"Thank you."

Our eyes opened and locked. Then, the boy slowly got up and started to walk toward his bike.

I stood, but I did not move. My rational mind was waking up. I noticed a dark-haired woman in steel-blue scrubs, standing still only feet from me, looking peaceful. She held what looked to be a portable defibrillator in her hand.

We caught eyes.

"It's impossible," she said, shaking her head. "He had no vital signs, and now he's moving around like nothing happened."

Her words jolted me back into my body, but my mind was still calm. I began to sense the commotion around me.

A man standing next to the woman said the words that shot me back into full reality. *"Oh my god—that man just brought the boy back to life!"*

Inside, I was calm, but I knew—in my heart—I was forever changed.

6

TELLING SEAN

Within moments, the crowd surged toward me. The calm that had enveloped the Parkway as I'd touched the boy was gone. I was pushed and shoved by people begging me to help them, heal them. I could feel their emotions and read their thoughts about cancer, chemo, surgeries, fear . . . I reached out and touched as many of them as I could.

By the time the police arrived, I was encircled by hundreds of people. A police officer shoved his way through the mass of humanity and pulled me to his cruiser. He put me in the back, jumped into the driver's seat, and locked us in. The car was immediately surrounded. People's faces were pressed against the windows, pleading for help. The cruiser rocked as it was jostled from all sides. I was feeling bombarded by their energy. I looked down at the floorboard and closed my eyes. I could not bear to take in and feel all their desperation. I felt my ego-mind scrambling to understand, but then the Gayatri mantra began to fill a part of my consciousness once again, and from a still-present calmness, I began to send love to everyone.

Veronica's words from my dream last night filtered into my memory: "Find the buried diamond of love in your heart . . . Love is the silver cord, you see" and "I was drawn by a force greater than fear to face the crowds. If I can do it, so can you."

After several minutes, another officer managed to climb into the front passenger seat.

"What the hell is going on?" the patrolman in the driver's seat asked. "Why are they screaming 'Heal me'?"

"They say he hit the kid on the bike," said the second officer, nodding toward me. "And then saved his life."

"Okay . . . so he resuscitated him and—"

"No, Captain, no one said he resuscitated him. They say he brought him back to life. Even a doctor, who was right there, said the boy was dead on impact. One person caught it on video, and it looked like this guy . . ."

There was silence before the captain turned to me.

"What's your name?"

"Reynolds Devlin."

"I'll need your driver's license."

I pulled it out of my pocket and handed it to him.

"Okay, Reynolds, we have to fill out our report. Then we need to get you home."

"I'm headed to a yoga studio in Hyde Park," I said. "I'm teaching this morning."

"I advise you to go home until things calm down."

"Thank you," I said the words the boy had said to me. "I think I'm okay to drive. How's the boy?"

"His bike's mangled beyond recognition, but he's alive and well and back with his parents. Guess that's why you're so popular right now," the second officer said.

After the crowd dispersed, the captain walked me to my car. It looked as if the damage created by the collision was minimal. Driving the black Subaru home was not a problem, especially with a police escort.

When I arrived at the house, Sean was in the library. I took a seat in one of the big leather chairs and pulled my knees to my chest. I took a deep breath and recounted what had happened.

"You did *what*?" Sean asked. "Are you okay? Did you hit your head?"

"I hit a boy on a bike on the Parkway. He came out of nowhere."

"Oh my god!"

I put my feet on the floor, sat up straight, and folded my hands in my lap. I took another deep breath, trying to be clear.

"As his weight hit the car, I was instantly connected to him."

"What do you mean?"

"I was energetically pulled out of the car to go to him. The Gayatri mantra was moving through me as I walked toward him—or at least his body. He wasn't moving at all. That's when I started to feel connected to everyone and everything, not just him."

"Connected? How?"

"I felt the emotions of everyone there," I said, looking up into the eyes of the most caring human I had ever met. "I felt the presence of the trees and the plants. Yet I was calm. My left hand moved to my heart, and my right palm out."

"Abhaya mudra," Sean whispered.

"I knelt next to the boy. I kept my left hand on me but put my right hand on his heart. That's when it got quiet, and I felt energy coming from everyone around us. It all came together as luminescent threads of light."

"Silver threads," he murmured.

"It was like the energy of the collective passed into me and out through my hand with each exhalation."

Tears rolled down my face. Sean reached over and put his hand on my knee.

"It's okay, Ren. It was an accident. No one's going to blame you. What happened then?"

"The boy took a breath and said, *Thank you.*"

"What?" Sean withdrew his hand with a jerk as he fell back in his chair, looking at me wide-eyed and shaking his head. "He's alive?"

I nodded. "He got up and walked away."

Sean sat up straight and leaned toward me. "Are you sure you're okay?"

"I feel better than okay," I said in a soft voice. "When it happened, I felt a deep sense of peace. I still feel it. The people on the Parkway felt the connection and the peace as well. But then—"

"Then what?"

"It got chaotic. The people in the crowd pushed toward me and started grabbing me, asking me to touch them and heal them, saying I raised the boy from the dead. They looked so desperate; some were crying. I could feel their emotions and read their thoughts. I touched as many as I could."

Sean had tears in his eyes. "Oh my god. I wish I had been there to help you."

"Thankfully, a policeman reached me and led me to a cruiser." Tears streamed down my face. "Sean, I'm not sure what I did or how I did it, but I know life is forever changed." I let out a deep exhalation, and the tears flowed. Sean sat on the edge of my chair and put his arm around me.

"You know, Reno, you may be in shock. We should get you checked out at urgent care."

"You don't believe me?"

"Well, for just hitting a biker and reviving him with a mudra and a bunch of silver lights, you're pretty calm. Shock's a weird thing."

"I know I'm weepy, but I feel good. Clear. I'd really like to sit in meditation to keep my center. Maybe I'll find some answers or at least a way to let go of all this and move on," I said.

"That's perfect. Why don't you go to your studio and sit while I check into all this?"

Sit, I did. I was still. As my eyes closed, I was absorbed in the Infinite. It felt right.

7

AN EXPLANATION

I went into my studio, still in a unique state of euphoria, feeling no boundaries between my physical self and the outside world. Sunlight flooded in from the two front windows and bathed the room, the plants, and me in warmth. The mint green walls enhanced the brightness. I stood before our four-foot by six-foot painting of Saraswati, depicting her graceful four-armed image, adorned in a white and gold sari, riding atop a snow-white swan.

I closed my eyes and took a deep breath. I felt as if I were plugged into a huge power source. Although I was aware of the world, it seemed as if everything about the physical realm floated through me like clouds. It was like nothing I had ever experienced. I still felt connected to everything, as I had been on the Parkway. Now, I felt the plants in the room, the trees outside, Sean downstairs, and the energetic world around me. My skin did not seem like a marker of my boundaries anymore; I had a strange sense of permeability. There was love energy emanating from everything, and it was converging in one common spot: my heart.

I took a seat on my meditation cushion and closed my eyes. My mind was at peace, and my heart was wide open—much too open to venture out into the world.

With my next breath, I allowed my rational mind to reflect on what was happening to me. Was this feeling of connection going to stay? Did I really bring back the boy from death? Why was I not paralyzed by fear when the accident happened? What led me to go to the young boy, kneel, and connect our hearts with my hands? Why did I recite the *Gayatri*?

Did my chanting of that mantra have anything to do with this? I'd been drawn to using the mantra for years, but for the last few months, the Gayatri had become an intricate part of my meditation practice. There was something different about that particular mantra.

The beautiful, thousands-of-years-old verse acknowledges the creator force, known as Divine Light, and requests that this light stimulate our intellect and bestow true knowledge. Gayatri is also the name for the divine mother, who wants all her creations to find peace. All other mantras, and there are thousands of them, are thought to merge into the source of the Gayatri.

I didn't choose this mantra. The Gayatri chose me. I'd heard it throughout all my years of studying yoga, but recently, a friend's slow, heartfelt rendition that sounded like a haunting plea to the divine had attached itself to my soul. I would automatically recite her version when I came to my mat. I inhaled, and my arms went overhead, "*Aum Bhur, Bhuvah, Swaha*" flowed from my lips. As I gently swan-dove on the exhale, I recited, "*Tat Savitur Varenyam.*" It was a dance that required no thought, only surrender.

I had been chanting it on my drive this morning, reciting it automatically, yet reverently, and as I got out of the car and approached the boy on the ground, I repeated it still. I could not ignore the presence of the sacred words. They wanted to be expressed through me. I now felt it was somehow intertwined with the profound levels of concentration and contemplation I was accessing in my meditation. The mantra and my recent dive into the Yoga Sutras were connected. I knew the general meaning of the Gayatri from my studies, but was there more to this mantra?

I got up from my cushion, sat at my computer, and typed "Meaning of the Gayatri mantra" into a search bar. I closed my eyes, sang the mantra softly, and set my intention for guidance. Then I hit enter. The first result was all I needed.

"The Gayatri's power springs forth from the specific articulation of its syllables over the lips, the tongue, the vocal cords and how it resonates with specific regions of the brain. Eventually, even reciting it silently will activate certain 'threads' and 'power centers' in the chanter's energetic body. The Gayatri has specifically been found to actuate magnetic resonance in the chanter after extended use. This resonance has been observed over the centuries to allow the long-term user of the chant to access supernatural currents."[1]

I opened my journal and scrawled the letters over three lines.

ACCESS
SUPERNATURAL
CURRENTS

Could silver threads flowing from everywhere be categorized as "supernatural currents"? Before my mind could rear its head any more than it had, I climbed back onto my meditation cushion and began my process of going inside. I intentionally deepened my breath, directing it first into the center of my brain to relax. Once the waves of my mental mind calmed to stillness, the breath spontaneously shifted to the area of my heart center.

A loud knock on the studio door sucked me back into my physical existence. I had no idea how long I'd sat in that deep state of meditation.

Sean stuck his head in. "Ren, it's been three hours. You can't just sit in here forever!" he said, his voice demanding yet agitated and shaky. "Okay, everything you told me pans out. There's a video of you on the Parkway that's gone viral! This won't just go away. The police must have released your name to the news . . . I mean, it's everywhere! The phone has *not* stopped ringing. We have hundreds, maybe thousands, of emails, and our social media pages are off the charts. Have you looked outside? The street's packed with every news crew in the city. The cops are trying to control the crowd, but—"

"Do you think one of the neighbors called them?" I asked.

---

1   www.themodernvedic.com.

"No one *had* to call! The street's impassable!" Sean's eyes widened as he shook his head. "Everyone wants an explanation, including me! They're calling it a miracle. A miracle! What the—?"

"Hey, don't be mad at me," I said.

Sean finally slowed down and took a deep breath. "I'm not mad, bud, but you have to make some kind of statement. Just pick an outlet. Any outlet. They all want you to say *something*."

"I don't know what to say. I'm just as confused as everyone!"

"Then, what do we do? We can't just hole up in the house and act like nothing happened!"

"What if I post something on social media?"

"That's a start, and I'm sure the news will pick up on it. It'll also buy us some time to figure this out." He took another deep breath and let it out slowly. His shoulders softened. "This is bigger than you think *or* want it to be. I don't understand what you've done, but—"

"I know," I said, joining his deep breathing. "I know."

"We could use some help right now," Sean said with a sigh. He turned, walked out of the studio, and closed the door behind him.

Yes, I thought we could use some help. I moved back to my computer and placed my fingers on the keyboard. I closed my eyes, bowed my head, and said aloud:

"Today, I call on the legion of feminine archetypes for help and clarity. I offer the Gayatri mantra to all of you, especially Veronica, who seems to be the harbinger of this experience, and *Saraswati*, the yogic goddess of wisdom and inspiration. I need inspiration."

As I finished the last syllable of the mantra, words shot through my fingers. *Her* words flew across the screen as I typed without thought:

> I would like to start by saying and deeply believing, "Everything I can do, you can do also."
>
> Who am I? What do I do?
>
> I follow the path of yoga as a spirituality and not a religion. With dedication and discipline, I experiment with the practices yoga offers to build my spiritual strength so I might know myself better and figure out what I want from my life.

This path helps me approach life more humbly as I have come to know that humans are not islands but, rather, we are all connected.

With that said, this morning, while driving and chanting a mantra I have come to use quite often—the Gayatri—I experienced a deep state of connection to everything where the usual parameters of my skin and physical space were nonexistent. After my car hit the young boy, it was this connection that moved me toward him, without dread, fear, or guilt about what had just happened. As I got closer to him, my hands spontaneously moved into Abhaya mudra, the Fearless Heart hand gesture of yoga. I knelt next to him, placing my right hand on his heart while leaving my left hand on my own.

I felt thin threads of light connecting me to him and to everyone who was there. I also sensed the threads extended out beyond the scene. The silver light flowed through me and to him. Our collective hearts joined together at that moment when I touched the boy.

I felt it. He felt it. We took a breath. The silver threads and the vital life force, known as *prana* in yoga, joined us together in that one instant. The action wasn't "I," but "We." It wasn't "Me," but "US."

Although I use words here, this experience is beyond rational description. I am not sure what it was or if it will ever happen again, but now, I know it is possible.

Maybe, just maybe, my dedicated practices of yoga have brought me to this point. If so, then why can't you do it too? We can continue to do it together!

I don't know if it was a miracle, but I do believe in them and the power of US.

I hit "post."

As my thoughts entered the world of social media, I wondered what would happen next.

I reminded myself this moment is all we have—be here, be present. Then a question floated through my mind: *Does the bird gliding high in the open summer sky wonder what will happen next?*

I closed my eyes. Deep breath in. Deep exhale to let go.

8

THE BOY'S STORY

Sean and I didn't own a TV. We found its distraction was too much of a challenge to keep our center. But our friends who had TVs were quick to text or call when any huge event was happening around the world. The headline, "Boy Raised from Dead by Yoga Teacher," was one of those events. Like everyone else, our friends had questions, but mostly, they wanted to help—even offering places to stay outside of the city.

The morning after the story hit the news, Carol, our bestie for the past thirty years, showed up on our doorstep loaded with bags of groceries and a cooler of homemade delicacies. She'd been our soul sister ever since she first introduced Sean and me so long ago. Over the years, we'd studied and meditated together on a regular basis. Carol was born a nurturer. She'd always claimed it's her Jewish DNA, but I believe it's also because her moon is in Cancer, the sign of the ultimate mother.

"Jesucristo," she said in her heavy Brooklyn accent. "First, I had to park three blocks away. Then I had to convince the cops I was your best friend. I asked, 'Who else would show up with all this food?' Thank god one of them agreed to help me get through the crowd. Otherwise, there's no way I could've gotten in here." She set everything on the floor. "Boys, what is going on? I mean, I know . . . but, Ren, what have you done?" Her voice was loving, and her big brown doe eyes beamed tenderness.

"I'm not sure, but I'm hoping all this attention goes away in a day or two," I said.

"Yeah," Sean said, nodding, "I'm sure it won't be long before another headline comes along to feed the beast of the media machine, and our life will go back to normal."

"Oy vey!" Carol said, putting her palms to her temples. "You two need to get your yogic heads out of the sand. This is not going away, and you need to stay informed so you don't get blindsided." She shook her head. "Now, give me your laptop," she said, commandeering Sean's keyboard.

"Carol, we've seen the video clip of what happened," he said.

"I hope so," she said, "it's everywhere. But wait—okay, gather 'round, my friends, because the celestial shit has hit the fan."

She stood between us as we watched a replay of an interview on *Good Morning America.*

"That's the kid!" I said.

On the interview couch sat the young boy, slight of build, with an energetic smile and a full head of dark-brown curly hair. He was dressed in blue jeans, a white long-sleeved shirt, and a polka-dot bowtie. There didn't seem to be a scratch on him. Next to the boy on the couch was a woman in her late thirties with an olive complexion, short dark hair, and an athletic build, wearing a heather-gray fitted suit jacket, matching pants, and a black open-collar shirt.

"That's the boy and the doctor from yesterday," I said, swallowing hard as I felt everything shift and change inside me.

Edward Bennet, the host of the show, who also looked a lot like George Stephanopoulos in his thirties, began the segment.

"So, Michael," the host said.

"You can call me Mike," the boy said.

"Okay, Mike," Mr. Bennet said with a laugh. "Now, tell us what happened Sunday morning on Columbia Parkway in Cincinnati."

"Well, my parents gave me a Kenda Kwest 700 for my birthday!" he said, scooting to the edge of his seat and leaning forward with a grin. "It was so rad, exactly what I wanted."

The host chuckled. "How old were you on Sunday?"

"Nine!"

"So, you decided to take the new bike out for a ride?"

"Yep, I wanted to see what it could do, so I headed over to a street with a huge hill that empties out onto Columbia Parkway. My parents don't want me to ride there because of the traffic, but I do it all the time." He paused and shared a guilty look with the audience. "I love speeding down the long hill and then cruising near the river."

"He's adorable," Sean said, "and so comfortable being on TV."

"Oh, the media is in love with him already," Carol said, squeezing both our arms. "Just wait."

"The bike felt great! But as I picked up speed going down the hill, something happened." Mike paused and now looked far too self-reflective for a nine-year-old.

"Did you have trouble with the brakes?" Mr. Bennet asked.

"I thought about squeezing the brakes, but I just couldn't get my hands to do it." Again, he paused. "I kept going faster and faster . . ."

"Could you see the traffic light up ahead was red?"

"Yep." The boy slowly nodded.

"Were you afraid?"

That question broke Mike's self-reflected trance.

"No! I knew this was going to be the ride of my life. I was *fearless!*" He grinned and lifted his left fist into the air triumphantly.

Fearless, I thought. *Abhaya mudra. The Fearless Heart mudra I held as I walked to him.* A nervousness I knew all too well swelled in my body as we continued to watch.

"I knew I was going to fly, me and my bike. Yeah!" Now, he was bouncing on the couch, barely able to contain himself.

"Like the boy in *ET?*" the host asked, smiling.

"Yep, just like him. I was laughing and then, I felt a burst that sent me and my 700 flying like a bird in the open sky." He spread his arms out to either side as if he were gliding. He took a deep breath and then landed back in his seat. "That's the last thing I remember till I woke up on the street with that man kneeling over me."

"Several people heard you say *thank you* to the man."

"Yep, I thanked him," the boy said.

"Do you know why?"

"Because he helped me," the boy said with conviction.

"But you got up and walked away on your own. How did he help you, Mike?"

"Uhmmm, I just know he helped me," he mumbled, shaking his head. "I get that people say I was dead, but look at me, I feel great! That's how I know he helped me." His eyes grew wide. "And the bike company wants to replace my bike for free! They said they're just happy to be part of a miracle."

Miracle. The boy said it. I felt goosebumps on my skin.

"Mike, do you feel you were part of a miracle?"

The boy looked around for a few seconds.

"I guess so. I got to fly without wings. I'll get my bike back, and, yay," he said, thrusting his arms overhead and grinning ear to ear, "I got a free trip here to see the Statue of Liberty!"

The audience cheered and applauded.

The host shook the boy's hand and then turned to his other guest.

"We also have with us—Dr. Gabrielle Jimenez, who, on her way to work that morning, saw the accident as it happened. Dr. Jimenez, thank you for joining us."

"My pleasure, Mr. Bennet."

"Doctor, you were the first responder to the boy. Tell us what you saw."

"I was in the front car stopped at the traffic light, going in the opposite direction. I saw Mike come down the hill, going through the red light, smashing into the car, and getting thrown. I saw the impact as he hit the street." She glanced over to the boy.

"That must have been intense."

She pursed her lips and nodded her head.

"And then?"

"I was on him in seconds. When I got there, he wasn't breathing. There was no heartbeat." She looked back to Mike and paused. "He was dead," she said, with the matter-of-factness of a scientist.

"Can you describe the scene as all this was happening?"

"It was frantic. People came running to help. Many were crying. I ran back to my car to get my defibrillator as a matter of procedure, not because I thought it would help. When I returned, the man who hit

Mike was walking calmly toward him. He looked so peaceful. He had his left hand over his heart and his right hand out in front of him. He knelt next to Mike and placed his right hand on the boy's chest. The man remained perfectly still. Normally, I would have been screaming at him to back away so I could at least try the defibrillator. But . . ." She paused. "I stopped and stood still. I felt as if I were in a holy place, like a temple, a cathedral, or a synagogue. I prayed. I don't even know what I was praying for. A sense of calm took over my body, and the commotion quieted as the man held his hand on the boy. Everyone was silent and still for those moments, a few seconds. I felt a strange yet loving connection to what was happening between them. Something I've never experienced. I heard the boy say thank you." Tears had welled up in her eyes. "And then, he got up on his own and walked away. He just walked away . . ."

"Other eyewitnesses have described a similar calm or peacefulness," the host added. "Some are calling what happened a miracle. Doctor Jimenez, would you call it a miracle?"

The doctor shifted in her seat and gave a bit of a frown. "I'm a trauma doctor. I see strange, intense things all the time. But this was unbelievable."

"So . . . ?"

"I can't explain it with science." She paused again and looked over to Mike. "So maybe we can call it a miracle."

Now, the doctor had used the word. Miracle.

"But no matter what, this has a happy ending, and God knows the world can use a few happy endings." She looked over at Mike and smiled, and he smiled back. Tears flowed down her face.

The studio audience was on their feet, yelling and clapping.

The clip finished. Sean, Carol, and I stood in silence. Carol reached for our hands and squeezed.

Then Sean reached over for my hand and held it tight. "Stay in the moment, Ren. Everything will be fine."

"Um, hmm," was all I had. I closed my eyes and took a deep inhale. Yes, I thought. Everything was changing, just like the chaos of the Universe around us. Everything was moving, spinning, and whirling.

And it is exactly how it is supposed to be. A new journey.

9

THE NINETY-YEAR-OLD WITNESS

yogah cittavrtti nirodhah
—Sutra 1:2

"The Miracle" quickly became the public catchphrase for what had happened between me and the boy. Social media and news outlets were abuzz with more eyewitness accounts and videos. Most descriptions were similar to the doctor's. Some witnesses also said they'd been healed.

"At first, I was horrified by what I saw," said one woman who'd witnessed "The Miracle." "Honestly, when I saw his little body crumpled on the asphalt, I had no hope, but then *something* changed."

One man who'd been there added, "I felt . . . connected to the kid and the man at his side. And I felt a weird, magnetic pull to the people standing around me."

Another male bystander said, "When the man touched the boy's chest, I felt a tingling sensation in my own chest. And afterward, I noticed my arthritis had eased up. By the next morning, I could stand up straight. For me, that's a miracle."

A witness from that day wrote on social media that she'd "felt pulled into a sort of rhythmic breath pattern that gave me this unusual sense of serenity. I was right beside that man, so I touched him on the shoulder to offer comfort. He then touched my hand, and suddenly, my chronic A-fib stopped! Just like that. My doctors said it would never go away without surgery. Well, it did. I've got one word for that . . . miracle."

The same day that Mike and Dr. Jimenez were on *Good Morning America*, Sean and I watched the local evening news on my laptop as they interviewed a ninety-year-old woman who had a unique perspective on the incident. The segment opened with a close-up of her face. The news ticker read, "Dottie Gant, Eyewitness."

"Wow," Sean said, "the Gants are the city's wealthiest philanthropists."

"I asked you here," the elderly woman said, "so I could share with you my vantage point. As you can see, being on the thirty-sixth floor, I have a bird's-eye view of where the hill of William Howard Taft Road and Columbia Parkway merge."

The camera angle widened to show her dramatically framed in a floor-to-ceiling window that overlooked the Parkway. Impeccably dressed in a coral, tweed, couture-fitted business suit, she pointed out the window and down.

"I was doing what I do every morning, reciting my prayers, right here in this chair." She placed her hand on an ornate Chippendale design chair situated in front of the window.

"I am grateful to have one of the most spectacular views of the city," Dottie Gant said as the camera panned the Ohio River, downtown Cincinnati, and Columbia Parkway. "Yes, every morning, I sit here with a cup of tea and my rosary." A beautiful, clear, glass-beaded rosary was wound around her left hand.

"Sunday was the final day of a novena to Mary, as the *Queen of Heaven*. I've been praying for world peace. It may sound trite, but prayer is about all I can do to help the world at this point in my life. I watched the boy as he sped down the hill and entered the intersection. I saw his impact with the car." She brought her left hand and the rosary to her chest. "I stood and stepped closer to the window, holding my breath as that poor little boy lay still on the ground. That's when I said out loud,

May the benevolent Queen of Heaven bring peace to those in front of me. I know it sounds crazy, but instantly, my whole body was overcome with tranquility." She paused and took a deep breath.

"I may be old, but I am *not* senile. I'm a businesswoman. I pay attention to current social and economic trends and still do my own investments. I like facts and figures. With that disclaimer . . ." She paused and looked directly into the camera as it moved in for a close-up. "I want you to believe me when I tell you, as the man knelt next to the boy on the ground, the people all around him began to shine like stars. I saw luminescent orbs on the road instead of people, *and* they were all connected by thin streams of light. It was stunning." She replaced her left hand on her chest with her right.

How mesmeric it must have been from her vantage point, I thought, *all the bright, thin streams of light.*

Her voice dropped to a whisper.

"It was the most exquisite thing I've ever seen, more beautiful than my view of the city, more beautiful than any place I've been fortunate to visit in my travels.

"I knew my prayer was heard. If I could still physically get down on my knees, I would have, but in lieu of that, I said *thank you.* All the news accounts reported that the boy had said thank you to the yoga teacher. I know with certainty I was saying thank you at the same time. Something extraordinary is going on here. That's why I need to speak out—why I called the station. We need to pay attention!"

Mrs. Gant took a deep breath and pointed toward the camera, her voice now shifting to that of a commanding CEO. "I've met three popes and four presidents in my life. Now, I plan to meet this *miracle man* and see what's going on. Who is he? How did *he* do this? We need more miracles in our world."

I was captivated by this woman and her recounting of her experience, but I wished she were talking about someone other than me. My head was spinning, so I opened my journal and wrote down my thoughts.

I am as confused as everyone else about what happened Sunday on the Parkway. I'm wondering if the bright lights emanating from everyone at the scene related to my Times Square vision and what Veronica said in my dream.

How do the Gayatri mantra, Abhaya mudra, and my experimentation with Pada Three of the Yoga Sutras play into this?

Have I opened a yogic Pandora's box?

The pen stopped. There was an emerging struggle between my mind and heart.

This is only the beginning, my ego-mind said. *Do it again! There will be more attention. You'll be famous and won't have to worry about money or work another day in your life. You can just heal people, be of service, and make the world a better place.*

My heart spoke softly but firmly: *Do not get derailed from what is truly important to your soul.*

At this moment, with my head full of chatter and the world calling me the miracle man, I couldn't be sure what was important to my soul. I needed to be clear and connect with the true Self inside me.

Go back to the beginning, I thought.

The first Sutra asks: *What is yoga?*

The second Sutra provides the answer: *Yogah cittavrtti nirodhah.*

Yoga is the complete mastery over the roaming tendencies of the mind.

I closed my eyes and went inward, not to escape but to regain my center.

10

RETURN OF THE COUNCIL

I sat in meditation immediately after Dottie Gant's interview and my journaling, but there was no depth to my journey. The same was true as I began my afternoon session. My ego fluctuated between making me a superhero and a total loser, and I was unable to turn off the mind and go beyond its veil of illusion. But I remained on my cushion and continued to chant the Gayatri mantra. Finally, the reality of the outside world began to dissolve, and I dropped into a place of no thought.

Suddenly, I saw in my mind's eye a flash—a fleeting image—of a set of highly polished twelve-foot-tall stainless-steel doors.

These were the same doors I'd seen in my dreams almost thirty years ago during my first Saturn Return, which is a time when the planet Saturn, the father of structure and discipline, returns to the exact place he was when we were born and demands our full attention.

What I remembered most about those long-ago dreams was entering through the large stainless-steel doors and sitting in front of a group of professional-looking people, all dressed in starched white lab coats, each with a legal pad and pencil. The room had no boundaries. There was no ceiling or walls—just a forty-foot-long mahogany boardroom table. The ten people—men and women—sat side-by-side on the other side of the table. I sat in a basic splat-back wooden chair facing them. The members took turns asking questions and sharing information that was "Saturnian" in nature: *What was I doing with my life, what plans was I making for the future, and was I on the right path for me?*

Those vivid dreams had been both intimidating and comforting. When I'd described them to Sean, I referred to them as "visitations."

During their first appearance, I'd asked why they were frequenting my dreams.

I distinctly remember a stately, well-groomed man with gray hair, who I later learned was Saturn. He sat at the center of the table and explained without hesitation that they were my board of advisors, my guides, *my council* if you will.

I'd asked about the lab coats and the boardroom setting, and at the time, he'd said it was the best way to get me to take them seriously.

Saturn had been right, of course. Thirty years ago, no way was I ready to see ancient gods and goddesses in flowing robes, with long hair and mala beads.

"Ren—"

"How do you know my name?" I'd asked.

"Of course, we know your name," Saturn said in a deep baritone voice that matched his commanding presence, broad shoulders, and massive chest. He explained further that they represented the eight planets and two luminaries of the solar system and their placement in my birth chart. They *were* my astrological makeup and, therefore, *were* me.

He then introduced himself as Saturn, which I'd strangely accepted without question. He said they'd come because of his natural return in the cycle of life.

A Saturn Return.

What I now remember most about these Saturn-led "visitations" was the guidance they offered for my spiritual evolution and their advice to use discipline to cultivate a meditation practice. One mesmerizing female council member had urged me to heed the teachings of yoga about deep contemplation. I still vividly recall her honey-colored blond hair, always perfectly piled on her head and held there by a pencil. She wore stylish black cat-eyed, horn-rimmed glasses. She'd counseled me to use my innate discipline to consistently practice meditation. She said this would expand my consciousness and deepen my understanding of love.

My initial dive into both yoga and astrology underscored their advice.

After two years and the completion of my first Saturn Return, I was relieved when the group of ten faded from my dreams. No matter how helpful—something about celestial guides visiting me in my dream state had me questioning my sanity.

Now, nearing my second Saturn Return, three decades later, the flash of the familiar stainless-steel doors during my meditation brought the council back into my psyche. They'd known so much about me then. I could only hope they would know how much I needed them now. Even though my meditation practices had evolved and developed deeply, maybe too deeply, I knew that *the miracle* had me at a crossroads—I needed all the celestial help I could get.

As I'd hoped, in that night's dream state, I found myself once again, after nearly thirty years, standing in front of the towering stainless-steel doors.

I took a deep breath, pulled open the giant doors enough to step in, and there they were. The council. All ten of them, still looking like a group of scientists in starched white lab coats, sitting behind the large conference table. The men were clean-shaven and well-groomed. The women had their hair pulled back into ponytails or wound into knots on the tops of their heads.

The atmosphere of the room was palpable with power.

"Hi, folks," I said with a wave. "It's been a long time. Can you maybe explain what's going on?"

I recognized Saturn immediately as he rose from his chair at the center of the table. "Yes, Ren, it *has* been a while, especially in your concept of linear time," he said. "Since our last meeting, you have deepened your astrological knowledge, so you know what we represent in both your psyche and your astrological chart. In time, all of our identities will be revealed. As you may remember, I am Saturn in Capricorn."

I gave a slight bow of my head.

"Yes, sir, I remember you well and have felt your presence every day of my life. I've often felt weighted down by you. But as I have grown and evolved, I've realized we have work to do. Your discipline and structure keep me on course. You are the taskmaster who provides the patience and endurance I need to reach my goals."

Saturn narrowed his eyes. "You are correct in my description, although a bit one-sided."

"Oh, I'm sorry, sir," I said. The last thing I wanted to do was tick him off.

"I get it," he said, "but you're only identifying with a partial, worn-out view of me. Remember, in tantra, there is always a combination of light and dark."

"I am your student, sir," I said. "What am I missing?"

"Besides ruling the structures of life, I also represent the father energy in the zodiac. In that role, I am here to help you decide whether to use your newly found powers for material gain or spiritual evolution. Will you climb the ladder of success for your ego gratification, or will you climb the spiritual mountain to enhance the Whole? Whether you see me as a loving, supportive paternal energy or a hard-core task master matters not. Either way, you face the Universal Law of cause and effect, Karma. And Karma is also my domain."

"Sir, I did not—"

He held up his massive hand. "In your life, I can be the Teacher or the Tester. As the latter, I ask you to trade your soul for power and money. In this role, some have named me Satan. But in my other role as a guide, to which you are currently blind, I teach the tantric nuances of light and dark and how to be in the world without becoming enslaved to the illusion of the material. I offer choices. *You* make the decision."

He paused and intensified his gaze. "Now, if you are feeling reprimanded or guilty, that is your decision. But feel free to project anything back onto me. I am used to playing the part of the heavy." He gave a deep chuckle.

I swallowed. "Um, I may have started off on the wrong foot."

"No, we have started off exactly as we need. My return is never light-minded. I am back for my second time, acting as gatekeeper to the rest of your council of heavenly bodies, including your co-chair." He looked to his left and then right to acknowledge the entire group.

"Co-chair, sir? I know you as the force that stands *alone* in my chart."

"We are all involved in your journey, Ren, but you are correct that you chose me to orchestrate much of this incarnation. You and I have a long history *and* a long way to go. As for the co-chair, they will reveal themselves in due time. Their presence is currently flowering in your heart."

I studied the faces of the others, wondering who my co-chair could be, but each council member remained expressionless.

"To address your initial question about what is going on, can you be more specific?" he asked as he crossed his arms over his broad chest.

"With respect to what happened on Columbia Parkway, did the boy come back from the dead or—?"

"What do you think?" asked a woman at the far end of the left side of the table, retrieving a pencil from behind her ear.

I was momentarily annoyed at the Socratic method she was using to engage me but, seeming to read my mind, she flashed a warm, loving smile.

"You've sensed my emotions," I said to her.

"I always do," she said. Her face was perfectly round, her skin milky white, and her silvery eyes sparkled like opals.

"You must be the Moon."

"Excellent observation. Now, what does your emotional inner knowing tell you about the boy?"

"I know if it's not your time to go, it's not your time. Astrology says you have to have a death aspect in your chart at the time of an accident, or death won't happen—like the one person out of many who survives a plane crash. Maybe it wasn't Mike's time to check out."

"You have been studying on so many levels," said the Moon. "Congratulations, your studies have helped you diminish the ignorance of *Avidya*."

"And I might add," Saturn said with a slight smile, "you have done quite well since our last appearance in educating not only yourself but others. You have made good use of my discipline, as explained in Sutra 1:13, to alleviate this first cause of suffering."

"Thank you, sir, for acknowledging my efforts to learn and grow. And yes, Sutra 1:13 seems to be very important, as do the yogic *kleshas* you are all mentioning, but that doesn't explain what's going on or why I'm involved."

"Facing the yogic *kleshas* and understanding Sutra 1:13 has more to do with what is going on than you know," said a woman at the opposite end of the table from the Moon. "For goddess's sake, we brought a statue to life to get your—"

"Ahem!" Saturn cleared his throat.

I did not remember this woman from my encounters thirty years ago. There was an air of power about her that exuded strength and confidence. Even seated, I could tell she was tall, maybe even as tall as Saturn.

"Besides study, the last time we visited you," the commanding woman continued, "we also advised you to meditate to calm your mind and access your inner strength. How do you feel that worked for you?" She bounced the eraser of her pencil on the table.

"Meditation changed my life. It led me to find a deeper place inside me," I said.

"But deep enough to overcome the many challenges of ego, coming at you from every direction, like a freight train?" she asked.

As I felt the familiar Saturnian fear constrict my solar plexus, I looked to the man himself, who had assumed Abhaya mudra. Instantly, my fear was replaced with the strength of conviction.

"Yes," I said. "Deep enough to face the challenges of *Asmita*-ego."

"Good!" she said matter-of-factly. "You will need to hone your meditations and tap into a deeper place in your heart to move forward." She leaned onto the table, and our eyes locked. "Look, I'm not as Pollyanna about you getting this right as are my colleagues."

"Get what right?" I asked. "And who are you anyway? I don't—"

"Just listen. We represent the different aspects of your astrological chart. We, your inner gurus, are the summation of the energies that constitute your Higher Self. The only answers we give you are the ones already inside you because *we are you*, and we live here." She gestured to her heart center. "That's why it's vital you open your heart this time and get on with the task at hand."

"The task at hand? I don't understand," I said, keeping her eye contact.

"You will," said Saturn, nodding. "Keep meditating. I give the discipline needed to apply the effort to cultivate a tranquil state of mind."

"I hear Sutra 1:13," I said.

"Yes," said a man with coarse, gray, wiry hair and chiseled, angular features, sitting next to the Moon, "move into the higher mind that is beyond the second klesha, *Asmita*-ego. It's the way to your heart. You're going to need it to walk the path of the remaining kleshas."

"The path of the kleshas, hmm, well . . . my ego is definitely screaming," I said to him. "With all the attention directed at me since I collided with the boy on the bike, *Asmita's* pulling me out of my heart."

"Continue to concentrate and meditate in the space of higher consciousness, where you will recognize the barriers of *Asmita*-ego and eventually learn how to dissolve them permanently," he said.

He must be Uranus, I thought, the awakener of higher consciousness and dissolver of barriers.

"Your mental supposition is correct," Uranus said, seemingly reserved yet self-assured.

"I see . . . *and* you can read my mind."

"We all can because we *are* you."

"Well, sir, barriers of *all kinds* are dissolving. I have moments where there's no separation between me and other people. I felt it with the boy," I said. "I have the overwhelming sense of being connected with everything right now. It's lovely, but . . . is this the dissolving of ego, or is this just part of my imagination?"

"YES!" said all ten. My eyes opened. I lay in bed, staring at the ceiling.

"Don't let that be the end," I said. "Damn, I need answers." *If my inner gurus are back and trying to get through to me, meditation is the best place for that to occur.*

So, instead of ruminating on the dream, I deepened my breath and let go of the mental chatter. A message bubbled up from my heart—*This isn't about knowing the answers. This is about allowing yourself to be open to all the possibilities.*

I let out a deep, long sigh.

The message continued—*This journey will lead you to uncover the diamond of your heart that radiates love and yearns for a connection with everything—a connection of Oneness.*

These thoughts of a new journey were underscored by the first rays of the morning sun peeking into our treehouse bedroom. With another deep sigh, my heart opened a little more, and I felt a hint of a smile come to my face.

11

THE BIRD

When I came downstairs, Sean was already in the garden with a cup of coffee waiting for me.

"So, how did you sleep?" he asked as I sat down.

"Do you remember my council visitations from years ago?"

"Ah, yes," he said, smiling. "The lab coat group." He sipped his coffee. "And?"

"Well, they're back!"

"Of course they are, and their timing is impeccable. Maybe they can give you some insights as to what's going on."

"Last night was like a reintroduction, along with warnings about ego challenges coming at me like a freight train."

"Those were their exact words?" he asked.

Out of nowhere, a sparrow flew between us and collided with the large gold-framed mirror that hung on our privacy fence. Its lifeless body fell to the deck.

"Oh man, that's number three in the last two weeks," Sean said. "The poor thing saw something, thinking it was real, only to find out unfortunately, it was just a reflection. Kinda like the veil of Maya that can cover our mind from reality."

"Great analogy," I said.

He stood and walked over to the bird.

"We all have a concept of reality that's just a reflection of what we like, don't like, and what scares us. The confusing thing is that reflection can be so convincing." He pointed to the tiny sparrow. "That bird didn't know the difference, and most of our life, neither do we."

"Wow," I said, "what a great way to look at the mind."

"You're not the only one studying the Yoga Sutras. I may not know as much as you or understand them to the depths of my being like you, but I'm trying really hard to break through this thick analytical mindset of mine."

"I know you study," I said. "I've never questioned your commitment."

"I know. It's my stuff, Ren. I've always been envious of your connection to the Universe, the gods, goddesses, whatever name you give it. And now this whole miracle thing is everywhere. I read today the Catholic Church is having a hissy fit because people are calling it a miracle without them certifying it. When did they get a monopoly on miracles?"

I shrugged.

"I wish the birds could see the mirror for what it is and fly around it." He knelt close to the sparrow. "What do you think? Can you lay your hands on the little guy and see what you can do? This should be easy. It just happened."

I froze in disbelief. *The freight train has infiltrated my bastion of love and support.*

"Are you serious?" I asked. "I don't know what happened with that kid, but I'm still Ren, just a regular guy. I can't raise things from the dead. Don't put expectations like this on me. I feel for the bird, but maybe it's his day to move on, and our mirror was his path."

"So, what if it was Mike's time to go, and our car was *his* path?" Sean asked.

"Even if I *could* bring the bird back to life, would it be right for me to meddle in the divine order? I'm not God," I said.

"You tell your students we are!" Sean said.

"What?"

"How many times have I heard you say in class that we all have a spark of the divine creator inside us? Maybe right now you're tapping into something that *can* do this." He pointed to the bird. "What about *that* as a possibility?"

"Tapping into something that can do what? Raise the dead? I don't want that kind of power."

"Too late," he said with rare sarcasm.

"The thought of that scares me, and *you* asking me this *really* scares me."

"I don't mean to scare you, but let me remind you of something else you always say to your students, which is . . . deal with *what is* and not with *what you think is supposed to be*. Ahh, we just circled back to the veil of Maya, didn't we?"

"Sean!"

"Try to step beyond your veil of illusion for a personal reality check!" he said. "Something happened between you and the kid on the bike. There are witnesses and a video. Add to that your long-term intense experimentation with *Dharana*, *Dhyana*, and *Samadhi* from Pada Three."

"I'm not sure I get your point," I said.

"Oh, I think you do. You told me months ago, before this happened, that you've been *dropping in* to places you didn't even know existed. You said you thought you were starting to understand, on a soul level, that the finite can never satisfy what we are infinitely inside. I can't even fathom what that means! But you do. I know you do!" He paused.

I was speechless in a way that only Sean could elicit.

"Then, on your way to class to discuss Pada Three, which describes how people who study like you do develop unexplained powers, *you* literally place your loving hand on some kid you hit with the car, who everyone says was dead, and he walks away after thanking you. And, oh, oh, oh . . . let's not forget your recent flying dream over Times Square, talking statues of Catholic saints quoting the Yoga Sutras and, as of last night, the return of your internal council. Then, we are back to my point. Let's deal with what is, Ren, please!"

I shook my head and looked over at the dead bird. "I don't want to know either way how this would work out."

"Okay," Sean said, "so, you just want to stay in this sense of limbo, even though the world outside our fence is clamoring for your attention and thinks you are the best thing to ever hit the planet?"

"Right now, yes!" I said. My heart was pounding in my chest.

"Okay, buddy," his tone softened.

"Sean, I know how deeply you feel about all living things," I said, trying to bring the attention back to the bird, "it's beautiful, but I just can't—"

"Okay," he said, "I'll decide what to do with the mirror tomorrow. I'm going to go take a shower."

I took a deep breath and looked at the small bird. How ironic. Just like Sean said, this creature flew directly into what it believed to be reality. We do the same thing as humans. When we don't take the time to step back and self-reflect, we continue to move toward and into a reflection that looks real but can be merely an illusion created by our mind.

After Sean went into the house, I walked over to the bird, cupped my hands about a half inch from it, and sang the Gayatri mantra. Then I scooped it up and walked over to the far end of our garden paradise and knelt in front of a huge big-leaf hydrangea.

"I give you back to the Earth," I said. "I bless you on your journey wherever it might take you."

Hundreds of birds in our neighbor's massive maple tree began to sing loudly. I felt their song move into my heart center and reverberate through my whole body as a feeling of joy. I then placed the bird carefully under the pink flowering plant. I stood and turned. With my first step, all the birds in the tree stopped singing at the same time. I paused and breathed in their silence. Then I heard it! One small chirp from directly behind me.

Don't turn around. Asmita! Your ego is looking for something. You don't want to know.

I picked up my pace and walked into the house. Was I going crazy?

Then a small voice in my heart said, *Perhaps you are finally living . . . fully.*

I leaned against the wall in the kitchen and closed my eyes. *Don't get caught by the illusion.* As the Sutras counsel, the *siddhis* you develop from your practices will only hinder your spiritual evolution by elevating your ego.

"Hey, Reno. You all right?" Sean asked as he entered the room.

"Yeah," I said, standing up straight and trying to look normal. "I was saying a little sendoff prayer to our sparrow friend. I gave him to the hydrangea. The deep pink of the flowers seemed like a perfect resting place."

"Thanks for doing that. So, did you feel anything or—?"

"Love," I said. "Just love."

Even as I said the words, I felt my ego wanting to take credit. I must be careful. *Is* my meditation deep enough to overcome the many challenges of ego that are coming at me from every direction, like a freight train? Yes, every direction, even from Sean. His request to save the bird was like an earthquake that was only adding to my current sense of schizophrenia.

Sean went back outside to deal with the mirror, and I headed to my studio and sat on my meditation cushion.

I took a deep breath. *My council's return last night was no coincidence.* As I exhaled, I said, "Tester or Teacher? This has Saturn written all over it."

12

THE MOUNTAIN GOAT

The door of my studio opened. "I thought you'd want to take this call," Sean said. "It's Carter." He handed me the phone and then closed the door.

I'm not alone. Carter is feeling me from halfway around the world.

Besides Sean, there were two people on the planet to whom I felt intuitively connected: Sara, my spiritual meditation mentor, and Carter, my astrological teacher. A vibrant, bearded, robust man in his mid-seventies who spoke seven languages fluently, Carter had been studying and teaching astrology for over fifty years. He was considered the undisputed master of esoteric astrology, known worldwide for the artful way he merged the yoga of evolutionary consciousness with practical personality astrology. His was not a path to merely predict events but to synthesize what was happening in a person's life and explain its significance in regard to their soul's journey. I had savored every moment of the nine years I had studied with him.

"Carter! I am *so* glad to hear from you."

"I'm sure you are, my friend. Is Saturn pushing you to the brink of implosion?" he said in his almost-British, but at times, New York accent.

"How did you know? I mean, of course, you know," I said with a laugh.

"Yes, when a client makes international news by raising the dead, I look to the current planetary energies to see how they are affecting their chart."

"So, you know about—?"

"Of course, my dear," he said. "Bora Bora may be remote, but even here, I am able to listen to the news and follow stories on the internet. These days, you're like divine providence. You're everywhere."

"Carter, I'm wondering—"

"I am sure you have questions, but I would like to give you what I see before we open it to a discussion. Is that all right with you?"

"Of course," I said.

"To begin, let's clarify a few things. We are both aware of the intensity and challenges found in your chart, and we both know that challenges and difficulties are part and parcel of life. Agreed?"

"Yes," I said, "I'm well aware of the difficult energies in my chart."

"We also agree that before we come into this life, we decide what we need to work on for the evolution of our soul, and therefore, we choose our birth chart as the karmic playpen in which to underscore the needed lessons. Correct?"

"Yes. The chart and the path I'm on are things I chose."

"Of course," he continued, "there is also the choice to stay blissfully ignorant if there is such a thing, and stay asleep and numb to our spiritual reality. But that is the path of *Avidya* and not *your* path."

"Staying blissfully ignorant has never been an option for me."

I wasn't sure where Carter's line of reasoning was going.

"I underscore the obvious—to make sure you don't feel sat upon by some celestial overseer but realize *you* are responsible for your journey. The last thing you need is to take on some martyr complex. Now, as I see it," he said in a more serious tone, "there is an extraordinary event or series of events coming your way."

"More extraordinary than what has already happened?" I asked.

"Yes. Pluto, the planet that coincides with the yogic god Shiva, is transiting through Capricorn, the sign of Saturn's structure. Having four plants in Capricorn, you are experiencing a tearing down and restructuring of things you have, until recently, been able to rely on to support you," he said. "The energies of Pluto and Saturn are churning up the old, tried, and true to create fertile ground where new things can grow. You're transforming how you are to serve the greater good of humanity by expressing the esoteric nature of Saturn as the spiritual mountain goat."

"Okay, Carter," I interjected when he finally took a breath, "I know that Capricorn is depicted as a mountain goat, but for the rest of it, remember, we're not all master yogi-astrologers. At least, not yet."

"Of course," he said with a light chuckle. "Let me break this down for you. The spiritual mountain goat helps others gain firm footing on their path upward by providing an example. Step here, then there. Show them how to do it, or more eloquently put: *everything I can do you can do also.*"

"Carter," I said, "just yesterday, I was guided by a goddess to use those very words in my social media post, but I'm filled with so much self-doubt that I don't know what to do with it."

"Remember, my friend, Saturn, as *one* of your chart leaders, plays a larger-than-life role in your current incarnation, and his shadow is to cast doubt."

"I feel his presence," I said, nodding. "But you mentioned he is one of my chart leaders. Who else is leading?"

"Without a doubt, it's that goddess who is whispering in your ear," he said. "Venus is your co-chair, my dear. Like Jesus *and* yours truly, you have Venus in Pisces. Compassion runs through your veins. You want to serve. You *have* to serve! Venus is her own undeniable force when she resides in the sign of the fish."

"You and Jesus have Venus in Pisces? Those are some big shoes to fill." I laughed. "But what does that have to—"

"Oh, no one can be sure about Jesus, of course, but the combination of lower and higher love represented by Venus in the sign of Pisces is what Christ's-Consciousness is all about—seeing the Divine spark in all creation and living in unconditional love as much as possible. If it sounds like *Samadhi* from the Yoga Sutras, it should," he said. "They're one and the same. Now, Ren, don't let your ego inflate over this combination."

"Oh, it's not," I said. "If anything, I feel it's beyond me to live that way. I aspire to unconditional love, but I've made some bad decisions and live with regret that still hangs over me."

"Hmm, you're dealing with the imperfection of being human," he said, sounding haughty. "Everyone makes mistakes, my friend. Get over it!"

I felt I had been slapped in the face.

"And now you're feeling small and reprimanded, correct?"

"Well, yes, I—"

"Get over that as well! Listen to me, and not the Saturn-influenced part of your ego," he said. "Everyone has the potential to attain this awakened consciousness, but with Venus in her exalted position in Pisces and the level of meditation I know you practice, you feel her unconditional love deeply and can access it readily. *But . . .* you also have a spiritual responsibility to share and show this deep love."

"As co-chairs, Venus and Saturn are not in simpatico," I said.

"*Au contraire, mon frère*," he said in perfect French. "These antithetical energies help you balance the quantitative side of your practical, earthy Saturn-led stellium with the qualitative spiritual realm of your loving Venus-led grand trine in water. Saturn's discipline is necessary! It's what keeps you doing your practices consistently, but discipline alone can be dry and lifeless." He cleared his throat. "Think of Saturn as your favorite college professor who expands your mind and inspires you to take your studies further, while Venus is your trusted friend who invites you out for cocktails and helps you put what you're learning in the classroom into the context of everyday life."

"Oh, that analogy is helpful," I said with a chuckle.

"I thought the mention of cocktails would be. Hmm, now, from what I see astrologically, and keeping the Yoga Sutras in mind, you are being asked to surrender into unconditional devotion. In yoga, it's called *Bhakti*," he said. "The devotion that encourages a deep surrender into the true meaning of life beyond the material world, the mind . . . *and* the *kleshas*."

It all sounded familiar.

"And," he added, "keep in mind that deep devotion is feminine. It's what you need to access Venus Energy.

"Saturn obviously has your number and has set your foundation.

Now, Venus is calling. Pick up the phone, put her on speaker, my friend, and listen to what she has to say." His voice was purposefully modulated. "With these *siddhis* you're exhibiting, you've clearly accessed *some* measure of qualitative love. *But* I am telling you, deeper layers of self-discovery are coming to you through her and most probably more *siddhis*."

"Oh goddess, no more *siddhis*, please—"

"They're coming, my friend. How they will come, only time will tell. I see big energy shifts through your chart. So, learn quickly to recognize ego, which disguises itself in the subtlest ways and only serves as an obstacle to what you truly need to be doing. Be vigilant in seeking it out, *and* do not think this is all about you. You are only one piece of what is happening."

Mystical revolutionaries.

"But what does all this have to do with miracles?" I asked.

"Eh, miracles are not so extraordinary," he said. "They're merely happenings that can't be explained rationally. The catch is, miracles are only attainable with a pure heart."

"That's what I don't understand, Carter. How did this come through me? I am *not* pure of heart, I'm not without sin, I'm not—"

"Boy," he said, his voice now stern, "you're going to have to yank this doubt of yours out by the roots. Our foibles are part of being human. Forgive yourself and move on."

I heard him take a deep breath.

"We could have unlimited miracles if collectively more of us purified our hearts by forgiving and connecting to the true source of being with no quantitative, selfish motives. That doesn't happen overnight, and until we are 100 percent there—we forgive ourselves when we trip or fall. The intent of the heart is what counts." A softness returned to his voice. "Deep down, we all know there is more to life than what we can see, touch, and taste. That's why *metaphysics* is surging with the millennials and Gen Z. Most of them have an astrology app on their phone and consult it daily."

"Really?" I asked.

"Oh, for the love of god, don't tell me you are not on Instagram or TikTok!" He sighed. "These young folk are trying to make sense of all the different dimensions of being human, some of which are knowing and believing in the unseen. Through an example of what is possible, like a miracle, you give them hope."

My head and heart were swirling with his words.

"Carter, plain and simple, I'm overwhelmed. I need some time to reflect."

"Of course you do, my boy. Meditate on what I've said and get ready."

"Get ready for what?" I asked, bracing myself.

"An accelerated path forward. Call me as you need me."

"I appreciate your understanding," I said, knowing he had my back energetically.

"I understand more than you know," he said. "One last thing." He spoke more slowly than before.

"Yes?"

"Cast a chart for the moment your car hit the boy. You'll see for yourself the spiritual significance of what is happening. I believe you will be quite surprised."

"I'll do that," I said. "Thank you."

"And in case you haven't looked at this yourself, the numerology of *thank you*, the only words Mike said to you that morning of the miracle, is thirteen. Something else to contemplate, my friend."

"The words *thank you*, the number 13, and I are good friends," I said.

"Thirteen and its compound four," Carter said, "vibrate to the unpredictable and ever-changing energy of the planet Uranus, which represents group consciousness and the collective. These energies are also significant, as you'll see when you cast the chart. Remember, Ren, all the planetary energies are involved, but Saturn and Venus lead you this time around. All right then, my friend, stay focused and know you are worthy." With that, he hung up.

I put down the phone, beelined to my cushion, took my seat, and closed my eyes.

How would I add more Venus devotion, counter the quantitative aspects of Saturn, and tame the ego-mind, as Carter suggested?

Come inside, whispered the voice in my heart. *Your heart will move you naturally from quantitative to qualitative love.*

In my mind's eye, I watched as my heart guided me from my car on the Parkway toward the boy on the ground. I internally chanted the Gayatri mantra as I knelt beside Mike and placed my hand on him. My heart, touched by devotion and combined with the energies of the many, had one qualitative, energetic objective—compassion for the boy. We shared transpersonal love for Mike. *His* energetic essence decided what to do with it.

That's when Mike rose from the pavement. The miracle was *not* his resurrection. Rather, the miracle was our Venus-inspired group energies coming together for the common good of him and *US*, our United Souls.

These actions came from a pure heart with no thought of self or ego. They contained an element of deep letting go that was much like the dew drop hanging on the edge of a leaf just before it slips and falls to the ground. Does the dew drop know, as it lets go, that it will then nourish the plant at its base? Does it trust it will add to the whole by its actions?

I heard another whisper: *Allow the Universe to unfold inside you without getting sidetracked by what your mind thinks.*

But my mind did think *and* question.

Was I up for this incredible ride Carter and my council talked about? Where did I, a fledgling yogi who doubted his worthiness, fit into the miracle?

Stop trying to understand. Instead, come inside and learn to surrender—I sensed this message from the divine feminine arise from deep within me. I bowed to Venus and asked her to step into the driver's seat of my journey.

I then sat in the stillness of my seemingly flawed heart and waited for a nudge, a shove, a sign, a voice, a stirring, or perhaps even another miracle.

13

THE CHART

The next morning, over coffee, Sean and I sat at the kitchen table and, as Carter suggested, ran a chart for the moment I'd hit Mike on the Parkway.

"What do you think this will show?" Sean asked as he typed the time, date, and place of the incident into an astrological website on his laptop.

"Carter said this chart will point out the spiritual significance of what happened that day," I said.

A circle divided into twelve sections, which showed the exact placement of the Sun, Moon, and the eight planets appeared on his screen. Colorful lines filled the interior of the circle, connecting the planetary symbols with mathematical configurations known as aspects.

"Wow, look at all those planets in the upper part of the chart *and* in the eleventh house," he said, pointing to a particular section in the upper half of the circle. "The eleventh house represents the collective consciousness of humanity, its hopes, dreams, aspirations, and rising above and beyond ego, right?" Sean asked.

"Exactly," I said, "all that energy points to manifesting the hopes and dreams of the collective into reality. And Venus and Neptune are exactly conjunct in Pisces, combining the elements of lower and higher love with mysticism and compassion."

"And wait, wait, wait . . . if we compare this chart with your birth chart," Sean said as he clicked on another document on his desktop, pulling up a copy of my chart, "that conjunction lines up exactly with your natal Venus in Pisces."

"For those two to be tightly together . . ." I paused and pointed to the symbols representing Venus and Neptune, which were snug up against each other, "and with *my* natal Venus smack in the middle of all that planetary energy, it sets up the Parkway event to be something otherworldly."

"Like a miracle," Sean said, staring at the chart.

I was silent.

"As hard as it is for me to say it, that's what happened," Sean said. "Something otherworldly. And now, we're looking at celestial proof. With most of that energy gathered in the eleventh house, which is ruled by Uranus, and taking place smack in the middle of two eclipses, it seems the Universe gave you a personal invitation to do what you did. And didn't Carter say Uranus vibrates to the number 13, which just happens to be your birthday, Veronica's feast day—"

"I know, I know," I said, "everything lined up."

"Amazing!" Sean said, slapping his hands on the table. "Astrologically, that day, the combined energies of all the planets were working together. The chart for that moment shows healing a group wound, altruistic surrender, and Saturn orchestrating a big transformation through death and rebirth as he sits in the eighth house. I mean, could Saturn have been more literal with raising the—"

"Okay, okay," I said, "I need to step away from this for a while."

"I know this must be overwhelming, but Carter's right. This answers so much."

"Does it?" I asked. "I'm still confused. What are you getting from all this?"

"I think the planetary energies of that moment were like a thunderbolt to your soul, making you a conduit to magnetize the energy of the group in order to heal Mike." Sean reached over and squeezed my arm. "Face it, over the past thirty years, you've tapped into the energy of Saturn. You've stayed focused, diligent, and committed to your yoga practices. That same commitment is now offering you access to Venus, the goddess of love. This moment," he said, pointing to the chart, "was the perfect convergence of all your guides."

I sat back in my chair and sighed. "Let's say you're right. Again, I ask, why?"

"I can't believe *I'm* going to say this to *you*, but—you're being too rational."

"*I'm* being too rational? That *is* quite a shift," I said with a smile.

"Carter just gave you a lesson in quantitative over qualitative, telling you to listen to your heart over your ego. Asking 'why' is a rational, quantitative tool of the mind. Believe me, I know. Let it go. Venus it up a bit." He winked at me.

"I know I have issues with *letting go*, but . . . I also know when I do let go, things open up," I said.

"Yep, and when we do, bam! Life becomes a beautiful journey."

"Yes, it does." I sat up straight and laughed. "Venus it up? You know, after talking with Carter, I sat for a short meditation and asked Venus to take over as the driver on this journey."

"I see, but to truly move from quantitative to qualitative, you can't just give Venus control of the steering wheel."

"What do you mean?"

"To really let go, you have to take your foot off the brake and give that over as well."

14

MYSTIC TRANSFORMATION

Consistent practice to the yogi is like blood to the vampire.
Once you taste the richness your practices bring,
you can't live without them.

—VENUS

After casting the chart, we sat for our morning meditation using the Gayatri mantra as our opening invocation. At first, my mind was busy with mental distractions, but by the fourth time through, the mantra rose in my heart and slowly replaced all other thoughts. "*Aum Bhur, Bhuvah, Swaha . . .*"

Then, I felt myself shift into another world.

Inside this other realm, my eyes opened. I sat on the edge of an unfamiliar four-poster bed in a strange house. It was cold, dark, and musty. I felt a warm dampness on the left side of my neck. I lifted my hand to investigate. There was blood on my fingers, but oddly, I was not alarmed. The sound of footsteps pulled me to the open window. I was in a peculiar state that was part meditation and part sleepwalking.

I was drawn to explore the dark shadows and deepest depths of the night, so I climbed out the window and descended a wrought-iron trellis to the ground below.

A gnawing desire grew inside me, but for what, I did not know. Once both feet were on the ground, I noticed a man standing beside me, dressed like a Catholic priest, in a tailored black suit and a white collar. His eyes were clear, and his skin had an unnatural porcelain sheen.

"You are morphing into an immortal creature of the night," he said. "One that needs blood to survive." He reached his hand toward me. "I have what you need."

"The yogi also morphs." I turned toward a lilting voice. To my surprise, it was the mesmerizing woman who sat to the right of Saturn at the council table, her honey-blond hair draped over her white one-shoulder tunic.

"Through your practices," she continued, "you experience a slow change that flows into all areas of your life. You work with the shadow to bring everything about you into the light and reclaim the hidden parts of yourself. Consistent practice to the yogi is like blood to the vampire." Her hazel eyes were hypnotizing. "Once you taste the richness your practices bring, you can't live without them. Why would you want to?"

I was compelled to take a step closer to her.

"The answers you seek are in the cave of your soul," she said. "Fearlessness is needed to traverse the dark of the cave, but that is where you will remember that you are a spark of the God Force, immortal in consciousness, and therefore need not fear transformation—even the transformation of death!"

"Oh, be sure death will come if you continue to follow her," the priest said, moving nearer to me. His gaze, too, was hypnotizing. "Your path will be better served if you follow me. Do as I say, and I will protect you from death *and* offer you the adoration of the world."

Any spell he had on me was broken.

"Do as you say, sir?" I said. "I follow nothing blindly, and as for protecting me from death, nothing can. It's part of our common journey to experience Yama, the god of death. And the adoration of the world will only derail me from my spiritual path."

"Yes," the woman said, "continue with your practices of mantra, mudra, *pranayama*, and *asana*. These are the practices of transformation and enlightenment. As lonely as the path may seem at times, it gradually leads you back to knowing you are immortal, you are never alone, and you are meant to live in bliss—all without blood stains, guilt, or shame."

She reached her hand to mine. I clasped hers in return. As we began to walk together, the dream shifted—the familiar stainless-steel doors appeared. We walked into the boardroom together. She took her usual place next to Saturn, and I took mine, facing them all.

"I see you've met your co-chair," Saturn said.

"So, you are Venus?" I asked my dream companion.

"Yes." She smiled demurely.

"Thank you for walking me out of that nightmare," I said to her. Then I turned to the full council. "I may not fully understand the symbolism of a vampire priest, but I know this all has something to do with the deep transformation stirring inside me. I get the feeling raising the dead is not the ultimate focus here."

"It's not," said Venus. "Rather, these recent events are bringing a profound transformational meaning to the phrase, *Everything I can do, you can do also.* When humans live and love from a place of deep inner compassion for all beings, when they choose to experience Oneness and not separation, when they join the energies of their hearts together—then magic happens—miracles occur."

"That explains a lot about the Parkway," I said.

"Yes, it does," she said, nodding, "and we're looking to you to get the word out, so we need your full, undivided attention to get you ready for the accelerated happenings that are about to unfold."

"Wait," I said, raising my hand to pause the conversation. "All this talk about getting the word out and accelerated happenings is making me extremely nervous."

"Here we go," the woman at the far right of the table said, rolling her eyes. She shifted in her chair, turning away from me.

"We know it makes you nervous," Saturn said, ignoring her. "But we will be offering you opportunities to prepare for all this as we continue to walk you through the kleshas."

"What's this all about?" I asked, shaking my head.

"Relax, Ren, you'll see soon enough," Saturn said. "First, Venus and I have some questions in an effort to lay some groundwork."

"This should prove interesting," said the still-agitated woman at the end of the table.

"Who *are* you?" I snapped.

"Keep your focus," my stately, gray-haired mentor said, drawing my attention back to him. "Now, tell us how you came to access your spiritual superpowers and enlightenment."

"Please don't call them superpowers, and I don't consider myself enlightened."

"Why?" Venus asked.

"I'm not the person everyone thinks I am. I have regrets and shame about those regrets. My astrological chart shows I'm working through the *samskaras* of intense past Karma to heal wounds and move forward. I'm just now learning to understand how wounds are part of my evolution and how to accept them, even the intense ones, with deep love and gratitude."

"That is the path of the enlightened mystic," Saturn added. "Few are born with true insight. Most work through diligent practice to increase their self-awareness."

"I'm in the 'diligently practicing' category," I said.

"Why are you working so hard to increase your self-awareness?" Saturn asked. "You could remain blissfully ignorant."

Not according to Carter, I thought.

"That's not for me," I said, shaking my head. "There's something rooted inside, pushing me to pursue the profound meaning of my existence and to reconnect with my cosmic origins. I believe there's some kind of innate desire in all humans to journey back home to connect with Oneness. I know that may sound out there . . ." I paused, remembering who I was speaking with.

Saturn smiled. "How are *you* connecting with the divine in your life?" he asked.

"Through the path of yoga," I said.

"You're on the right track, Ren," Venus said. "We know you are diligently working, but it's time to put down your ego-fed doubt, deal with your unfathomable sense of regret, and accept your path."

"The regret of saying 'no' to my nine-year-old nephew still haunts me," I said. "I wear it like a shroud, and I can't confide in anyone about it. That's not something I can just snap my fingers and let go of."

"Yes, you can," said my still-unnamed female nemesis.

"Ren," Venus said, pulling my attention back to her, "to rid yourself of guilt and regret, say you're sorry on a soul level, and then let it go. Those feelings are not you, but only part of your process."

I leaned forward, put my head into my hands, and took a couple of full breaths. My brain felt full.

"I'm so confused," I said as I looked back to the council.

"Humanity needs more mystics who, like you, live in the everyday world," Saturn said. "Mystics help change the world and put it on track for right human action."

"Yes," Venus added. "Teach by example, move from the heart, and look into your past to find the deep patterns and wounds that need to be transformed. Make your life a prayer. Connect with the internal witness who sees each moment for what it is and makes each moment of life sacred. Can you see this is your journey?"

"I want to say yes," I said, "but this mystical transformation feels so dark and lonely."

"Very dark and lonely," said Venus, "because the personal relationship mystics have with the divine is a threat to organized dogma and society's need to control the masses. But, nonetheless, more mystical revolutionaries are coming into their own, and as you recognize each other, you will not feel lonely, but empowered. There will be challenges to all of you as you become more visible, but remember the light and dark of tantra and meet the challenges with love." She stood. "There is no greater power than love. We are all with you." She gestured to both sides of the conference table. "Right now, the feminine is especially supportive of your transformation and healing. The feminine needs your help, Ren. The first step is to be willing to forgive everyone, especially yourself."

The space behind my eyes went black. I was back on my cushion, and Sean was reciting the closing prayer of our meditation:

"May all beings have happiness and the causes of happiness.

May all beings be free from suffering and the causes of suffering.

May all beings know the sacred space that lies beyond suffering.

May we all have equanimity beyond hatred, anger, attachment, and fear, and

May we all know the equality of all that lives."

From a place deep in my heart, I spontaneously added, "May we be the inspiration to ourselves and to all beings that leads us to the path of everyday miracles."

15

ANTICHRIST AMONG US

Later that afternoon, Josh stopped by the house to check on us. Josh was the only child of my brother, Dave, and the nephew I'd spoken of to Venus, the one who held my deepest guilt and regret. The car accident had brought our whole family to its knees. Josh had gone to live with his maternal grandmother. I'd never forgotten that she had not been his first choice. I was.

Josh walked in, loaded down with a warm smile and bags of groceries, just like Carol. "I was thinking you probably aren't able to get out, so I thought I'd bring by some supplies." With a slightly reddish complexion, light-brown hair, and freckles, he was the perfect blending of his parents. "Looks like my timing is good. The street's pretty clear right now."

"Oh my god, this is perfect," I said as I helped him with the bags. "It's usually a circus out there. So many people gawking at the house."

"Tell me about it. Ever since you did the Jesus thing on the Parkway," Josh said, "we've had strangers and reporters knocking on our door. I mean, it didn't take long for the media to connect us to you."

"The Jesus thing?" I repeated back to him. "You're making me laugh."

"What else would you call it?"

"I'm still not sure what exactly happened. I try not to think about it too much—it pulls me off center."

We walked into the kitchen.

"Do you remember that massage you gave me a couple of weeks ago?" he asked, helping me put everything away.

"Absolutely, how's your shoulder?"

"Ever since that massage, my range of motion has increased, *and* it's not keeping me up at night."

"Excellent!"

"Yeah, it's great." Josh paused and looked at me with puzzlement. "But for me to get more range of motion after twenty years . . . it's pretty much . . . um . . . a miracle."

"Hold on, let's not go there, please!"

"I'm telling you, something's different in here," Josh said, rubbing his left shoulder.

"That's great. Clients have told me I have a magic touch, but a miracle touch takes it too far," I said with a smile.

"Okay, but I wanted you to know. I think there's something to all this hype about your 'magic' touch."

I focused on the groceries.

"I'm sure this has changed your life," Josh said, handing me the last of the provisions. "Are you still chanting the mantra you wrote about in your post?"

"You read my post?" I asked as I sat down at the table and gestured for him to do the same.

"Everybody's read it, dear uncle. That *and* the Parkway video are trending everywhere."

"Well, I'm not even sure I know what trending means, but to answer your question, yes, I'm sitting a lot in meditation, but chanting the Gayatri constantly as well."

"What does the mantra do?"

"The Gayatri is a specific request to the Supreme Being to enlighten our intellect and inspire us with wisdom."

"Sounds like something the whole world should be chanting right now. I know I could use it," he said.

"One way I explain it to my yoga students is the prayer spirals from the heart of the chanter through the entire universe as an appeal for peace and divine wisdom for all."

"Spiraling from the heart, appealing for peace—do you think that you've tapped into something through your chanting?" he asked.

"I don't know, but I've been chanting it spontaneously for months. On the day of the *Jesus thing*," I said and nudged his shoulder, "I was chanting it as I hit the boy and as I went to him."

"It's amazing—however it happened. I bet it feels good knowing you helped a kid who really needed you," he said a bit wistfully.

I heard Venus's words, *Say you're sorry on a soul level, and then let it go.*

"Josh, I hope you know . . . I wish I could have . . ."

"Ren, I was talking about you and the kid," Josh said as he touched my hand. "I think it's great you helped him."

"I know, but . . . I still deal with guilt about you . . . and Lisa."

"How *is* Lisa?" he asked, attempting to change the subject.

"She's great. She called several times to check on us after what happened on the Parkway. You know, Lisa, Sean, and I have developed a tight friendship. She and I were friends before she and I ever dated, and we'll be friends forever," I said. "I hope you both can forgive—"

"Let's not go there," he said. "How 'bout you teach me the mantra? That will help me out."

"Okay," I said, "but as I see it, you've been tapping into wisdom since you were a kid."

"Come on," he said, looking away from me, seeming self-conscious. "Teach it to me."

We spent the next half hour going over the Gayatri. I loved joining our voices.

"I should get going," Josh finally said. "The boys are out of school today, so Whitney has her hands full."

"How is your beautiful family?" I asked.

"Just great," he said. "Both boys are completely obsessed by what happened on the Parkway. I think Harry's watched the video a hundred times. It's hard to compete with video games with a six-year-old, but I think you've done it.

"You know, Whitney's grandparents have that piece of land not far from here, near Lexington," he said as he stood. "You and Sean are welcome to go there anytime you like. Might be nice to get away from all this craziness."

"How about tomorrow?" Sean said as he walked into the kitchen. "Not that I'm eavesdropping, but I was, and we could use a break."

"Tomorrow would be perfect. I'll let Whitney's grandparents know." Josh reached into his pocket and took out his key ring. "Here's a key to the gate," Josh said, sliding it off the ring and handing it to me. "You'll have the place all to yourself, and once you're beyond the gates, no one can bother you."

"Sounds like heaven," Sean said. "Peace, quiet, some time in nature, and a chance to just be us."

"Hey," I said to Sean the next morning as we packed a cooler for our road trip, "I've been meaning to apologize."

"For what?"

"I know I got whacked out when you asked me to help the bird. It's just I thought the ego freight train the council talked about was referring to all the people out in front of the house, reporters constantly knocking on our door, and the media hounding our friends and family for info on us. I never expected it to come from inside the house, so—"

"It's okay, really. I should be the one apologizing," Sean said. "I know I pushed a button. I didn't mean to be part of the freight train, but we are both under intense pressure. Anyway, this little getaway will be perfect, just the two of us with Mother Nature, no media, no negative emails or calls—"

"What do you mean, no negative—"

"Nothing. It'll just be us and the vibes of the daisies, the coral bells, the oak, and the maple."

"Is there something I should know?"

"Not right now, my love. Let's go sit with Brother Sun this afternoon and Sister Moon tonight."

He was right. We needed this break. I let his comment go.

"Whatever you do," Sean said as we left through the side kitchen door, "don't make eye contact with anyone on the street. Today's not the day to do any healing. It's about getting some R&R. I purposefully backed into the driveway last night, so it should be easy to scoot into the car and pull out."

As we jumped into the car, any hope of relaxation was gone. Across the entire windshield, written in soap, were the numbers 666. Looking across the street, I saw a dozen or more men, women, and children holding signs: *God Hates Fags. The Antichrist Lives. Die Faggots.*

My heart sank.

Two men held an outstretched eight-foot sign reading:

And the great dragon was thrown down, that ancient serpent, who is called Devil and Satan, the deceiver of the whole world . . .

"Wow," Sean said, "talk about a freight train. Looks like the news teams are going to get some great footage." He pointed to three cameramen positioned strategically between them and us.

"Wow is right," I said. "You know, my buddy Saturn's been called both Satan and devil throughout time. He gets a bad rap everywhere, even from me. Oh, Father Saturn, be with me today. Provide me with your discipline *and* patience."

"Saturn, Satan, Devil, Devlin—it all sounds similar," Sean said. "You know, maybe you are the antichrist. Oops, I guess you have to believe in one before you can be one, right?" He smiled at me and squeezed my hand.

Even with our attempts at humor, fear knocked on the door of my heart. A different side of ego, one I had not anticipated, reared its head. *Not everyone likes you. In fact, these people hate you!*

I looked past the soapy sixes and tried to see these people with compassion. What kind of fear, anger, and hatred were they harboring? How deeply affected were their minds by these negative emotions?

Closing my eyes, I was unexpectedly transported back to 1993, when Sean and I had encountered this same group, the Phelps family from Kansas, at the Gay and Lesbian March on Washington. Their intentions to protest the march had been highly publicized, but I never anticipated being that close to them personally.

Back then, my practices of yoga and meditation were new and spotty. I was still caught up in black and white, right and wrong, good and bad. I remember the rage I felt that day in Washington, DC, as I'd walked within two feet of a tall, slender man in his midforties, who stood front and center of their group.

"I have questions about your so-called faith," I'd said to him. He'd looked over and past me.

"Do not look at him!" the man shouted to his group. "Look away from the infidel. Do not meet eyes with the devil!"

"What? Don't look at me?" I asked. "You can't even look me in the eyes while you spew your hate? Are you afraid you might see a real human being? Maybe you'll see one of God's creatures. Have you ever thought you might be wrong?" My voice got louder. "What if Jesus *really* meant *love your neighbor*? Do you think Christ would say *die faggot*?"

"Sing," the tall man yelled. The group of thirty or so broke into "We Shall Overcome."

"Look at me!" I screamed over their song as I paced the length of the group, trying to meet eyes with at least one of them. "Are you afraid to face the thing you fear? Cowards, see me!"

Sean tried to pull me away, but I broke from his grip and ran toward them, ranting, "See me! See me, cowards!"

Sean and a friend finally managed to drag me from the hateful protesters as I sobbed, heartbroken, asking them one last question that they never heard, "How can you hate so much . . . and why?"

CNN had broadcasted the encounter throughout that day. The clip ended with a close-up of the front of my T-shirt that read, *Hate Is Not a Family Value*.

Today, we met again, directly in front of my home. I was much different now, I hoped. I now knew this was an opportunity my council was giving me. One I must take to face a regret and a wound. Today, my reaction *must* be different. Today, I needed to respond and not react. I couldn't let my heart be filled with rage and anger.

I opened my eyes, and I sat for a moment, looking out at them. Then, remembering the word *Namaste* printed on the shirt I was wearing, I opened the car door.

"What are you doing?" Sean asked, grabbing my shoulder.

"I'm going to approach this group of fellow humans in the energy of Namaste: *the Divinity in me recognizes the Divinity in you.* I'm going to reassure them they have nothing to fear and that fear is what separates us from each other. These aren't *bad* people," I said to him, "these people are dealing with *Avidya*, the klesha that means 'to be without knowledge.' Ignorance allows fear to live in their hearts. It's *Avidya* that has these people doing what they do. They're afraid."

"Ren, those people hate you."

"They don't know me. I want them to recognize our common essence. I want them to realize we are created from the same source."

"I'm pretty sure that's not going to happen today," Sean said. "Please, let's just go."

I got out of the car and slowly walked into the street. Traffic stopped. The camera crews pulled in closer. The group on the other side immediately started singing "Amazing Grace." I chanted the *Gayatri* mantra. Unlike in Washington years ago, when none of them would look at me, a small child, maybe six years old, looked me right in the eyes. I felt a recognition, a heart connection between the two of us. The thread was strong. I saw it. She saw it. It pulled us toward each other.

She dropped her mother's hand and sprinted into the street toward me.

"Stop!" her clan screamed. "Don't run toward the devil! Stop, Clary! He has bewitched you."

I dropped to my knees on the asphalt, and she ran straight into my open arms.

"My name is Clary. I love you," she said as we held each other tight.

"I love you too, Clary. You are very, very special."

"We all are. We are God's children."

"Yes, we are, and children of the goddess too."

The singing had stopped. I looked over the young girl's shoulder to see the entire group staring at us. They see us, I thought. They see *me* with *her.*

"Clary, come here!" A frowning woman approached and grabbed the little girl by the hand.

"She's beautiful," I said with a smile.

The woman looked me in the eyes for a split second, a split second longer than any of them ever had.

"She is special and has a deep gift of love to give to all people. Let her love everyone. *I* love you all," I said. "It's all about love. Just love."

The woman pulled Clary toward her and hurried to join the others across the street.

I stood and raised my voice. "Let us all be like this little child, full of love and goodness toward all living beings." Although I spoke right to them, once again, not one of the group would meet my eyes.

I turned toward our car. Standing on the driver's side, Sean brought his hands into Abhaya mudra and bowed his head. I returned the mudra, then turned to face the crowd and bowed.

"Let all of us learn to live without fear in our hearts," I said. "You can hate me all you want, but you can't stop me from loving you. You can't stop love."

As Sean and I got back in the car, he placed his hand on my shoulder.

"That was lovely," he said.

I started to cry gently, which soon turned into deep sobbing for all the fear in the world that separates us, human from human.

"Something shifted," I whispered through my tears. "I did not match hate for hate."

As we sat in the driveway for a few more moments, I saw Clary smiling, waving, and blowing me kisses while her mother tried to stop her. I waved back.

"Clary sees no boundaries," I said. "She feels the connection and the happiness it brings. Children access love so readily until the programming of society sets in."

"Should we skip this outing and just go back in the house?" Sean asked.

"Maybe. I'm a little rattled. I could use time on my cushion."

How strange, the games of the ego, I thought, where you are never sure if you will be the cat or the mouse in its constant back-and-forth in your mind. And what just happened between me and that little girl? How can Clary have so much love when she seems surrounded by so much hate and anger?

I heard Venus softly whisper, *The untouched innocence of a child gives her a deep capacity for unconditional love. Innocence of heart is available at any age. Aspire.*

Yes, I thought, she was untouched by her upbringing. I saw the depth of unconditional love in Clary's eyes.

"Well, boyfriends, you made national news again with your message of love," Carol said when she called a few hours later. "CNN's running a clip of Ren and a little girl hugging in front of your house. The headline says it all: 'Phelps Child and Miracle Man Find Love in Common.'"

How different this incident is from the one in 1993. That one depleted me of energy and hope. This time, I was full of optimism. Clary's gift of unconditional love was a karmic second chance for me, provided by the grand master, Saturn, with a touch of Venus in Pisces. Her love helped strip away ugliness from my heart today. Perhaps her clan would one day see that we were more similar than different. At any time, we can release the chains of ignorance that bind our hearts so we can love to our fullest potential, just like Clary.

Much love, beautiful one.

And . . . Thank you.

16

DOTTIE

The rest of the day, we stayed in the house and tried to shut out anything that was happening on the street. Sean did laundry and got caught up on emails and text messages while I sat in contemplation. It was peaceful.

Late that afternoon, Sean opened the door to my studio, balancing two cups of coffee.

"Do you have a few minutes for a debriefing?"

"Of course, chief-of-staff," I said. "What's going on in the outside world?"

"Well, social media's abuzz, and the street out front is once again packed with people. There's nothing like making national news again to boost your popularity."

"I was really hoping things were going to calm down."

"It might if you'd refrain from public miracles."

"*One.* One public miracle."

"Ahh . . . so you finally admit it," Sean said.

"Oh, man . . ."

"I'm kinda kidding." He winked. "Hey, how about some good news?"

"Please."

"We got a text from Ashley," Sean said. "She's in town this week working for Home Redo Catalog. She has four tickets for a concert at Bogarts on Friday night and wants us to join her and Stephanie for a night on the town. What do you say?"

"Oh, man, you know how I love those two, but I don't think being out in public is the best thing right now," I said with a sigh.

Ashley and Stephanie were Sean's nieces by birth and mine by spirit. Ashley lived in New York City, working as a stylist for magazines, catalogs, and movies. Stephanie was a personal assistant to a CEO of a major retail chain, raising a family in Cincinnati. Both were creative and energetic and were two of our favorite people.

"Ashley suggested we go incognito," Sean said, "and wear wigs and sunglasses."

"Sounds like when we renamed Thanksgiving, Thankswigging, making her friends in the City wear wigs to our otherwise traditional celebration," I said.

"Exactly. No one will know who you are. If Diana and Fergie could sneak out of Buckingham Palace, you and I can get out of here for one night and go to a concert with our soul sisters," he said with a smile. "I get why this makes you nervous, and I *know* we have to be careful, but we could use a fun night out to let our hair down—pun totally intended." He reached over and squeezed my hand.

"Bud, if the circumstances were different . . . but with everything that's going on . . . I'm just not comfortable."

"Okay. I'll tell her probably not, but I'll leave it open just in case you change your mind between now and tomorrow."

"I hate letting you down," I said, "and I'd love to see them, but—"

"Don't give it another thought—let's leave it in the hands of the Universe," Sean said, "it'll take care of itself. But there is another invitation I've already accepted."

"Really, and what would that be?"

"We're going to see that swanky penthouse with the bird's-eye view of Columbia Parkway."

"What?"

"Dottie Gant, the ninety-year-old who gave the local interview, wants to give us some business."

I squinted. "How?"

"Her personal assistant, Susan, called earlier, and apparently, Mrs. Gant perused our website and wants to schedule a weekly in-home, four-hands massage for the next six months, paid in full, up front."

"In her penthouse? I'm not sure if—"

"I told her we have a four o'clock opening tomorrow, and she took it."

"Wait, tomorrow? I'm not sure. It hasn't even been a week and what about the crowds outside?" I asked.

"Exactly, Ren, because of the crowds, clients can't easily come to the house. And the reality check on our economics is your celebrity status has brought us no monetary gain unless you want to accept the offer to host that psychic game show based in Sedona." He smiled. "Mrs. Gant wants a weekly house call with little chance of public confrontation. Susan gave me the code to the private underground garage. She said there's security all over the place. It's perfect."

"It sounds good, but come on, this woman we've never met wants to schedule out for six months? Does she really want a four-hands massage, or is she expecting some kind of miracle?"

"What kind of miracle could she possibly want at ninety? Unless—*she wants to live forever*," Sean sang out as he bobbed his head. "And when *I'm* ninety, if I can afford it, *I'm* going to have a weekly massage."

I shook my head. "Looks like the Universe is trying to get us out of the house. First Ashley, now this."

"The Universe works in mysterious ways," Sean said. "*Maybe* there are opportunities afoot that we'd miss if we just stayed cooped up."

"All right," I said with a sigh. "This should be very interesting."

On Friday, we pulled up to the garage of Mrs. Gant's building. The code her assistant provided opened not just a barrier arm but full metal security doors.

"I feel like we should be driving an armored truck," Sean said as we parked.

Situated on the side of one of Cincinnati's seven hills, each unit of the building had a commanding view of the city, the Ohio River, and Columbia Parkway. Mrs. Gant's flat occupied the entire thirty-sixth floor.

A petite woman in her forties, with dark hair pulled into a ponytail, wearing wire-rimmed glasses, and dressed in a tailored gray skirt, a black cashmere V-neck sweater, and a single strain of pearls, greeted us at the door of the condo.

"I'm Susan Saunders," she said. "We'll have you set up in Mrs. Gant's private drawing room, which is ensuite to her bedroom."

She ushered us into a room that was bigger than most New York City apartments.

"Mrs. Gant will be in shortly. Is there anything I can bring you?" she asked.

"Thank you, we're fine," Sean said. I shook my head in agreement.

Once we had the massage table set up, we each perused the room.

"Whoa," Sean said with a low whistle, "this is a Modigliani—"

"And there's a Matisse and Renoir over here," I said and then meandered over to a mahogany Chippendale chair that was placed in a floor-to-ceiling bay window. On the seat was a prayer book and a clear glass rosary. After seeing the caliber of her artwork, I wondered if the beads of the rosary were diamonds.

"Hey, Sean, this must've been where she saw it all happen," I said, pointing out the large window and down to the spot where my life, her life, and the lives of many others converged last Sunday.

"That is *exactly* where I witnessed the miracle," a voice from behind us boomed.

We turned. Mrs. Gant stood in the double doorway, looking like a 1940s movie queen, dressed in a floor-length, off-white satin dressing gown with wispy feathers circling the collar and each sleeve.

"So, do you think you raised that young boy from the dead like everyone says?" Before I could answer, she continued, "I've been reading accounts from some of the other people you've touched. They say you've cured them from all kinds of sicknesses."

"Hello, Mrs.—"

"Oh no," she said as she strode into the room, "you *will* call me Dottie. The three of us are on a fast track to becoming best friends."

"Nice to meet you, Dottie," Sean said.

"Yes, nice to meet you in person," I said, feeling as if I should bow. "To answer your question, I believe it was a combination of me, the crowd, and even you that allowed the boy to walk away from the scene."

"But *you* were the conduit for bringing the miracle energies together," she said with a nod.

"Perhaps, but I believe any one of us is capable of doing things that neither science nor our rational mind can explain," I said.

"I am in full agreement," she said as she sauntered toward the massage table.

She looked timeless. I was mesmerized.

"Oh, at my age, I've seen lots of *those* types of miracles: telephones to computers and smartphones, diseases that used to take out whole populations, cured by vaccines, transportation that moves at unbelievably high speeds around and above the Earth. But let's talk about the kind of miracles like Jesus did." There was a slight pause as she tilted her head and increased the intensity of her gaze on me. "You," she said, pointing at me, "seem to be able to carry it off like my favorite Messiah."

Her favorite Messiah. Who were her others, I wondered but dared not ask.

"You know, Dottie," I said, "there are theories that between the age of twelve and twenty-nine, in a period called the *lost years*, Jesus studied yogic philosophy and learned deep levels of meditation, so he and I *might* have something in common." I grinned and leaned toward her. "I've been playing around with deep levels of meditation myself."

"Playing around!" she said sternly and unamused. "Raising a nine-year-old from a catatonic state, if not death, is not playing around. Do you realize how serious this is, young man?"

"I didn't mean to come across insincere . . . I just—"

"I've met three popes in my lifetime because of my *connections*." Her stare was direct. "*Connections* is a code word for money. You with me? Excuse me if I'm wrong, but I don't believe you have *that* type of connection, nor do you need it." She raised one eyebrow and placed her right hand on her hip. "I hear from very reliable sources that because of your *talent*, the current pope wants to meet you!"

I gasped under my breath. *The pope!*

"Do you think it's because of your *playing around* with certain spiritual practices? I don't think so! He has questions for you. And he should!" she said. "He should be finding out how to teach his leaders to do what you've done. Thank God you're a Catholic." She shook her head and looked up as if to heaven.

"I'm not Catholic," I said, "not anymore. I don't adhere to any religion. I'm cultivating a spirituality for my Soul."

"Whatever," she said with a wave of her hand. "You were baptized into the Catholic faith and confirmed Reynolds James Patrick Devlin."

Sean and I glanced at each other. *How did she know my confirmation name?*

"Once a Catholic, always a Catholic," she said, again pointing her finger at me. "You have the ritual in your blood. It never comes out. Besides, the Catholic Church needs you right now!"

"You're right about Catholicism," I said, "it shows up for me when I least expect it. But as for *it* needing *me*, I'm not sure the pope would want a gay, feminist yogi teaching priests about spirituality and meditation."

"You're wrong about this pope. He's a wise man. He doesn't care who you sleep with, nor should he. The church's stance on homosexuals and women will change sooner or later if they hope to keep Catholicism alive."

Sean and I exchanged a knowing smile.

"And as for you instructing student priests, can you imagine a world where all priests could cure sickness and alleviate pain?"

"That would be a different world, Dottie, but remember, as your favorite Messiah said, *everything I can do, you can do also*."

"Well, we need teachers like you to get everyone on board," she said. "The pope has a whole system in place, ready for you to tap into." She talked as if this whole thing should be structured like a corporation. "Don't shut down on this idea. You have to teach what you've learned so the rest of us can start doing these things for ourselves."

"Hmmm . . ." I muttered

"Don't hmmm me, boy, listen," she said, placing her hands on her hips and honing her laser-intense stare even more. "You need some help with this. You may have an *in* on the spiritual connection, but you need help on the business end."

"The business end of spirituality? Really?"

"Like you haven't seen it before," she said, rolling her eyes.

"I am afraid I have, and it's called religion. But we're here today to give you a massage and relax you, not talk religion or business. How about we save this conversation for another time?"

"Are you blowing me off?" she asked, her eyebrows raised, her hands still on her hips.

I smiled. "I promise that's not what I'm doing. I just want you to relax. That's our job today."

"Okay, two things, and then I'll get on the table. First, we make a date to talk about this miracle thing over a glass of limoncello."

To that, I smiled in agreement.

"Second," she continued, "not that I'm putting any pressure on you, but see what you can do about my right hip. My doctor says I'm too old to have it replaced. Again, no pressure, but since we both believe in miracles . . ." She winked. "It's worth a shot."

In a flash, I felt a wave of love from her.

"Sure thing, Dottie. I would've never known there was any issue with your hip by the way you walk."

"I may not be able to do miracles, but I can teach you a thing or two about mind over matter. Let's get this massage going. Remember, I'm supposed to be relaxing today under your four hands. So far, all you've done is get me all riled up." This time, she smiled. "I like you two already. Now get to work!"

17

WAKE UP

"Well, that was different," Sean said as we waited for the elevator. "Different's one word for it," I said. "How did Dottie know my confirmation name? That information's not public. It's only in church records."

"And what about her saying the pope wanted to meet you?"

"I'm hoping that was merely conjecture on her part."

"Whatever," Sean said as the elevator doors opened and we stepped in. "At least now I won't be surprised if I answer the phone and the pope's on the other end. *Buongiorno padre . . .*"

I rolled my eyes. The doors opened on the garage level, and two young women jumped in front of us.

"Surprise!" they yelled, with huge smiles on their faces.

"What the . . . ?" I said, taking a step back.

"Ren, it's Ashley and Stephanie," Sean said, wearing a big grin. "We're heading to the concert."

I didn't move as I checked out their get-ups.

Stephanie was stunning, wearing large, black-rimmed sunglasses and a white-blond Jean Harlow wig that completely covered her usual shoulder-length, dark-brown locks. Ashley, who was naturally blond, looked very Uma Thurman in a short, cropped black wig along with bright red lipstick and pink cat-eye sunglasses.

"You know I love seeing you both, but I'm not sure this is the smartest thing to do," I said. "I'm worried about being in public. Maybe we should go back to the house and—"

"Ren," Sean said, "this is perfect. We'll leave the parking garage in Stephanie's minivan incognito, no one will suspect, and we'll be with two of our favorite peeps."

"Oh, come on, it'll be fun!" Ashley said, handing Sean and me each a wig and sunglasses.

This could be fun, I thought, and as reclusive as we'd been, no one would expect to find us at a concert.

"All right," I said. "Let's do it. Tonight's all about enjoying ourselves; it has nothing to do with miracles. I'm trusting you three."

Sean and I climbed into the back seat of the minivan and slipped on our wigs and sunglasses.

"How do I look?" Sean asked, adjusting his spiky blond wig and white-framed glasses.

"Very Flock of Seagulls. What about me?" I asked, fussing with my curly auburn locks.

"Uhmmm . . . with the round tinted glasses, you're a cross between a surfer dude and John Lennon."

"My kids didn't even recognize me," Stephanie added from the driver's seat. We all laughed as we left the garage. No one seemed to be following.

I took a deep breath, feeling the freedom of anonymity.

We found a parking spot two blocks from the venue and joined the lengthy line of concertgoers.

"Thanks for getting this together," I said to Stephanie and Ashley as we inched our way to the doorman. "The car switch and disguises were brilliant."

"We also have to thank Mrs. Gant . . . I mean Dottie," Sean said. "She had no problem with me giving Stephanie the code to the garage."

"I see," I said, "several masterminds made this happen. So, Ash, who are we seeing tonight?"

"The opening band is BeatNik Gypsys. They're kinda circus-burlesque.

But it's Soul Retrievers who you guys are going to love. Their lyrics are so soulful."

"And both groups will get you moving," Stephanie said, snapping her fingers and swaying from side to side.

"Your magical uncle and I really need this tonight," Sean said, matching her movements.

Even with wigs and sunglasses, I felt we were tapping into our normal life again.

"This is great," I said, looking at each of them. "Thank you."

We shared fist-bumps.

BeatNik Gypsys, complete with jugglers and unicyclists, was already onstage when we entered the theater. We blended into the crowd and danced to every song.

At intermission, the four of us headed to the bar. "This is just what we needed!" Sean said, smiling as he walked arm and arm with Steph and Ash. This was definitely the right thing to do. I smiled to myself. Who knew a month ago how crazy our lives would become?

"To love!" Sean said as we raised our Coronas to toast.

"To love," the four of us said in unison.

"I'm curious," Sean turned to Ashley, "what made you choose tonight's show?"

"I've seen Soul Retrievers a couple of times, and I just knew you'd really enjoy them and their message. But . . . I also need to fess up—these are comp tickets from my producer friend in New York."

"You can't beat free," Sean said.

"Yeah, Devon's a great guy. You met him at one of the Thankswig-gings. Anyway, he's been following the miracle stuff—"

"Who hasn't?" Stephanie said and winked at me.

I nodded.

"Devon also produces Soul Retrievers," Ashley continued. "And Ren, their lead singer, Nina, is a huge fan of yours."

"Wow, Ren, you've got rock star fans," Sean said, squeezing my shoulder.

My solar plexus tightened.

Ashley smiled. "Yeah, when Nina found out Devon had a connection to you, she asked him to send me the tickets and bring you. Isn't it cool? It's such a small world. Meant to be, really."

An alarm went off in my head that matched the knot in my stomach. I suddenly felt trapped.

"The band knows we're here," I said, glancing around. "They may not know where we are in the crowd, but they know someone used the tickets. They can track the barcodes."

"Don't worry," Ashley said. "No one will recognize you. We're invited to go backstage afterward, but we don't have to."

"I think I'm going to leave now," I said, shaking my head.

"Chill out, Ren," Sean said, "you're overthinking this. Ashley could have brought anyone."

"But Nina requested Ashley bring *me*, remember? People know I'm here!"

"Oh, I see where this is going," Sean said and cupped his hand behind one ear. "I think I hear the freight train of ego rolling through. Ren, don't let your ego steal this time from you."

He was right. I'd lost any feeling of contentment and was now *only* thinking of *me*: my security, my anonymity.

We finished our beers and re-entered the ocean of people gathered around the stage.

"I hope we can remain anonymous in this mass of humanity," I mumbled. I began to feel very uneasy, remembering the crowd surging toward me on the Parkway. Tiny beads of sweat rolled down my temples.

The lights went dark. Then, a stark, single white spotlight beamed onto Nina, the lead singer of Soul Retrievers. The crowd erupted with excitement.

She's stunning, I thought. Her floor-length black slip-dress was covered in delicate silver threads that ran the length of it. Her chestnut hair was styled into a blunt chin-length cut that accentuated her high cheekbones and full, deep red lips.

At the close of her first song, she cried out, "Hello, Cinnnncinnnn-naaaati!!! The place where miracles happen!"

The crowd cheered.

I took a deep breath. Sean squeezed my hand.

She began to canvass the entire length of the stage as she spoke directly to the audience. "We need more miracles to shift the energy of this crazy world we live in. Miracles *are* possible!"

The mention of "miracles" intensified the nervous feeling inside me.

"We went to Columbia Parkway this morning," she said, gesturing behind her to the band, "and stood on the hallowed ground where Miracle Mike came back to life. It was awesome!"

She placed one hand on her heart and bowed her head.

"Remember—whatever he can do, we can do also, so let's join *our* beautiful threads of light together and make miracles happen."

I wanted to take a deep breath, but instead, I felt myself holding it, waiting for . . . what? I wasn't sure.

"It's time for all of us to come back to life," her voice was full of excitement, "so we too can perform miracles. To do it, we must wake up to our true self."

Then she stooped down toward the front of the stage, putting her finger to her lips. There was silence.

"Guess what?" she whispered.

"What?" the crowd mimicked her hushed tone.

"We think the miracle man is here tonight."

Everyone erupted again except the four of us.

"Damn," I said under my breath.

Ashley reached over and touched me on the arm. "I'm so sorry," she mouthed.

I winked at her as if everything was okay, but inside, I was afraid to talk or move. I didn't want anything to blow our cover. I finally took a deep breath to help calm the fear and anxiety. *Why was I anxious?* These folks obviously believe in love and miracles. *It's all good.* With that reminder, the claustrophobia that had been bubbling up was unexpectedly replaced by a sense of exhilaration. I took another full breath.

"Join me in a mantra!" the singer said. "I'll start, and you repeat. WAAAAAAKE UUUUUUUUUUP!" She then held the microphone toward the crowd.

Everyone echoed her words.

"WAKE UP . . . TO THE POWER OF LOVE!" Nina then secured her mic onto a stand and placed her hands into Abhaya mudra.

The thousand gathered followed her lead. The sense I had of being trapped was being replaced with a tingling euphoria of Oneness with the crowd. The boundaries of *me* dissolved as I felt a connection to everyone around me.

Standing close to the mic, still holding the mudra, Nina spoke to the group, but I felt she was talking directly to me.

"Don't live in fear. Love your life and believe in love. We can't control the chaos in our world *but* we can *love*. So, love unconditionally, in total abandon, and let miracles happen."

The bass drum hit with a single *boom*. The lights shifted to spotlight Nina as she began singing a cappella.

In the deep recesses of my soul
I found clues to being Whole.
Descending down to my heart's hallowed ground
I open myself up—to be found.

With two full resounding beats from the bass drum and floor tom-toms, the stage came alive in a blazing light show. The rest of the band joined in as Nina pulled the mic from its stand, started jumping up and down, and roused the audience into excitement.

Amid the dancing and music, I stood holding the mudra, letting her voice wash over me. Her words described the relationship we can have with our inner Selves. Once we hear its voice, it encourages us to live our lives fully. She sang of threads of light weaving through us. Over and over, she sang of waking up and learning to fly.

It's all about Love, Ren, I heard from my inner voice. *When we gather in the name of* love, *anything is possible, even bringing little boys back from the dead.*

I felt the connection.

Our group of four stood close, holding the mudra. Our feet were the only ones that were still. Nina replaced the mic on the stand as she brought her hands back into the familiar mudra. The music softened to only the piano. A narrow spotlight lit up Nina's face as she sang the last line of her love song to Self:

I finally see the sky of life.
I know now I will take flight!
Love!

As the piano held the final chord, the singer's eyes connected with mine. She pointed directly at me. The spotlight followed the direction of her gesture. It happened in a matter of seconds, but for me, it seemed in slow motion. Now, in the bright, hot light, Sean, Ashley, Stephanie, and I dropped the mudra and grabbed hands. Then, as if possessed by some undeniable force, I ripped off my wig and sunglasses and brought my hands into the mudra once again.

"Ren, what the hell are you doing?" Sean said. "Remember the freight train of ego! Your council warned you about this. Let's get out of here . . . now."

"I'm a big part of this," I said.

"What?" Sean said incredulously. "We're out of here!" He grabbed my hand.

Continuing to point at me, Nina began chanting, "Ren, Ren, Ren . . ." The crowd joined in.

Sean also began screaming my name, but not with the same intent.

"Ren! Let's go. Now!" he said, trying to pull me through the crowd toward the exit.

"No!" I said, staring at Nina. I had to stay. *Compelled.*

"Bring him up here," she said from the stage, gesturing for me to come forward.

As if levitating, I was lifted by those standing near me. My hand separated from Sean's as I was passed overhead, from cheering person to cheering person, until I was delivered onto the stage. Nina and I embraced as the chant changed from my name to "Love."

What miracles would take place in the hearts of these lovely beings? I thought, looking out at what I hoped was an emerging group of mystical revolutionaries.

"Miracles don't come from the mind but from the heart," I said into the microphone. "As we wake up and learn to hear our heart, we come to *know*—Miracles Happen—Miracles are happening every minute . . ."

I wanted to share this moment with Sean. I glanced to where, just moments ago, Sean and I had been standing together.

He was gone.

18

THE VEILED ONES

"Sean. I'm surprised you're still up," I said, coming in the side door to the house and walking into the living room. "It's after midnight."

"It's 1:00 a.m.," Sean said, not looking up from his book.

"Sorry it's so late, but we went backstage and hung out with the band after the show."

"I know. There are already posts on social media."

"How did you get home?" I asked. "I was worried."

"Were you?" he asked, still not looking up. "I took an Uber to Dottie's and picked up the car."

"You should've stayed. I wanted to get you up on stage with me, but you were gone."

There was a cold silence.

"I guess I'll go up to bed," I said. "I feel like I'm walking on eggshells—"

"Oh, I'm sorry *you're* uncomfortable," Sean said, finally looking at me. "I wouldn't want you to cut your precious feet on anything sharp. Why don't you just levitate, or am I not enough of an audience for one of your miracles?"

"Clearly, you're upset," I said, "although I'm not sure why."

"Did you even once wonder why I left?"

"Of course, but Ash and Steph said you told them to keep an eye on me and bring me home, but I—"

"Come on, let's stop the bullshit! What the hell's going on? I have to drag you to that concert in the first place, then the band strokes your miracle-inflated ego with chants of *Ren, Ren, Ren* . . . and you decide to blow your own cover and bodysurf to the stage. Who are you?"

"I felt safe. It was a group of like-minded people. Maybe they're all mystical revolutionaries."

Sean dropped his book. "Oh, holy Hindu goddess, are you for real?" He slid to the edge of his seat and raised his hands high.

"Will someone help me, please?" he yelled, looking up to the ceiling. "Open his eyes to reality, cover him with holy water, do something to wake him up."

"Sean, I hate to see you so—"

"So what? Concerned for your safety, our lives . . . I'm serious, Ren. I wish your council or one of the feminine vanguard you've been talking to would give you some kind of smack in the face because all their precautions about the klesha of ego are not sinking in."

"I don't see ego in what I did tonight."

"That makes this even more dangerous," he said. "Go to bed. You'll need to be rested to deal with tomorrow's headlines and your new pop star status."

"Are you coming soon?" I asked.

"I'm going to sleep on the couch. I need some space."

In our more than thirty years together, we had only slept apart for a handful of nights. I walked the stairs to the third-floor treehouse bedroom with a heavy heart.

It was no surprise I had trouble falling asleep as I ruminated on the night's events and my motives. I'd been connecting with others who may be walking the path of the mystic, hadn't I? "May the Gayatri mantra instill my intellect with wisdom," I whispered to the empty bedroom as I began to chant. Within three rounds of the mantra, I'd slipped into a twilight state and found myself once again kneeling in the back of my childhood parish church, Corpus Christi. I looked up at the statue of St.

Veronica, expecting her to speak. Instead, I heard the rustling of fabric to my left. I turned to see St. Clare of Assisi staring at me. Her gaze beckoned me closer to her. I stood, moved from St. Veronica, past Mary Magdalene, until I was close to St. Clare.

She was beautiful and serene. Her garment was made from heavy, gray wool, and like Veronica's, it went all the way to the floor. Her head was draped with a deep purple veil, laid atop a white coif that framed the olive complexion of her face and dark eyes. I could see the subtle rise and fall of her chest under the mantle of her nun's habit. I looked into her eyes, and she into mine. Then she lifted her arms out in front of her, parallel to the floor, revealing a three-foot long, tight-weaved, black muslin veil.

"Step closer," she said.

I moved within inches of her and the black cloth.

"In place of holy water, I cover you with a veil of vision. May it bring light and clarity into your being," she said, leaning forward and covering my head. "Heed the messages."

I inhaled deeply and bowed my head to accept the veil. With my next breath, I heard a different female voice. As if removing the hood of a jacket, I pushed back the veil and found myself standing among a small group of people, listening to a woman who was speaking English with a heavy Italian accent.

"Clare's Basilica is 800 years old," she said. "Construction began in 1257 over the pre-existing Church of San Giorgio and was completed in 1260, just three years after her death. The remains of St. Clare were placed here after the cathedral's completion and are still here today. The original crucifix from which Jesus is said to have spoken to St. Francis hangs over the altar in one of the cathedral's side chapels."

Behind the speaker, the sun shone brightly through the large rose window, casting a pink-red hue onto everything inside and bringing life to the hundreds of gold stars painted on the royal blue ceiling. *Such a vivid dream.*

"Is Clare the female version of Francis?" a familiar voice asked the guide. I turned to see Sean. *Why is he here?*

"Clare was devoted to finding *her own* connection with the transcendental and helping others to find it as well," the guide said to Sean. "She and Francis were both individual examples of yogic surrender."

Yogic surrender? How odd for her to describe them in those terms.

"Sounds like they were ahead of their time *and* ahead on the consciousness curve," Sean said. "Just curious, did Clare perform miracles?"

"Well, besides saving Assisi from a violent invasion by holding up a monstrance, housing the sacred host, legend says Clare could see things happening miles away through what many called her inner sixth sense."

"Sixth sense, huh? Sounds like Pada Three. I bet she did a lot of meditating," he said with noticeable sarcasm.

"Sean," I said, walking toward him. "What are you doing here?"

"What do you mean?"

"You asked someone to throw holy water on me, but instead, St. Clare placed a veil over my head and . . . now we're on a tour of her Basilica in Italy and—"

"Are you all right?" Sean looked as confused as I felt.

"Forget it," I said. I took a deep breath and let go of my need to know what was going on. Instead, I enjoyed the fact that Sean wasn't mad at me in this dream.

"Come on, let's walk around," Sean said, "this tour is boring." He took my hand, and we walked the perimeter of the nave.

"I feel something in here," he said as we strolled.

"You're sensing centuries of human contemplation infused into the bones of this structure," I said.

On the far side of the nave, we saw a side chapel with a large group gathered around its entrance.

"Let's check it out," Sean said.

There was no order to the queue. It was like a human amoeba, gently sliding people through a doorway that acted as a sieve.

"Let's dive into the unknown," I said, pulling on Sean's shirt sleeve and leading him into the mutable mass of humanity. Eventually, we were funneled through the wooden doorway into a small chamber, dimly lit by two wrought-iron candle stands at the far end of the room and hundreds of votive candles flickering on the three-foot-thick sills of the dark stained-glass windows that lined the right side of the room. A soft murmur of whispers filled the air. We were slowly jostled forward toward a mahogany lattice with diamond-shaped openings.

"What is this place?" I asked, turning to Sean, only to find the crowd had separated us, and he was now half a room away. We waved to each other as we inched forward.

I could see the people at the lattice reach for something being offered from the other side of the wooden tracery. As I moved closer, I saw two nuns dressed in full-length belted black tunics and veils behind the ornate structure. They also wore black sateen gloves and an intricate piece of black lace that, from a distance, concealed their facial features.

Little Sisters of Poverty, the followers of St. Clare, I thought.

A half step at a time, I drew closer until I could finally make out the visage of the nun closest to me through her lace veil.

Her beautiful features were dark, too dark to be Italian. I watched her with fascination. She made eye contact with no one as she quickly moved along half of the twenty-five-foot screen, silently passing cards through the intricately carved openings to those on the other side. I soon realized they were holy cards, like the ones given out at Catholic funerals. Usually, one side of the card featured a depiction of either Mary or Jesus, and the other side had an appropriate prayer.

Finally, I stepped forward. She made her way toward me. With only the screen separating us, I saw her almond-shaped eyes and exquisite facial features. *She looks Indian. Is this the Hindu goddess Sean called on for help?* Then, unexpectedly, her eyes raised to meet mine. Keeping eye contact, she slid a card toward me. Her lips parted slightly, and for a split second, I thought she was going to speak. But with no words, she released the card, gazed back at the floor, and moved on. I slipped the card into my pocket.

I was funneled back through the chapel doors and saw Sean making his way out of the cathedral. I followed him to an open-air plaza of the Basilica.

"Something weird is going on, Ren," he said, his voice shaky. "That nun wanted to say something to me. I know it. She stared directly at me." He shook the card in his hand. "This has something to do with goddesses and your council wanting your attention. Was your nun Indian?"

I nodded.

"Yeah, how many Hindu nuns are in Italy? And two just happen to be working at the Cathedral of Saint Clare on the same day?"

"Sean . . ." I was just as confused. "Maybe—"

"Let me see your card."

I pulled the holy card from my pocket and held it out to show him an illustration of St. Clare holding a monstrance of protection.

"What's printed on the back?" he asked. Before I could answer, he said, "Mine says, *in* English—"

Face Asmita—Drop Ego
Do not Go to Italy
Expect a Miracle
Wake Up!
P.U.T.P.

I looked at my card to see four of the five same lines printed in cardinal red.

"Mine says the same thing but nothing about Italy."

Sean turned to an older woman who was walking near us.

"Excuse me. Do you speak English?"

"Piccolo," she responded.

"May I please see your holy card?" He pointed to the object she held in her hand. She handed it to him. He turned it over.

"*Grazie mille*," he said as he handed it back to her.

I watched him comb the plaza and ask several others to see their cards. He shook his head as he walked back to me.

"Of all the cards those nuns are handing out," he said, pausing and taking a deep breath, "ours are the only ones that don't have the Prayer of St. Clare on the back."

"That's strange," I said, trying to remain calm.

"Yeah, it's *strange*! It's even stranger that ours say, *Expect a Miracle!*" He raised his hand to stop me from interjecting. "And wake up—which is what goddesses, councils, and lead singers in rock bands are telling you to do. And what about drop ego-*Asmita*? Coincidence?"

"Sean—"

"No, no, let me finish," he said. "Does P.U.T.P. have some Catholic meaning?"

I shook my head.

"I didn't think so! This is *not* random!" he said. "There are only three people on the planet who know what P.U.T.P. means to us: you, me, and Carol. PICK UP THE PACE. That's what Carol says when she's trying to get us to hurry up. Where are these messages coming from and why?"

Sean began pacing.

I remained silent and took deep breaths.

"Of the hundreds of people going through there," he said, gesturing toward the cathedral, "those Hindu nuns knew to give these two specific cards to us? Who are they?"

"Sean—"

"We weren't even together, and they knew! And mine says *don't go to Italy*, but yours doesn't. What's going on, Ren?!" He was shaking.

"I know it's weird, buddy, but don't freak out!" I said.

"I *am* freaked out." He looked down at the card, then back to me. "It's as if something is watching us."

I hugged him. My mind was also full of questions. *Why are we in Italy at a Catholic cathedral? How am I supposed to pick up the pace? Am I stuck in a spiral with ego that I can't see?*

"I know it's unsettling," I said, "but it's okay."

"Should we go back in there and ask those nuns some questions?"

"Our answers aren't in there. They're in here." I touched the middle of his chest. "Deep inside is the only place I can think where we might find some answers."

"You're better at that than I am. What can I do?" he asked.

"Well," I said, "to start with, help me keep an eye on my ego and, for both our sakes, be very, very careful what *you* ask for."

With that, Italy was gone. I was alone in our treehouse bedroom. I ran down to the first floor, where Sean was sleeping on the couch.

"Sean," I said, "I'm really sorry about what happened at the concert."

Sean sat up and rubbed his eyes.

"I just got lost in the moment. But remember when you pleaded to a Hindu goddess to wake me up?"

"Yeah?" he said groggily.

"Well, I just had a dream where we were both in a church in Assisi, Italy, and there were two Hindu nuns passing out holy cards to hundreds of people."

"Okay, Italy, Hindu nuns, holy cards—"

"Yes, and everybody's had the Prayer of St. Clare on it, except ours. Mine read 'face *Asmita*—drop ego, expect a miracle, wake up, and P.U.T.P.'"

"Okay, that's pretty weird. And mine?"

"All that plus . . . don't go to Italy."

"Don't go to Italy? But you said we *were* in Italy. What the heck does that mean?"

"I have no idea, but I think it's a direct response to you invoking a goddess before I went upstairs," I said, sitting down close to him. "There's some kind of message in this for us. I feel it."

"This keeps getting weirder and weirder. Will our lives ever be the same?" he asked.

"They may never be what they were pre-miracle, but we're in this together," I said. I lay down and placed my head in his lap. "Sean?"

"What?"

"Can I sleep on the couch with you?"

He put his arm around me and kissed the top of my head.

Life was good, I thought. Weird, but good.

19

THE CHURCH COMES A KNOCKIN'

E ven after my ego-inspired antics at the concert and a dream of mysterious messages on a holy card, things were normal between us the next morning over coffee. Sean browsed emails while I jotted down some thoughts on Pada Three in my journal.

Are the superpowers of yoga gifts or hindrances?

Everything I've read says the powers of the Samyama-siddhis are obstacles that appeal to the ego and hinder the yogi's journey to Self-realization.

If siddhis develop in your practice, it is advised to observe, experience, and then move away from them.

I am definitely observing and experiencing these powers, yet, I do not know how to move away from them.

"Hey," Sean said, "Carol's been helping me sort through the massive volume of emails and passed along a couple of interesting inquiries. The first one is from the *Beacon of Illumination* podcast. They're inviting you to be on next week's edition, which airs live on Tuesday."

"Book it! I don't have to leave the house for that one," I said, "and I love they're getting the message out that meditation is for everyone!"

"Agreed. I'll get back to them today. Next is a request for private meditation sessions. The guy's message sounded really sincere, and you know how lucrative private meditation is for us. He gave a phone number. So, how about I call him, feel him out, and maybe set an appointment?"

"Sure, why not?"

Sean stepped out of the room to make the call, and in what could only have been three minutes, he stepped back into the kitchen.

"That was quick." I looked up from my journal.

"He picked up on the first ring. He's eager to get started, so I scheduled him for Monday," Sean said.

"That only gives me two days. That's not much time to prep."

"Once tomorrow morning's Rise and Shine yoga class is over, you'll have all afternoon to prepare for his session."

"Who is this person? Does he have any meditation experience?"

"His name's Joseph Piedmont. He said he had some experience but wants to start with the basics. *I'm ready to go deep*, were his words."

"Joseph Piedmont? Should I know him?" I asked.

"Let's look him up."

Sean typed his name into a search on the phone.

"Huh . . . now, it might just be a coincidence . . . ," Sean said and paused.

"Come on," I said.

". . . but the archbishop of *this* diocese of the Catholic Church has the same name. Coincidence or synchronicity?"

"Why would an archbishop come to me for instruction in meditation? Priests meditate all the time. Wouldn't they have hours and hours of instruction in the seminary?"

"Well, my naive one, maybe there are other reasons an archbishop wants to talk to a guy who just raised the dead. And remember what Dottie said about the pope wanting to meet you, *and* you've been dreaming all things Catholic lately . . . just saying."

"Does he understand it might be a circus out front?"

"I told him to park in the driveway," Sean said. "I'll put our car on the street."

"This should be interesting," I said shaking my head.

"Are you going to ask him if he's the archbishop?"

"Of course not, Sean. That wouldn't be right. Anyway, I won't have to. You'll check out photos of him on the diocese's website, so you'll know if it's him when you answer the door."

We both laughed, and he nodded.

"Are there any Catholic mantras or mudras you should brush up on?" Sean asked.

"I'll stick with my usual Tantric yoga curriculum and Sanskrit. But we know there are enough rosaries around here to use as malas." I winked at him and smiled.

Later, as I sat at my desk preparing for the next day's yoga class, I did a search on Joseph Piedmont. I wanted to have a clear picture of him in my mind. Why would an archbishop want to study with *me*?

A vampire priest, Hindu nuns, and now an archbishop . . . what did my council have in store for me next?

20

IF I COULD CURE
THE SICK . . .

The wound is where the light comes in.
—Rumi

I awoke before sunrise on Sunday morning. I felt a profound calmness.
Sean was fast asleep, so I slipped out of bed and moved to my meditation cushion on the opposite side of the room—a sense of connection,
contentment, and a *knowing* that everything was right washed over me.
My ego mind was not functioning. Instead, I was plugged into the Universal Life Force and felt the *buzz of existence*. Then, without thought, I
said softly, "Roll back the stone from the cave of your heart. Enter the
sacred sanctuary with curiosity and reawaken the connection you have to
every living creature."

"Hey, are you okay?" I heard Sean whisper.

"Absolutely," I said. "I'm just finishing a strange meditation."

"Oh really, strange in what way?"

"As soon as I took my seat, I recited a verse that sounded like yogic philosophy, but it may be from one of the Gnostic Gospels."

Sean let out a sigh. "Aren't those the ones that were never included in the Bible?"

"Yeah. They only resurfaced a little over a hundred years ago," I said, "but wherever the verse came from, it's very comforting and just what I needed to get ready for today."

"Are you sure you're up to teaching today? I can tell Kate you're not ready yet, especially after what happened at the concert."

"No, I'm ready, and I promise to keep the reins on my ego," I said. "Besides, it'll feel good to be surrounded by the teacher trainees and the class regulars. I must say, I'm grateful *you'll* be with me."

"Every step of the way," Sean said, getting out of bed. "Let me go get the morning started."

"I'll be down in a couple of minutes," I said.

As I entered the kitchen, Sean was pouring coffee. "There's a text from Kate. She said there are already hundreds of people, some in wheelchairs, waiting in the parking lot. She wants to know if you want to take the week off."

Sean placed a cup of coffee in front of me as I took a seat at the kitchen table.

"It might be a good idea," he said. "The hoopla is bound to settle down sooner or later."

I sat up, placed my hands in Abhaya mudra, and took a deep breath. "I am not afraid of my life or what's in my heart. Let's do this. I'll text Kate that we'll be on our way soon."

"Anything I can do?" Sean asked.

"Pray for clarity and a miracle."

"What kind of miracle?"

"That we face this day without ego and can be of service to whoever's there."

"Boy, all of this certainly is weird."

"Yes, it is," I said, "but let's think of this as one grand adventure and keep the pure joy of *Ananda* in our hearts. Joy is always a welcomed companion when facing the unknown."

I gathered my mala beads and an old journal I'd found the previous day, and we headed out to the car. The air was still and quiet.

"Wow, this is so . . . normal," I said. "There's no one here."

"That's because everyone's probably waiting at the yoga studio. We'll need to be careful. There's no place for you to hide there."

"No place to hide . . . hmm," I said, taking a deep breath.

We slipped into the car and began our journey.

"May I read something to you from my first journal?" I asked.

"Your first journal," Sean said and smiled. "Who keeps such things?"

I raised my hand and chuckled.

"Something I wrote in it came up in the teacher training class last week, so I went back and found the entry."

"And—?"

"Well, most of the entries are chronological lists of the events of my days," I said as I opened the book, "but on page nine, I wrote, 'If I could have anything in the world, it would be inner peace. I want to be calm and relaxed and not worry so much. Inner peace. It sounds lovely. If my prayers are reaching you, Jesus, please grant me inner peace.'

"It's all written in my nine-year-old cursive," I said. "And here, a few pages later, I wrote, 'I am confused that Jesus got so angry with the crowds that followed him. They just wanted to be healed. Surely, he understood that. If I could cure the sick, I would do it all day long and be happy to.'"

"Wow," Sean said, "so, you've always been precocious." He smiled. "And it sounds like you had a premonition about your life."

"Perhaps I did," I whispered.

At that moment, we passed through the intersection where I'd hit Mike, and a sense of sacredness descended. We fell silent. I closed my eyes and internally chanted the Gayatri—behind the words of the mantra, I heard my nine-year-old self: *If I could cure the sick, I would do it all day long and be happy to.*

Another voice said: *Be careful what you ask for.*

The street and parking lot surrounding the yoga studio were jammed. Sean maneuvered the car near a policeman who was directing traffic. Well over six feet tall, the cop was massive. His hat sat atop a mound of thick blond hair.

Sean rolled down the window. "Looks like you have your hands full," he said to the officer. "We're here for the yoga class. Any suggestions on where to park?"

The cop stepped over to the driver's side of the car. His reflective sunglasses hid his eyes, but I could still see faint laugh lines on his temples. "Your guess would be as good as mine," the cop replied. "All these people are waiting for the miracle man to show up."

"That's who I have with me," Sean said. The officer stooped to look over at me. Then he walked around to my side of the car. I rolled down the window.

"I've seen the news stories," he said, removing his sunglasses. "It's incredible! The kid just got up and walked away. Fellas, pull into that driveway. I have it reserved for emergency vehicles, but I'll make sure it's fine."

Sean pulled into the drive, and we got out of the car.

"I'm Jake," the officer said, walking toward me. When we shook hands, an image of a beautiful female with auburn hair appeared in my mind's eye. *Someone very close to Jake.* A gray shadow covered the right side of her body.

"Nice to meet you, Jake. We appreciate your help," I said.

"Hey, my wife, Caroline, is in the crowd," he said. "She didn't get a seat in the classroom, but she's waiting right outside. She's a beautiful redhead, pink top, and . . ." Tears welled in his eyes.

As I lightly touched his forearm to comfort him, the shadow surrounding the auburn-haired woman made sense. "She has breast cancer," I said, not knowing how I knew. But—I also sensed there was something else.

"Yeah . . . it's aggressive." He wiped his eyes. "When we saw the news about you and the kid, she said, *I need to meet that man.* Caroline's the most kind, loving, and spiritual person I've ever met, and we have three kids under nine . . . she wants to see 'em grow up. Would you . . . ?"

I felt the heaviness and vulnerability of this man's heart as if his emotions were mine.

Pada Three.

"Of course, I'll see what I can do."

He put his hand on my shoulder. "Thank you," he said. "Let me call a couple of officers over so we can help you both get through the crowd."

Within minutes, two more officers joined us. The five of us crossed the street toward the studio.

"That's *him!*" I heard from the crowd. "That's the miracle man."

Aum Bhur, Bhuvah, Swaha. The Gayatri sounded in my mind at first and then came forth from my lips as a whisper. Sean joined me. We needed the power of the mantra in this moment.

We walked into the mass of people. There was no pushing or shoving like the day on the Parkway. Instead, there was an unexpected silence—a reverence. Mesmerized by the love I felt coming from everyone, I allowed it to flow into my heart center, then back out to those surrounding me. I made eye contact with as many people as I could and felt a unique connection to each person. It was as if a cosmic spider had spun an intricate web of light that touched and joined us together.

"Hey, Sean," I said, "I'm *feeling it.* I'm *feeling it* for each of them. It's deep."

"I know, buddy," Sean said, "I'm feeling it too."

As we neared the studio door, I saw her, the woman with the auburn hair.

"Jake, bring Caroline inside with us. Sean can set her up in a chair," I said. "And will you let everyone know, while I make no claims to having special healing powers, I'll be around after class to connect with as many people as I can?"

"Thank you," Jake said. "I'll let them know, and I'll stay as long as you stay."

We entered the yoga studio and were greeted by Kate. Her long black hair was loosely piled on her head, and her cheeks were flushed with color. The three windows on the left side of the room were wide open, allowing the sweet morning air to filter in. The teacher's mat was set along the wall, which was painted with the chakra system. Yoga mats and people filled the space.

"All right, everyone," Kate said, "please stay on your mats and find your meditation posture. Class will begin soon."

Sean worked to make room for Caroline as Kate and I slipped into the office.

"This is intense," she said. "How are you?"

"Surprisingly well this morning."

"So, do you think you're really healing people with your touch?"

"That's what people are saying. I'm still not exactly sure how, *but* I feel it's connected to the Sutras, especially Pada Three."

"You're a poster child for it," she said with a chuckle. "The teacher trainees feel they're seeing the *siddhis* come to life firsthand."

"Me too, and I don't think it's over yet."

We walked out into the studio. Sean had Caroline positioned in one corner of the room. I smiled at her and took my seat at the front of the class.

"What a beautiful day. And what a treat to have the windows open so nature and everyone outside can join us," I said. "This morning, let's open ourselves to the love we receive from our inner spark. Breathe love, hope, and faith into the fabric of your being. For true healing to take place, we *must* know love. Close your eyes. Let's begin with the sound of the Universal vibration and chant three oms. Breathe out, now in . . ."

The oms came from everyone, even from those in the parking lot. The sound was full, clear, and vibrant, just like the beings chanting it. I was humbled and filled with gratitude for life. Throughout the whole class, I had a sense of joy and euphoria. We finished the seventy-five-minute session by chanting the Gayatri mantra.

Afterward, I asked Caroline to join me in the office. Her beautiful auburn hair was draped over her left shoulder. Although she was thin and pale, her green eyes were clear and alert.

"Kate said we could use her massage table," I said. "I thought I'd do a few minutes of energy work with you."

"I'm honored you're making time for me," Caroline said as I helped her onto the padded table. "I want you to know I'm *not* expecting a miracle. But I feel like I've carried some kind of . . . I don't know . . . wound around for my whole life. And I'd like to heal that so I can be at peace."

"Inner peace is a salve for many things," I said, "even ancient wounds that are part of our shadow. Our wounds are doorways we need to walk through in order to experience true freedom."

She closed her eyes. "Yes," she said, "once we roll back the stone from the cave of our heart."

"And enter the sacred sanctuary with curiosity," I said, sitting at the head of the table, knowing I needed to pay close attention. With my hands out wide, in line with her temples, I slowly moved them toward her ears as a representation of blocking out the noise of the world. An inch away, I felt a powerful magnetic force. *Was it resistance or her strong, energetic field pulling me in?* I then moved my hands to cup her eyes. The same potent current was present. I breathed deeply. Caroline's breathing synced with mine.

I closed my eyes and saw colorful, swirling energy patterns on a black backdrop inside my mind. Then, distinguishable images of people started to emerge. I felt uncomfortable. Somehow, I was simultaneously within two worlds: the reality of working on Caroline in the office and inside a vision of a child, a young girl, curled up in a small ball on the floor of a bedroom. Someone was knocking on a door. I heard a mature female voice say, "Let me in, please let me in."

I *knew* the heart and mind of the girl. Her heart felt as if it would burst from the pain it held. Her mind was confused. *Why am I afraid? I know they love me. Why can't I let them in?*

In the vision of my mind's eye, I couldn't take a deep breath, although my real body was breathing deeply and rhythmically. *What is happening?*

I opened my eyes. Kate's office looked normal.

Moving to Caroline's right side, I placed my left hand on her right shoulder—my right hand on her left hip, and gently rocked her. As I worked to balance the energy in her body, my eyes were drawn to a multitude of thin scars that ran along her right forearm.

"Those are old scars," she whispered, her eyes still closed.

Was she reading my mind? Why not? I was obviously *inside* hers.

"There's no judgment . . . just relax," I said.

I moved my right hand to her right forearm. Her breath became staccato. These *were* old scars. There was no physical discomfort but something deeper: the raw, energetic pain of a psychic wound.

I kept my breath deep and smooth. I closed my eyes and once again entered the *other* reality. I saw a young me hiding behind the chair in the living room of my childhood home. I stuck my head out from behind it to see the young girl now sitting several feet away, huddled in a ball, sobbing. *She's alone and afraid. I know that feeling.*

Still hiding behind the chair, I felt stabbing sensations in my little boy arm. I looked down, expecting to see abrasions, but instead, I saw words tattooed. Words that I recognized.

Pratyayasya paracitta jnanam

The words were from Pada Three. They described the *siddhi of knowing another's mind.*

Caroline and I were sharing this internal *other* world. Experiencing together the time she'd inflicted pain on herself as a young girl, a time when she'd felt lost, a time that still lived inside her.

I opened my eyes and glanced at my arm, but of course, there was no tattoo. Caroline lay still.

Closing my eyes, I was once again the young me behind the safe haven of my chair. The walls of the room whispered, *Save Her.*

I took a deep breath, darted across the room, and grabbed her by the hand. "Come with me!" I said, dragging her back with me behind the safety of my chair.

In the office, I lightly stroked Caroline's arm. Behind the chair—in the living room of my mind's eye—we clutched one another.

I opened my eyes and saw tears rolling down Caroline's cheeks. We shared several deep breaths and then, with a hint of a smile on her lips, she whispered, "Thank you."

"How do you feel?" I asked.

"Very safe. Thank you for taking me to your sanctuary behind the chair," she said. "After all these years of feeling alone and unwanted, being there with you released something."

"You saw the chair?"

"Oh yes. I left a lot of unwanted baggage there."

"Good," I said.

"I didn't have a bad childhood. I mean, there was no abuse that I recall," she said. "But I've carried a boulder of self-loathing around since I can remember. The cutting was a child's attempt to escape feeling."

"We all have wounds," I said. "Some of us have physical scars that show on our bodies, and others have them on their hearts. The wounds on the heart are always harder to heal."

"I felt a shift," she said. "In its own way, this was a miracle."

My ego stirred. *Go back to sleep*, I told it. *Today is about selfless love.*

"I hope you know how much this means to me," Caroline said as I helped her off the table.

"It means a lot to me too. My wounds heal a little as I learn to love myself, listen to the voice within, and offer it back out. That's yoga."

Jake was waiting for us as we stepped out of the office. He took Caroline into his arms.

"Thank you for all of your time," he said, looking over to me. "Now, let me help you."

We found Sean, and the three of us walked outside into the waiting crowd. Caroline stayed behind in the studio. With Sean and Jake at my sides, I touched the first outstretched hand that came toward me—and then another, and then another, and another—hundreds of hands reaching out in a peaceful silence. Some I gave a handshake, some a touch on the shoulder or a cheek, yet others were full-body hugs. The type of touch was orchestrated by the Universe. It came naturally without thought.

For hours, I stayed, making contact with everyone through touch. The web of connection was vibrant and palpable. The whole time, I felt a melding and a dissolving of barriers. A constant thought ran through my mind: *I'm feeling it—for everyone—*that deep, overwhelming sensation Sean and I share when our hearts are wide open to each other, and we can't feel anything but love.

There were some tears, but the overall experience was one of joy. I was in a deep meditation with my eyes wide open. This had seldom worked for me, but now, I was making not only eye but also *heart* contact with hundreds of individuals as we shared a moment of unified bliss. There was no judgment, no barriers, no grasping—only the unspoken recognition of our common divine essence.

May all beings have happiness.

21

A MAN OF THE CLOTH

You must ask for what you really want.
Don't go back to sleep.
—Rumi

"How'd you sleep?" Sean asked the next morning.

"Like a baby. No dreams, no visitations, just deep sleep."

"Have you looked out front yet?" he asked.

"Nope."

"It's almost clear, maybe all you need to do is touch everyone on Sundays after class and we could have a fairly normal life."

"If helping people with my touch is the new normal, I'll take it. How's everything else?" I asked.

"Well, after Friday night's concert appearance and yesterday's mass healing at the studio, you're super-hot with the media again," Sean said. "Carol and I are overwhelmed with social media, emails, and requests for you to talk to any media outlet you want."

"Even Fox?" I asked, raising my eyebrow.

"I may have deleted those requests," he said. "My mind's a blank." We both laughed.

"I think we did the right thing by choosing the *Beacon of Illumination* for my first media contact. What can I do to help you and Carol?"

"Just focus on getting yourself prepared for today's client, who we're pretty sure is an archbishop."

"An archbishop . . . ," I said, shaking my head.

"Ren, don't let self-doubt get the best of you. He may be some higher-up in the church, but remember, he sought you out. Do your thing and stay true to yourself."

"Thank you." I sighed.

I gathered my journal and moved to our garden. I opened it to the page where I had written the Yoga Sutras Veronica had quoted to me before any of this new journey began.

Sutra 1:12 Both practice (abhyāsa) and non-attachment (vairāgya) are required to still the habits of consciousness.

Sutra 1:13 Practice (abhyāsa) is the sustained effort to rest in that stillness.

These wise yogic words, recited by an animated statue of a Catholic saint, were great reminders, and now, I had the opportunity to pass this wisdom on to a possible man of the cloth.

What an interesting phrase, I thought—man of the cloth. Historically, it applied to anyone who wore a uniform to denote their occupation, but eventually, it referred specifically to the black clothing and white collar of a holy man. *What is holy, though, other than a judgment from human to human?* Did a particular way of dress denote someone holy? Who knew what lurked behind the collar or the cloth?

"Ren," Sean said, sticking his head out the kitchen door, "he's early! He's in your studio, and we were right about him being the archbishop."

"How do you know?"

"He's wearing a white collar."

"I see. Well, I'm off to teach meditation to a man of the cloth," I said.

"Good luck, and may the saints be with you." He gave me a love nudge on the shoulder as I moved past him.

I took several deep, cleansing breaths as I ascended the stairs to meet Father Piedmont. Why was I so nervous? *Don't bring in baggage from past experiences with Catholicism.* The man had made an appointment for meditation instruction, so that's what I planned to give him. We'd start with the basics, like I did with all my students.

I opened the door to my studio and stepped in. A man in his late sixties with a full head of silky gray hair sat in a chair. His face was long and thin, his eyebrows bushy, and his blue eyes deeply set above large dark circles. He stood.

As I closed the door behind me, he knelt.

"Father Piedmont, please, we'll begin seated."

He then moved into full prostrated *pranam* in front of me.

I had a flash of myself doing the same thing in front of the saints in the back of Corpus Christi.

Why was he doing this? "Father . . ."

"Please, call me Joseph. Let *me* call *you* Father," he said.

I felt chills.

"All right, Joseph, but call me Ren. Come sit in this chair so we can talk." I reached for his arm to help him up, but he shook his head and remained outstretched on the floor.

"Please forgive me. Please, please forgive me," he whispered.

I felt a similar energy as I did yesterday with Jake, now feeling *this* man's emotions as if they were mine.

"I forgive you. Can you forgive yourself? That's what truly counts," I said.

He began to sob. I moved to my knees and stroked his gray hair with my right hand. I placed my left hand on the middle of his back and gently rocked him.

"Forgiving yourself is the first step," I said. "Then, say you're sorry on a soul level for what you're hiding deep inside and set yourself free." These Venus-inspired words were as much for me as for this priest.

After a few moments, I helped him back to the chair and handed him a box of tissues. We sat face-to-face, but he did not meet my eyes.

"Why are you here, Joseph?"

"I'm trapped by my desires for personal gain and recognition. My soul is dead asleep. I can't be true to my calling while I feel like this," he said. "I want to help others, but I'm a fake. I've been a fake for the thirty-six years I've been a priest." He placed his hand on his heart. "Something needs to be released and forgiven so I can do what you do. Please help me."

Tears once again welled in his eyes.

"Let's take some deep breaths together," I said, "for calming."

We began.

"Close your eyes," I instructed. "Hold your inhale for a few seconds, then exhale slowly. Soften from the inside and feel your body fill with love and light. Experience the grace of being alive in this moment, just as you are.

"Bring your awareness back to the room," I said after several rounds of this intentional breathing. Our eyes met for the first time—I saw a deep sadness. "Tell me about your meditation training in the seminary. Did you study the traditions of the Catholic mystics?"

"We had little-to-no meditation training, nor did we explore the saints on any mystical level," he said. "Merely saying the rosary was our contemplation. We did spend time in prayer, called vespers, but that was listening to readings from the gospels. We were never instructed to go inside and reflect on our personal relationship with God."

"So, after thirty-six years," I asked, "why are you now interested in meditation and exploring this personal relationship?"

"I saw the clip of you with the boy," he said. "I've read your social media post a hundred times, and I saw the news story of you touching all those people yesterday. They say you've cured them. I want to experience what you're experiencing. I want to learn your techniques so I can serve those who entrust their souls to me."

"What do you think I'm experiencing?" I asked.

"Something beyond religion, something mystical and transcendental, something I know is possible but eludes me. I've been praying for direction for decades." He paused. "I want to share something I've never told anyone. I think you'll understand, and it will shed light on why I'm here."

"Okay," I said, my interest definitely piqued.

"Ever since I was a boy, I've had vivid dreams. They're clear and illuminated. For most of my life, they've been dreams of inspiring conversations with the saints. That's why I was drawn to the priesthood," he said. "I always remember minute details from these dreams, but more importantly, pieces of them come true, although I never know which pieces.

"Saturday before last, I had one of those dreams. In it, I was in a park, sitting at a picnic table reading a book called *The Life of St. Francis: The Yogi*. To my knowledge, there's no such book.

"As I sat reading, a bird landed directly in front of me on the table. It was the most natural thing to be reading about St. Francis and having a bird only inches from me. After several moments of mutual eye gazing, it spoke, *'Joseph, find guidance from the one who gives me refuge from the cold. Seek the one who has rolled back the stone from the cave of his heart and opened a clear channel to love.'*"

I took a deep breath and sat up straight as the archbishop continued.

"'He can open you to the possibilities of your life. He can bring you the peace you seek by helping you be of service to the greatest number of humanity. Wake up from this death sleep that covers you and learn to breathe. Veritas vos Liberabit.' As the bird flew off, I woke up."

Veritas vos Liberabit. The truth will set you free, I thought.

"I wrote down the dream and wondered who the bird could be talking about and how the meaning would reveal itself."

"Fascinating dream," I said. My head was spinning with all the synchronized information. *Refuge from the cold . . .* roll back the stone.

"The next day," he said, "as I was preparing for noontime Sunday services at the cathedral, I was shown the clip of you and the boy on the Parkway. I knew it was you I had to meet. You're the one who could help me wake up from the death sleep that covers me. You can teach me to breathe." He bowed his head. "I seek your guidance."

An intense tingling covered my entire body.

"What kind of bird was in your dream?" I asked.

"A bright red male cardinal. I'm still not sure what he meant by 'seek the one who gives me refuge from the cold.'"

"For the last nine years," I said, "from late fall to early spring, a male cardinal has made his home on the light fixture of our side porch."

"So, you're the one who gives him shelter," he said, shaking his head. "There's one more thing, but this must be kept completely confidential."

"Of course," I said.

"I'm being considered for a newly vacated seat in the American College of Cardinals. This just came about last week. Although nothing is finalized, I have had my initial interview with the pope, so it's likely I will be wearing cardinal-red robes before the end of the year."

That kind of promotion would definitely fan the flames of his desires for personal recognition, I thought.

"Can you see how it all fits together like a puzzle?" he asked.

Like a big cosmic puzzle.

"You've been sent to me," he said, leaning toward me.

I leaned back instinctually as if putting distance between me and a fire that had suddenly become too hot for comfort.

"That gives us much to ponder," I said, trying to keep myself present. "Let's work on breathing techniques and the use of mantra for the rest of our session."

We practiced for forty minutes. The priest was receptive to every instruction I gave.

"I'd like to give you more breathing and concentration exercises to practice for homework," I said as our time came to an end. I retrieved a handout I had prepared for him from my desk. "Focus, *Dharana*, as it is called in yogic philosophy, is the key that opens us to deeper practices of meditation. So, as you work to focus, I'd like you to work with the mantra, *Aim*, the bija sound of the goddess Saraswati, to help open you to inspiration and wisdom. Be consistent, Joseph, practice daily and use self-inquiry to monitor the subtle changes you notice."

"I will be diligent," he said as we shook hands. "You're exactly who I need. Our destinies are intertwined."

His grip intensified. I had a flash of standing between the porcelain-skinned vampire and Venus, and then looking into the eyes of the nun in Assisi as she handed me the holy card.

"May I set another appointment in the next day or so?" he asked. "I need to continue with you as often as you have time."

We set an appointment for our next session, and I sent him on his way.

Back in my studio, I sat at my computer and searched: "Spiritual meaning of a male cardinal."

Wake up! was what I read. *Wake up to your power and stop hiding from your destiny. With a cardinal as your guide, learn to fly with him. He is the teacher of focus and clarity.*

As for our real side porch cardinal, he'd stayed longer than usual this year, but last night, Sean and I had both noticed he was gone. And . . . today, I was visited by a man dreaming of talking cardinals. Had our feathered visitor from the side porch manifested into a human being named Joseph Piedmont? Would he transform even further into a cardinal of the Catholic Church?

The man of the cloth and I had similar intentions—to Wake Up and be of service to humanity. The message of a cardinal had brought us together. I bowed my head. *Let the mystery unfold. Synchronicity abounds!*

22

PODCAST

There was a light knock on my studio door as Sean stuck his head in. "I'm dying to know! How did it go?" he asked. "Did he pick your brain of all your secrets?"

"No, nothing like that, but it was definitely illuminating," I said.

"Illuminating?" Sean asked as he sat down at the other side of my desk. "I'm intrigued."

"He asked me for forgiveness."

"Forgiveness, for what?"

"He said he's a fake and isn't living up to his role. Then, he had a dream—"

"A dream?" Sean shifted in his chair.

"In it, he was reading *The Life of St. Francis: The Yogi* when a red cardinal told him to *find guidance from the one who gives me refuge from the cold. Seek the one who has rolled back the stone from the cave of his heart.*"

"Oh, Jeez."

"I know," I said. "The cardinal also told him to wake up!"

"Are you serious?"

"Something's brewing with this guy. I wonder if we're destined to work together."

"Wait, wait, wait . . . that's not sitting well with me."

"He's seeking tools to live a life full of truth. I think he's on a yogic path."

"A Catholic priest on a yogic path?"

"I know, I know, but the synchronicity of the dreams . . . the bird, and he said he's even being promoted to a cardinal! He just had an interview with the pope, so—"

"What?" Sean pushed back into his chair, putting his hands to his face. "Are you making this up? Of course not . . . this is just *your* life."

"It's *our* life," I said.

"I'm telling you, this is not what it seems. He's trying to seduce you or hypnotize you into somehow helping *his* church."

"We'll see," I said, "I have another session with him in a couple of days."

"Okay, whatever," Sean said, shaking his head. "Let's move on. The producer of the podcast called with all the details for tomorrow's interview. The podcast is audio, but you'll be on a video call with Sonja, the host, so I thought I'd set you up in here with the painting of Saraswati as your background. Sonja will get to see the enchanting image, and the goddess will literally have your back."

"I love you, Sean."

"I love you too, Magic Man." Sean winked.

"Sean!" I shook my head.

"I'm not talking about miracles. I'm talking about the mesmerizing way you continue to open my heart, *even* when I think you have your head in the sand." I knew he was referring to the archbishop.

"Always," I said, meaning it but also as a diversion.

"Forever."

The next morning, I was experiencing a mixture of exhilaration from my meeting with the archbishop and butterflies about my upcoming interview with Sonja.

Sean placed the ring light, filled two glasses with water, and set up my computer, so all I had to do was sit down and talk. He sat across from me, behind my computer screen. His presence and the goddess at my back were the moral support I needed.

As we went live, Sonja Mathers, a woman in her late fifties, greeted me with a bright smile. Her blue eyes, short silvery hair, and small, round, dark-rimmed retro glasses gave her an air of wisdom. She wore a dark mock turtleneck with a single rose quartz pendant.

"Hello, Ren. Thank you for choosing the *Beacon of Illumination* as your first interview. We're honored." She placed her hands in prayer position in front of her face and bowed her head.

I returned the hand gesture. "I love your podcast, Sonja. It's wonderful how you're spreading the word about the life-changing benefits of meditation. I thought this was the perfect outlet to start a dialogue."

"I couldn't agree more." She smiled, quickly transitioning into a raised eyebrow and pursed lips. "A little background for our audience—until just a few days ago, you were a complete unknown. Then you brought a boy back to life. Now, news and social media are barraged with innumerable accounts of incredible healing all attributed to your touch. Everyone wants to hear from you, but until now, you've kept the world waiting."

"Well, I did post—"

"Yes, in your only social media post, you said you practice yoga. My staff did some research and found that you study and teach Tantric yoga. You're also a longtime meditator, studying for many years with meditation guru Sara Howard, who our audience is well acquainted with."

I suddenly felt exposed.

"What originally brought you to meditation?" she asked.

"Fear," I said without hesitation. "It was my constant companion growing up."

"Did you grow up in a hostile environment?"

"No, it was nothing like that. It was a combination of being a security-minded Capricorn, whose shadow is fear, and my mom working dinner shifts as a waitress after my parents divorced. So by the time I was eight years old, I was alone many evenings."

"You were alone in your house at eight years old?"

"Yes, but I was a mature kid. But I *was* still a kid. Those nights I was alone, I was afraid, so I'd hide behind a big old chair in the living room, waiting for my mom to come home. By the time I was ten, the fear manifested as ulcers and bouts of exhaustion."

"So, fear really was your childhood companion. Did you have any tools to cope?"

"Well, one day in the eighth grade, apparently, after a discussion between my mom and the principal, I was asked to stay after school. Sister Colette told me she had a suggestion to help me relax."

"And what did she offer you?" Sonja asked.

"She called it a full body scan, but you and I call it Yoga Nidra. *Relax your feet fully*, she said, *and now move your attention to the lower parts of your legs and relax them.* She took us through the whole body in about fifteen minutes. Then we'd hang out all relaxed for another five minutes with no words. We did this every day for about six months."

"That first taste of meditation came early," Sonja said. "Do you remember what you thought about the experience?"

"I liked it, but when I was alone at home, it wasn't easy to access, so most of the time, I just curled up behind the chair."

"Then how did you come to meditation as an ongoing practice?" Sonja asked.

"By the time I was in my early twenties, it was literally *learn to relax or die*. Every loud noise made me jump, and I took everything to the worst-case scenario. That's when I found yoga, and my *real* meditation journey began."

"And that journey led to what happened on Columbia Parkway," Sonja said, "and now you're showing the world what's possible when we focus on meditation and walk the path of a heart-centered life."

"I guess so," I said.

"What do you mean?"

"Yes, I meditate, but I don't know if that's what brought Mike back to life. It's certainly helped calm my mind, given me a more objective perspective on my life, and helped me relax. But I still struggle," I admitted.

"Struggle? With what?"

"Uh . . . being human, self-doubt, self-criticism, regrets, coming to terms with the internal taskmaster."

"And in the meantime, even while struggling with all the things that make us human, *you* perform miracles."

I sensed an inauthentic tone in her voice. I sat up straight.

"You know, Sonja, I think it's important to meditate for the sake of what it does to calm your mind and expand your consciousness," I said. "Meditation saved my life. That's a miracle in itself. And it can do the same for anyone who'll give it a chance with their time, energy, and effort. *But* if you meditate *only* to perform miracles, you're missing the point. Besides, meditation or no meditation, we all perform miracles whenever we give love and receive love."

"What a beautiful sentiment," she said with a tight smile.

"It's more than sentiment," I said. "It's what I believe."

"I really do agree, Ren." Her Cheshire smile added to my uneasy feeling. "So, do you diligently study and follow the teachings outlined in the Yoga Sutras? Is yoga your spirituality?"

"Yoga's a big part of it. I combine its tools and techniques with astrology to create my spirituality."

"Speaking of tools and techniques, in your social media post, you described using the Gayatri mantra and a hand gesture called Abhaya mudra. Is that how saving the boy came about?"

I took a deep breath.

"As much as you'd like to distill this down to some formula, it isn't that simple, Sonja."

"I realize it wasn't simple—but I want to help our listeners understand you and meditation's part in this event."

"Meditation is a *huge* part of this," I said, "specifically calming the brain chatter to allow the inner guides to be heard over the mind."

"So, you have inner guides that are helping you?"

"We *all* have them when we learn to listen. For most, the guide is the gentle voice of intuition we hear in our heart once the ego-mind is quiet."

"Is that how it guides *you*?"

"Yes, for the most part, but my intuition also presents itself as an internal council representing the archetypes of my astrological chart. Right now, they're guiding me through a journey of the yoga kleshas."

"Really?" Sonja said, sounding a bit incredulous. "That's quite unique."

"I don't know if it's unique or not," I said, "but it works for me. Our guides can come in all shapes and sizes. I'm also receiving guidance from goddess energies coming through a group of female Catholic saints that were—"

"Oh . . . I see . . . ," she said slowly, sitting back in her chair. "Is that the Catholic connection? Are you discussing these female saint guides with Archbishop Piedmont?"

I looked over my computer to Sean, who was shaking his head with his hands up in the air. He picked up the phone and started typing.

"Archbishop Piedmont?" I asked, taking a slow breath.

"Yes, this morning, there were photos online showing the archbishop leaving your house yesterday. Are these saints, the archbishop, and the Vatican's recent investigation of the miracle on the Parkway connected?"

Sean held up the phone screen so I could see a photo of the archbishop leaving our house.

"Investigation?" I swallowed hard.

"Oh yes," Sonja said, clearly knowing she had thrown me off. "The Congregation for the Causes of Saints at the Vatican has opened a case—but you must know all of this since you're working with the archbishop."

"Can we get back on track with our discussion of meditation?" I asked.

"I see," she said as she removed her glasses and placed the end of one arm on her bottom lip, "you aren't at liberty to discuss this publicly, is that it?"

"Something like that," I said, closing my eyes and shaking my head slightly. I had thought this podcast was going to be easy.

"What the hell was that?" Sean asked after the interview.

I put my head into my hands. "I don't know," I said.

"The Congregation for the Causes of Saints? Are they going to make you a saint?"

"You have to be dead *and* Catholic to be a saint."

"Well, you're not dead, but you seem to be more Catholic every day."

I looked up. "I'm no saint, and I am *not* Catholic, but one thing I definitely am is confused."

23

CAROLINE

The interview with Sonja, the miracle, the media, the celebrity status, the questioning, the self-doubt, the struggle with my ego, and now the re-entry of Catholicism into my life had my internal balance fluctuating from second to second. It all caught up with me that afternoon.

"I'm going to the treehouse," I said to Sean.

"Time to meditate?"

"Nope. I need a good old-fashioned nap."

Even in the daylight, it was easy to make the bedroom dark and cozy. I closed the blinds, crawled into bed, and was somewhere else in a matter of minutes.

I was sitting on a park bench, looking out over fields of exquisite colorful flowers, light purple irises, orange and yellow tiger lilies, and snow-white Lady Shasta daisies.

I closed my eyes and took a deep breath to fill myself with the alluring fragrance of the flowers. Then I felt a comforting caress of soft hands on the tops of my bare feet. I opened my eyes to find a woman dressed in a flowing black gown kneeling in front of me. Her dress was similar to that of my statue friends, Veronica and Clare, but instead of a veil, her long, wavy auburn hair was pulled to the left and draped over her shoulder.

"Your touch feels good. But what are you doing?" I asked.

Her emerald-green eyes met mine.

"Washing your feet and anointing them with oil."

She pulled a small pitcher of water and a white cloth closer to my feet.

"Do not become desensitized with all that is happening. Feel each step as you move through your journey."

She poured the water over my feet.

"Something sacred is being birthed, and you are one of *my* midwives." She began to dry my feet with the white cloth.

"Keep *my* essence in your heart. Much healing needs to take place, and it cannot take place without *me*."

"Who are you?" I asked.

"I am one of many who make up the feminine collective that opens hearts to deep levels of love that can change the natural order of the world."

She placed three drops of oil onto each of my feet and began to massage them.

"Keep these words in your heart. Therein lies the secret to your mystery."

"Mystery?"

"She, like everything, will resolve again into her own nature."

"*Who* will resolve?" I asked.

She stood and placed her hand on my cheek.

"What transpires in the next few hours will help you believe in the connection that is guiding you. Continue to teach in full humility and bring a clearer understanding to all who seek. Help seekers find me."

I reached to place my hand on hers—but as my eyes opened—*my* hand was on *my* cheek.

Still feeling her essence, I got out of bed, picked up my journal, went to my meditation cushion, and wrote down pieces of the dream. A golden beam of light made its way into the room through a small space in one of the blinds and lit up the page. My heart was full of appreciation and gratitude.

"Reno," Sean called from downstairs.

I closed my journal and headed down the steps.

"Sorry to wake you," Sean said as I entered the kitchen.

"That's okay, it was just what I needed. What's up?" I sat down at the table.

"I spoke with Jake, the police officer who helped us outside the yoga studio."

"How's Caroline?"

"She's in hospice."

My heart sank.

"What? But we just—"

"She wants to see you," Sean said. "Jake said she has an overwhelming *need* to wash your feet."

Any internal balance I'd regained from my nap and visitation with the green-eyed woman was gone. *She will resolve again into her own nature.*

"I *have* to see her," I said. "She's going, she's resolving."

"What are you talking about?"

"I'll explain in the car. Let me get my journal."

On the drive, I told Sean the entire dream.

"The woman in the park had Caroline's hair and eyes, and she was quoting the Gospel of Mary Magdalene. She said, *She will resolve again into her own nature.* Now I know she was talking about Caroline getting ready to transition."

"Why the feet washing?" Sean asked.

"There's a practice in yoga called *vandana*, where you wash the feet of your teacher out of respect. It's also a ritual some cultures did right before death."

"But washing the dying person's feet, not the other way around, right?"

"Yes, that part I don't understand," I said, "but Caroline's tapping into some deep stuff, so I know there's something to all this: Female saints and Hindu nuns showing up with messages about digging them out of obscurity and finding out last week that Venus in Pisces is the co-chair of my council." I shook my head. "Did you know that in medical astrology, Pisces rules the feet?"

"What? This is like some kind of cosmic puzzle," Sean said, glancing over at me as we sat at a traffic light.

"It is, but we don't have all the pieces yet."

"I am trying hard to keep up," Sean said. "Who's the woman in the dream?"

"She said she's one of many of the feminine collective, and what transpires in the next few hours will help me believe in the connection that's guiding me. I just hope I can—wait. Sean, look," I said, pointing to a large white van in the next lane. The artwork on the side was abstract, but I knew exactly what it was. "There's another piece of the puzzle."

The light changed. All the cars started moving.

"Catch up with it, Sean."

"I'm trying. What is it?"

At the next traffic light, Sean saw it too: a graphic of a kneeling female figure holding someone's feet.

"Jesus," he said.

"Maybe . . . but right now, *she's* the one we need to focus on."

"Everything is so connected, it's freaky," Sean said.

"Carl Jung and the *Vedas* say the web of connection is always there, but we have to be willing to see."

"We're seeing it," Sean said with a sigh.

I rolled down my window and got the driver's attention.

"Excuse me, what organization are you with, sir?"

"I'm with The Magdalene Hospice Center," he said.

"O-M-G," Sean said, "that's where we're headed."

"What?" I said, looking over at him.

"That's where Caroline is."

I felt chills up and down my spine.

As the light changed, the driver handed me a card.

"More orphic words on a card?" Sean asked as I rolled up the window.

"Yep, it says, The Magdalene Hospice Center, serving with humility and bringing a clearer understanding to all who seek—that's what the woman in my dream told *me* to do."

"So, you had a dream with Mary Magdalene washing your feet?"

"I guess so," I said, "but that's confusing."

"How much clearer can the Universe be?" Sean asked. "She washed Jesus's feet and then showed up in your dream to wash your feet."

"But Mary Magdalene didn't wash his feet."

"I thought she did, and he forgave her for being a prostitute," Sean said.

"That's what the church *wants* us to believe but if you read the gospels, there are several Marys," I said. "Mary Magdalene was actually a wealthy patron of Jesus, not a prostitute. There was a plan by the early church leaders to downplay the role of women, especially the Magdalene. That's why the Gnostic Gospels were never included in the Bible. The masses were only given the stories these men wanted us to have *until* a copy of the Gospel of Mary Magdalene was discovered in the late nineteenth century in Cairo, and another copy was found at Nag Hammadi in Egypt. The omitted texts make a strong case for her being his number-one disciple *and* maybe even his partner. In one part, it says he loved her more than all other women."

"You're blowing me away," Sean said. "So why did they alter it?"

"Besides downplaying the role of women, the omitted books counseled you to develop a personal relationship with the divine source. They *encourage* mysticism."

"Got it. So there would be no need for priests."

"Bingo! The men wanted to maintain control," I said. "The church still doesn't recognize the omitted books as part of their teachings."

"But if these Gnostic Gospels are out there, why don't more people know about them?"

"Two thousand years of propaganda takes a *long* time to change."

"I'd like to read them."

"I have a copy at home."

"Of course you do." Sean reached over and squeezed my leg.

"It's interesting how yogic they sound. They're eloquent about our mystical connection and the power of the feminine."

"It sounds like *she* is trying to get your attention."

Goosebumps rose on my skin. "I want to know more about the feet washing and Mary Magdalene. I want more puzzle pieces." I sighed. "Wouldn't it be cool to visit the Vatican and go through all those old books and notes and see what else they've done to obscure her?"

"Sure, we'll just pop in and visit with the pope too!" Sean chuckled. "Maybe Dottie or your archbishop can arrange it."

I smiled. "I know it sounds crazy, but this is the kind of stuff former history teachers fantasize about: old manuscripts and correcting historical distortions."

"Just be careful what you wish for, especially these days."

We walked through the doors of The Magdalene Hospice Center. I chanted the Gayatri mantra softly under my breath as we walked down the hallway toward room nine. Suddenly, everything began to feel both familiar and ancient. The antiseptic smell was replaced with scents of frankincense and myrrh. The tiled floors blurred into ancient stones. The overhead fluorescent lighting morphed into thick pillar candles and hanging torches. I focused on putting one foot in front of the other as I walked this strange, sacred pathway. Everything was as it should be.

We stood at the threshold of room nine. Caroline was propped up in bed and Jake sat in a chair beside her. Caroline's long auburn hair was draped over her left shoulder, and she was holding Abhaya mudra. Her eyes were closed, her breathing peaceful, and she had a hint of a smile on her lips.

I took a deep breath.

Jake waved us in. As we approached the bed, her eyes opened, and her smile widened. Near the bed was a chair, a basin of water, and a towel. Jake gestured for me to take a seat. I did. I removed my shoes. Caroline rose from the bed, took her husband's hand, walked over, and knelt before me. She motioned for me to place my feet into the water. Jake handed her a small bottle of oil. After placing several drops in the water and moving the water with her hands, she began to massage my feet.

I was totally absorbed in the moment.

"One journey ends as another begins," she said, continuing her ritual. "Every moment is pregnant with potential. You can change your perception with the closing of your eyes. The body and soul have full memory of your journey and purpose. Only your mind forgets."

For several seconds, she was silent, then in a whisper, she said, "The feminine is coming back to nurture, to soothe, and to open hearts to deep levels of love. She *can* and *will* change the natural order of the world to save it. Keep these words in your heart."

More phrases from the Gospel of Mary, I thought.

"The secret to your mystery is that *She* is taking Her rightful place in the order of life. You and many more like you are called to be of service."

She looked up. I then heard without words, *I'm feeling it*, and then, *Me too*.

After she dried my feet, I helped her up. She glided back to her bed and once again assumed Abhaya mudra.

I stood by her side, savoring our heart connection. I leaned over her and whispered, "I am at Her service."

She looked deeply into my eyes, and I into hers. Human-to-human, soul-to-soul, spark-to-spark.

"I see the thread," she said. "It's beautiful. It exists *in* and *between* all creatures. Thank you."

Her *thank you* was similar yet different to when Mike said it on the Parkway. The boy got up and walked away. Caroline was getting ready to take flight.

Spread your wings, angel. Fly to heights unimaginable.
Shanti, shanti, shanti. Peace, peace, peace.

Jake walked us to the front door of the hospice facility.

"How long has she been holding the mudra?" I asked.

"She started holding it occasionally after seeing the video of you with the boy, but here she's been holding it the entire time."

"It's the mudra of fearlessness," I said.

"Fearless," he said, nodding. "That's what she's become since you were with her at the yoga studio. She told me she'd healed her trauma and now knows that her connection with me and the girls will continue even after she's gone. To see her this resolved is a miracle!"

Resolved.

I hugged him.

"She sees the threads of light that connect us all. The mothering essence is guiding her," I said. "She's showing us how to fearlessly face life and its transitions with understanding and strength. Some will face this same transition with fascination, some with fear—and yet others, like Caroline, full of grace. She'll be more than fine."

"I know it," Jake said and embraced me. "I really, really know it." He began to cry onto my shoulder.

"You'll be fine too, my friend," I said as I squeezed him a little tighter.

"Yes, I will. I'm richer for loving her and living this experience."

He took a deep breath as we stepped back from each other. Sean moved in and gave him a hug. Then Sean and I placed our hands into Abhaya mudra. We bowed slightly and said, "Namaste."

"Namaste, my friends," Jake said, returning the gesture.

Sean and I sang a different chant as we drove home.

We all come from the goddess,
And to Her, we shall return,
Like a drop of rain,
Flowing to the Ocean

24

THE DOOR

We returned home from hospice, lit candles on our living room altar, and sat for a meditation dedicated to Caroline. We chanted the *Maha Mrityunjaya*, a mantra devoted to lifting the spirit of a person transitioning and ensuring a clear and safe journey.

"We offer the *Maha Mrityunjaya* to our friend Caroline," I said at the end of our session. "Even while our hearts are breaking, we recognize that suffering and ecstasy co-exist, and both make life worth living. The transitions of life are miracles when made sacred."

"Namaste," we said in unison, then blew out the candles.

That evening, I fell asleep wondering about the beautiful woman in the park, Caroline, Mary Magdalene, the anointing of feet, and all the connected events of the day. As I shifted from consciousness to unconsciousness, I again found myself in front of the stainless-steel boardroom doors. I took a deep breath and pushed them open.

All ten were in attendance, but this time, not all of them were in lab coats. The Moon was now dressed like Venus in a white tunic. Both allowed their hair to cascade over their shoulders. All of the men had longer, less groomed hair and five o'clock shadows. Saturn and Uranus were dressed like Greek gods. The rest were still dressed like scientists.

"Hello, my friends," I said.

Saturn motioned for me to take my regular seat.

"I had a dream, and a woman was washing my feet. Was it Mary Magdalene?" I asked.

"Perhaps Neptune should take that question. He directs the world of dreams," Saturn said, gesturing to his right. A man sitting next to Uranus stood. By the time he'd picked up a five-foot trident resting next to him, his lab coat had transformed into a belted waist tunic, his white hair had grown to shoulder length, and his beard had become full, resembling tangled seaweed.

"Wow, that was quite a transition," I said.

"Anything is possible in my world of dreams," he said, "as you well know. And discerning what is unconscious gibberish and prophecy takes skill."

"That's why I'm asking if it was Mary Magdalene," I said.

"Why do you think it *might* be her?"

"All the details fit: her manner of dress, the myths of her washing feet, Caroline asking to wash my feet, and then the graphic on the van. The synchronicity's coming fast and furious, and I don't want to miss the significance of what I'm supposed to be doing."

"That's definitely in *my* realm of quantitative mind stuff," said a man sitting to the immediate left of Saturn, who was furiously writing down everything that was said like a court stenographer. He was much smaller in stature than the other men. His facial features were soft and delicate, with no trace of a beard. He looked to be a boy. "Why do you *think* you're supposed to be doing anything?"

Androgynous Mercury, the god of communication and the lower mind.

Mercury nodded, seemingly aware of my internal dialogue.

"Isn't all this happening for a reason?" I asked.

"You decide."

Enough of this. I stood, "If you're my guides, shouldn't you be giving me answers?"

"You come to us for opportunities," said Saturn, gesturing for me to sit. "We're very interested in your process of self-discovery."

"On this road to self-discovery," I said, plopping down in my seat, "how about answering at least some of my questions instead of dancing around them?"

"What do you want to know?" Mercury asked, fidgeting with his pencil.

"Why would Mary Magdalene visit me? Why would all these women visit me?"

"Maybe she's looking to *you* to help challenge all the misinformation about *her* and change the way the world sees *her* and the whole feminine essence," said Venus.

"I'd gladly take that on if I thought I could make a difference," I said.

"What's standing in your way?" she asked with a slight smile.

"Well . . . lack of factual knowledge," I answered. "It's difficult to know what's real in human history since it's written by the victors. In this case, our early history was written and rewritten by men. Who knows what else has been hidden or destroyed to propagate male dominance and their hierarchy?"

"So, you seek *evidence* for your intuitive hunches before you will consider taking on your assignment?" she asked.

"Assignment? I don't—"

Saturn cleared his throat. "Ren, answer her question. Do you want evidence to back up your internal knowing?"

"Yes. I wish I could read the original manuscripts in the Vatican archives. I bet all the omitted books from the Bible are there—maybe even accounts of the lost years of Jesus that reveal he studied some form of yogic philosophy. I'd love for *all* of us to know what was removed in order to justify the supremacy of men and the male priesthood."

"Okay," Venus said with a wink.

"Okay? What does that mean?"

"See that door?" asked the still-mysterious woman.

I looked over my right shoulder. Where there had been nothing was now an immense, thick, heavy door with four twelve-inch honey-colored wooden planks secured with black wrought-iron supports that formed a large "E." A dense metal latch on the right served as the doorknob.

"What's behind it?" I asked.

"One of the opportunities we can provide," she continued. "Open it and step inside."

I'd be more comfortable if Venus were presenting this invitation, I thought.

"Well?" The impatient goddess pressed.

"I would love to, especially if I can find some answers."

"Open it and take a step into the darkness," said Saturn.

"Darkness?"

"Darkness holds so many possibilities," added the Moon. "As you know, yoga teaches you can't know the light without experiencing the dark."

I stood and slowly walked toward the door. *If I can't trust my inner guides, who can I trust?*

The door was even more massive up close. I ran my hand over the smooth wood, then tugged on the wrought-iron latch. With enormous effort, I managed to pull it open. I peered inside at a solid wall of impenetrable blackness that the light from my side of the threshold did not pierce.

"Go in or not," said the mysterious woman, "but do something for goddess's sake!" She exhaled hard.

I looked at her. *Exactly who is this aggressive woman?*

"I'm going. Give me a minute."

I turned back to the door and stepped to the edge of the threshold, being careful not to step over it. I stared into the blackness. I tried to see something, anything, but there was nothing.

The Buddhist concept of *no-thingness* came to mind: *It is in what seems a void that all possibilities exist.*

"I trust you folks," I said over my shoulder as I continued to observe the darkness.

"And we trust you," said Venus, "that's why you are here standing on the threshold of truth. *Veritas vos Liberabit.*"

"Yes, the truth will set me free," I said as I brought my hands into Abhaya mudra. I took a deep breath and repeated the words I had taught so many of my students facing unknown circumstances:

I am not afraid of my life or
what is in my heart.

With an exhale, I stepped off the precipice. As I began a free fall into blackness, my heart raced, I fell head over heels—tumbling, tumbling, tumbling. Then, I heard the chant that is so much a part of my heart and being. The Gayatri mantra came at me from everywhere, all sides—soft, sweet, calm.

Aum Bhur, Bhuvah, Swaha

Tumbling, tumbling, tumbling . . .

Tat Savitur Varenyum

As I fell into no-thingness, the temperature cooled. The air whisked over my skin.

Tumbling, tumbling, tumbling . . .

My fall decelerated and the tumbling stopped. My feet touched softly on solid ground. The air was moist and now much cooler, almost cold. In a blink, a single, faint red ultraviolet light illuminated the space. I stood in front of yet another wooden door. This one was shorter than the one in the council chamber. Its planks were black and covered in moss. I pushed it open to find a dimly lit hallway. There was a musty scent in the air. I walked several hundred feet before I saw what looked to be a floor-to-ceiling bookshelf pivoted in the middle. What an odd doorway, I thought. I stepped through and closed it, realizing it was an undetectable revolving bookcase concealing the hidden passage from which I had just come.

I took a few steps into the room. The smell of the air changed from musty to an earthy, woodsy fragrance. LED lights cast a soft, yellow-gold aura, illuminating hundreds of manuscripts that filled the enormous bookshelves. The spines of the books were in Latin—the leather covers were cracked and distressed.

I addressed my council. "Ladies and gentlemen, where am I? What am I doing here?"

There was no answer, so I continued my exploration. Beyond the first room was a series of small, glass-enclosed stark spaces, each containing only a wooden table, a chair, and a lamp. *These are like the viewing rooms in the rare books library at the University of Cincinnati!* I'd spent countless hours doing research for my master's thesis in rooms like these.

The hallways between these rooms were lined with short wooden shelves and document drawers, which would house papers that must be stored lying flat. The cool, temperature-controlled air and dim lights—which protected the manuscripts—felt familiar and comforting. I walked into one of the glass-enclosed rooms to search for clues.

"Signor."

I jumped.

"Let me know where you'd like to start."

I turned to see a man dressed like a Catholic priest. *Where had he come from? He seemed to be expecting me.* The priest had black hair, dark eyes, and an olive complexion.

"Father . . . ," I said, my voice faltering, "where *exactly* are we?"

"Do you mean what *part* of the Vatican Library?" he asked.

Oh, my goddess, the council did it.

"Yes," I said, "what part of the Vatican Library are we in?"

"You are in the limited access area, Signor. This section houses rare manuscripts pertaining to the first through sixth centuries CE. This is what you requested, no?"

"No . . . yes . . . I mean." *Sixth century! What an opportunity!*

"I have deep gratitude for the privilege to be here to study these documents," I said with a slight bow of my head.

"Of course. Cardinal Piedmont gives you the highest references and accolades. He wants you to have access for your studies. So, where would you like to begin?"

"Let's see, how about the notes on the Council of Nicaea, then the omitted books of the Bible and the lost years of Jesus? I'd also like to read any early accounts written about the Magdalene, especially notes of Pope Gregory." I wanted to learn more about how and why he came up with his interpretation of her as a prostitute and not the wealthy benefactor she was. "And finally, I'd like to see any materials on the relationship between the Magdalene and Jesus."

"I will get these together for your perusal." He turned and left me in the small research room.

Obviously, I needed to be careful what I asked the council for.

Cardinal Piedmont? Interesting. Not only had I fallen through a rabbit hole and landed in the archives of the Vatican Library, but it also seemed I'd fallen into the future where my archbishop/student had transformed into a full-fledged cardinal.

Aum Bhur, Bhuvah, Swaha

As I waited, I called on the essence of Earth, Sky, and Heaven. *May my mind's highest faculties and intuition be guided by the light of the Divine, the supreme intelligence.* I was sure this experience would be enlightening.

The priest soon returned with a small cart of books and documents. What a wild ride, I thought, I'm sitting among ancient writings that most people don't even know exist! As I began reading the first documents, I realized I was comprehending both classical Greek and Latin. How could this be? Was it part of this dream state?

Or the siddhis of Pada Three, came a whisper.

I spent hours poring over the documents. As soon as I finished one set, the priest brought more. Some papers looked like modern copies, while others appeared to be thousands of years old. I read notes from early church leaders on the decisions made to purposely omit certain writings that emphasized the hotly contested role of women, especially the Magdalene, as both an intimate equal partner and a disciple.

What I read in the Gnostic documents about the god-man known as Jesus, who spoke of loving one another, showed that he did not differentiate between men and women. To me, he appeared to be a feminist, treating women as equals and accepting their patronage and their service. Certainly not like the Catholic Church I'd grown up in.

There were so many beautiful yogic writings in the documents I was reading, advising humanity to acquire peace within themselves and stating that there was no sin but only our desires and attachments that derail us from finding inner peace and collective Oneness.

Why exclude something so inclusive?

Many of the omitted documents from the New Testament spoke of love and forgiveness. They suggested, like the teachings of yoga, to look into your heart to find compassion for *all* the children of humanity.

My mind was spinning. Here was proof that the church had

downplayed the equal place of women on purpose. The male hierarchy had worked hard to bury the whole divine feminine essence. The divine feminine had been omitted from our human narrative. I reached for the cell phone in my back pocket to take a picture or two of the ancient texts, but it wasn't there. *Damn.*

This must be why women were inundating my dreams and meditations. The world needs to wake up and acknowledge the goddess energy that exists in all of us. And apparently, I had been chosen to help in the waking up. Is this what She meant by saying that I am one of Her midwives? Something clearly needed to change. *We need Her in our world now.* Perhaps, She *is* the light thread, the nurturing matrix that holds us all together.

Suddenly, the priest rushed into the room, out of breath and carrying a black cassock.

"You must go. They know you are here." His nervousness was palpable. I felt *my* heart rate begin to race.

"Who knows I'm here?" I asked as I stood.

Sweat beaded on the priest's forehead as he thrust the black robe at me. "Put this on and come quickly! I have to get you out of here without them seeing you, or you may never leave."

"Hey, this is a dream," I said as I put on the robe and stumbled after him. "Can't I just go out the same way I came in, through the rabbit hole back to my council?"

His eyebrows furrowed. "I don't know what you're talking about," he said, "but if we aren't out of here in two minutes, neither the cardinal nor I will be able to help you."

I swallowed hard and my fingers fumbled as I tried to button the robe while we ran toward the back of the library.

"Hurry!" the priest whispered in a desperate tone.

"I am," I said. We were now facing the wall of books that I'd stepped through hours earlier. He pushed on a particular book, and the bookcase pivoted open.

We entered the dim hallway. He closed the wall behind us. We had only taken a few steps when we heard a door unlock and footsteps coming toward us. He and I stood still, breathing hard in the dark, damp corridor. I assumed Abhaya mudra. To calm myself further, I said in a whisper, "This is only a dream."

A voice inside said, *Is it?*

The priest pulled me close and whispered in my ear, "We must do something. Tap into the *parama suksma* and intercept the light from all observers. Do it now!"

He was quoting from *Pada Three*, I thought. This Catholic priest was instructing me to move into a deep meditation to make myself invisible by using the sharpest form of my intellect to deflect the light from registering me in the retina of those around me. I had read about this and taught about it, but I had never experienced it. Why would he think I could turn myself invisible?

"Trust me," he whispered, "I know you can do it if you let yourself go deep and set your intent. Do it now! Do not let doubt cloud your ability. Be gone with your image until I tell you it is safe to be with me again."

I dropped into my deepest state of concentration. I went so deep, so quickly, my mind kicked in momentarily. I heard his words again: *Do not let doubt cloud your ability.* With that, I moved from my mind and entered my heart space. I slipped deeper and deeper inside.

A lightness from *Muladhara*, my root chakra, moved up the ladder of my spine and through all the major energy vortices of my being. I felt my chakra wheels spinning. My physical being became lighter and lighter. *Am I levitating? Stay in the heart,* came a commanding voice from inside. *Do not get distracted by the ego.*

I remained deep in my *samyama*. A light energy slowly emanated from my third eye, the *Ajna* chakra, and poured out from the space between my eyebrows, surrounding me in a crystal-clear egg of celestial light. Vaguely aware of what was going on outside me, my attention was fully connected to my heart center. A rapport was taking place between my companion and two other men. I dared not open my eyes. They spoke in Italian, but I understood fully.

"Monsignor, we thought we would find you with a special guest, but you are alone. How disappointing," one of the men said, his voice high-pitched, sharp, and stern.

"A guest?" my companion said. "I am alone, as you see, and heading back to the offices."

"Perhaps there is someone in the antiquities library we should meet?" the other man said with a sarcastic, condescending intonation.

"There is no one in the library. I just left there myself," my guardian retorted.

"We've heard you've been collecting sources on the council of Nicaea and manuscripts on the Magdalene and taking them to the viewing rooms."

"Your sources are correct. As the head archivist, I do not feel it's odd that I am working with the things entrusted to me. Do you?" He did not wait for an answer. "I am doing my job, reviewing the conditions of our collection in rotation."

I relaxed deeper into some cavern of my being where I had never been until now.

They could not see me. I was invisible to them.

"I see, Father. We will check the library for ourselves," the interrogator said.

"Do what you like. I will keep on my way. I have a meeting in ten minutes. If you will excuse me."

"A meeting with a certain cardinal, Monsignor?" one of them asked.

"Good day, gentlemen," my companion said. I heard his footsteps as he walked away.

The interrogators hurried off in the direction of the secret door. I stayed where I was, breathing deeply and somehow staying out of sight.

Seconds later, my priest, the Monsignor, returned.

"Make yourself visible to me. Come to the surface. Let the light find you so I might see you," he said.

I opened my eyes and saw him several feet away. He rushed toward me.

"Oh my god, it's possible, these things written in the Sutras. Come, come, they will be back this way soon. I need to get you out of here."

"Will I ever know what is going on?"

"I have no idea, but the things you are doing are getting much attention from all sides of the politic here. Unfortunately, not all men who wear crosses are to be trusted."

"I am well aware of that."

"The truth will set us all free," he said. "Stay pure of heart and keep the compassion you have tapped into foremost in your consciousness."

"Father, could you see me back there when you were talking to those men?"

"Not at all. You were invisible. It was amazing. I saw your image fade from your head down."

"I am not sure how that happened—"

"Not all who have eyes can see." He pointed up ahead. "At the end of the hallway, there will be two doors. The one you recognize is unlocked. Open it. It will take you to safety. Now go." He gave me a light shove.

"But—"

We heard footsteps approaching again.

The priest put his finger to his lips and pointed frantically up ahead toward the door.

I ran in my priestly garb as fast as I could in the dim light. The footsteps from behind were getting closer. Then I saw the familiar ancient door where this fantastic journey had started.

"*Arresto! Arresto!*" The quickly approaching men were yelling.

I took a deep breath and surrendered into something bigger than myself. I pulled open the wooden door and jumped into total blackness. Once again, I was in the no-thingness of life.

Whoosh! I was falling, tumbling. My body relaxed. There was the sound of the space around me breathing, then a humming sound engulfed me, and once again, I heard the mantra: *Aum Bhur, Bhuvah, Swaha.* It was like a lullaby sung to me by the Universe. Yes, I was falling—but was the direction up or down—but more importantly, I was without fear and without doubt. I was safe in the arms of something invisible yet tangible.

After moving in this timeless tumble for an undefinable amount of time, I slowed until I was once more upright. I stretched my arms out into the darkness until I found the massive door. I slowly pushed it open and peeked around it. My council of advisors was staring at me.

"So, Ren, what did you learn on your journey?" asked Saturn.

"Wait, wait, wait," I said as I slipped off the black robe. "What the hell was that about?"

"Be more specific!" Saturn said.

I put my face into my hands. *Will I ever get a straight answer out of these people?*

I looked up. I was in bed, staring at the ceiling. I had returned home again through the looking glass—or through the magic medieval door, to be exact.

Now I had more questions than before. What *was* my reality these days? *Breathe and relax, Ren. Breathe and relax.*

"Wow, that was some dream or reality bleed-through. What do you think?" Sean asked after I told him about the council meeting and the Vatican Library.

"It was so real and vivid. I felt the paper of the manuscripts and the cool air of the temperature-controlled room. I understood Italian. I could read Latin and Greek. I also felt real anxiety when the priest said we had to get out of there." I shook my head.

"And then he told you to go invisible, and you just did it?" Sean asked.

"Actually, he said, tap into the *parama suksma* and by your deep level of *samyama*, intercept the light from all observers."

Sean's forehead crinkled. "And you knew what that meant?"

"It's from Pada Three, Sutra 21, stating in deep states of *samyama*, you can intercept the light from those around you so that nothing of your image goes into their retina. You're invisible to them."

"You're starting to sound like a Jehovah's Witness reciting exact scripture passages. Nothing wrong with the Witnesses, I'm just saying." Sean smiled. "So, when the priest instructed you to intercept the light, you did it. Wow, wouldn't it be cool to do that in real life?"

"I guess so," I said with a shrug.

"Come on, give it a try right now." Sean gave me a little love shove on the shoulder.

"You're cracking me up," I said. "Just go invisible?"

"Yeah!! I think this should be a piece of cake compared to raising the dead in front of hundreds of people," he winked.

"You know," I said, "there was a similar feeling to the day with Mike and the disappearing act in my dream."

"How so?"

"I was nervous when we were running, but as I stood there doing as the Monsignor instructed, a steady calm came over me. Something inside me shifted, and I let go, like I did when I got out of the car and walked over to Mike."

"Keep that sense of calm," Sean said. "It's good for you."

I nodded. "I need to write about this in my journal."

"And prepare for tomorrow's session with the archbishop," Sean said. "Are you going to tell him about being dropped into the Vatican Library and him already being a cardinal?"

"I could. He's a firm believer in dreams, but I don't think I will, at least not yet."

"Come on, you could say, 'Padre, I had a grueling time at the Vatican last night, all because of you.'"

"I don't think so," I said, shaking my head.

"I'm just kidding. Come here, Reno," he said, motioning me toward him and then pulling me into a full-body hug. I laid my head on his shoulder.

"I must admit, I don't know what to make of the people chasing me. Somebody did not want me to see the truth written in those manuscripts about the plot to kill the feminine."

"So, you think what you saw was real?"

I moved back and looked him in the eyes.

"I do," I said, nodding. After a pause, I added, "I really, really do."

25

CATHEDRAL

Later that afternoon, an odd text arrived from Archbishop Piedmont.

> I would like to meet tomorrow as scheduled, but I can't come to you anymore. I am hoping you can come to me. A courier will drop off a package. I know it's strange, but please follow the instructions inside.

Not knowing what else to say, I replied, *OK.*

Within twenty minutes, a man knocked on the door. Without any salutation, he handed me a medium-sized box, then returned to his black sedan.

Inside the unmarked box was a note. I read it aloud to Sean.

> *I'm afraid I've been recognized coming to your home. Presently, my actions are under much scrutiny, and I must be careful until my lifetime appointment is official. After this, I will have more freedom and the ability to make changes to the outdated structure with which I am affiliated. My soul is responding to the practices you have introduced me to, especially mantra. Please follow the outlined protocol. It*

will enable us to continue our work—inside is a cassock and a key. I will send a car for you. Once in the car, put on the cassock. The driver will pull into a garage that is attached to the back of the church. The key will unlock a door which will lead you into the sanctuary. I will join you shortly if I am not already there.

If someone should ask who you are, tell them you are Fr. Conleth from the Holy Cross Province of Passionist Priest. I appreciate your understanding and look forward to the changes we can make together in the world.

"No, no, no!" Sean said. "The changes you can make *together* in the world? What is he talking about? You've seen him once—"

"Calm down . . . I think—"

"First the Vatican, now a cathedral, locked and unlocked doors, sneaking around in priest robes. What is up with Catholicism?"

"I don't know. I'm trying not to let my imagination get the best of me." I pulled the robe out from the box. "Except . . . this is exactly what I had on in my dream."

Sean planted his hands on the kitchen table and stood up.

"I don't want you to do this."

"Come on, buddy, it'll be fine." I smiled. "I'm going to teach the future cardinal the Gayatri mantra. He said his soul is responding, and I think *this* mantra could be his path inward. Who knew a Catholic priest would respond to *goddess* mantras?"

"For goddess's sake, Ren, Catholics make a claim to the Mother of God, he *should* respond to it." He was shaking his head. "Something's not right."

"It'll be fine. I promise."

"Why are you so set on doing this? The church ditched you thirty years ago."

I nodded.

"This could be one small way to help bring the feminine back to a religion that still has a lot of influence around the world," I said. "A cardinal who believes in goddess mantras could be a game changer."

"I think you're delusional. And I say that with lots of love," he said. "But one chanting cardinal doesn't have a chance against a patriarchy that you yourself said buried Her alive."

"Let's just see what happens. If he does get this promotion, he'll be gone soon and out of our lives. Until then, maybe I can help him."

Sean shook his head. His body language softened.

"All right. But be careful, Ren. Lots of people are threatened by what you've done."

"I know," I said, "but right now, I think the archbishop is sincere."

"Promise me one thing."

"What's that?"

"If it gets weird, just cover your sweet self in a celestial light and disappear."

I rolled my eyes and shook my head.

The next morning, I folded the cassock, then gathered my session notes and a small singing bowl. I put it all into a black Tibetan monk bag and waited for the car. Fifteen minutes before my appointment, a car horn sounded. It was the same car and driver that dropped off the package. I climbed into the back seat and slipped on the robe. Again, there were no words between us as the driver wove through alleys and back streets, making sure we weren't followed. Finally, he pulled into a private garage.

I stepped out of the car, pulling the key the archbishop had given me from my pocket. The cement floor and stone walls made the air cool, almost cold. I shivered as I unlocked the only door on the back wall. I walked down a narrow hallway until I found myself in a small vestibule with an elaborate hand-carved stone archway, the opening of which was covered by a thick, rich, dark red tapestry.

I pulled it to the side and slid into the splendor of St. Mary's Cathedral, Basilica of the Assumption. It was just as grand as I remember from the few times I was there as a child. I stood at the front of the church and marveled at the eight-story nave, housing vast expanses of stone canopies that seemed to defy gravity. My eye was drawn to the massive sixty-by twenty-foot stained-glass window depicting the Assumption of Mary and the Council of Ephesus that proclaimed her *Theotokos* or *Mother of God*. Because of that status, at her death, she was *assumed* into heaven rather than going through physical decay. *Sounds like a miracle.* This Basilica, named for Her, was a replica of Notre Dame in Paris. Although a third the size of its French sister, it maintained much of the grandeur of the original, with a massive rose window and vaulted ceilings. As I took in the incredible richness of this majestic edifice, a spontaneous om passed over my lips. The om journeyed out of me, reverberated throughout the massive structure, and back again to my heart.

Sensing my internal energies being pulled toward contemplation, I realized there was something ethereal about this space.

Are we going to meditate in the cathedral? I hoped so. I could go deep here.

I sat in the first pew and closed my eyes to enjoy the silence. I heard an internal whisper and followed its instructions:

Parama Suksma . . . Samyama . . .
Intercept the Light . . . Deflect the Light

A door at the back of the sanctuary opened and closed. Footsteps came within feet of me and stopped. *Keep your eyes closed,* I thought.

"Fr. Conleth? Are you here?" A man projected his voice throughout the church.

I opened my eyes and saw a priest, maybe six feet tall, standing only two feet away. *He didn't see me!* He did a one-eighty.

I cleared my throat. He turned back.

"What? You . . . weren't just there . . . I—"

"Hello, I'm Father Conleth." I reached out my hand.

He reluctantly accepted my gesture. His name and internal thoughts registered in my mind: *No, you're not. I know who you are.*

"You are correct, Father Blair. We can drop the pretense. Call me Ren."

He stepped back. The priest looked to be in his thirties. He was round, and his cheeks and the tip of his nose were red. He stared at me with wide eyes and open mouth.

"Uh . . . I . . . uh . . . the archbishop has been detained on a series of calls with Rome," he finally said. He stood up straight and took a deep breath. "It's official. He's been appointed to the College of Cardinals and will spend the next three years on assignment in Rome."

Was last night's dream a premonition?

"I see," I said, nodding. "He just found out today?"

"Yes. He'll be creating a new curriculum for clerical education, focusing on the contemplative arts. Meditation," the priest said with an I-just-dropped-a-bomb smile.

He turned, took a few steps, but then glanced back over his shoulder at me.

"I'm still here," I said with a grin and a wave.

He walked quickly to the exit.

Holy shit, I thought, he *really* is going to be a cardinal, *and* in charge of a meditation curriculum? I took a deep, deep breath and let it out with an audible sigh.

I perused the cathedral as a distraction. I strolled the perimeter until I came to a group of statues at the back of the church. Veronica caught my eye. I felt the recognition of old friends. It was almost as if she smiled. Perhaps she did. This time, we weren't meeting in a dream but rather in the flesh, or more accurately, my flesh and her plaster.

"Hello, Veronica, I'm remaining steadfast as you and all the 1:13s suggest. I'm getting the message that the feminine essence, with all its strength and compassion, is ready to return as the alternative to living in fear and hatred."

I knelt.

"I'm ready to help," I said as I placed my body into pranam and began chanting the Gayatri mantra.

"Ren?"

Did one of the statues call me? I lifted my head. It was the archbishop.

"Hello, Joseph," I said as I stood.

"That chant is beautiful. What is it?"

"It's called the Gayatri. It's a request to the divine to illuminate our intellect with wisdom."

"I may need that one," he said.

"You're in luck. The Gayatri is today's curriculum."

We sauntered toward the front of the church.

"Joseph, the other night, I had a bizarre dream that took place in the Vatican Library where you were referred to as Cardinal Piedmont. You were responsible for getting me access to documents I wanted to see and study."

"That's *very* interesting," he said.

"Yes, especially because Father Blair just told me it's official: you're going to be a cardinal and relocating to Rome."

"It's true, and I'd like to talk with you about it."

We reached the front-side chapel and took seats facing each other.

"In the brief time we've connected, I'm coming more fully into my spiritual self. The depth of meditation you are helping me achieve is changing my world. Part of it's the technique, but the other part is *your* presence."

"You're doing it. I am only guiding," I said.

"But your guidance and energy are facilitating my shifts. I need to continue with you *in person*. I believe I can now make a difference in the archaic structure of the church."

"I believe you can too, my friend."

"In Rome, I'll have a small staff, both cleric and lay. I want you to come with me, at least for a while."

My mouth dropped open.

"Before you object," he said, "let me tell you, your living expenses will be taken care of, and you will receive a sizable stipend as my spiritual tutor."

"Whoa, whoa, whoa—I'm flattered, but I have a partner and—"

"If it's necessary to bring him, we can make that happen. You'll have your apartment. You'll be an employee of mine, so, yes, indirectly an employee of the Catholic Church, but there are no strings or stipulations on you or your lifestyle."

"My lifestyle?"

"They know who you are. And they also know about the events on the Parkway. I will be working directly with the Vatican's education department. My vision is to have you do in a classroom setting, what you do with me. Together, we can make big changes. I think you'll find yourself quite popular and perhaps with more students than you can handle."

"Wow, padre." The Italian word for priest seemed appropriate here, and it reminded me of Sean.

Joseph laughed. "Will you at least consider it?"

"I . . . uh—"

"Great! I'm sure this will make for good conversation over dinner tonight." He smiled.

I shook my head. *If he only knew.*

"Now that you've rocked my world, let's get to today's lesson," I said. "We both need to open to divine illumination and to the plan of the Universe."

"Yes, we do!" he said. "Maybe that plan involves Italy. Maybe it includes making changes in a world full of fear."

"Maybe," I said, smiling at him.

We chanted for over an hour.

Dhiyo Yonaha Prachodayat

I returned home the same way I came.

Sean was waiting at the front door.

"I'm so glad to see you," he said. "Your dream really freaked me out."

"Speaking of the dream, it's official: Archbishop Piedmont is on his way to being Cardinal Piedmont."

"Wow! That's wild," Sean said, leading me toward the kitchen, "so it was a premonition and not a dream."

"I hope not. I don't want to be chased through that library."

Sean laughed. "You'd have to go to Italy for that," he said.

"Well, Piedmont is. He's moving to Rome for three years and—"

"Wow again," Sean said, "that's another—"

"And he offered me a position as his spiritual tutor, as well as teaching in their education department. Think about it! You and I could move to Rome with a private apartment, a salary, and—"

"Holy Saraswati! Are you making this up?" Sean shook his head and leaned back against the counter. "Whoa, whoa, whoa, whoa."

"That's exactly what I did and said."

"So you're serious? Oh no, oh no." He started pacing.

"Bud," I said in my calmest voice, "I think this has really rocked you off center."

He stopped and looked at me with eyes wide.

"Yeah, it has!" he said. "And what about you? That church completely rejected you when you came out. Aren't *you* the least bit thrown off by all this weird synchronicity with Catholic undertones?"

"I was at first, but then Piedmont and I chanted for an hour, which helped. Do you want to chant?"

"Ren, we can't do this!" he said, shaking his head.

"Joseph says we can make a difference. Maybe they're finally ready to embrace the feminine. Maybe we can use this opportunity to midwife the goddess back into a religion that's denied Her for centuries. We could teach about the Gnostic Gospels and Tantra. He also said *the powers that be* at the Vatican know who we are, and they'll embrace his offer to us. I'm fascinated about teaching classes there."

"Of course, the church knows who you are! And what better place to be than under *their* roof so they can keep an eye on you? Look, *Jesus*, I don't want to hang out with the Pharisees." Sean paused. "Please tell me you're *not* considering this."

I was silent.

Sean took a deep breath. "You *are*, aren't you?" He paced the length of the kitchen again. "This is all so weird, the dead/living kid, the archbishop being your student, a dream of you in the Vatican doing a Claude Rains act."

"Claude Rains?"

"The Invisible Man! Can we please slow down? This whole thing is giving me the heebie-jeebies, and I don't understand why you're so calm! How could you even consider this? What about our life here? What about our students and clients? Do we just up and leave them? Oh, and what about the headlines once the media finds out?" He gestured one hand over his head, "Miracle Man Takes Job at the Vatican. And will your first class be called Raising the Dead 101 or how to spy on your friends while standing in the room with them?"

I wanted to smile, but I did not dare. "At least consider it," I said.

"Ren, are you really taking this seriously?"

"What's for dinner? I'm starving."

"Holy Hindu Mantra, you're avoiding the question. I know I'm in trouble now."

I fell asleep that night with an image of a beautiful woman with hazel-colored eyes cradling me.

Her lips parted slightly, and, in a whisper, she said, "Do not forget me."

"Never," I replied.

She to me: "So many have."

Me to her: "I never will."

26

P.U.T.P.

The next morning, we were up by 6:00 a.m. Over coffee, I prepped breakfast while Sean perused emails.

"Anything interesting?" I asked.

"Well, there are lots of thank-yous for healing them on Sunday. And you hit some universal themes with the podcast. Seems people are surprised you're a regular guy and not superhuman."

"I'm glad that came across," I said with a chuckle.

"And there are tons of requests for more info on meditation, the kleshas, astrology, and mystical revolutionaries, so I'm putting a suggested reading list up on our website."

"That's a great idea," I said.

"Overall, *most* reactions are positive."

"Most? Keep me tethered to reality, Sean."

"Well, there's always negative hate stuff. Carol and I delete those. But . . . how about this?" he asked. "William Miller from NBC is asking for an interview."

"NBC? I'm not ready for a national interview," I said.

"But you *are* ready to pick up and move to Rome?" Sean said, still looking at his computer.

"Let's not go there now."

Sean raised an eyebrow. "Mr. Miller says they want your thoughts on *everything I can do, you can do also*, and how you see that happening."

"I don't know—"

"This is your big chance," he said, pointing to his screen. "They want to record the interview here at their local affiliate on Monday morning and feature it that night on the national news. They're even going to send a car to take you back and forth to the studio. It seems pretty easy!"

"You really think I should do this? We already have zero privacy."

"Yes, *these* are the kinds of offers you should be considering. This is a way to really get the word out."

"The word?"

"Yeah, your message of love! Everywhere you go, you're connecting with people; the studio, the concert, people want to be near you . . . look at all these emails . . . something's coming through. The world needs to change its focus from hate and anger to love. Do the interview, Ren. Talk about the yoga practices you feel are a large part of what's happening. Get people thinking about increasing their levels of love. Encourage them to practice *something* that can help change the way they think."

"So, I should go on national TV and talk about my practices that may have given rise to my ability to help people? That all this *healing* is because of love?"

"Yes! And everything I can do, you can do . . . don't forget that."

I nodded and took a deep breath.

"You're already in the public eye with all the videos of you with Mike. Sonja said your podcast has the highest ratings they've ever seen! Take the next step, and maybe, just maybe, you're not the only yogi out there experiencing a shift. Make yourself visible . . . no pun intended." He smiled. "Seriously, maybe the mystical revolutionaries your council talks about will come out and help even more people. We both know that humankind is at a crossroads. Maybe this will give some people a new direction."

He reached for my hands across the table.

"Help everyone see if we all deepen our capacity to love, we can make this planet heaven on earth. This is a huge platform. We all need more love. We all need miracles!"

I took another deep breath and let it out with a sigh. I squeezed his hands.

"I know you're right, but we're on a high precipice," I said, shaking my head. "I'm afraid we're about to dive into something bigger than we can handle."

"Try to look out from that precipice without fear and doubt, Ren. This has got to be a better path than working for the church."

"Again, let's not go there," I said.

"Okay, but I do think you should say yes to *this* opportunity. You teach that when each of us works to increase our consciousness, we change the world. I know not everyone will listen. There will always be dissenters *but* there are *so* many who *are* ready to make a change and move forward. As Carol would say to us, it's time to *Pick Up The Pace*."

"But I—"

"Ren, P.U.T.P. I'm not saying you have all the answers, but you can share what you *do* know and perhaps open a few hearts along the way."

We sat looking at each other.

"Well, what do you think?" Sean asked.

"I think you're my favorite yogi." I smiled. "Thank you for reminding me of the power of love and for being such an even force in my life." I squeezed his hands even tighter. "You're right, let's pick up the pace."

"And," his eyes widened, "if this interview is as big a hit as I think it will be, we'll ask for Katie Couric next time!"

"Next time? And why Katie Couric?" I asked, narrowing my eyes.

"Well, she interviewed you in your New York flying dream, so I did some research. Katie's a Capricorn too, and her Sun and your Jupiter are conjunct. It's a cosmic match," he smiled and raised his eyes toward the ceiling.

"I see, so when I tell her about my conversation with Veronica—the talking statue—she'll understand perfectly!"

"Oh yeah, she'll get *all* the far-out stuff you share with her," he said.

"Carol called," Sean said over lunch. "She contacted NBC, and the interview is set for Monday. She said they'll email you a rough outline of questions later today. We also talked about Sara Howard's mediation retreat in Winchester, Kentucky, next weekend. It's only a two-hour drive. What do you think?"

"That could be the break we're looking for!" I said. "Maybe Sara can shed some light on everything that's been happening. Sign us up."

"Carol's already taken care of it. She's going to pick us up early next Friday. The three of us will share a little cabin."

"We'll need to reschedule Dottie's massage that week."

"Done," Sean said, "and remember, we're staying for a glass of limoncello after her massage today."

I nodded.

Sean picked up the phone. "Wow, there's a text from Carol. She's already seen two promos for the interview."

"That was quick," I said, taking a deep breath. "I'm nervous about the interview," I confessed.

"Don't be, bud. The goddess is eternally guiding you."

"You're right." I smiled. "She's holding me in her arms."

Sean walked over and pulled me close.

"She's not the only one holding you." He squeezed me. "This is so exciting," he whispered in my ear. "Your message of love is about to go national."

"*Her* message," I said, snuggling into his neck. "*Her* message."

27

LIMONCELLO

"Boys, I'm going to be as quiet as a mouse today," Dottie said once on the massage table. "I'm looking forward to our chat afterward over my favorite libation."

"That sounds perfect," I said, smiling at Sean.

After the massage, Dottie took us to her living room, directing us to sit on a stately, cognac-tan leather sofa positioned in front of three floor-to-ceiling windows that faced downtown Cincinnati.

"Just give me a minute to change," she said. "Make yourself comfortable."

From where we sat, I could see three distinct sitting areas, each with a long couch, matching armchairs, and a coffee table. There was a highly polished black grand piano with gold trim in one corner of the room. The floor was dotted with bright floral Turkish rugs, and the interior walls featured artwork similar to those found in Dottie's sitting room. It was an odd mixture of motifs, giving it an air of old-world aristocracy that matched our new friend's persona.

Moments later, Dottie entered through the kitchen, wearing a short-sleeved navy shin-length dress featuring an O neckline and pearl buttons that ran from the tailored waistline to the hem. She was carrying a crystal carafe in one hand and three delicately carved aperitif glasses in the other.

I noticed she had no limp, but I chalked it up to her talent for mind over matter.

"I just love it when the help has left for the day," she said as she placed everything on the coffee table. "I like my privacy. I want everyone out of here by 6:00 p.m. so I can let my hair down and let go of all the pretense that comes with all of this." She opened her arms wide. "Do you know what I mean?"

"Not at all," Sean said with a chuckle.

"Of course, you don't. You," she pointed to Sean, "came from a solid middle-class upbringing, but Ren, you were poor."

"But I never knew it," I said with a laugh.

"That's good. I bet your mother was a hard worker as well as a strong Catholic," she said as she filled the glasses.

I looked at Sean, who rolled his eyes.

"She was both," I said, "but also a *very* liberal Catholic."

"That's a rare species," she said. "I'm assuming social issues weren't her thing, and I'm with her. But let's not go into all that. I want us to get to know each other."

"It sounds like you already know a lot about us," Sean said.

"Well, anyone can get your family history. I want to know how you came to raise the dead."

Sean shook his head and pointed to me.

"I see, so you're not a mystic?" she asked Sean.

"No . . . I'm just a—"

"In his own way, he is," I said.

"I'm sure you have your own magical powers," she said with an impish smile. "Let's toast."

We stood and put our glasses together.

"To our new friendship *and* changing the world with love," she said.

"Cheers," we said in unison, then took a sip of our drink.

"Dottie," Sean said as we took our seats, "Ren recently met your friend Archbishop Piedmont."

"Great," she said as she threw back the rest of her drink and reached to pour herself another. She then turned to me. "Are you getting along?"

"Yes, we have a lot in common," I said.

"Doesn't surprise me. He's a little mystical in his own way."

"And now that he'll be a cardinal—"

"Sean!" I snapped.

"Really," she said, "when did that happen?"

"You didn't know?" Sean asked. "Aren't *you* responsible for getting the archbishop and Ren together?"

Dottie turned to me. "I called a few people and suggested they employ you, but that's as far as it went. I know several American bishops, but not many of them are liberal enough to take advice from a woman." She settled back into the plush leather armchair. "Boys, help yourself to more limoncello. There's not much alcohol in it, so you need a few glasses to *really* enjoy it." She winked.

"I'm good, thank you," I said.

Sean poured himself another glass and topped hers off.

"The new cardinal even offered Ren a job in Italy."

"Sean!" I said. "Please stop."

"Well, all right. Good man, Joseph," Dottie said. "Honestly, I'm not privy to any agenda they have for you. Darling, they only call me when they need a donation." She raised both eyebrows with a slight, forced smile. "So, what kind of job did he offer you?"

"Oh, I don't think this is common knowledge, so—"

"To be the cardinal's spiritual advisor while living in Rome," Sean said, "and also to teach the priests all his secrets."

"Hot damn," she said, slapping her thigh. "Excuse my French, but maybe somebody *did* listen to my suggestion. This is a record. It usually takes the church centuries to make a move. I'll miss you, but this position is much more important work, *and* I'm moving better than I have in years. You've mended something in this old hip." She placed her hand on her side. "I feel like I'm seventy again."

I laughed. "I'm still thinking it over, and Sean's not keen on it so . . ."

She leaned toward me, now looking serious.

"My dear boy—you can't say no—this is bigger than you—this is an opportunity to change the world."

I glanced at Sean, who had closed his eyes and shook his head.

"You study the stars. Isn't there some cosmic connection you can see that shows this is perhaps your purpose, why you were born?"

Sean cleared his throat as he sat straight up.

"Purpose?" Sean asked. "To enhance a religion that persecuted people for centuries and refuses to deal with reality? In fact, as I see it, they created the reality they wanted and spoon-fed it to the masses to control them." He tossed back the entire contents of his glass.

Dottie looked at him, then turned to me and placed her hand on my knee.

"I see what you're facing," she said, "it's called a rock and a hard place." She chugged the rest of her limoncello and put the glass down firmly on the coffee table.

I closed my eyes and took a deep breath.

28

AND MY SPIRIT PONDERS

"Your private chariot just pulled up," Sean said on Saturday morning. "Shouldn't Piedmont be doing Mass or something? Isn't Saturday a holy day?"

"In Judaism, but Catholics only have a Saturday afternoon Mass to count for Sunday."

"Sounds like convenience to me, so they can party tonight and sleep in tomorrow."

"Sean, can you at least *try* to stay neutral with this?" I asked. "For some reason, his path and mine have crossed, and neither you nor I believe in random coincidence."

"I just don't get the sneaking around or him thinking you would uproot to move to Italy. You barely know each other."

I shrugged. "I'm just trying to listen with my heart." I moved toward the door. "Okay, I have to go, the car's waiting."

"Ren . . . don't forget me."

I turned to see tears in his eyes.

"Oh, Sean, I never could," I said.

"Okay," he said, nodding.

My heart was heavy as I left, wondering how such a thought could even be a part of his psyche.

When I arrived, Joseph had two high-back chairs with red crushed-velvet seats positioned in front of the statue of Mary as Queen of Heaven. We sat facing each other.

"Why the secrecy about our meetings?" I asked.

"Right now, neither of us needs more publicity or reporters hounding us," he said. "It's best if we keep our affiliation private."

I was uneasy with this explanation. I couldn't pinpoint why, but I trusted She was guiding me and had brought us together for a reason. "Why have you asked me to go to Italy when there must be advanced spiritual advisors available through the Vatican?"

"Ren, I learned early on I must pay attention to my dreams. Some are prophetic, while others teach me something about myself. The dream of the talking cardinal was both. When I first saw the video clip of you with the little boy, I knew that I needed you. At the time, I had no idea why, but I listened."

"I know what you mean about paying attention to dreams," I said.

"The bottom line is that I'm questioning some long-held beliefs right now, and your knowledge of Catholicism and yoga has opened me to new possibilities. Any spiritual advisor appointed by the Vatican is going to be threatened by what's bubbling up inside me."

He leaned forward, placed his elbows onto his knees, and brought his hands into prayer position.

"I've spent many years praying to something outside of me," he said. "Like many others, I never thought to look inside my heart. I knew I was missing something deeper. So, I asked for guidance, direction, whatever you want to call it, something to help me find and connect with my soul."

"I know exactly what you're talking about. I've spent my whole life searching for that connection. That's how I came to the path of yoga," I said.

The archbishop smiled. "I know you have, and now you're helping me experience a revitalized zeal for my life and my spiritual practices. I don't want to let that go now that I've found it *and* you." He sat back in his chair and took a deep breath. "Ren, I will soon be in a position where I can implement far-reaching change in an institution that must change or die. It has so much potential to help the world if it can just move forward with the times."

"I agree, but how receptive will the old boys' club be to adding yogic thought to their structure?" I asked.

"It'll be a process," he said, "and it doesn't mean *everything* must go. It just gives a different lens, a different way of looking at what is already in place. I'm still studying the scriptures, but they are coming to mean something different from what I thought of them originally.

"For instance," he closed his eyes and spoke softly, "Psalm 77:6, *I will remember my song in the night; I will meditate with my heart, And my spirit ponders.*" He sat quietly, savoring the words he recited.

"Lovely," I said.

"My new meditation practices, the mudras and mantras, are tools that are helping me meditate with my heart," he said. "I do remember my song in the night. That phrase from Psalms is about a personal relationship with a god who is inside me and not outside and above."

He really is shifting in a major way, I thought.

"This path is leading me to study myself with depth. I ask myself, *Why do I do what I do? What's driving me?* This week, I studied the kleshas and realized they drive most of my actions. Ignorance, ego, attachment, aversion, and the fear of death are driving me and most humans. Do I want to live that way? No! Especially now that I know there's another path."

"You're comprehending at such an accelerated rate. It's incredible," I said.

"I realize seeking guidance, not from the outside but from the inside, will eventually wipe away the overall need for priests as spiritual leaders." He paused. "*Unless* they guide others to find their hearts and help their flock to ponder their spirit. Priests can become viable again in people's lives if we change their focus and educate them differently. As you know,

Catholicism has a desperate feeling about it right now. It's hanging on by its fingernails. A pope with a vision can help, but the true change needs to come from a deeper place than that. Each priest must have practices that take him to his place to ponder. He then must teach and share from his own experiences, just like you have done and then shared with me."

"You're a force the church needs right now," I said.

"Yes, but I need help," he said. "I need to walk into my new life with someone who can show them this is not just Eastern theory—someone like you, who has already raised the dead and acquired other *siddhis* from the Sutras. Ren, religion is far too intellectual. We have the opportunity to teach them that spirituality has to come intuitively from the heart. It must be experiential, with *everyone* honoring each other's path."

"One truth, many paths," I said.

"Yes. I now believe that with my whole heart."

"I know you do, Joseph. And that one truth includes all of us. The feminine energy must be included. Women must be given a place to administer love and guidance. The priestess is as powerful as any priest."

"Absolutely! But one step at a time."

"By not recognizing the feminine, the Catholic Church has disenfranchised more than half of the world's population. I believe Mary Magdalene was an apostle. I believe she held on to the esoteric spiritual teachings of her teacher while the men around her caved into the kleshas."

The archbishop grinned. "That sounds like perfect material for a class you could teach in Italy."

"Hmm . . . ," I said.

"Are you at least considering coming to Rome?" He raised an eyebrow.

"That's a tough one," I said.

"Think of it as doing a yoga teacher training course for Catholic priests," he chuckled.

"And will the priests accept it and embrace it?" I asked.

"I know *somebody* in the Vatican likes the idea. Those who aren't open to it will eventually move on. We need to attract the ones who *do* get it," Piedmont said.

"The ones who *remember their song in the night, who will meditate with their heart and ponder their spirits?*" I asked.

"Yes, those are who I believe we will attract. Let's change the world, Ren."

Her message could get out there quickly, I thought, disseminated through the church's already existent structure. Perhaps *this* is what all the recent guidance has been about.

"Okay, my friend, but the women of the church must be involved," I said. "I have a group of goddesses who want to make sure the feminine is included, and so do I. They need to be a part of this! Women are changing the world."

He smiled. "I couldn't agree more."

"Now, let's get down to business and do some chanting," I said. "Sitting with Mary as Queen of Heaven, let's chant a hundred and eight rounds of the Gayatri mantra."

"I look forward to joining our voices together," he said.

And so we did.

Aum Bhur, Bhuvah, Swaha . . .

29

CHAOS

"Did he bring up Italy again?" Sean asked as I walked in the door.

"Yes, and he was very excited," I said. "He talked of all the change *we* could make in how the church educates priests."

"We? You're not seriously considering this, are you?"

"He told me to think of it as a yoga teacher training program for priests. He really believes *we* can make a difference."

"You've got to be kidding! The church will never change—don't you see he's trying to seduce you? Stop this idiotic insanity before it gets any weirder."

"But what if this is the path the feminine energies want me to take?" I asked.

"Or what if it's the church manipulating you so you'll teach priests how to become even more controlling?"

"I don't think so, Sean. Joseph and I have so many things in common, and our thoughts on serving the collective are in sync."

"Oh, so now it's Joseph?" Sean stood in the middle of our library, shaking his head.

"I think I need to sit in meditation to sort this out," I said.

And I did, for at least an hour.

Yet, I found no resolution for the Italy issue.

The next morning, there was a coolness between us that verged on frigid. I prepped for the Rise and Shine yoga class while Sean made a few phone calls. When it was time, we left the house in silence and began our drive to the yoga studio.

"I spoke to Jake," Sean finally said, "he won't be joining us this morning. It's still just too tough without Caroline."

"Of course," I said. "I couldn't imagine where to begin if I had to face life without you."

A weighted silence returned. I looked out the car window at the light on the river and reflected on how everything had shifted just weeks ago on this same drive.

"I also spoke with the police this morning," Sean said, "and asked if they could post an officer or two around the studio . . . just in case."

"Do you think that's necessary? Last week was so peaceful."

"The pushback from the other side has grown the past few days."

"The other side?" I said. "Why are there sides? Shouldn't we all be together?"

"I'm dealing with reality," Sean said, as he made the turn off the Parkway. "I think it would be good to have them around."

Kate had a reserved parking place for us right out front. The area around the studio was just as crowded as last week. But this time, there *were* two sides, two separate groups. Near the building, the gathered crowd was quiet and peaceful. Across the street, people held placards of hate and shouted passages from the Bible over a megaphone. My heart was heavy as we entered the classroom. "It's a little different today," Kate said.

"I've asked for a couple of police officers to hang around after class," Sean said.

"Are you going out into the parking lot again?" she asked.

"Yep, I want to spread as much love as I can."

At the end of a once-again packed class, Sean and I made our way outside with the assistance of two police officers, one male and one female.

Like last week, I touched the first outstretched hand, then another. Toward the back of the crowd, I heard shouting. With deep breathing, I worked to focus only on the people surrounding me who were full of love and wanted connection. After about fifteen minutes and making our way to the center of the crowd, a sharp sensation of fear pierced my heart. Like a flame to a candle wick, the anger of the protesters ignited an energy change in the crowd. The shouting and screaming drew nearer as the mass of people heaved their way forward. The officers grabbed my arms, but Sean was pushed several feet from us. After another huge surge, several people, including Sean, were shoved to the ground. I saw him disappear.

"You have to help Sean," I said to a male police officer.

"10-34 in progress," the officer shouted into his radio. "We need backup."

The officers tried to move back to the studio, but there was a wall of resistance, and we couldn't budge. I finally glimpsed Sean, but now he was at least twenty feet away.

"Get back in the building!" Sean screamed.

The two officers secured their grip on my arms as the three of us formed a mini phalanx. They lifted me slightly off the ground and aggressively pushed us toward the building like a human battering ram. I felt the pressure of bodies all around me. "Touch me, touch me," people said as they pushed and shoved. My T-shirt ripped as someone from behind grabbed it, yelling for help. The three of us kept moving, forcefully inching our way through the mob.

"Help Sean," I screamed.

"It's you they're after. We have to get you inside."

More screams, pushing, and cries.

"Sean! Sean! Sean!" I was yelling.

Sirens wailed in the distance.

I had no center. I was in flight mode. On the brink of passing out, I heard his voice.

"I'm right here, Ren. Keep going, keep pressing forward. We're almost there!"

Sean was somehow able to get in front of us and move toward the studio door. I saw Kate guarding the entrance, waiting. When we reached her, she unlocked the door, and the police officers shoved Sean and me over the threshold. We tumbled to the floor, and Kate bolted the door. The officers went back into the crowd to try to restore order.

"Go into the office and lock yourself in," Kate said. "This is a thick security door, but let's not take any chances."

I heard more sirens approach as we rushed into the office and turned the deadbolt.

I leaned against the closed door, shaking. *What is happening?*

"Ren, it's okay, buddy. Take a few breaths."

I heard myself reciting the Gayatri, but it seemed distant and far away, as if it was coming from someone else.

"Sean, I need help!" I said, unable to catch my breath. He held me softly by the shoulders as tears streamed down my face.

"This is too much." I was sobbing, gasping for breath. "It's beyond me."

"This will all pass. We just need to give it some time. Breathe deep, buddy. Go inside your heart and relax."

Fear gripped my insides like a vise, and I slid down to the floor.

"I can't do this. It'll kill me." What felt like ancient despair seemed to be pouring out of me. "My soul is crying."

"You have to get this out. Just cry," Sean said. He sat down, pulled me onto his lap, and began to rock me.

"Ahhhhhhhhhhh . . ." Primeval hurt burst from my soul. "I'm not strong enough." The sobbing continued.

"Release me!" I yelled. "Let me out! Let me go!"

A voice said, *This is not beyond you! You are love! You can do this!*

Sean continued the rhythmic rocking.

Keep waking up! Enter the cave of your heart.

I could not discern if this was Sean's voice or—

"I'm too weak!"

This, too, is part of your process. Feel it. Experience it and learn from it.

"Why? I want to be free," I screamed.

You are always free.

My sobs gradually slowed.

"I'm losing my mind," I said, but more softly.

Lose your mind, my love. Find your heart.

My entire body, every limb, every hair, every cell, took a deep breath.

Let go with an exhale.

I did.

You are in the arms of your beloved, your healing shaman. He gives you the soul-healing love you need.

"Ren, don't take on the world's opinions. This intensity is not you." It was Sean's voice. "Don't take on all this pain. Come on, say it with me. *Neti, Neti, Neti, Neti* . . . This is not me, this is not me."

He kept rocking me and repeating it. I finally followed his lead, "*Neti, Neti, Neti* . . ."

"So much fear. So much angst," he whispered as his lips touched my forehead. "We all have it, but we have to remember: in the cave of the heart, there's joy. Don't leave me. Come home."

I relaxed into him and let myself slip into darkness.

I had no idea how long we were in the office. Eventually, Kate let us know that things had quieted down, and the crowd had dispersed.

"The officers are outside," she said. "They're going to escort you to your car, just as a precaution."

"Thank you," I said. "I'm a mess."

"Of course you are! It's hard looking at the world through the eyes of love when, unfortunately, there are still people addicted to anger and hate. Don't forget you're human," Kate said with a wise, sideways smile.

"Amen, sister," Sean said.

"I never expected it to be like that," I said as we walked to the car.

"We were lucky today," he said, reaching over to rub the top of my head. "We're being picked up at 6:00 a.m. for tomorrow's interview. Are you still up for that?"

"More than ever! Hate won't stop me."

30

WHAT IF MIKE HAD DIED?

The alarm rang at 4:30 a.m. I was not as rested as I would have liked, not because of council meetings or dreams of goddesses but rather my mental rumination of the chaos at the studio. Over a quick breakfast, I told Sean I didn't want to put anyone else in danger, so for now, any public contact had to be put on hold. Thankfully, today's interview was a different way to make a connection.

As planned, a car picked us up at 6:00 a.m. to take us to the TV station. The sun had not yet come up, and the street outside the house was quiet.

When we arrived, we were greeted on the set by Haley Smithers, the lead news anchor of the local NBC affiliate and host of a popular morning show, *AM Cincinnati*. She was a petite thirty-something blond with silver-blue soulful eyes that were accentuated by her tailored lapis-colored skirt suit, a white silk blouse, and a necklace of chunky pieces of polished turquoise. The set was brightly lit, with three cameras arranged to capture every angle. We sat across from each other in black leather-like drafting chairs.

"We have some time before we begin. Do you have any questions?" Haley asked.

"I'm good," I said. "Ready whenever you are."

"Great, remember this is being taped for later and will definitely be edited, so my questions may not be sequential. Don't worry, you can't mess up," she said, reaching over and touching my knee. "We'll take a break between sets of questions."

I like her.

"Quiet on the set," said a voice from the sound booth.

Haley turned her focus to one of the enormous cameras and froze into a closed-lip smile until given a signal.

"Millions have seen the video clips of the unbelievable recovery of the nine-year-old boy whose bike collided with a car on a busy thoroughfare in Cincinnati. The man responsible for his return to life, meditation and yoga teacher Ren Devlin, is here with me today." She turned to face me, her smile widening. "Thank you for joining us, Ren. The video and witness accounts about you and the boy speak for themselves. The bigger question is how."

"I don't have a formula, Haley, which is what most people want, but I do believe, in that moment, my years of diligent yoga practice allowed me to access a deep dimension of love that was supported by everyone who wanted Mike to get up."

"Love? How do you get to that level of love?"

"In my case, by cultivating a deep relationship with my inner-self through meditation."

"Are you saying if we learn to sit quietly, we can raise the—?"

"Oh no. I'm saying that meditation can lead you to believe in your energetic connection to all beings *and* the Universe. This connection is the transformative energy of love that not only changes you but changes the entire world."

"Powerful," she said, nodding. "You've claimed everything you have done, everyone can do as well. Can you give us some insights on how?"

"First, you need to *want* to change from living in fear and hate to love. Then find the practices that open you to love and commit to them."

"I've taken my share of yoga classes and do some meditation," she said, "and I'm not doing what you've done. This isn't as easy as it sounds."

"Keep at it," I said with a smile. "And you're right, it's *not* easy, but there's nothing easy about being human. Dealing with the stresses of a modern world is hard enough, let alone trying to attune your energies to a level where you can believe in yourself, the human race, and not become *all-consumed* with the struggles of the current state of the world."

"What do you see as the current state of the world?"

"We're severely divided and pitted against each other," I said. "Rather than support one another as equals, we let ego-driven world leaders, who are desperately hanging on to outdated concepts of power, divide us with a constant diet of fear and anger. But at the same time, huge shifts and changes are taking place that can't and won't be stopped. Change is a Universal reality, and consciousness is spiraling upward and will continue to do so."

"Ren, is what happened with you and Michael Cuberry a miracle?"

"It depends on how you define 'miracle,'" I said. "I see the birth of a baby as a miracle. Are you asking if what happened with Mike is beyond our current understanding of scientific knowledge—was it supernatural?"

She nodded.

"It looks that way," I said, "but yogis have been exploring the interior terrain of the human mind for thousands of years. They believe that spontaneous healing, telepathic communication, and multidimensional travel are part of our evolution. Maybe science just needs to catch up. Remember, electricity or a smartphone would have been viewed as a miracle not too long ago."

Haley smiled. "So, do you think—in the future—we may be healing each other like you've done?"

I shrugged.

"Interesting," she said. "Well, that certainly opens this up to lots of questions, but let's change direction." She shifted in her chair and leaned forward.

"I've seen footage from outside your home and the yoga studio both this week and last. I was sorry to hear that things got out of hand yesterday."

"Yes, that was unfortunate, but I'm not going to allow hate to keep me from living," I said.

"How are you coping with all the attention?"

"I do the same yoga and meditation practices now that I did before the day on the Parkway."

"And that keeps you calm?"

I nodded.

"I'd like to go off-script." She then sat back and folded her hands in her lap.

"As a person who dedicates his life to helping people through yoga and meditation," she said, her tone more serious, "how do you think you'd feel if Mike had died?"

I froze. Mike dying had never crossed my mind. At the thought now, a deep sadness welled from my core. My witnessing self was fully activated. I heard myself whisper, "No." A tear slowly made a trail down my face.

"Research shows," she said, "those who involuntarily cause another's death are never the same. If the boy had died, would you still believe so strongly in your practices? Would you feel the same about love and healing?"

Every ounce of energy sank into my solar plexus as I sat, unable to move or speak.

"Let's cut here for a moment," I heard Haley say.

"Ren, are you all right? Ren?"

As Haley placed her hand on my knee, a flash of bright light burst through what I knew was my third eye, instantly transmuting my sadness into gratitude for the way things turned out. Even as chaotic as my life had become, at this moment, I was ecstatic that Mike had lived.

"Ren?" Haley repeated. "Do you think you can finish the interview?"

I closed my eyes, took a deep breath, and asked the goddesses to inspire me.

"Yes," I said, "let's finish."

"Okay, here we go. Let's begin with you answering the question about Mike."

"Of course, it would be different if Mike hadn't made it," I said. "Either way, we would have all been changed: Mike, his family, the crowd, me, my partner. But this was the way it was meant to be. He was meant to live. It was his fate, or to use the Greek word, *Moira*."

"Moira?" she asked.

"In mythology, *Moira* is a collective of three goddesses who determine a person's destiny." I took a deep breath and smiled. "Moira-destiny is represented by a beautiful thread of light. The first goddess spins the thread, the second dispenses it throughout life, and the third cuts it when it's time to die."

"Does this have anything to do with the silver threads people described seeing on the Parkway?"

"Yes, and the silver threads were all being dispensed. There was no cutting."

"What a beautiful image."

"It is," I said, "and I'm eternally grateful for how it turned out. But had the thread been severed and my Moira was to walk the path of involuntarily taking a life, it would have been challenging but noble nonetheless."

"Noble?" Haley asked as her brow furrowed.

"All life paths are noble. The more we accept the reality of our lives with compassion rather than try to run from it, our life path becomes our greatest teacher," I said. "Can you imagine a world where we learn compassion for ourselves . . ." I placed my hand on my heart. "And then offer it to everyone?"

"Is that your vision for the future?" she asked.

I now placed both hands on my heart.

"It's the yogic vision—a time when we honor our differences and diversity with deep compassion rather than kill each other over them." I sighed. "That may be way off in human years, but it doesn't matter. Detach from it happening today or even in your lifetime. The Universe doesn't work on our clock. Instead, dive into meditation, explore yourself, drop judgment, and surrender into trusting that all of life and every path is sacred. Savor your own Moira, honor everyone else's, and work to make the world a utopia all beings can enjoy."

"Cut," said a voice in the darkness. The bright lights went off.

"Perfect," Haley said.

31

ITALY CALLS

That evening after the interview aired, Sean and I sat around our kitchen table, overwhelmed. Thousands of emails flooded in, social media was a buzz, and I received a phone call from Archbishop Piedmont.

"Hello, Joseph," I said. Sean rolled his eyes.

"Ren, I saw your spot with Haley Smithers. Bravo, dear teacher," he said. "Your reply to her query of what if Mike had died was so soulful. You are right. We can never be sure how we will react to any event in our lives, but honoring the outcome is so important. I'll be using this insight and the story of the three goddesses of Moira in my counseling."

"Thank you, Joseph. The question threw me at first, but a deep sense of gratitude and divine inspiration came over me. That's when I said we must believe that whatever comes our way as our destiny is noble, and we should honor it."

"Speaking of honoring destinies," he said, "I'm convinced ours are intertwined. I know you still haven't made a final decision, but I've taken the liberty to give your contact information to Father Assaglio, the director of education for the Vatican, and I'll send you his."

"The director of education at the Vatican?" I felt butterflies in my stomach.

"Feel free to reach out to him with any questions, and once you decide to accompany me, he'll be the one to set up classes and curriculum. *Your* curriculum, of course. I hope I haven't crossed a boundary."

"No, you're fine. Sean and I are close to making a decision. But this is a big step, and we want to make sure we move forward as the Universe and our Moira would have us do."

"I completely understand. I hope we can be up and running within a few months and making the changes we both know are so needed in our world."

"Thank you. A conversation with the director may be beneficial. I could get his thoughts and make sure the student groups are co-ed."

"Ren, certain things are still being hammered out, but I know we'll do great work together. Remember, we'd like to keep this off the media's radar as much as possible. Peace, my friend. I'll see you Wednesday for our next session."

I hung up the phone.

"I'm not going, Ren," Sean said, looking at me from across the kitchen table.

"What do you mean? We have to do this."

"No, we don't. Piedmont's the serpent in the garden. I hear the seduction. 'We'll do great things together, dear teacher, blah, blah, blah blah, blah.'"

"The feminine energies in my dreams are pushing me to ignite change in the church. What better way than by teaching future priests?"

"You're not going to change the church, Ren. It has too much invested in an androcentric hierarchy."

"Now you're pissing me off," I said.

"*I'm* pissing *you* off? What about your council, Veronica, Clare . . . ? Don't you think they'll be pissed off?"

I shook my head. "Sean, we need to at least try. This is my big chance to make a real difference."

"*My* big chance? I see," Sean said. "This is about you!"

He started to leave the kitchen, then turned back to me.

"Oh, I forgot to tell you, the National Institute of Neurological

Science called. They asked if they could study your brain functions while you meditate."

"Really?"

"Yeah, but I told them you've already volunteered to be a lab rat for the Vatican," Sean smirked.

32

THE COUNCIL'S COUNSEL

S ean stormed out to the garden, and I retreated to my meditation
cushion. Almost instantly, I was seated in front of my council. Gone
were the lab coats. All the members were now adorned in togas, chitons,
peplos—looking godly.

"What's happening?" I addressed my inquiry to the whole council.
"Sean thinks the klesha of ego is pushing me to go to Rome. But I've
already wrestled with my ego, and I'm *not* taking credit for all the healing.
I know it's not me. I'm over all that."

"Oh, I see," said the still-nameless goddess. "You think you've con-
quered ego with your incomparable knowledge of yoga and can now save
the world by working within the very institution that has purposely buried
the feminine?" Flaming red hair surrounded her perfectly proportioned
oval, porcelain face and full, unsmiling lips. Her haunting gray eyes were
formidable, glaring out from under her gold helmet. She clutched a five-
foot spear. From under the table, I spied her shin greaves. She was dressed
for battle. I hoped it wasn't a battle with me.

"Again, my ego's not the issue," I said.

Her left eyebrow raised as she shifted her grip on her spear.

"So, you're living without a point of view," she said, "your ego is fully under control, the fluctuations of the mind have been tamed to resemble the motionless, stillness of an undisturbed body of water, and judgment, in all forms, has been dropped."

"I didn't say that."

"Yes, you did."

"No, I . . . *who are you*?" I asked.

"Who do you think I am?" she taunted.

"Well, there's the Moon," I said and pointed. "And Venus is seated next to Saturn. That's it for the female representations of the planets as I know them."

"Wrong!" There was a sneer of superiority on her face.

"THEN WHO ARE YOU?" I yelled.

Her smirk turned to a self-satisfied grin.

"Brava Athena," Saturn said, raising his eyebrow, looking at her, and then back to me, "you broke his calm exterior."

"Athena?" I asked. That explained the military outfit.

"Yes!" she said. "Each of us has a male and female representation. I am the female Mars, though naturally much wiser, I say with full heartfelt humility. With *your* natal Mars in sappy non-confrontational Cancer, I'm here to show you what female warrior energy can do."

"What the—?"

"Aah, aah, aah . . ." Saturn said, pointing his finger at me. "Be respectful."

"That's right, Ren, do what your daddy says," Athena said, narrowing her eyes.

"Stop!" Saturn said sternly. "Everybody, take a deep breath."

We all did.

"I will remind the council, as the celestial makeup of his chart, we incline his actions, we do not compel. We will keep free will; his free will front and center as we continue."

Everyone on the council nodded in agreement but one.

"Ren," asked Mercury, "do you feel you have all the information you need to make a decision about Italy right now?" He held a pencil poised above a notepad. Was he taking the minutes?

"Yes. My association with the archbishop and our uncanny similarities are not random. He's heading to Rome to become a cardinal—the timing is perfect," I said.

"Make sure you move from your heart and that the decision is based in love," Venus said. "When the ego is involved, *we*, especially the feminine, get pushed to the back of the bus."

"Thank you!" Athena said, rolling her eyes and crossing her arms.

"Besides the church wanting me," I said, directing my comment to Venus and trying to ignore Athena, "I believe the feminine essence is pushing me in this direction. Where better to make great strides for change than in the institution which limits and hides Her?"

"Perhaps the Sun would like to ask Ren a question or two," Saturn said, looking to his immediate left at a man who appeared older than Mercury but younger than the other males at the table. His features were handsomely proportioned and framed by his wavy dark blond hair. There was a natural aura of light, almost like a halo, surrounding his head.

"I suppose it's fitting," I said, "given that he's the celestial representation of the ego."

"How important is it for you to be accepted by an institution that abandoned you?" the Sun asked with an even and measured tone.

I frowned. "What does that—?"

"Back when the church abandoned you, was your ego injured?" the Sun asked.

"For a time . . ."

"Ego can be quite cunning," he said with a nod.

"Are you utilizing your higher mind in these decisions?" Uranus asked.

"Ren," the Moon interjected, "could there be a blind spot when it comes to a belief system that has been part of your DNA for hundreds of years?"

"What you don't understand," I said, "is the church is *ready* for change, *and* you sent me to the Vatican Library in the first place."

All ten folded their hands in front of them on the table and sat expressionless.

They're not listening. How can my council turn a deaf ear to a reality that could bring Her back in such a powerful and enormous way? Were they suddenly falling into a conservative, backward way of behavior?

Saturn cleared his throat.

Athena unfolded her hands, placed her elbows on the table and her hands over her mouth.

"Joseph and I are so similar. There's a sense of destiny here, don't you see it? You've come back to me at this time. Other saints-goddesses are guiding me—the three statues, the three fates . . ."

Athena's face turned red.

I stood. "Listen to me, folks, this is an opportunity. Joseph agrees with me. We can make this happen. I would love to have your support."

Athena stood. "Don't screw this up again!" she said, pounding her fist on the table.

"Again?"

"This isn't your first time at this rodeo. There are lots of past-life lessons swirling here. Can't you feel it, Mr. Intuitive?"

"Athena!" Saturn growled as he rose from his chair. They glared at each other.

"Are you just going to stand there and let him—?"

"We, *and* I emphasize . . . *all of us* . . . will honor the law of Karma," Saturn said. "We will not interfere with free will. Now, take your seat."

Athena plopped down and turned her body away from me and the rest of the council. Saturn now directed his intense gaze at me and pointed.

"As for you—"

Venus stood and placed her hand on Saturn's outstretched arm.

"Ren," Venus said, as she placed her other hand over her chest, "listen to your heart and make sure the direction you follow is paved with love."

I placed my hands on my heart center. "Goddess, I believe this is much bigger than *my* journey, that I, with the help of Joseph, can make a huge difference. I believe the path I'm walking is the path that *must* be taken."

"Arrghhhh . . . ," Athena bellowed. An intense clap of thunder resounded through the council chamber. I felt a swish of air at the top of my head as a huge snowy owl flew from behind me toward the council. Its fully outstretched wings blocked the celestial light that had been illuminating our meeting. The chamber went dark.

33

INVOKING A GODDESS

I walked outside to the garden. Sean was sitting in a chair next to our fire pit, staring into the raging flames.

"It's so beautiful," I said, "with the way the flames bob and bend and move so freely like they're dancing."

Sean was stone silent.

"I know you're upset," I said, taking a seat opposite him, "but I'd like to have an objective, rational conversation about this."

"Really," he said, still gazing into the fire. "You're good at many things, but being objective and rational is not on that list."

"Sean, going to Italy is temporary. Once we get the program up and running, we can come home."

"We need a mediator," Sean said. "I want you to discuss this absurd idea with Sara at the retreat this weekend. She'll talk some sense into you."

"What if she agrees with me and says we should go?"

"Italy's not happening."

"But what if this is what all the mystical dreams and encounters are pointing to?"

"Have you thought to ask your council directly?"

"I did, but they said I have free will, and they can't—"

"Can't what?" he said, looking at me. "Tell you not to go? Tell you this is a mistake, that you're being seduced by some mammoth machine that's used to getting its way, *or* they can't tell you your ego has you by the . . ." He looked back to the fire.

"You're starting to sound like Athena," I said under my breath.

"What?"

"The agitated woman at the table . . . She's Athena, the female warrior version of Mars. She's the only one who doesn't think this is a good idea. Actually, that's an understatement; she was furious. She slammed her fist on the table and shrieked so loudly, she created a clap of thunder and then blacked out all light with her white totem owl."

"Sounds like my kind of goddess," Sean said, looking up. "Excuse me, but doesn't your council work as a unit? Aren't they the different facets of you?"

I nodded.

"Well, if one of them dissents, shouldn't you be listening?"

"She's never liked me," I said.

"She's part of you. Doesn't Mars-Athena represent your masculine, straightforward, take-action energy?"

"Oh, my goddess. You're right. She said my Mars is in sappy, no-action Cancer," I said, watching the flames pulsate and crackle in a mesmerizing dance. "She's teaching me in her unique way." I stood. "I'm going to Italy, Sean. It's my fate."

"We're *not* going! Think of me as your own personal Athena!"

"I want you to go, but I'm going with or without you."

"What?" he said, sitting up straight. "You'd leave me, our life? What about Always and Forever?"

I saw the heart-wrenching pain in his eyes. I had to stay strong, so I took a deep breath.

"I'll always love you, even from five thousand miles away. But I believe this is what I need to do. I'm going."

I pushed back tears. Sean's were flowing down his face.

"What about listening to your heart?" His bottom lip quivered.

Be strong, I told myself.

"What about your council, your dreams . . . the holy card from the nuns in Assisi! It was printed right there . . . *Do not Go to Italy*, remember?

"That was *your* card, Sean."

"What?" he said, shaking his head.

"Your card said, *Do not Go to Italy*. Mine didn't."

He dropped his head in his hands and sobbed, his shoulders heaving. I walked away, holding in my tears, knowing that eventually, alone in the house, I, too, would let out the pain that ripped at my soul.

What am I doing? Doubt be gone. I have to do this . . . for *Her*.

I stopped at the bottom of the stairs and heard Sean's muffled yells outside.

"Please, somebody help me! I'm losing him! If there's some council . . . or saints . . . mystical revolutionaries . . . guide me . . . Athena, help me prove to Ren the church is using him!"

I felt him—his heart severed in half with no hope. I placed my hand on my heart and ascended the stairs to the second floor. I went to the back window that faces out onto the garden. From there, I could see Sean still sitting near the fire, staring into the flames.

As I climbed the stairs to our treehouse bedroom, my heart ached with Sean's sadness, which I felt as my own. But I also knew I was not the one who could help him right now.

34

ATHENA

As I lay in bed, Saturnian self-doubt filled me with questions. *What was I doing?* Sean was like yoga to me; he sustained me. Was I really prepared to go to Italy without him? I would create what could be an irreconcilable wedge between us. But how could he not see that this was what I needed to do? The goddesses were pushing me to Rome. I wanted him to go with me, but I knew he wouldn't change his mind.

I cried myself to sleep.

"Wake up, Ren."

Sean?

I opened my eyes, blinded by the bright midday sun overhead.

"Where are we?" I asked.

"You said you wanted to go to Italy. We're back in Assisi," he said. "This is the Piazza del Comune."

I did a three-sixty, taking in my surroundings. The building in front of us, with six ornate Corinthian columns flanking the entrance, looked to be thousands of years old, much older than the medieval structures that created the rest of the Piazza.

"Is this a temple?" I asked.

"It is *my* temple, even today. Originally built in 25 BCE as a temple to the feminine, it was dedicated to Minerva, the Roman goddess of Wisdom. Then, in the fourth century, as Christianity spread through the Roman empire, various Catholic monastic orders used it," Sean said with an uncustomary curtness.

My temple? I thought. *And Minerva's the Roman equivalent of the Greek goddess Athena.*

"How do you know all this history?" I asked, furrowing my brow.

"I'm not who you think I am."

"I see," I said, realization dawning. "Well, goddess—"

"You can call me Sean for now."

"Sure, *Sean*," I said, nodding. "Tell me more."

"In 1539, after several hundred years of neglect, Pope Paolo III ordered the Temple of Minerva to be restored and rededicated to the Virgin Mary, Queen of Wisdom. The temple then took the name Santa Maria sopra Minerva, literally meaning Mary over Minerva."

"The Pagan Goddess of Wisdom was tied directly to Christianity's Queen of Wisdom," I said. "Imagine that."

"Yes, the ancients rightfully believed that wisdom was feminine. They called her Sophia, then Athena, then Minerva, and in yoga, you call her Shakti. More specifically, the piece of Shakti that represents wisdom in yoga is the Hindu goddess Saraswati. But no matter what name you call wisdom, they're all feminine."

"So, this is the former home of a goddess of wisdom?" I asked.

"It's not a former home. We're still here, all of us," Sean said. "Please, step inside."

"Are you coming with me?" I asked.

"Just you."

We stepped forward to the fifteen-foot arched wooden door that served as the main entry to the temple. The massive door contained a slighter entrance within it. Sean opened the smaller doorway and made a sweeping gesture for me to enter.

"Hey," I said as I took a micro-step toward the threshold, "I know last night was hard, but—never mind."

He again gestured for me to enter. I took a deep breath and stepped into the vestibule. Sean closed the door. I was inside . . . alone.

The interior looked like a typical Catholic cathedral with a long center aisle and massive stained-glass windows along the length of the nave. One striking difference was the life-size statue of Mary, dressed in a sky-blue robe and a white cape, wearing a crown of electrically illuminated stars, standing center stage above the main altar.

A female has the spotlight here.

I felt the energy of many goddesses as I roamed the church. Toward the back was a side grotto with another statue of Mary, this one dressed in black and white with a veil draped across her arm, reminiscent of Veronica and Clare. I knelt at a large wrought-iron votive stand and lit a candle in gratitude for all the mythical and real female goddesses in my life. Then I walked to the front of the church, sat quietly in the first pew, and closed my eyes.

Remain still with your eyes closed, I heard Her whisper inside my heart. *Go deep, tatra sthitau yatnah abhyāsa. Bring yourself to a stable and tranquil state—sthitau,* the voice advised.

My mind raced—*Sutra 1:13.* I began to take long, deep breaths to release all thought. *Let go of your inner sense of self.*

I dropped through several layers of consciousness into an all-encompassing sense of no-thingness.

I felt a resistance to this new, unfamiliar frontier.

Step up a rung on the ladder of evolution. Move away from the instinctual programming you inherited from your ancestors. P.U.T.P.

I took another breath and exhaled, then opened my eyes to find myself in front of the council doors.

Why was I suddenly fearful?

A large bird screeched behind me, and its talons clawed at my back, thrusting me through the chamber doors with the force of ten humans. I lay crumpled on the floor.

"Welcome."

I looked up to see Athena, no longer appearing as Sean, sitting alone at the huge council table. She stood, draped in her ornate white tunic, her protective aegis strapped across her chest, and her warrior helmet shining. She smacked the blunt end of her five-foot-tall spear on the floor, beckoning her three-foot snowy owl to perch inches from her on the table.

"Where's everyone else?" I asked, coming to my feet.

"We need some alone time, just you and me." She feigned blowing me a kiss. "Welcome to my old stomping grounds."

"Why in Assisi? And why so much drama?"

"Drama?" Athena yelled. "Your council's been cajoling you to take action and wake up. We've pulled in several goddesses and a couple of saints, but nothing seems to be working. So, I brought you here, to this hallowed ground of the feminine, to inundate you with our energy."

She moved around to the front of the table carrying her spear.

"This was my sacred space for centuries until the Christians thought they could bury me beneath the Queen of Heaven," the goddess said, cocking her head to the right. "Little did they know, they increased our energy. Mary and I aren't adversaries. Au contraire!" Athena leaned against the table. "We are one and the same. They can demote her to queen and strip away her goddess status, but those who come here to pray are not fooled by semantics. They come here to connect with Us—the feminine. Whatever our name, we are strengthened here."

"I felt it when I walked in the door," I said. "So—?"

"I want you to feel the ancient energy of the feminine coming from east, west, above, and below, and to remind you that part of your new global platform *and* your karmic clearing is to dig us out of obscurity."

"I'm trying, Goddess, that's why I'm going to—"

"YOU'RE NOT TRYING!" She stomped her feet until the room shook as if it would crumble.

"Please . . . ," I said. "Let's just calm down."

"I'm frustrated!" she yelled. She took a deep breath, set the spear against the table, and folded her arms across her aegis. "We have too much riding on this for you to be weak and sloppy. You aren't doing well on even the simple tests we have set up for you. You might need more intense training with Saturn."

"What do you mean? If I'm moving through the kleshas, as the council's told me, I've—"

"Yes, klesha one, *Avidya*, you've done an excellent job of educating yourself, but you're failing miserably at klesha two, *Asmita*. Your ego has you believing you can change the church."

"I don't agree," I said. "My ego is in check, and I am acting as the council and the goddesses want me to."

"Wrong! Your ego wants to make amends with an institution that would rather see you dead."

"What is it you want?" I felt my anger rising.

Athena picked up her spear and pointed it at me. Her widened eyes gave her the look of someone gone mad.

"I want you . . . we *all* want you . . . to pick up the pace and get this right. *That's* what we want!" She shook the spear. "Pay attention!"

"I—"

"The rest of them are playing by the rules of Karma," the goddess said. "They don't want to break any universal spiritual tenets." She rolled her eyes. "Well, *I* don't like rules."

I stood silent.

"They're used to me asking for forgiveness—after the fact. That's what I plan to do now."

"Is the rest of the council coming back soon?" I asked, taking a step back. My instincts told me to run.

"Are you feeling abandoned, Ren?" Athena took a step forward. "There's no chair in here to hide behind. It's just you and me. And . . . the cauldron."

"Cauldron?"

She smacked the end of the spear on the floor. To her left appeared a barrel-size, four-legged black iron cauldron. Images of the astrological symbols adorned its stout belly, along with ancient-looking depictions of owls.

"The cauldron symbolizes the womb of the Goddess—where all life begins and where history is held. Through the ancient art of scrying—gazing into it—you can see images from the past, present, and future. Come and look into it!"

"No, thanks," I said. I didn't want anything to do with the cauldron, nor did I want to get any closer to her. "I'm good."

"That wasn't an invitation." She pointed her spear at me once again. "Come here!"

The owl took flight, circling several inches above our heads.

"No!" I said.

I'd thrown gas on a smoldering fire. My eyes locked with Athena's. With calculated steps, she walked toward me until the sharp point of her outstretched weapon lightly pushed on my third eye.

I started deep, rhythmic yogic breathing and reminded myself there was more to this life than my physical being. I wanted to maintain some semblance of centeredness, even as I felt *Abhinivesha*, the fear of death klesha, pulsating in my chest.

"Are you going to run your spear through my brain?" I asked with all the calmness I could fake at the moment.

"I might. Maybe running it through your brain will do something to your consciousness," she said with a sneer. "Once again, I may find myself asking for forgiveness and apologizing later, or you could do as I asked and gaze into the cauldron."

"I'm not afraid of death," I said, still matching her stare.

She pushed the spear point harder. I felt a drop of blood trickle down my forehead. I remained silent.

"You aren't the only one who has ever raised the dead," she said, "but you *are* the only one who's been captured doing it on video. That was sloppy, sloppy, sloppy! The greatest Masters of the world are supposed to remain unknown to human history."

"But I'm not a Master," I said, keeping her gaze.

"Yes, *that* is certainly true," she scoffed. "Yet you *have* awakened deep levels of compassion that allowed your life force to act like a master. But you have a huge blind spot—the church. You're hearing what you want to hear and in denial about the rest."

"But Joseph says—"

"Wake Up, P.U.T.P.—work to create more miracles in the world through Her love. Pick the right invitations, Ren. Don't get distracted by your past connection to the church— it's long—and not very pleasant."

"Athena, Joseph assures me women will be included, and I'll have the freedom to teach Tantric techniques that include the goddess."

"*Ingenuo, ingenuo,*" she said, as her left eyebrow slowly raised, and her eyes widened even more. "Naive!"

I swallowed hard.

She lowered her spear, reached out her left arm, and energetically pulled the cauldron across the stone floor until it was within inches of us. Her majestic, feathered companion landed on the lip of the iron bowl.

"Step up. Allow my faithful totem and magic pot to illuminate your blind spot and show you the abridged version of your Italian future."

Feeling there was no alternative, I stepped to the rim of the cauldron, took a deep breath, and looked inside.

"It's just black water," I said. "I don't see . . ."

Slowly, from the bottom, a two-by-two-foot multicolored mandala emerged and floated just below the surface. The outer red square, symbolizing the Universe, featured pink and blue lotus flowers in each corner, while an inner gold circle was filled with ornate Sanskrit letters. Further in was another square holding yet another circle and then another square and another circle . . . using my breath and honing my vision, I gazed into the focal point until the periphery dissolved. A figure slowly materialized, bubbling up from the core. It was . . . the porcelain-skinned vampire priest from the dream I had days before the church re-entered my life. His piercing eyes drew me into the heart of the mandala, where I was spun into a cyclone of energy. I was no longer observing the image. I *was* the image.

I watched myself, dressed in all black, walking through an airport. Then, snippets flashed before me.

"These are details on your classes," said a priest, handing me a manila envelope. "Information on the students will be given to you by Father Assaglio tomorrow morning." He turned to leave, then turned back. "Not all men who wear crosses can be trusted. There are those here who have attachments, aversions, ego, and ignorance. What holds us back from our heart is Universal."

I closed my eyes to block out the vision, the cauldron, and Athena.

The goddess pounded her spear on the ground. "Open your eyes."

I did. I was pulled back into the swirling vision of the mandala.

I stood in a room filled with desks.

"I am Fr. Assaglio," said a priest in his early seventies, who resembled the vampire priest from my earlier dream. He frowned and handed me a piece of paper. "Here is your class list. I will not stay. Until I can raise the dead, I have been told to allow you to teach what you like."

I saw myself scan the names. "There are no women on this list."

"None were interested."

Nine men walked into the room and took seats at the table desks lining the room. Assaglio turned to them and said, "You have been hand-picked by Cardinal Joseph Piedmont for this pilot program on meditation. You will no doubt hear things that go against church doctrine. Do not be offended. Ignore it."

"Oh, on the contrary," I heard myself say, looking at the class, "be offended!"

I closed my eyes to block out the vision. Was this really a look into my future reality? I heard the pound of Athena's spear on the ground.

I opened my eyes and saw myself in conversations with three of the student priests. Father Lanzetta said he was Assaglio's assistant, Father Ferrara admitted he levitated when praying, and Father Arsenio, I recognized from my dream of being chased in the Vatican.

"Father Arsenio, you are the head archivist of the Vatican Library, correct?" I asked. "I would like to visit it at some point."

"As before, you have full access to the collections."

As before?

Leaning over the mandala-producing cauldron, I felt a sharp stab in my stomach. I tried to lift my head, but it was locked into position over the black scrying pot.

Then, a glowing computer screen appeared in the blackness with a message. I read the words.

> Signore Devlin,
> It is futile to contact Cardinal Piedmont again about the absence of females in your program. Let me be clear: there will be no women. When our personnel are teaching your curriculum, we may

allow women, but that will not be decided by you but rather by the powers within the church.

Father Assaglio

If what I was seeing in the waters of Athena's cauldron were real, Joseph was lying to me. Whatever held my head in place over the cauldron suddenly released. My face fell into the water, scattering the image of the mandala.

I stood, my face dripping. Athena threw me a towel.

"Well?" she asked.

"You've definitely planted a seed of doubt in my psyche," I said. "This might have been the original plan, but I'd like to think that with free will, maybe he's changed his mind. I've seen great strides in Joseph in just the last few weeks, and—"

Athena let out a long sigh as she walked back to the council table.

"Look, I didn't ask for any of this to happen."

"We never do," she said, now with a gentler intonation. She took her seat. Even her eyes softened toward me. "We never ask, and we never know when the miracles will come. Ego can never be part of it. If you want it, it won't happen. It's when you align your energies and desires with the ultimate Oneness of the cosmos that miracles occur. That's what can bring little boys back to life."

"Why does it still feel as if the church *needs* to be my next step?" I asked.

"The church doesn't want to make changes . . . *we* do," she said. "The energies you've tapped into are a radical affirmation of what is possible when life is a balance between the feminine and the masculine. A certain aligning, with the stars . . . ," she made a sweeping motion with her hand toward the sky, ". . . has allowed you to move beyond the limiting, lopsided thoughts of this earthly, male-dominated world."

The snowy owl flew from the cauldron to the table, landing next to her. She stroked its head.

"Why me?" I asked.

"*You* are all we have," she said. "*You*, and all humans who feel their hearts waking up, are all we have. *You* and all of them *are* enough."

My eyes began to fill with tears at the magnitude of my task.

"I want human consciousness to realize what is missing is *Us*," she said, "the Moon, Venus, all the mother goddesses, the warrior goddesses, the caretaker goddesses. We need men to stand firm in their conviction to recognize women, the feminine, as equals," she continued. "It's time for us to come home to your hearts." Two more white owls flew in and perched on the back of the chairs normally occupied by the Moon and Venus. "We'll help you replace fear with love and deep knowing. Don't forget us."

Athena looked to her totem, then to the other owls, and then back to me. "We each traverse the deep, dark recesses of our souls. When we are ready to face whatever is there, we light a candle. Face any hate you encounter head-on with a pure heart. You have a parliament of love and wisdom behind you."

We smiled at each other, then I heard, *Open your eyes.*

35

ENLIGHTENED
SELF-INTEREST

Eyes wide open, I lay in bed, trying to make sense of my time with Athena. Finally, I got up.

"Hey, bud," I called out as I walked downstairs. In the kitchen, there were no candles lit, no smell of incense or coffee. No Sean.

There *was* a note on the kitchen table.

Gone to help Carol. I have the phone. Be back later.

I considered sitting behind a chair in the living room and creating a safe space, but instead, still holding his note to my chest, I moved to the library for my morning meditation.

I took my seat in one of the leather chairs in front of the fireplace and closed my eyes. I placed my hands in Abhaya mudra, trying to invoke the fearlessness I needed to face a possible future without Sean. I repeated a mantra I hoped could build my self-assurance.

"WE'RE NEVER ALONE. WE'RE NEVER ALONE . . ."

But the deep grief I felt and the memory of what I saw in Athena's cauldron limited the depth of my inner journey, so I got up to prepare for my session with the new cardinal.

When I folded Sean's note to take it with me, I saw more writing on the back.

> Athena's totem a white owl
> Snowy owls in KY—rare to never.
> A group of owls—a parliament

Did Athena visit Sean last night, too? Is that why she initially came to me disguised as Sean? My mind raced. The sound of a car horn jolted me back to reality. I gathered my things and headed out to the waiting black sedan. The car once again dropped me off in the cold garage at the back of the cathedral. As before, I walked the short hallway that led to the nave of the church. Joseph Piedmont was already there, head bowed, reading from the copy of the Yoga Sutras I had given him.

"Good morning, Ren," he said with a big smile.

"Hello, Joseph."

"I thought sitting in front of the Queen of Heaven again would be the perfect place to practice today."

"It is," I said, positioning my chair to have Joseph opposite me, the statue behind me, and a full view into the cathedral. "I need her to have my back today."

"Have your back?" He chuckled. "I hope you're as excited about working within the Vatican as I am. Have you been in contact with Father Assaglio yet?"

"Indirectly."

"Well, I hope you didn't go to any expense calling Rome," he said. He reached into a briefcase sitting next to him and handed me a phone. "A gift for you. It's fully activated with international calling and messaging. It has all the bells and whistles."

I looked at the phone, then back at him.

"I know you and Sean share a phone, but I thought it best you had your own . . . just in case."

"Just in case what?"

"Well . . . in case you have to make calls to Rome in preparation for your classes . . . or in case you end up going to Rome alone."

"Alone? What makes you think I would go without Sean?" I asked, putting the phone in my pocket, then crossing my arms.

"Oh, I hope that isn't the case, but I've had intuitive feelings that he may be resisting the Moira you and I share."

"Your intuition is right. Sean's not going. He doesn't trust *you* or anything about this situation."

"I hate to hear that, but *you* trust me, right? What we're about to embark on is bigger than either of us. We *must* move forward in enlightened self-interest."

I had the visceral sensation of fingernails on a chalkboard.

"We *both* have a lot to lose personally, Ren, but so much more to gain spiritually."

"I could lose the love of my life. What do you have to lose?"

"My integrity. I'm assuring the Vatican that you're genuine and can help us make changes."

I heard the *whoosh* of bird wings and saw three white owls land on the railing of the choir loft. *They're in his blind spot.*

"Ah, your integrity . . . of course," I said.

Joseph pulled on his collar and shifted in his seat.

"Which is directly tied to any hope you might have of moving up in the church hierarchy."

Joseph smiled. "I assure you any ambition I have *is* in enlightened self-interest. You have to trust me."

"You're right. I *do* have to trust you," I said, staring at the owls. "Unfortunately, a growing seed of doubt's been planted."

"Why? I've been upfront with you."

"Have you? Even if you have, Father Assaglio doesn't want me anywhere near the Vatican."

"So, you have spoken with him?"

"He told me until he can raise the dead, he's been instructed to allow me to teach whatever I like."

"Did he really say that? I can't believe he . . . let me call him." He reached inside his pocket for his phone.

"Don't you believe me, Joseph?"

"I just can't believe he'd tell you that. He's been instructed to . . ." He frowned.

"To say anything to get me to come with you? Even lie?"

"What I was going to say . . . is not give out details until things are finalized."

"Are you hiding something?"

"Of course not," he said, shaking his head. "What else did he say that has you so riled and doubting my word?"

"He gave me the class list."

"Now, there's no way he would do that, I know for absolute certain."

"Let's see, there's Fr. Lanzetta, Assaglio's assistant. Fr. Ferrara, who levitates and is the most likely to develop other *siddhis*."

He looked at me slack-jawed.

"And Father Arsenio from the archives, whom I know very well."

"How could you possibly know him?"

"I get around," I said with a slight smile.

"Look, I don't know why he would say these things or give you all this information, but nothing is finalized."

"Are these men in the first class?" I asked.

"They're on the list, but like I said, nothing's finalized. Keep in mind, Ren, we're dealing with a two-thousand-year-old structure. Change takes time."

"And in some cases," I said, "so much time, the mind forgets what needs to be changed, and we once again become oblivious to the problem."

"What are you talking about?" he asked.

"I had a dream, a vision where things don't work out as you say they will."

Two of the owls took flight from their upper perch and landed softly just behind Piedmont. He glanced over his shoulder but did not see them.

"This is all about some dream?" he asked, shaking his head. "You're beginning to sound a little unstable."

"Really," I said, shifting in my chair and feeling my ire build. "Didn't *you* have a dream where a talking bird directed you to me? Or did you make that up?"

"No, I did not make it up, but—"

"But, what? You're not the only one who has dreams and visions that come true," I said. "Right before we met, I had a dream of a vampire priest who tried to persuade me not to go with the goddess and another dream where I was chased in the bowels of the Vatican and escaped by following Father Arsenio's directions to disappear into thin air."

"And you did it, didn't you?"

"Did what?"

"My assistant swears you appeared out of thin air your first time here."

"Let's not lose our focus here," I said, shaking my head.

"The church needs you. You *have* to come to Rome with me and teach the techniques from Pada Three. Just imagine your legacy."

"My legacy? And I don't *have* to do anything, Cardinal."

From the statue behind me came a whisper. *Let those who have eyes see.*

"In my vision, Father Assaglio also told me there were *no* women in the first session."

"I assure you there will be women."

The lone owl on the banister of the choir loft paced back and forth.

"In my heart, Joseph, I want to feel you're genuine."

"What can I do to reassure you and get you to join me on this journey?"

"Answer two questions."

"Okay," he said, straightening his shoulders.

"First: do you believe truths can be discovered through your dreams and birds can be messengers?"

"Yes."

I nodded.

"Next: when we get to Rome, if there *are* no women in the program and the powers stonewall us, will you resign your new position in protest? That will make headlines that will get the world's attention and make the goddesses happy."

He frowned and swallowed. After a few moments, he looked me in the eyes and said, "I'll do it."

The three *all-knowing*, trusted totems of the goddess of wisdom took flight. Two landed at the feet of the statue behind me, and the other landed directly to my right. I stroked its head.

Joseph recoiled in his chair, almost tumbling backward. I heard his short, shallow breaths and saw genuine disbelief on his face.

"Thank you," I said, placing my left hand on my heart.

I stood. He followed. I reached my hand toward him, and he moved back.

"What are you doing?" he asked.

"Just trust me."

I reached my hand to him again.

"No," he said.

"This isn't a magic show, Joseph."

"Really? It looks like one right now," he said, his eyes darting to the owls. "You have to go with me. We must do this."

"Nothing happens unless your heart is pure," I said, stepping toward him.

He moved back.

"Why won't you accept my hand, Joseph?"

"Pada Three, Sutra 19. By *samyama*, you can occupy the mind and have knowledge of the mind of others," he said. "You want to touch me so you can read my thoughts."

"And your heart," I said. "I know *without* touching you that your heart is full of ego."

I wrapped my outstretched hand around an energetic version of Athena's spear and felt a legion of goddesses at my back.

"It's time to tell the truth about Mary Magdalene, Mary, the Queen of Heaven, Minerva, and the rest of the females the church has tried to bury alive. Are you aware the Vatican sits on the temple site of the Roman goddess Cybele? Let's talk about literally burying them. They're not happy! Trust me, you do not want to feel their spear point pressed against your forehead. I'm seeing very clearly right now that real change will only happen in your boys' club when there is a Pope Clare! Wake up, Joseph!"

We stood at either side of a quickly widening precipice, looking at each other.

"Believe me, I will work to have women included. I promise. If not this session, definitely in the next. You're right. Assaglio is not supportive, but I assure you, I'm working with other people who are. My hands may be tied right now, but the pope is committed to change, and he's working for it."

I reached into my bag, pulled out a piece of paper and a pen, and wrote.

"Give this to the pope," I said, handing him the note. "Tell him it's a personal message from a goddess, actually a legion of goddesses."

"P-U-T-P?" Joseph read aloud. He looked up, puzzled.

"Yes. Pick Up the Pace. The heat's on. I suggest he *and* you do it now."

"Do what?"

"*Pick up the pace!*" I yelled, my words reverberating through the cathedral.

"There are things you don't understand—"

"You are so right, *Mister* Piedmont. I don't understand how you and this hierarchy are ignoring the very change that's needed. It's right in front of your face!"

"Ren, *you* can make a difference."

"How? By creating a male priesthood who can perform miracles? Stop trying to lure me in. We're both stuck in the kleshas. Your ambition is right in my face, reflecting mine to me. Ego has us in a stranglehold, and I'm breaking free right now!"

I reached into my pocket, pulled out the phone he had given me, and dialed.

"Sean, can you come get me? I'm ready to come home, really, really ready to come home."

I hung up and handed the phone to the dejected-looking man standing in front of me.

"That's the only call I will ever make on that phone. Goodbye, Joseph."

I walked slowly through the Basilica. When I reached the thick red drape leading to the hallway, I turned. Piedmont was sitting with his head in his hands. One white Athena-owl was still there, perched on the arm of the statue of the Queen of Heaven.

Remorse for what I almost did covered my heart like a shroud. I closed my eyes.

Let me have you. The hazel-eyed goddess once again held me in her arms. *You did not forget me.*

I never will, I replied, *but we failed to make any change.*

What you label failure is the stepping stone to success at a later time. You moved from the heart. She placed her hand on my heart center.

The despair I feel is heavy, I confessed. *I was blinded by ego and ready to abandon the love of my life. I turned a deaf ear to my guides. How can I ever trust myself again?*

It is all part of the plan, she said with a hint of a smile.

In my mind's eye, we sat breathing in unison. I felt a deep understanding, connection, and euphoric sense of inner peace from her.

Stay centered, my love. The plan is accelerating. We are all with you.

I opened my eyes and looked into the nave of the Basilica. I extended my arms overhead, interlaced my hands, pointed my forefingers to the heavens, and gave one swift cutting motion down to the floor, energetically severing any last ties with this institution. I unbuttoned the cassock, let it fall to the marble floor, turned, walked through the drape, and down the stone hallway. I did not look back.

36

IT'S OVER

I got into our car, strapped in with the seat belt, and looked straight ahead.

"So, what happened?" Sean asked.

"It's over. I cut through the thick maya of illusion that blinded me."

"How can you be sure?"

"Oh, I'm sure. I even did the Kali mudra in Athena's honor to cut through the bullshit."

"I hope so," he said.

"I hope . . ." A wave of deep emotion welled in my chest. "That you can forgive me."

"I was blindsided."

"I know. And I was so completely consumed by ego that I couldn't see the truth."

"Ren, I'm ecstatic to hear this, but do you *really* think it's over with the church? That's what you thought over thirty years ago."

I turned to look at him. "I understand your doubt, but it's over. Sean Carson, *you* are what I want. Whatever this miracle thing is about, I want to go through it with you."

"This *miracle* thing is intense," he said. "I need some time to recover."

"Take all the time you need, but know that I will never leave you."

"Up until a few days ago, you leaving never crossed my mind, but . . ." Sean tilted his head to the right. "Up until last night, I never thought *I'd* have a mystical experience."

I reached into my pocket and pulled out his note. "Did it have something to do with white owls?"

"If you're reading my mind, stop it," he said.

"No, it's on the back of your note." I held out the piece of paper.

"I guess we have a lot to talk about," Sean said.

37

A MEA CULPA MOMENT

"The owls in the yard were real," Sean said as we sat across from each other on our meditation cushions in our library. "I was only a foot away from them. But how did the owls get into the cathedral?"

"If Athena, the Moon, and Venus can transform into birds, they can get into a cathedral."

"I'm just having a hard time believing I was part of some mystical happening."

"You'll get used to it," I said with a smile.

"Oh, jeez . . . ," he said, shaking his head.

"Sean . . ." I took a deep breath and exhaled slowly. "I want to say again how sorry I am about this whole Italy thing."

"I know you are, but I can't stop wondering if you would have gone if Athena and the white owls had not stepped in."

"I can't imagine life without you."

"You came close to finding out."

I felt Athena's spear pierce my heart.

"Let's close our eyes," Sean said, "and let the dust settle. How about we do nine rounds of the Gayatri to move into meditation?"

So we began.

At the end of the last round, I directed my breath into my spiritual heart center, the *Hridaya*, to help it heal. The stress that gripped it loosened slightly. My chin dropped to my chest as traces of remorse, guilt, and doubt continued to swirl around me.

"Don't get caught in a *mea culpa* moment." *Saturn?* I looked up to see the full council convened.

"You eventually recognized how your cunning ego was controlling you, and you cut your ties with it," continued Saturn.

"You made a deeply ingrained human error," said Venus, "to believe solely in your ego. Now, you must say you're sorry on a soul level and move on. The emotions you're feeling are part of the process, but they are *not* you."

"But I may have lost Sean," I said. "It may never be the same between us. How can he trust me? How can I trust myself? I never, in a thousand lifetimes, thought I'd ever let something come between us. I made big, *huge* mistakes." I shook my head. "This all needs to stop. I want our normal life back. We can move, start over, and go back to our simple existence. I'm through, so stop—"

"Oh my," Saturn said, "you're starting to give *me* anxiety, and we *all* know we don't need that." The council chuckled. "It's obvious the dark side of the Moon is eating you alive through your emotions."

I looked toward the Moon, who bowed her head and smiled.

"My associate, the Moon, is not upset with me speaking the truth," Saturn said. "Each of us has our balanced and out-of-balance side." He gestured to both sides of the table. "*We each* know what they are. The Moon, reputed to be the ultimate nurturer, can also be a nightmare when you let her run your life, and obviously, you're allowing your emotional nature to run wild with fear and self-doubt."

"I want off this merry-go-round," I said.

"You signed up for this, Ren," Saturn said, leaning forward. "You asked me to be your main advisor this incarnation, and I don't say yes lightly. I'm the ultimate disciplinarian of your chart. I'm conjunct your Sun in

Capricorn; therefore, I even have control over how you express your primal life force and vitality. I pull the strings on *all* your internal drives."

"Is that why the Sun is so quiet in these meetings?" I asked.

"I am quiet," said the Sun, "but not absent! I give my power to Saturn willingly. We all have a part in your journey." His wavy blond hair glowed brightly.

"What about Athena?" I said, looking to her. "She wasn't quiet in this journey."

"We're used to her impetuous nature," Saturn said, raising an eyebrow, "and sometimes—we even count on it."

They shared a sly smile.

"*But* you put me in charge," Saturn said. "You chose a clear direction for this lifetime—to make a great push forward."

"I don't remember—"

"Well, we're here to remind you," Saturn said. "*You* chose to advance your soul and the souls of those in your biological lineage by facing the kleshas head-on, honoring the goddess, ridding yourself of regret and self-doubt, and offering yourself through intense service to humankind." Saturn's stare was intense. "So, here we are. I'm here to assist you and make sure you do all that you've set out to do."

"If Venus is my co-chair, what part does she play?" I asked.

"I am the discipline of your meditation," Saturn said, "and she is the purity of your heart. Together, for good or for bad, we came through you to raise the boy."

There was shuffling of chairs and clearing of throats.

"I am not downplaying any deity here," Saturn continued, projecting his voice toward the others. "We *all* have a part in this miracle of yours, but Venus and I are the major conductors. That is truth."

His clarification calmed the others.

"With all due respect," I said, "I am not sure raising Mike from the dead was the best thing to do."

"Neither are we," Saturn said under his breath.

"What . . . ? You made a mistake? I . . . you and I . . . ?"

"Relax! There are no mistakes, merely different paths to life's lessons," he said, tilting his head slightly to the right. "It'll be interesting to see how this plays out."

"You don't know?" I asked.

"There's always free will. It's the wild card that makes it interesting for everyone involved, including us."

Everyone laughed—but me.

"Oh, goddess! This is not helping me relax, knowing you don't know how—"

"Shhh, shhh, shhh." Saturn placed his finger to his lips. "We have more to do. You must tap into your discipline more than ever." He sat straight, then pointed at me. "Just like ego came at you like a freight train, the kleshas of attachment and aversion are quickly approaching."

"Don't, you're freaking me out," I said. "I'm serious, Sean and I need a break. Let me teach, meditate, and chant—"

"Perfect, do all of that," said Neptune, "but remember to keep an eye on your ego. You know how tricky it is."

"This is not just about you, but the collective," said Uranus.

"Step into the space between heaven and earth and follow your soul," said Venus.

"Ren." Saturn stood. "Your practices are vital for your evolution. Heed the words I have written on your skin."

"What . . . what words?" I asked.

He held out his left forearm and ran his right forefinger up it.

I looked at my arm and saw **Discipline Equals Freedom** tattooed there.

I gasped and was jolted back to my cushion in our home.

"Ren," Sean said, opening his eyes. "Are you all right?"

"I hope so," I said. "But we'll see."

38

REQUEST FOR HELP

"What do you mean, you hope so?" Sean asked.

The doorbell rang. Sean peeked out the front window. "I think it's an emissary from the cathedral."

"What?" I asked.

Sean answered the door. "Come in, Dottie. What brings you to the west side of town?"

"I was born on the west side and I'm proud of the tenacity it gave me to live this long," she said, stepping into the library.

Dressed in a tailored navy blue pantsuit, she looked ready for business.

"Have a seat," Sean offered.

"I don't have time to sit," Dottie said with a shake of her head.

"Hi, Dottie," I said. "I thought we'd have this conversation tomorrow during your massage."

"What are you talking about?" she asked.

"Aren't you here to talk me into going to Rome? Because I am definitely not—"

"Oh, for heaven's sake, did they mess that up?" She flicked her hand. "I'm here because I need your help, *and* I am willing to pay for it."

"What are *you* talking about?" Sean asked.

"I need a miracle," she said. "My son Walt had a massive heart attack yesterday."

Sean gasped. "Oh, Dottie, we're so—"

She held her hand up. "After a lengthy surgery, they said he was stable and would be fine. Now, this morning, they can't get his breathing regulated. He's on a ventilator, and they tell me he won't make it through the day. I told the doctor he *would* make it." She pointed at me. "Because I have you!"

"Me?"

"Yes! If there's any time ripe for a miracle in my life, it's now, right now. I've had three of my four children die already. God has to leave me the one I have left. Walt needs to stay around to keep working with all our charities. I'm too old to keep going at this pace.

"I saw you raise the boy from the dead! I know you can do this. Besides, Walt's still alive, so that'll make this easier." She took a deep breath. Tears rolled down her face. I noticed the weariness of worry and the fatigue of being up all night in her eyes. I also felt the heaviness of her heart.

"I can't do miracles at will," I said softly.

"Please, hear me out," she said. "Give me your hand."

Using me to balance, she knelt. She bowed her head and placed her hands in a prayer position in front of her heart.

"Dottie, you—"

"I *know* God has been good to me. And now He sent me you. I know you're close to Him. I can feel it."

"We're all close to Him or Her or It . . . we just need to open our hearts," I said.

"I'm opening my heart right now and asking Him *and* you to give me one last wish. I want my son to outlive me. I will never ask for anything again, no matter how long I live." She looked up at me. "I know you don't care much about money, but if you give me this miracle, I'll make sure you're set for life. Help me, Ren."

I knelt.

"There's nothing I'd like more than to give you this miracle. But I can't make it happen like the stories of Jesus. The miracle you witnessed was a combination of a lot of energies coming together to create something none of us can explain. You were part of it!"

She dropped her head.

"Dottie, as unfair as it seems, this may be Walt's time to go. When we're challenged, we see if we have the grace to continue when all seems lost."

"I see . . . *and* . . . I understand," she whispered, "but there's always hope. Right?"

"Life would not be worth living without it," I said.

"Well, right now, I'm living in the hope that my son may have a chance if you touch him and we pray together. Watch this." She stood quickly, without assistance, and turned around in place. "No pain since the last massage. You coming into my life has divine intervention written all over it. I know there are no guarantees. But will you come with me anyway, just to be with him? Both of you? Please?"

"Of course, but I'm going as your friend and not a miracle worker. Where is Walt anyway?" I asked.

"Cleveland."

"When do you want to go?"

"Now!"

"Okay, well . . ." I looked over at Sean.

"Pack a few things and come out to the car. I'm thinking you can pull this off in a few days," she said, once again sounding like a CEO.

"Cleveland's a five-hour drive," I said.

"Only forty minutes by plane." She smiled and winked. "We're headed to the airport. I've hired a little jet. Pick up the pace, will you?"

"P.U.T.P.," I said. "Pick Up The Pace. It's what a bossy girlfriend of ours says when she wants us to hurry up."

We all exchanged smiles.

"I like her," Dottie said. "Bossy women get things done. P.U.T.P., boys! I'll be in the car." She walked out the door.

39

FLYING HIGH

Within thirty minutes, we were cleared through private security and sitting inside a two-engine jet on the runway. The three of us sat around a medium-sized table in captain's chairs, Dottie in the middle.

"I don't usually fly like this," she said as we waited for takeoff. "Walter and I are much too frugal for this kind of travel, but right now, I'm grateful to have the resources to do this. More divine intervention, as I see it."

"Gratitude is always good," I said.

Suddenly, a wave of doubt came to mind: *What if I can't help them?* Then, a voice, *this is not about you.*

"Boys, what would you like?" Dottie asked as the flight attendant approached shortly after takeoff.

"Water for me, please," I said.

Sean nodded.

"I'll have a limoncello straight up," Dottie said. "I tell everyone it's my secret to longevity."

"How about we sit quietly to hone our focus," I said after the flight attendant placed the drinks on the table.

"Of course, boys. Do what you do."

"*Mahamrityunjaya?*" Sean asked as we took our malas from around our necks.

"Well, that's not a Hail Mary," she said with a laugh.

"No," I said, "it's a Tantric mantra, said for healing the ill or honoring the recently passed."

"Lean toward the healing part, will you?" she asked. "You're gonna get him up and moving."

"Dottie, remember—"

"I know, no guarantees, *and* we're doing this together. I gotcha. I'll even join you in your prayer circle," she said.

Sean and I closed our eyes and silently began the mantra. I heard Dottie ruffle through her purse. I squinted and watched her pull out her beautiful, clear beaded rosary. She took a sip of her limoncello and settled back into her seat with *her* holy beads.

"Holy Mary, Mother of God," Dottie recited *her* mantra over and over.

Mary and I aren't adversaries, I recalled Athena's words. *Au contraire, we are one and the same.* With that, I found *myself* flowing back and forth from the healing Sanskrit mantra to Holy Mary, Mother of God.

"Boys, can you feel it?" Dottie whispered.

I opened my eyes fully to see a childlike radiance on her face.

"We're doing it." She reached once again into her purse, then placed a photo on the table. "This is Walt. He's a good guy. I can't begin to thank you enough for doing this."

We each returned to our chants within the sacred space we created for her son, but this time, I heard Dottie say on each bead, "Holy Mary, Mother of God, let him live."

Our magic carpet ride of healing intention soon landed and came to rest on the tarmac. There was a car waiting as we deplaned.

"I'm Mikayla," said the driver, a thirty-something woman with red hair wearing a black cap and jacket. "I'll escort you to the clinic. It's about a half-hour drive."

When we finally pulled up to the hospital, Sean said, "Damn, news crews."

Three white vans, painted with *Eyewitness News* and other logos, were surrounded by ten or so people—cameras and microphones ready.

"Maybe they're not here for us," I said.

"Of course, they're here for us," Dottie said. "I wasn't exactly discreet coming to your house. But screw the press! Driver—"

"It's all taken care of, Mrs. Gant. This place is no stranger to celebrities," Mikayla said. "I'm taking you to an entrance around the back. There are people waiting."

"Smart woman," Dottie said. "Besides, we'll have a bigger story for the press on our way out."

"Dottie," I squeezed her hand. "No matter what happens in there, this has to remain private. Promise me."

"Ren's right, we want our life back," Sean said. "This has to stay between us."

"I understand. This is not to be a spectacle. This is the new Vegas. What happens in Cleveland stays in Cleveland. Right, driver?"

"Absolutely, Mrs. Gant."

"I'll make sure the doctors know as well," Dottie added.

Several security guards approached as we pulled up to the rear entry. Dottie got out on her own, declining any assistance, and beelined for the door.

"Call me when you need me. I'll be here in the parking lot," the driver said to Sean, handing him a card.

"Thank you," Sean said.

We jogged to catch up with our spry friend.

A female security guard and a woman from the hospital administrative staff took us to the Intensive Care Unit. On the elevator, Dottie repeated, "Please let him live. Please let him live."

A man about six feet tall, with black hair and oval tortoise-framed glasses, wearing a white lab coat, stood waiting as the doors to the elevator opened.

"Mrs.—"

"Is he alive?" Dottie asked.

"Yes, but—"

"Take us to him. You *know* who I have with me." She pointed to me.

"We've done all we can. I don't expect him to make it much longer."

"That's what you told me this morning, and he's still breathing. Now, where is he? We have miracles to perform."

The doctor pushed a button on the wall to open the large security doors into the Intensive Care Unit. We walked down the hallway. He stopped and turned, blocking the door to Walt's room.

"Mrs. Gant, I don't want you to get your hopes up," he said. "I'm not sure what these men have told you they can do, but at your advanced age, I'm concerned about the effects the letdown will have on *your* health. We've done everything medically possible, and beyond all the medical issues I explained to you on the phone, your son doesn't have the will to live. He's given up. He's dying."

"Shut up! You don't know that! The last thing we need is a doubting Thomas. And . . . at my *advanced age*? Let me be the one to remind you, doctor, there's more to life and death than what science can do. I've seen it." She pointed to me. "I've seen *him* raise the dead. If you're as smart as you think you are, you'd pay him to touch all the terminally ill patients in this hospital. That might finally get you into the *New England Journal of Medicine*. Get out of the way." She moved him aside.

Dottie was right; we needed no doubt in our minds. We needed as much love as we could muster in these precious moments.

"He won't make it . . . ," the doctor said to Sean and me.

"Shhhhhhh," we both said as we crossed the threshold.

Dottie stood motionless two feet inside the door. The sight of her son hooked to all the machines *and* the palpable feeling of death in the room overwhelmed her. Two nurses stood near the bed.

"Is death here?" she asked me.

"He's close but not in the room," I said.

With that, her innate warrior goddess nature returned.

"Everybody out! Everyone except these two," she ordered, pointing to Sean and me. "Now, now, now . . . go. He's my son. I want to be with him. Go!"

"It's fine," the doctor said to the nurses, motioning for them to exit with him. "Let them do whatever it is they think they're going to do."

"And take that skepticism with you as well," Dottie said over her shoulder as she moved closer to Walt.

One nurse, a young, tall brunette wearing braces, stopped at the door. "Mrs. Gant, I'll need to come in and take his vitals occasionally, *but* I'll pray with you the whole time I do it. I want him to walk out of here. I've seen the videos. I believe!" The door closed.

Tears streamed down Dottie's face as she gazed at what seemed to be the mere shell of her son. Walt's eyes were closed, and he lay perfectly still. "This doesn't look good, boys. Now what?"

"Continue your Hail Mary mantra," I said, "and let go of any expectations. Just be with Walt. Place your left hand on your heart and your right hand on his."

She stepped close to the right side of his bed and placed her hands.

"Holy Mary, Mother of God, let him live. Holy Mary, Mother of God, let him live," she repeated several times.

"Let's send him love for his journey, no matter what it might be," I said.

Dottie kept her focus on her son. Sean stepped to the bottom of the bed and placed his hands on the tops of Walt's feet. I moved close to Walt's left side and held Abhaya mudra—the only sounds were the blips and beeps of the life support machines *and* our collective breathing.

We stood in this reverent silence for more than three hours.

"Darling," I finally heard Dottie whisper. I opened my eyes to see her leaning over Walt, close to his ear. "I know this is challenging, and you may feel discouraged, but get better, Walt, so you can give away more of our money. Give it *all* away if you want. My eyes are wide open. I see what's important. I hope you can, too. If you're tired and need to go, I understand. You won't disappoint me. *But* if you have the will, please, please pull it up and come back to life." She bent even closer to him. "If I could trade places with you, I would, I truly would. I love you."

Walt's mother kissed his cheek and returned to her upright position.

I closed my eyes and relished the love I felt in the room. When we'd first arrived, I felt Yama, the god of death, standing near, but I no longer felt his presence. The Gayatri mantra swelled in my heart.

Aum Bhur, Bhuvah, Swaha . . .

Soon, it passed through my lips, and I began to chant aloud. Sean joined me. Eventually, so did Dottie.

May the light of the Universe illuminate us and fill us with wisdom.

There was no concept of time. We chanted. We paused. We chanted.

The energy in the room gradually shifted, and I began to feel the connection I'd felt that Sunday on the Parkway.

"Excuse me, I'm sorry to interrupt. But I need to check his vitals again," the young nurse who'd promised prayers said, poking her head in the door. She'd returned several times throughout our time with Walt to check machines and collect numbers.

Now, the nurse walked over to Walt's side, took a small cloth from her smock, and gently wiped his face.

Veronica and all the nurturers are here today. Human kindness, no matter how small, is a miracle to behold.

"He'll be fine," Dottie said to the nurse.

The nurse looked over the many monitors, noted something on her tablet, then pulled a cell phone out of her pocket and dialed.

"I think you should come in here," the young nurse said into the phone.

The doctor and the other nurse entered within seconds. The young nurse handed the doctor her tablet with her notes.

"He's better," Dottie said as a statement, not a question.

"Mrs. Gant," the doctor said, "*something has* shifted. His vitals are much stronger now. Of course, we need to keep an eye on him. I still don't want you to get your hopes up just yet. It looks like, I mean . . ." He glanced at me, then down to the floor. "Well . . . it's not like he is going to get up and walk out of here today."

"Maybe not today," Dottie said, patting Walt's hand. "I asked the Blessed Virgin to let him live. I wasn't specific about how quickly I wanted his recovery. But he *will* walk out of this hospital. I know it here." She gestured to her heart. "There's more to the world than provable science." She looked up. "Doctor, do you have a rational explanation for the changes you see in him?"

"Well, uhm . . . Mrs. Gant, there's always a chance a patient may get better. The body is a miraculous vehicle. It's always striving for homeostasis, so yes, there are instances—"

"Excellent," she said, "that's what I wanted to hear. I want you to flush out all your scientific BS and *really* believe it *and* stick with it. What took place here today had nothing to do with the three of us being here.

There were no miracles." She continued her intense stare. "What's happening with Walter is all explainable in some medical jargon. Do you understand?" Dottie narrowed her eyes at the group.

"Of course," said the doctor. The nurses nodded.

"Now, please, give us a few more minutes alone with my son."

The three of them left. Dottie ran her hand across the top of Walt's head as if he were a little boy.

"There was a shift," she said, looking at Walt. "I felt threads of light coming from all three of us to him, into his heart. Even from that nurse when she was in the room. My *desire* for him to live turned into a *knowing* that he would. And you're right . . ." She looked at me and then Sean. "*We* did this. We did it together."

Tears welled in her eyes.

"All I can say is—thank you."

Sean and I stayed for several more hours, mostly sitting in silence. What do you talk about when you feel your prayers have been heard and answered by the divine?

At the first glimpse of sunrise over the horizon, Sean and I decided to go home. The miracles of moving vehicles and flying machines would have us back home in our nest within hours.

Dottie stayed with her son. She sat by his side with pure love and devotion and waited for the first glimpse of sunrise in his eyes.

40

THE EARTHEN MOUND

"If that was the lesson on attachment and aversion," Sean said as we settled into the jet, "it was much easier than the lesson on ego."

"We're not getting off that easy, facing two kleshas. I just know it," I said, leaning back in my seat.

We sat in silence for the rest of the flight, too tired and mentally foggy to process anything. Dottie's driver picked us up. Sean turned on the phone as we settled into the back seat of the car.

"Anything interesting?" I asked.

"There's a couple of texts. Carol's picking us up early tomorrow and Sara confirmed that there won't be any celebrity hunters on the retreat."

"How nice," I said with a sigh. "I can't wait."

Once we were in the house, being awake all night caught up with us.

"Let's get a couple of hours of sleep," Sean suggested, "I'll set an alarm so we don't sleep all day. We'll check in with Dottie and Walt a little later, too."

Within seconds of my head resting on the pillow, I found myself walking through a dense forest just after sunrise. The morning dew was heavy on the foliage and the air was cool and moist as it crossed my nostrils. Clothed only in jeans, a T-shirt, and gym shoes, I was chilled but not uncomfortable. Walking through this exquisite canopy of nature, my awareness spontaneously shifted from my breath to the sound of leaves crunching beneath my feet, and back to my breath, in a peaceful walking meditation.

After several minutes, I came face-to-face with a mound of earth four times my height. Its surface was wet and covered with florescent green moss. It wasn't part of some hillside. Rather, it stood alone, free from the surroundings, as if the earth had birthed it out of itself.

I knew walking around it and continuing wasn't an option. I had come here today, through this wooded area, to see it. I stood observing it and felt it observe me. I took a few steps closer. Now, I noticed, under some long-hanging moss, a four-foot-wide opening, an entryway into the Earth itself. I tried to see in, but it was the same impenetrable blackness as behind the medieval wooden door in the council chambers. I stepped closer, hoping to see something, but instead, I felt a magnetic pull radiating from the opening. I could resist its tug from where I stood, but I knew if I stepped any closer, I would be drawn inside.

Then I felt the magnetism increase, so I stepped back several feet. I had to step back again, and then again . . . until, from the top of my lungs, I yelled, "No! No, No, No! I am not going in. You can't make me. No, No, No!"

I shouted at the opening of the earthen mound as if it were a living thing because, like everything else in the cosmos, it was a creation of the feminine essence. Therefore, it is alive and contains consciousness.

One part of me wanted to be drawn into the warmth and comforting darkness of the Earth's Universal womb. But a lightning bolt of terror lit up another part of me.

What if I never return? Stay with what you know.

But to stay with what is safe suffocates the life force that is meant to change and grow.

The council says more lessons with the kleshas are coming; this may be an opportunity. But I've already gone through so many life-altering transformations, I'll just say no.

Out of frustration with this internal back and forth, I jumped up and down and stamped my feet like a five-year-old in a tantrum.

"No, No, No! I won't go! You can't make me. I said no. I mean it!" I let out one final sustained scream, "Noooooooooo . . ."

Then I stood still, staring at it. The only sound in the forest was my rapidly beating heart. After a few moments, my breath returned to an even inhale and exhale, and my heart rate slowed to normal. I stared at the hole, telepathically communicating with this mysterious opening.

Softly and under my breath, I said two words: "Not yet."

Jolted awake, I sat straight up in bed. *Not yet?* Why would I think I would ever voluntarily venture into that hole?

Sean stirred.

"Is it time to get up already?" he asked.

"Not yet!"

I lay back into the comfort of our bed and pulled the covers close. I slid my hand under his and whispered, *not yet?*

41

THE WAITING ROOM

Carol picked us up before sunrise on Friday. Her bright-red jeep was full of love and peace bumper stickers, and the headlight eyelashes matched her own. The street in front of our house was quiet, so getting into the car was easy. Sean climbed into the driver's seat, and I slid into the back. Because of our early departure, I waited to tell Sean about yesterday's dream until now.

"Do you boys ever have a normal day?" Carol asked. "I mean, gods and goddesses, cardinals, mystical owls, Cleveland, and now an opening in the Earth that's beckoning you in . . . whew!"

"This is the first I've heard about the seductive hole, and what do you mean, not yet?" Sean asked, looking at me in the rearview mirror. "If that invitation comes up again, don't go, okay? It feels ominous."

I nodded, even though I felt saying no would not be an option.

We pulled into the retreat center around seven.

"That was an easy drive," Sean said as we unloaded the car. "And we have two hours to settle in before Sara's opening session."

"I'm thrilled we're doing this," Carol said. "I've been looking forward to it all week."

"Welcome, and thank you for joining me," Sara said from her teacher's seat in front of the room. Sara, in her early seventies, was tall, slender, and stately.

Carol, Sean, and I sat shoulder-to-shoulder in the first row.

"This is a special group." She gestured to the twenty of us seated in front of her. "I know each of you personally, and I know your meditation practices. Many of you are advanced in your spiritual pursuit. *But* a label like *advanced* can suck you into the quicksand of ego where you sink quickly into your attachments and aversions."

I took a deep breath, feeling like she was talking directly to me.

"My invitation this weekend is to go back to the basics of your practice." She stood. "With that in mind, why meditate?"

"It's good for me and helps me relax," someone behind us said.

Carol raised her hand. "It keeps me sane."

"Excellent reasons," Sara said, "but don't forget the core intent of meditation is to keep us in touch with the feminine life force, our inner beloved we call Shakti. *She* exists in all things. On the macrocosm, she is found in the tides of the ocean and the magnetic lure emanating from the core of the Earth."

"Holy shit," Carol whispered as she squeezed my hand.

"On the microcosm, she is found in the pulse of our heart and the rhythm of our breath. For many in this room, all we need to do to stay in touch with *her* is close our eyes and connect to our breath. But no matter how consummate we may be in meditation, we're human, living in a modern world, so we have blocks and distractions. That's why no matter what level we may feel we are, we have to stay committed."

Sutra 1:13, discipline equals freedom.

Sara began to sway and move her hands as if conducting a celestial orchestra.

"Through meditation, we learn to dance with the Shakti-life force. We move effortlessly with the rhythm of who we are, and through the steadiness of our practice, we invite the feminine energy to dance through us."

She returned to her seat.

"Close your eyes," she instructed. "Slowly breathe in and out through the spaciousness of your heart. Set your intention for this weekend, perhaps to notice what hinders you from moving forward. Open yourself to an inner vision that is full of Shakti so you can see a clear path for your journey back to the source of love."

We sat breathing for several minutes.

"Open your eyes," Sara said.

When I looked at her, her authentic, divine self was beaming.

"Now, I invite you to go outside and surround yourself with the feminine energy of nature. Find a place to sit comfortably. Keep your intention in your heart and rediscover all the self-love that is available to you from the inner beloved. Stay with this practice until you hear the conch shell calling us to lunch. Make sure to take your journal to jot down any insights. After lunch, we'll reconvene here."

She placed her hands in prayer position and bowed. The group returned the gesture.

"Gents, I'll see you at lunch," Carol said. "I'm going to let the Universe take me where it will." Dressed in khaki shorts, a black T-shirt printed with *Love Wins* in two-inch letters across the chest, and fluorescent red gym shoes, she headed out of the room.

Sean and I walked along a path that led to a clearing. Through the trees, we could faintly see the back porch of our cabin.

"I think this is our meditation spot," I said.

"Absolutely not," Sean said.

"Why?"

He pointed thirty feet ahead of us.

I looked and swallowed, standing speechless.

"Doesn't that look like the earthen mound you described in the car this morning?" Sean asked.

I still had no words.

"That's what I thought," Sean said. "Let's go." He took my hand and turned from the mound.

"We have to stay here," I said.

"No, we don't."

"Come on. I don't feel any magnetic pull, do you?"

"No, but—"

"We don't need to get close, but seeing this mound is no accident."

"Nothing ever is, and my newfound intuition is not liking this," he said. "Promise me you won't get any closer, and for goddess's sake, don't change *not yet* into *okay now*?"

"I promise you, and I mean it."

We took our seats about ten feet apart, facing the mound, and settled into our meditation postures. We closed our eyes and did one om together.

My inner awareness quickly dropped into my spiritual heart center. I heard a whisper: *Pay attention.*

My internal eyes fluttered open.

Sean and I were in an unfamiliar, starkly lit room, seated in padded vinyl sled chairs, holding hands. I looked around—to our left was a set of institutional-looking double doors. There were no windows, but several eleven-inch by seventeen-inch framed photographs of white wispy clouds floating in pale blue skies hung on the beige walls. On a small side table, a few magazines were laid out: *Yoga Journal, Mountain Astrologer,* and *Tricycle.*

"Where are we?" I asked.

"We're waiting to go in and make our selections," Sean said, reaching for a magazine.

"I thought we were meditating on Sara's retreat."

"Keep meditating while we wait. You're going to need to be centered."

"Centered for what?"

"For this meeting with your council. We're going to talk about our next incarnation. We'll decide what kind of issues and challenges we want to face that will take us to the next level of our personal soul evolution."

"We're going into the council to pick the circumstances for our next incarnation?"

"Yep. We can even modify our current path if we want."

He lifted the magazine he was reading toward me. "Have you read this issue of *Mountain Astrologer* on how to use astrology to realize one's potential?"

"Don't distract me," I said, shifting to face him. "Don't you usually pick the next incarnation when you're in between lifetimes? Are we dead?"

"We're not dead, Ren." Sean chuckled. "From what I understand, this selection takes place throughout our life—in dreams and deep states of concentration. It's a process, like the evolution of consciousness."

"What does the council have to do with this?" I asked.

"We scheduled this appointment to keep everyone in the loop."

I sat back in exasperation. *Why was this making me nervous?*

"Because everything makes you nervous," Sean said smiling, still looking at the magazine.

"What? You just answered my thought. I didn't say anything out loud."

"Um, hmm," he said.

Deciding what's vital to the personal evolution of our soul is a big deal.

"Yes, but remember you're never alone in this process. You're always connected."

I turned to see a woman seated behind an L-shaped white laminate reception desk. She wore a black short-sleeved top with a white ring collar, a white and black paisley scarf tied around her neck, and a silver name badge pinned to the left side of her blouse.

"The Universe provides tools and clues, like synchronicity," she said, "but you have to be brave enough to see them." She smiled and tilted her head.

"Once again, I only thought that," I said. "Who are you anyway?"

"I'm Sharon, the cosmic receptionist."

"Well, Sharon, the cosmic receptionist, please get out of my head. I have enough mind reading with my council."

The thirty-something receptionist with fuchsia hair continued to smile. Sean picked up a different magazine.

"Hey, speaking of synchronicity," Sean said, "this article on the karmic complexity of dealing with the kleshas fits right in. It says we have to deal with the kleshas of *Raga* and *Dvesha*, attachment and aversion, and let go of everything to move forward to the deepest levels of love."

"Well, we're supposed to be meditating on what blocks us from finding self-love," I said, "and that article sounds like a definite clue to me."

He gave my hand a squeeze.

"Remind me," Sharon interjected, "which one of you requested some extended alone time in the *Chonyid Bardo* of the Peaceful Deities between incarnations?"

"Alone time in a visionary state of tranquility?" I asked. "I didn't even know you could request something like that." I looked to Sean. "Did you?"

His hand slipped from mine. His eyes moved to the floor.

"Okay, I guess you did," I said, "this is really pushing my abandonment buttons. Were you going to tell me before I started making *my* selections?"

"I thought a little break would be nice, that's all," Sean said. "The last few weeks have been exhausting, and just a few days ago I thought I might have to finish *this* incarnation alone, with you leaving me for the church."

A huge wave of understanding and compassion washed over me.

"I know," I said, "you've been through a lot." I placed my hand on top of his.

"A break would be good for you. You deserve time in a state of perfect knowledge. Above everything else, I want you to be happy. I mean it, Sean, with my whole heart and soul. Take a break."

He looked up with a huge Cheshire smile.

"Good man, Reno, you just dropped a bit of clinging. That's a very good sign when working with attachment and aversion. It means *Raga* and *Dvesha* don't have a *complete* grip on your heart."

I looked over at Sharon, who was also grinning ear to ear.

"Is this a trick? Are you two testing me? Do you know something I don't?"

"You went with deep love and compassion," Sean said, "the aspects of true Venus in Pisces Oneness, instead of the individual longings of the emotional Moon. Excellent, bud." He gave me a thumbs-up.

I took a deep breath and let it out with a sigh.

"So, Ren, let's talk about this. What do *you* want from the next go-round on Earth?"

"I want it to be just like this one. I want to do it again . . . with you, if you'll have me."

"I'm with you," Sean said, "I'm going to request another go-round just like this one."

"Remember years ago," I said, "when we decided to dive deep into meditation so we could find each other faster next time?"

"That's *Raga*," he said, shaking his head.

An intense constriction gripped my heart. I closed my eyes to deal with the pain. One word in capital letters appeared in my mind's eye.

ATTACHMENT

Suddenly, my heart felt it would burst from grief as I was overwhelmed by a flood of goodbyes Sean and I had experienced over many lifetimes.

"Oh my," I said, "I'm not consistent in going with deep compassion over my desires, am I? Does this mean I won't get what I request?"

"Klesha number three, *Raga*, and number four, *Dvesha*," Sharon chimed in. "There's a problem when your attachments and aversions become an obsession, and you can't let go."

"I got it, Sharon," I said. *She's getting on my nerves.* Probably because what she said was true. Sitting in this brightly lit celestial waiting room, I felt I was the only one in the dark.

"Sean, what if I'm so attached to you that I don't get—"

"You get a say in this," he said, putting his hand on my shoulder.

"I wish I could shake this self-doubt once and for all."

"So do I," Sean said, "along with facing the kleshas, it's one of the issues you came in to transform this time around."

"If you know so much, tell me, what's going on? What's in store for me the next time?"

Sean took a deep breath. "*Raga* and *Dvesha*, you're not going to deal with them next time. You're going to deal with them *now!*"

Now, I took a deep breath.

"The council's bringing in some help from the past," he said. "You have to deal with some regrets and . . . I don't know all the details, but if you want us to remain together, Ren, you have to drop it all right now!"

"Drop my attachments and aversions?" I asked.

"Yes, and forgive yourself for . . . again, I don't know what but some guilt that blocks you from your inner beloved. Do you know what I'm talking about? Because I'm not sure."

I swallowed. My breath was shallow.

"I do know, and I'm scared. What if I can't—"

"No self-doubt!" he said sternly. "Keep Athena and every other warrior goddess close. If fear wins, we lose! You have the will, the courage, and *definitely* the love to live fully, with *or* without me!"

"Without you?" I stood.

"Know it in your heart. Change *Raga* into the desire for true, unconditional love. Go with love. You're a good person. You've never hurt anyone, so—"

"Stop, stop! You don't know everything about me."

"What don't I know?"

"Never mind, just tell me, what's about to happen? Tell me!"

I verged on panic.

Sean stood, placed his hands on my shoulders, and gently squeezed.

"I'm not exactly sure. I'm just getting bits and pieces, but it's going to challenge both of us. Remember, wherever you end up . . . I love you deeply."

I began to cry.

"The council's ready for you," the cosmic receptionist said, gesturing toward her right. The institutional double doors had transformed into the familiar stainless-steel chamber entry.

Sean's hands were still on my shoulders as he stared into my eyes.

"Remember, I love you deeply but more importantly, remember to deeply love yourself. *Love you*, Ren! Love your divine spark. Keep doing your practices to keep the feminine close. Forgive yourself and face your attachments. I know that's the key. Hold the key in your heart. I will be with you—just breathe me in. I'm always right here." He touched my chest.

My mind was numb.

We turned, held hands, and took a few steps.

"This is our first time here together," I said.

"Um-hm," he said with a steady gaze on the open chamber doors, "keep that key close, so this isn't the last."

"Okay."

"I'll love and support you no matter what," Sean said, squeezing my hand firmly. "I promise."

"I'm sorry about the whole church thing—"

"Drop it; it'll only get in the way," he said. "I *know* you're sorry on a soul level."

"Excuse me," Sharon said now behind us, "the members just sent a message that they want to see you one at a time."

"But—," I said.

"There's no use protesting," Sean said, continuing to squeeze my hand. "It's part of the plan. Go on in, lover."

A wave of surrender washed over me. Our hands slid apart. I walked over the threshold of the chamber doors alone.

"This is the start of it," he said, projecting his voice. "Hold tight to that key—love and forgive yourself."

I turned for one last look, but the doors slammed shut.

It's not the past or future we are to look upon, I thought, but as yoga teaches, we are to be fully present in the moment.

I placed my hands into Abhaya mudra, pressing my left hand firmly into my heart center to remember Sean's key. Softly, I repeated a new mantra: *I love myself, I forgive myself, and I can face my attachments.*

Goddess, I hope I believe this in my heart of hearts. I need to believe it now more than ever.

42

ANOTHER DAY ON
THE BIG BLUE BALL

My eyes opened onto the earthen mound, yet the vision of the doors slamming shut lingered. I still had a sinking feeling in the pit of my stomach. Would I ever see Sean again? I looked over to see him sitting in meditation and felt a weight lift. I got up and walked over to him.

"Hey," I said as I touched him on the shoulder.

"Oh, wow," Sean said, opening his eyes and shaking his head. "I had the weirdest experience. I've never had a meditation like it. I thought I was going to meet your council and see what goes on, but the doors slammed shut behind you, and I was left alone in some bizarre waiting room."

"*What?*"

"Yeah, we were waiting to talk to your council about our next incarnation and—"

"There was a female receptionist named Sharon," I said, "and you were reading *Mountain Astrologer*—"

Sean stood and nodded. "About realizing your potential through astrology and dealing with the kleshas . . . and I could read your mind."

"Yep, you and the cosmic receptionist both did it. It was annoying."

"Could we have had the same experience inside a meditation?"

"Sure seems like it."

"This is another rung up on the freakiness ladder," Sean said.

"What about the warnings about *Raga* and *Dvesha*?" I asked. "There was a foreboding sense of separation."

Sean reached for my hand. "That would never happen."

"How can you be sure?"

"Because I'm committed to *us*!" he said.

"So am I. I mean it. I won't let *anything* come between us ever again."

Sean began to pace. "I told you we shouldn't sit near this . . . thing." Then he stood so close our noses almost touched. "I don't know why I need to say this . . . but no matter where you go, I'll find you."

"Buddy, I'm not going anywhere," I said.

"Something's percolating. In *my* meditation, I gave you a key to keep in your heart."

"Yes, I know." Tears filled my eyes.

"Hold on to that key, get rid of self-doubt, love yourself, do your practices . . . do it for both of us."

"Okay, buddy, okay! This is *really* weird!" I said.

"How did your meditation end?" Sean asked.

"After the doors slammed shut, I turned toward the council with my hands in Abhaya mudra and repeated, *I love myself, I forgive myself, and I can face my attachments.*"

"Then you didn't hear me beating on the doors, screaming, *Don't go, please don't go.*" Tears began to roll down his face.

I wrapped my arms around him.

"It's just a meditation, Sean."

My words were meant to comfort us, but holding him tight, I *knew* both of us felt in our heart of hearts there could soon be more than a set of shiny stainless-steel doors separating us.

"Does anyone want to share something from this morning's exercise?" Sara asked, opening our afternoon session.

Sean's was the first hand up. "I've had some . . . uhm . . . mystical things happen lately, then during this exercise, Ren and I had the same experience within our meditation. I'm thinking that's unusual, right?"

"How similar were they?" Sara asked, shifting in her chair.

"To every detail, except the very end."

"That *is* unusual," she said, now leaning forward. "For two people to share such an experience, this could point to a karmic lesson that needs to be addressed together."

"I'm not usually the nervous one, Sara," Sean said, "but this sounds like—"

"*You* and Ren are on an accelerated path. This could simply be the next step," she said. "Be patient and attentive. Let's have breakfast tomorrow. That will give *me* an opportunity to meditate on it. You can fill me in on all the details then, but if anything happens before, let me know right away."

"Like what, Sara?" I asked.

"Ren," she said calmly, "everything's fine. Keep breathing and stay in the spaciousness of your heart."

Sara then expertly guided the class away from the discussion of our *unusual* experience. Neither Sean nor I closed our eyes during any of the remaining group meditations.

Over dinner, we filled Carol in on our experience and shared our fears that something, somehow, was going to separate us. Afterward, the three of us retired to our cabin.

"Hey, you two," Carol said, standing in the doorway of her bedroom, "I feel your tension, but you know Sara will explain it, and everything will be fine tomorrow. It's not like one of you is just gonna disappear!"

She gave us each a kiss on the cheek and closed her door.

In an effort to regain our confidence, we sat for a twenty-minute closed-eyed meditation before climbing into bed. But every few moments, we caught each other looking to make sure the other was still there.

We lay down, rolled to the middle of the bed, and kissed.

"Always," Sean said.

"Forever," I said.

We held hands.

"Buddy?"

"Yeah, Reno?"

"I look forward to tomorrow and another day with you on the big blue ball."

"Me too, bud."

One deep breath and I felt myself slip from this world to the other . . .

43

LIFE WITHOUT

I stood with my hands in Abhaya mudra, the familiar stainless-steel doors behind me. I once again faced the council of ten.

"We know you encountered the earthen mound," said Venus.

"Yes, and while sitting near it, Sean and I had the same weird meditation."

"Refusing the Earth's invitation in your dream led to the need for the mutual experience," she explained. "The mound is offering you both an opportunity to clear karmic residue specific to *Raga* and *Dvesha*. We are pleased you said *not yet*, which denotes your willingness to eventually venture in."

"Look, goddess, I know what I said, but I'm not ready—"

Venus placed her hand on her heart, which evoked an unseen force that rendered me speechless.

"Willingness is an important part of spiritual involution," she said. "It's time you *willingly* move through the gateway the mound offers." Her intonation had its usual hypnotic allure. She lowered her hand, and I was again able to speak.

"Is this opportunity really all about our *next* incarnation?"

"Actually, you have things to redress within *this* lifetime first," Athena now spoke. "There are obstacles you must both face to clear the path to the future." Her gentle words slowed my breathing, and a feeling of reassurance descended. "Soon, you'll again be at the earthen entrance into infinity. There will be a note. Contemplate it and let it unfold. Along with your practices, draw on the patience of Saturn . . ."

I looked at the god, and he bowed his head.

Athena continued. "*And* the power of the feminine, to unearth the deeper meaning of your past and the current kleshas you are to face."

"You're cloaking something in poetic camouflage," I said. "What if *this* lesson is beyond me?"

"No lesson is beyond you," Athena said, "just remember to fill yourself with love rather than fear and keep close all you've cultivated through your years of practice."

I sighed and sat down in my chair.

"Oh, come on, my celestial counterparts," said a man near the center of the table who, until now, had not said a word. He stood, taking a stance like an emperor addressing the Roman senate. He was muscular, with a curly light-brown beard and dazzling blue eyes. He held a lightning bolt in his right hand. "I cannot remain silent any longer." His voice resonated with a bass tone, and he now gestured like a Shakespearean actor. "You're acting like this is his sepulchre when, in reality, our ward is about to begin an adventure to expand his mind and usher in a profound understanding of what human life is and *all* that it can be."

"Jupiter!" I said, applauding at his over-the-top performance. He took a full melodramatic bow as he smiled from ear to ear. "For the god of expansion, adventure, and high drama, you've been uncharacteristically quiet, sir. You and Pluto are the only council members I've not heard from."

"We speak in our due time, right, Pluto?" Jupiter said, looking at a man with penetrating green eyes, straight, shoulder-length dark hair, and prominent cheekbones seated next to Venus.

"My colleague is the consummate non-verbal communicator, but I like words." Jupiter raised his lightning bolt overhead and winked. "In *my humble* opinion," he said, taking another full, melodramatic bow from the waist, "you're ready! Yes, yes, I know Saturn rules, la, la, la . . . and

Venus is your co-chair, more la, la, la . . ." He glanced at both of them before continuing. "But *I* rule your Sagittarius moon—therefore, I know you will find what's coming emotionally exciting! And . . ." His eyes widened as he pointed at me, ". . . you get to teach!"

"Teach!" I said.

"Yes, besides letting go of some petty regrets you might have," he said with a wave of his hand, "another part of your lesson takes place in my realm of teaching and higher learning, so love where you are going and do what you do best—teach and do it well. You, my dear friend . . ." His voice had risen to a thunderous boom, and his hands gestured overhead. ". . . are about to embark on—"

"Wait one moment," Saturn demanded. It was the stoic tone I heard so often in my head and heart. "I doubt very much you'll approach what's coming in the *Indiana Jones* style that Jupiter suggests. Let me remind you this journey is happening for a reason. Make sure to experience everything down to the depths of your physical cells and into the memories of your past lives. You are about to dance with the sister kleshas of *Raga* and *Dvesha*."

"Attachment and aversion, I know, I know, but why?"

"You faced ego to unbury the feminine, especially in your own heart. Now, you have the opportunity to climb higher and upward like the spiritual mountain goat. This is the next phase. You've been preparing for this," Saturn said.

"If I've been preparing, sir, why am I nervous? Why can't I face this like an adventure and jump at it as Jupiter suggests?"

"It's not your style," he deadpanned.

There were chuckles.

"Well . . . ," I said, with a sigh.

"It's not a flaw, Ren," Saturn said, "but with me overseeing most of these proceedings, surrendering into ecstatic dance scares you."

"The apple doesn't fall far from the tree," I replied. Saturn cleared his throat. "You are me, and I am you, Lord Saturn. Does it not scare us both to dance like Jupiter?" I began to feel more confident.

"Touché," he said with a rare hint of a smile, "but trust me, you're as ready as you'll ever be. Breathe deep, keep your heart open, and dance as you will. We are all with you. Hold the key your beloved gave, close."

"Thank you," I said, acknowledging him and then the entire council.

With a downward sweep of Saturn's hand, my eyes closed. In one blink, I was back outside, only inches from the entrance of the earthen mound. Within reach, balanced on the root of a plant, was the note Athena mentioned. The parchment paper affixed with a wax stamp looked and felt to be from another century. The seal was embossed with a stylized monogram—RD.

My initials, I thought.

Raga and Dvesha, said a voice inside.

Have *Raga* and *Dvesha* been so important to my evolution that my name has held a clue for me my entire life?

Then, as if someone flicked a switch, I felt the pulsating, magnetic pull from the hole. I backed up several feet.

Ren, if the invitation comes up again, please don't go. Was Sean tapping into his fears or his intuition? I wondered.

I opened the antique envelope and unfolded the parchment. The text was illegible, but as I stared at the page, I started to make sense of the Old English script—something I was familiar with from my graduate studies. The ability to read the fifteenth-century cursive came back . . . *or* was it Pada Three once again seeping into my life as needed?

Welcome to your other life, RD,

All humans forever move back and forth between the role of the teacher and the student. Teacher, it is time to go back to school to learn lessons of the soul, RD, and reconcile the injuries of the heart.

Many paths are possible. You are always surrounded by the many, and never alone. Choosing *loneliness* will kill your spirit. Experiencing *aloneness* will set you free.

Love yourself, forgive yourself, and face R&D.

Always and forever

Although I was unclear of its meaning, I placed the note on my heart and then slipped it into my pocket. Sean's key and *always* and *forever*, both written at the close, were comforting.

"*Come inside.*"

"Who said that?" I held my breath.

"*Come inside!*"

This time the words were louder and unmistakably coming from the earth itself.

Come inside, come inside, come inside, come inside, come inside.

I was pulled several steps toward the dark opening of the earthen mound as the magnetic force grew stronger. I leaned back, but I was drawn closer and closer. I felt fear *but* also excitement.

And then . . .

Allow the Magnetic Radiance of Oneness to envelop you, a soothing voice inside me said, *let go.*

With my next exhale, I surrendered. What felt like the winds of a cyclone sucked me over the threshold and thrust me into solid blackness. I was suspended, levitating in a state of weightlessness, hovering in an eerie silence.

Then, off in the distance, I heard soft, tranquil violins. The lullaby relaxed me in my suspended state. Suddenly, the volume on the celestial stereo increased, and thousands of violins played at such a fevered pitch that the vibratory force of the frantic stringed instruments propelled me horizontally, at a superhuman speed, into the depths of the Earth. Cool, brisk air whisked over my body as the sound pushed me deeper and deeper through the darkness at what felt like the speed of light.

I was hurtling back, but back to what, I had no idea. Then . . . *Whoooosh!* I slowed to a standstill. Except for my heavy breathing and pounding heart, all was silent. Then, I felt butterflies of anticipation in my solar plexus. I looked toward my feet to see just a sliver of light, which began to grow as a curtain or mystical veil began to rise. I followed its ascent up into the ethers, then looked straight out in front of me.

More than a hundred people were seated in an amphitheater, silent and staring at me.

"Professor Devlin," said a petite woman in her midtwenties, seated in the front row, "this would be a good place to stop. You're already five minutes over."

"No, no . . . let him finish, Paulette," someone shouted. "We have to know how it ends. Finish the story!"

I was standing at a podium in a large classroom in McMicken Hall at the University of Cincinnati. *How?*

"Next time, my friends," I said. *Why did I just say that?* "Just like a good mini-series, I need to keep you coming back for more. Have a great day."

I gave myself a light slap on the face and shook my head as the students moved out of the room.

What has my council done?

"Dr. D, I'll have these quizzes graded by the end of the week," said the young woman, walking up to the podium.

"That would be great, Paulette, but give me a handful," I said.

I know this woman. How?

"I can do them. I know you still have to tackle a lot of research for your new book."

A new book? Quizzes? My former university?

"I'd like to grade ten or fifteen to see if they're grasping the material," I said, hoping they'd give me clues to what I was teaching.

"Sure," she said, handing me a small stack off the top, "but they're getting the material, Doc. You have them in the palm of your hand, as usual." She smiled. "Are you going back to your office?"

"Probably." I wonder where my office is.

"May I walk with you? I'd like to borrow a couple of books if that's okay."

"Yes, of course," I said, still feeling out of place in my body.

"I respect you so much," Paulette said as she led the way. "I mean, there aren't many highly credentialed historical experts who also write popular historical fiction. I'd love to do that too."

"Well, then I'm sure you will," I said, starting to put some of the clues together: history, fiction, all things on my path in the 1980s.

We climbed a flight of stairs.

The fog lifted a little when I saw "Dr. Reynolds Devlin" written on a familiar door. This was my former history mentor's office when I was a student. *Is it now mine?* Paulette unlocked the door with a key, and we walked inside. Bookcases filled one wall, two large windows were opposite the door, and a large dark wooden desk with a clunky push-button phone faced the bookshelves. Paulette went over to the books, and I walked behind the desk, hoping for more clues.

There was a small piece of paper taped to the phone.

Dr. D, your wife wants you to call her.

MY WIFE! I held my breath.

"Paulette?"

"Yes?" She pulled a book from the shelf and turned toward me.

"This note says my wife called. I don't—" I stopped and blinked slowly, hoping to compose myself.

"Yeah, sorry, I meant to tell you before you went into lecture. Lisa said it's nothing urgent, but she wants you to call before you leave campus. She may need you to pick up Josh."

"Josh?"

"Your star athlete son may need a ride home from practice." She smiled.

Wife? Lisa? Son?

I grabbed the edge of the desk with both hands and felt the blood drain from my head.

"Are you all right? Dr. D?"

"I need to sit down."

"If you have other things going on, I can pick up Josh for you," she said.

I was on the verge of hyperventilating. Josh was my brother's son, not mine. I tried to slow my breath.

"Will you get me some water? I feel lightheaded."

"Of course. I'll be right back."

As she stepped from the bookshelves, I saw it. I got up slowly, walked to the middle shelf, and picked up the framed photo. Three familiar faces stared back: a younger me, with my arm around my former girlfriend, Lisa, and my nephew, Joshua, looking about nine years old. Somehow, they were now my wife and son? How? What is this? *Raga* and *Dvesha*? Where was Sean?

"Here's some water, Doc." Paulette held out the glass to me, a look of concern on her face.

I gulped it.

"Paulette, did you ever meet my brother and his wife?" I asked, dreading the answer.

"No, Dr. D, but I bet they were great people. Josh is such a fantastic kid," she said, placing her hand on my shoulder.

I turned toward the bookshelves and began to cry.

"Can I do anything for you?" she asked. "You don't seem yourself right now."

"I'm *not* myself," I said. "Go on home. I'll see you tomorrow."

Transfixed on the photo, I heard Paulette pick up her book bag and close the door behind her. I sobbed. I sobbed ancient tears for my brother and his wife, for my nephew who was now my son, for Lisa, and for Sean.

This existence could have been, but . . .

Why was I here? And where was Sean? *Oh, dear goddess, will I ever see him again?*

44

SEAN

"Ren," Sean whispered from his side of the bed, "remember we're having breakfast with Sara this morning."

Sean could tell by Ren's breathing that the love of his life was still fast asleep. Sean went out to the kitchen to prepare some hot lemon water. Carol had left a sticky note on the fridge.

Doing a pre-dawn walking meditation. Xoxox, Carol

Sean moved to the back deck of the house, lit a couple of tea lights and incense, and then went back to rouse Ren.

"Reno. Hey, sleepy boy." Sean said, sticking his head into the bedroom, "it's time to start another day on the big blue ball."

No movement.

Sean approached the bed. Ren's breath was slow and deep. After sleeping beside Ren for more than thirty years and sitting next to him in meditation a thousand times, Sean immediately recognized this meditative breath. Ren looked so peaceful with his body emulating a perfect *savasana* form—lying on his back, his arms long by his sides, legs extended.

Sean sat on the edge of the bed and placed his hand on Ren's heart. Ren's breath deepened at the touch.

"Ren?" Sean said. There was no reaction.

Sean got on his knees, slid one hand under Ren's neck and the other under his lower back, and gently rocked him.

"Buddy," Sean whispered in his ear, "are you all right?"

He didn't seem distressed, but something *was not* right.

Sean heard the back door close. "Carol!" he yelled out. "Go get Sara."

"What's going on?" she asked from the threshold of the bedroom.

"I don't know. His breathing is fine, but I can't wake him. It's as if he's in a deep meditation. Deeper than I've ever seen."

"What do you mean? I don't underst—?"

"Stay calm and get Sara. If this has anything to do with meditation, she'll know what to do."

Carol bolted out the door.

"I know it's scary," Sara said, "but judging by his rhythmic breathing and peaceful state, this looks like a meditation coma. It's a deep state sometimes used to work on intense issues."

"How long can it last?" Sean asked.

"From my personal experience, usually a few hours, but sometimes several days. It depends on the intensity of the issues."

"How can he survive like this for days?" Carol asked.

"His heart rate and metabolism have slowed to a minimum, so right now, it takes very little to keep him going. He could actually stay in this state for weeks without any damage to his body," Sara explained.

"Should I call the doctor? Take him to the hospital?" Sean asked.

"Not yet. Trust me, they wouldn't know what to do with him, and the last thing he needs is to be put on lots of drugs that won't help. I'll come back during every break, but in the meantime, keep his surroundings peaceful and pick a mantra to chant. It'll help him, *and* it'll keep you two calm."

"I should've insisted on going with him to see his council yesterday,"

Sean said, "but for some reason, I hesitated. After the doors slammed shut, I couldn't open them. I tried."

"Sean," Sara said, "remember the council is Ren's, not yours. Some things must be done alone. I'm not saying this to make you feel better, but you weren't meant to go with him. Do you remember anything from that meditation that might be a clue to what he's working on?"

"The main theme was *Raga* and *Dvesha*. I sensed these were the issues his council wanted to address. I also gave him a verbal key to put in his heart and keep close."

"Can you share that?" Sara asked.

"I told him to love himself, forgive himself, and face his attachments."

"Hmmm . . . that's significant for sure," she said. "Start a mantra, and every once in a while, whisper that key phrase in his ear. You two are going to hold space for him, but remember to take breaks, eat, drink plenty of water, and even go outside once in a while."

"Is it okay to touch him? I rocked him earlier, and it felt good."

"Absolutely. It'll be good for all of you. I'll be back, but come get me if anything unusual happens."

"More unusual than having the love of my life in a meditation coma?" Sean asked.

"Keep breathing, you two," Sara said as she left.

Sean sat next to the bed and held Ren's left hand. Carol crawled onto the bed and held Ren's right hand.

"This is going to work out fine," Carol said. "We both trust Sara and know Ren's working on lots of intense stuff. Raising the kid from the dead was just the beginning. He's going to be okay, no matter how this goes."

"No matter how it goes . ." Sean said in a hushed tone.

They started softly chanting the Gayatri mantra.

Aum Bhur, Bhuvah, Swaha . . .

Every few rounds, Sean spoke in Ren's ear, "Always and forever."

After a few more repetitions, he whispered, "Love yourself, forgive yourself, and face your attachments."

Then, after several more, Sean sighed. "Come back to me, Ren. Come home."

45

DR. DEVLIN

I was physically shaking. I made my way over to the desk and sat down. I closed my eyes to block out a reality I did not understand *or* want. *This won't last long.* I'd figure out what the council needed me to learn about *Raga* and *Dvesha*, and then I'd open my eyes and be back in my life with Sean.

I deepened my breath and envisioned bringing the inhale in from my crown chakra and letting it travel down the front of my spine's energetic channel, the *Sushumna Nadi*. As I exhaled, the breath traveled up the back of my spine, creating an energetic massage.

What if this is your new reality? said the saboteur voice of my mind.

I sat up straight, re-focused, and began again. I used my breath to create space between me and these thoughts.

This is so close to what could have been. That's why this scares you. Admit it, Dr. Devlin.

Negativity infiltrated my mind.

Once again, I focused on the spinal breath, inhale down, exhale up. The thoughts began to float away like clouds into the open sky. *I know how to do this.*

For a few moments, I calmed myself with my breath. My heart rate slowed. Then, my mind got hooked on the sounds of students in the hall and outside the window, reminding me I was still in this nightmare reality.

Breathe, go deep.

I opened my eyes slightly and saw the photo of my *new family* staring at me. Anxiety re-entered my body.

I'll try something different, I thought. I started to breathe in and out of my heart center. This technique was always more visceral for me. I attempted to open myself up to a sense of gratitude for this experience, even if I didn't understand it. Continuing the gratitude heart breath for about twenty minutes, I sat in the internal emptiness that contains everything and tapped into a deep, soothing solitude where I could access my inner guides.

You're a fake.

My body began to shake.

You know you abandoned them both. Did you think your past actions would just go away? Wrong! It's called Karma.

My ego mind had reared its ugly head.

Come inside . . . Come inside . . . I heard a faint voice in my heart say.

"Take me back to Sean." I whispered.

Not yet, my heart said softly.

Never, the ego said loudly.

My breath became shallow.

Allow the Magnetic Radiance of Oneness to envelop you. Let go, my heart whispered.

"Argh . . . I am letting go!" I screamed. "I'm tired of being told to let go. I can't let go any more than I already have. Take me home. Now!"

I slammed my fist on the desk. A deep sense of loneliness descended. Instantly, the heart voice vanished. Its absence became its presence.

"Where are my guides now? Have you abandoned me? What about 'You're never alone'?" I recognized, yet could not control, the sharp edge of defiance in my voice. I slid deeper into the desperate void of loneliness.

"What is this? My new reality?"

Silence.

I opened my eyes and stood.

"Saturn, don't leave me in this reality. Life without Sean is worse than death. Don't let me die here." I grabbed my chest.

Silence.

"I told you this would be beyond me. I failed. Wake me up."

My anger was mixed with tears *and* fear.

I looked at the ceiling of the office and felt it closing down on me. Shaking my fist, I screamed, "Venus, Athena, the Moon, I did not forget *you*, do not forget *me!*"

The phone rang. I grabbed it, expecting one of the three to be on the other end.

"Hi, Dr. Devlin," said an unexpected yet familiar female voice. "This is your fabulous wife, wondering why you haven't called as requested."

Even with all my angst, I recognized Lisa's voice and humor. It was momentarily soothing. More tears welled in my eyes.

"Ren, are you there?"

"Lis, I'm having one of the strangest days of my life."

"Strange to an Aquarian is extremely relative," she said. "Is the pressure of the new book getting to you? Promising two so close together is a lot for anyone, even you, Dr. Fantastic," she said with a chuckle.

Could this woman, who was one of the least judgmental humans I have ever known, be answering my plea to the goddesses?

"Where's Josh?" I asked.

"He's with one of his friends and decided to spend the night."

"Great, how about you meet me at Highland Coffee House in a few minutes? I'll head that way now."

"An afternoon date with a doctor? How can I refuse? See you shortly."

I grabbed my jacket and what I presumed was my briefcase and headed out the door. Moments later, I stepped into the coffee house where I had spent many hours during graduate school, immersed in its quirky beatnik atmosphere and surrounded by Bohemian-Uranian types who came here to drink espresso and express their eclectic individuality. I took a seat at the front window table, where Sean and I had sat only weeks ago. The love seat and mismatched bistro chairs were the same, just much newer now.

What was I going to do? I felt I needed to be honest and tell Lisa everything. I hoped she could tap into the wild and unpredictable energies of her Uranus-ruled Aquarian Sun.

The bells on the door signaled her arrival. It was good to see her, even under these bizarre circumstances. Her wavy champagne-blond hair was perfectly coiffed, and her skin was smooth and creamy white. She wore high-waisted navy jeans with an oversized powder-blue blouse belted to accent her size zero waist. The light-blue top set off the color of her stunning aquamarine eyes. She looked exactly as she did when we dated in the eighties. I guess I did, too, I thought. I reached up and felt my full head of hair.

Well, there's at least one thing in favor of reverse time travel.

I stood.

"Well, Dr. D, this is unusual," she said, smiling. "I'm rarely invited to this den of scholarly decadence."

I kissed her on the cheek. "I thought this would be the perfect place to chat about what's going on," I said as we both took a seat.

"Oh no!" Her smile faded. "It's that time of year again, isn't it? Are you thinking of running away to Europe or some monastery? Come on, let me have it."

"No, it's nothing like that," I reassured her.

"Then what's on your mind, hon? All I know is you said you were having a strange day, and then here we are at a place you usually only come with colleagues, grad students, or your racquetball buddies." She gave me that familiar, confident, seductive, slow wink. "But no matter what, I'm glad to be here with you."

Looking across at her blue-green eyes, I was grateful we'd remained close in my *real* life and that she and Sean were good friends.

"Okay, handsome, I love the eye gazing, but I want to get to the chase of this strange day. Fill me in. Are you about to rock my world?"

"Rock it more than marrying me and adopting my nephew? You think I have more in me to surprise you?" I asked.

"*Now* I'm sure you do," she said. "Ren, I know this isn't the path you thought you'd take. You swore you'd quit school, move to Europe, or do something else non-mainstream. But after the accident—and Josh, well, you had to give him a stable environment. I know getting married was not on your radar, *and* it was quite a surprise to everyone, including me, *but* we do love each other." She folded her hands on the table and leaned in.

"Your life is full. Besides raising a great kid, you live through your books. You and your muse create unbelievable adventures that people love. You raise some spirits in this ultraconservative political environment—fuck you, Ronald Reagan." She smiled coyly. "You give people an escape. And you and I are good the way things are. You keep writing, teaching, and playing as much racquetball as you need. I don't care. I want you to be happy. But let go of the what-ifs. Love who you are right now."

I was taken aback. As close as we were when we dated, this situation and her understanding of our relationship were new. I also felt she was tapping into something. I heard hints of Sean's key and the feminine guidance in her words.

"I wish I had one ounce of your objectivity," I said as the waiter sauntered up.

"What'll it be today?" His nonchalant demeanor was the perfect fit with the Bohemian ambiance.

"Lis?" I asked.

"Order for me," she said.

"I'll have a grande Americano with an extra shot. My lovely friend here will have a cappuccino." I winked at her.

"Ren Devlin, are you flirting with me?"

"It kinda seems that way, but—"

"Oh, don't qualify it, let me bask in it," she said with a wry smile. "So go on, tell me about the strange day you are having. If you're lucky, I *might* tell you about a wild, sensual dream I had last night. Sorry, you weren't in it." She feigned blowing me a kiss.

"All right!" I reached over and squeezed her hands. "Thank you for being such a good friend."

"That's how we started. And that's how we'll always be, no matter what."

"Thank you for saying that," I said. "I need you to tap into your eccentric yet objective Aquarian energy right now—"

"Ren, you're stalling."

"Right, here goes . . ."

I filled Lisa in on everything about my *real* life in another time and dimension—my deep practices of yoga, meditation, my council, *and* my relationship with Sean.

I paused to assess how she was receiving this real but fantastical web of information.

"Go on," she said, leaning back and folding her arms across her chest.

I felt my brow furrow. Then, I told her of the miracle, my wild journey into the earth, and how I came to be *here*.

The waiter brought the coffees.

Lisa unfolded her arms and sat up. Simultaneously, we took a deep breath.

"I'm going to be honest," she said, "this is out there for you, *but* fascinating! I mean, *I* have no problem with the homosexual part, but are you going to be okay with it? I know this is fiction, but you know how people are, and we both know it hits close to home. But . . ." She leaned forward onto the table. "You're on the pulse of something. Gay rights are a hot issue, *and* the time travel is intriguing as hell. Are you doing new research into yoga and Sanskrit? Is that going to be your historical link? Yoga and meditation are so mysterious to most people. I *love* that part. Do you have any idea where it will go from there? How do I react to all this when you tell me? What about Josh? Does it disrupt our lives or somehow add a deeper element? I can't wait to hear more. Is this all from chapter one?"

She picked up the cappuccino and carefully took a sip.

Big tears formed in my eyes. I felt more alone than ever. I reached into my pants pocket and handed her the parchment envelope and letter.

"I recognize this old script from your research, but . . ." She handed it back to me.

"It's from the mound," I said and read the words aloud.

When I finished, I looked up. Lisa's initial excitement had shifted to a questioning stare.

"If I would have married a woman, it would have been you. Your Aquarian-Aries self-confidence and self-reliance give you the warrior goddess persona that helped me in my most insecure times. If we're raising Josh, if I have my doctorate, and I'm writing successful historical fiction in this alternate incarnation, I know your guiding energy is all over it, but from where I came from this morning, I didn't choose this or you. 'Always and Forever,' is what Sean and I say to each other in letters and before we go to bed at night. I love you, Lisa, but I love him in a way that comes from the depths of my soul. I'm asking you to try to understand this and forgive me for any wrong I have done to your beautiful heart. I believe you and Josh are the injuries of the heart that need to be forgiven."

"Well . . . Ren . . . somewhere inside, I know there's truth here." She reached across the table and took my hands. Tears slipped down our faces. "But how can I forgive you for something you've never done? Even if this is *somehow* true, Josh and I have you, you're here, you *did* choose us, so . . . I have nothing to forgive you for."

I slumped back in my chair and felt a gripping pain in my chest.

"Ren, the letter said forgive yourself. Can *you* do it?"

Her words were reminiscent of the goddess heart voice I heard so readily until a few hours ago.

"I don't know," I said, still crying, "but until I figure this out, I live here. But I'm not who you think I am. I am not Dr. Devlin. I never have been."

"Okay," she said. "If this council put *you* here and took *my* Ren, who is a professor and author, where is *he*?"

I shrugged.

We stared at each other. Was it five seconds, five minutes, or five hours?

"How long will this go on?" she asked, breaking the silence.

"A moment, an eternity . . . I don't know."

46

SEAN'S ATTACHMENT

What really frightens and dismays us is not external
events themselves, but the way in which we think
about them. It is not things that disturb us, but our
interpretation of their significance.
—EPICTETUS, *ART OF LIVING*

Sara checked in on Ren midafternoon, but there had been no change. She returned after the last session on Saturday to sit and chant.

"Help me understand what's happening to Ren," Sean said. "Aren't spiritual practices designed to help us grow and expand? Look at him! He's listless! Is that what deep practice does to you?"

"Try to stay calm," Sara said. "Remember, Ren's sensitive to his surroundings in this deep state."

"Then, can we step out on the back porch?"

Carol switched places with Sean as he and Sara moved outside.

"I'm frustrated and tired of being calm," Sean said as he crossed his arms and looked out into the woods.

"I miss him, Sara. I miss us," Sean said. "Our lives have been turned upside down since the miracle and that whole thing with ego and the Catholic Church. I thought I lost him then, but thank the goddesses, he snapped out of it. Now, this is something I never expected. I thought this retreat would renew us. Instead—"

"Sean," Sara said, "why don't we sit down and relax?"

Sean shook his head as he sat on the top step of the porch next to Sara.

"Lately, my intuition has been waking up," he said, "and it's telling me he's not okay. Something's not right. How can we help him?"

Sean wiped tears from his eyes.

"I know it may seem useless, but the best thing we can do is chant, pray, and hold vigil. To be in a meditative state like this for more than a few hours means he's dealing with something intrinsically karmic to his consciousness."

"Do you know if he's all right and that he'll come back to me? If I know that, I can hold vigil forever."

"I don't know for sure, Sean. He may be working on a recapitulation meditation; it can go several ways."

"Recapitulation? He's reliving something?" Sean asked.

"Sometimes, to clear the pathway to a new level of consciousness, we have to bring things we've hidden into our awareness. We all bury things that disturb us, but that doesn't mean they go away. Actually, they control us more from our subconscious and form blocks to our evolution."

"Blocks to his evolution? How can he have blocks when he's raised the dead?" Sean asked.

"We all face walls. It's the way things are set up. All of us are working to break free of the chains that bind us. Ren's doing the same thing."

"So, once he works out these blocks, he'll come back to me? Is that what you're saying?" Sean asked.

"That's up to him. Will he clear the blocks, or will he fight them? Intuitively, I feel the lessons of attachment are for *both* of you. Can *you* let go of him, even just a little? Can you know *you'll* be okay even if he doesn't come back and have gratitude for what you've already had?"

Sean leaned forward, cupped his face with his hands, and began to cry.

"Sean, I'm just saying you may have a bigger part in this than you're aware. Forgive him for anything you may be holding against him in your heart, and look at your attachments."

Sara reached over and touched Sean's shoulder.

"The sharp beauty of pain lets us know we're experiencing deep levels of love," Sara said, "but suffering rips at our soul as we deny the reality of change and chaos in the Universe. Have gratitude for all you've shared together, even gratitude for him lying in your arms in this state. This moment is all there is."

He looked up at Sara.

"My emotions have me by the balls right now," he said. "I'm sorry, but that's exactly how I feel. I want to scream and rant and rave. I know it won't do any good, but it's how I feel. This isn't fair."

"Ren's been seeking deeper meaning in life from an early age. He could be getting exactly what he asked for."

"But this isn't what *I* want."

"Do you know the Zen story of good luck, bad luck?" she asked.

"Yes," he sighed, "I know it's about accepting the events of our life and moving on. Are the things that happen good luck or bad luck? In the short term, they seem like the worst possible thing, but we never know how they'll play out in the long term. I get it, Sara. But right now, I feel helpless."

"We can choose to let our *emotions* carry us, or we can let our *practices* carry us," she said. "What we think and how we feel gets us caught up in the dramas of worst-case scenarios. We can't know what this situation may lead to. Be here, Sean. Be with Ren as he is. I know it's hard, but he needs you to be present for what's unfolding. Try not to see it as good or bad but as what is. And keep listening to your newfound intuition."

"Have you ever experienced this deep state of meditation?"

"A couple of times, and I am here with you now." She smiled.

"I feel him," Sean said, "and he's looking for me. I know he is."

"You guys," Carol said as she ran out onto the porch, "he just squeezed my hand."

Sean jumped up and ran back into the bedroom. Carol and Sara followed.

"I told him we love him," Carol said, "and he had to come back to us."

Ren's body quivered slightly. Was he responding to Carol's words? Sean wondered.

"It's a sign, Sean!" Carol said.

They sat quietly for a few moments, waiting for something more. But there was nothing.

"Can we chant the Gayatri mantra?" Carol asked.

After 108 rounds, only stillness and silence remained.

"I'm going to head back to my cabin," Sara whispered. "Make sure you get some sleep. I'll be back tomorrow."

"It's dark. Let me walk you back," Carol said. "I'll grab the lantern."

After a time, Carol returned, climbed back onto the bed, and held Ren's hand.

Sean sat silently. "Being with Sara is inspiring, isn't it?" Sean asked.

"Always, but I just had a chat with her that was a bit unsettling."

"Why?"

"She said part of this process might be about you and I learning to let go."

Sean swallowed.

"Letting go? Of Ren? Now?" he asked, then leaned close to Ren's ear.

"I can't. I just can't, bud. I can't let go. Not yet."

47

ANOTHER RED X

I sat at my in-home office desk. I put another red *X* through today's date on my curriculum calendar.

"Day thirty," I said, slumping into my chair. I kept hoping to wake up and be back in my life with Sean. This was so different from any other time I'd gone deep in my dreams or meditations. The days were weirdly normal, as if this *were* my life. I'd go to bed. I'd teach. Go to meetings. Field calls from editors with questions about the books I was supposed to be writing.

What was I missing? Would this ever end? I kept asking these questions, but no one answered.

The door opened, and Josh popped his head in. Even at nine years old, he was the spitting image of my brother, his father, with his round face, reddish complexion, light-brown hair, and freckles.

"Hey, Ren, are you coming to my game? The team's hot, but *I'm* on fire." He smiled.

"I bet you are, buddy, but I don't think so."

Josh stepped into my office. "Up until a few weeks ago, you were at every game. Are you ticked at me?"

"Oh, no, no . . . ," I said, standing and walking over to him. "Every game?"

"Yeah, every game. What's up? You've been really weird."

"I'm distracted," I said, putting my hand on his shoulder. "It's not you, it's the book stuff and—"

"And that you're bat shit crazy," Lisa said, walking in behind Josh. The two of them laughed.

"Hey, Josh, how about I meet you in the car?" she said. "I need to talk to Looney Tunes for a minute."

Lisa closed the door.

"Something has to give," she said. "With as much as we've talked about your other life and your journey with yoga, I'm trying hard to stay open-minded, but I don't know if you're really having a mystical experience or if I should have you checked for some neurological issue. You're so distracted—it's like Josh and I have totally lost you."

"Lisa, my true essence is not here. It's somewhere in the future, in another life. Here, I'm living a life that's so close to what could have been my reality it scares me. As the weeks pass, I wonder, am I in a meditative state in my other life with Sean? Am I functioning there? Have I disappeared, or am I dead?"

"In this *other* life," Lisa said, "you say you went so deep in your practices, you healed a kid, turned invisible, blah, blah, blah, so, why do you think you're stuck? Can't you *go deep* and make this all normal again?"

"That's the scariest thing for me: my inability to access deep states in my meditations. One part of me wants to find the comfort of my *samyama* practices, and another part of me has given up hope on them. I haven't heard a word from any of my guides or my heart voice in weeks."

"I certainly don't know what to do about silent guides," she said, shaking her head, "but I do have a suggestion."

"Great."

"Come to Josh's game. It'll make him happy and give you something to focus on besides yourself."

I sighed. "I can't. I need to figure this out. I need to focus and get out of here."

"You're right," she said, pointing her finger at me. "You *do* have to figure this out. Go back to being with Sean or get on board with being with us."

"I'm trying," I snapped.

"Okay, Ren, but remember, loneliness and regret kill the soul."

I sighed.

"Will you stop channeling the goddesses, please?"

"I'm not channeling them," she said, raising one eyebrow. "I am one."

48

SEAN—MIRACLE OF LOVE

S ean slept next to Ren, holding his hand. Several times throughout the
night, he felt Ren lightly squeeze his hand or make a slight whimper.
Each time, Sean would sit up, hoping Ren was back, but nothing. The
next morning, Sean and Carol resumed their chanting vigil. Sara quietly
came into the cabin before the morning session of the retreat.

"Sean," Sara said, "I didn't go into detail with the retreat director, but
I told her the four of us would be staying a few days longer. I think it's
important to keep Ren just as he is."

"Thank you," Sean said, turning to meet her eyes. "I'm trying to stay
in the moment and listen to my intuition. I know him. Our souls are
energetically linked. He wants to come back to me. I don't even know
how, but he's communicating with me. He's on another trip designed by
his council, but he's stuck."

"Stay with your intuition," Sara said. "Your soul connection could
have something to do with bringing him back."

"Oh, I know it does," Sean said as he stroked Ren's head. "I have to
stop comparing myself to him. I witness the unbelievable synchronistic
energies and miracles that swirl around him, and I wonder why I don't

have those kinds of experiences. I need to validate my *own* experiences and not compare. I'm ready."

"Ready for what?" Carol asked.

"To face the self-doubt that stops me from going deep. It's time to look at my insecurities, invoke the power of love, and dive in."

"It's a beautiful intent, Sean," Sara said, "but you have to let go of your attachment and do it with selfless love."

"I understand. I witnessed Dottie go through the process with her son in Cleveland. And just as Ren and I held space for Dottie and Walt, you two are holding space for Ren and me. I'm hoping for a similar miracle of love."

"It can go many ways," Sara said, moving close to Sean to touch his shoulder.

Sean looked up at her, then at Carol, and then back to Ren.

"Yep, I might bring him back, or I may have to say goodbye to him forever."

49

MAGICK STORE

Every day of our lives is only the beginning.
—Ren Devlin; Journal entry March 2

I sat at my desk at home and stared out the window, watching twilight descend onto the planet. Once again, I drew a red *X* through the date.

"Month three," I said and opened my journal to write.

> *I guess this is my life. This is my reality, living with Lisa and Josh and teaching as a tenured professor at the University of Cincinnati. Not being with Sean is also my reality. I fear I will never accept this to be true.*

I got up, went upstairs, and climbed into bed. Lisa was awake, but we did not exchange any words. I pulled the covers up to my chin. I closed my eyes and tried to focus on my breath. For months now, there's been no connection to my practices. Instead, there was an unending chatter of the mind voice that kept me up for hours and left me exhausted the next day. Tonight, after several deep breaths, I tried something different. I imagined every detail of Sean's loving face and his bright blue eyes. To my surprise, I quickly fell into a deep sleep and found myself in a dream, sitting cross-legged on the floor, staring at Sean.

"I love you," he said.

"I love you too, and I'm so glad to see you."

"Remember, we're always together," he said, "the immortal piece of *us* will always be united. There can be no separation or sadness when we know this to be Truth."

His smile and presence soothed me.

"Your words about our everlasting love flow like an exquisite Upanishad," I said. "Take me back with you, Sean."

"Not yet," he said.

My heart felt like it was in a vice grip.

"Not yet? Will I ever be back where you and I are in our happy little house? I don't even mind all the reporters following us to our yoga classes. I just want the beautiful exchanges with you and our clients and students."

"Ren," Lisa said and nudged my arm. "Wake up."

Sean vanished.

"Damn it."

"I guess you were dreaming," she said, "you were talking about reporters and yoga classes, and—"

"I finally dreamt of Sean, but—"

"I am *so* sorry to interrupt," she said. "I had no idea you were communing with your lover from another life."

I rolled over and looked at her.

"This has to be strange for you."

"Damn good thing I'm lying down, or I'd fall over," she said. "That's the first semi-selfless thing you've said since you dropped into *this* life months ago."

We sat up and turned toward each other.

"Last week, I picked up a couple of books about yoga at that quirky bookshop up the street. If you were such a great adept, like these books describe, you dropped it like a hot poker when you arrived here."

"I know, and I wish I could—"

"Oh no, no, no . . . ," she said, "you opened the floodgates, buddy. It's all about me right now, so you just listen."

"Okay," I said.

"I've been awake most nights wondering what's real and what's insanity. Is it you or me who's gone over the edge, *and* should one or both of us be in counseling?" She sighed. "*But* I also have a gut feeling that somehow this is all true. It's like the Wizard of Oz, except instead of dropping a house on a witch, you dropped your consciousness from a different dimension into my husband."

We sat silently for a few moments.

"Whoever you are, I really want *you* to go back to *your* life," she said. "I'm so ready to take *my* Ren back. We were happy, and I definitely *know* he loves me and Josh. There's no love with you. None!"

She threw the covers off and got out of bed.

"Yow, that stung," I said, looking down.

"Well, if you think I'm going to apologize, I'm not, because as much as I'm against any kind of physical violence, all I want to do is slap you to snap some sense into you."

"Whoa, Lisa, you said you were a goddess, but I thought you'd be the loving and supportive Venus. Now you sound like angry Athena."

"Watch out," she said, pointing her finger at me. "They're all in here." She then lightly pounded her chest with a closed fist. "Venus, Athena, Saraswati, Durga, and even a little Kali."

I sat up straight against the headboard.

"You've done more than a *little* reading," I said.

"Um-hm," she said as she walked out, slamming the door.

I slid down into the bed, covered my head with a pillow, and cried.

The next morning, when I got out of bed, Lisa and Josh were gone. I walked through the house feeling isolated and lonely. This is how I felt as a kid behind the chair, I thought, but then I found yoga, and it taught me we are never alone. What's happened to me? I'm caught in a riptide that's pulling the life force out of me. I wandered into my office, stood on my yoga mat, and thought about doing a couple of sun salutations. My heart and head weren't into it. Maybe I'd try to sit in meditation. Useless, I thought. I haven't been able to go deep in meditation since I arrived here, and each failed attempt only depresses me. Part of me blamed my practices for me being here in the first place.

I went to my desk and looked at my calendar. Class wasn't until late afternoon, but I could go in early and work on the curriculum, anything to get my mind on something other than the hopeless situation I was in. I decided to walk the fifteen minutes to campus, so I gathered a few things and put them in my briefcase. The bright sunshine and fresh air would be good for me.

As I walked along Ludlow Avenue past the shops and restaurants, a thick gray and white fog bank, at least three stories tall, rounded the corner of Clifton Avenue and moved toward me. It covered buildings, people, and cars as it rolled through the streets. No one seemed alarmed.

Was I the only one seeing it?

When it was just about to engulf me, I grabbed the doorknob to the nearest business and stepped in.

Tibetan bells announced my entrance. Within seconds, I realized I was in the New Age shop where the physics professor/astrologer had read my chart when I was a graduate student.

It looked just as it did then, with tall, dark wood bookcases along each wall and several library tables placed here and there. Little signs hung from the ceiling denoting yoga, spirituality, astrology, etc. To my left was an eight-foot-long glass display case filled with pentagrams, chalices, crystals, spell candles, incense, and goddess figurines. A small round table next to this case had several neatly folded T-shirts featuring an image of Earth with the words, *All One People.*

A man in his late twenties stood behind the display case. He was dressed in a brown tweed three-piece suit with a red pocket square on the jacket. His hair was long and pulled back into a ponytail, showing off his high cheekbones and green eyes.

"Hi, welcome to LeftHanded Moon. I'm Orcus."

"I'm Ren," I said. "Orcus, is that your given name or chosen?"

"Given." His gaze was intense.

"That's not a light name to carry around," I said.

"To the right person, it is. It's a Roman version of Pluto or Hades."

"I know. I've studied mythology."

"I see," he said, "then you know Orcus is the avenger of broken oaths."

"Broken oaths," I mumbled.

"So, *you* summoned the fog," he said, pointing out the plate glass windows behind me. I turned. The fog was still there and so thick you couldn't see the sidewalk.

"It took me by surprise. I've never seen anything like it. That's why I stepped in."

"Exactly, that was its mission," he said.

"Its mission?"

"In witchcraft, fog can be the gray area that shrouds our eyes from seeing our future, or it can be a place of transformation, where the veils that obscure our vision are thinner."

"I've had several experiences involving veils lately, that's for sure," I said with a chuckle.

He continued his vehement stare.

"Fogs also blur the boundaries between one period of time and another. Any experiences with *that* lately?" he asked.

"Maybe I did bring the fog," I said, taking a step back from him.

He slowly nodded.

"How can I help you?"

"Well, like I said, the fog . . . but since I'm here, several years ago, I had an astrology reading from a man who had an office in the back. Would he be available?"

"You're referring to my uncle. He's like a father to me, raised me since I was nine, but unfortunately, he's teaching all day."

"Physics," I said, "yes, I remember. He was extremely helpful the last time I was here, and I could use guidance from someone I trust."

"I read the tarot," Orcus said, "may I offer you a reading? No one will be in until this fog lifts, and it won't lift until you leave."

"I don't know. I was thinking astrological advice . . ."

Where there had been no music, I now heard the etheric voices of Jane Siberry and k.d. lang singing "Calling All Angels." *Was this some kind of synchronicity finally coming through, calling the fog, calling all angels?*

"Sure," I said to his offer, but I was feeling *unsure* of this whole experience.

Orcus gestured to a small round claw-foot table in the back of the store. It was draped with a dark blue silky fringed cloth that featured an image of a golden astrological wheel surrounded by stars and moons. There was a deck of cards in the center.

"Trust me, Ren. You can ask or tell me anything," he said as we sat.

He picked up the cards and shuffled them, keeping his gaze on me the whole time.

"Are you a Scorpio?" I asked. "Your demeanor and your eyes—"

"Um, uhm, there *is* no other energy for me."

"Especially with a name like—"

"Focus," he said.

"Excuse me." I was taken aback by his authoritarian tone.

"Pardon my impertinence, but as you know, Scorpions have little capacity for small talk. I feel deep things are happening for you, and I hope I can help."

"I appreciate it, and you're right. I'm desperate and at a loss as to how to break a spell that binds me to an existence where I don't belong. I bet that sounds cryptically crazy," I said.

"The strangest things happen in this store," he said. "My uncle and I believe it's a vortex of transformational energy. You believe in energy, don't you?"

"Boy do I," I said, "and my story can definitely add to the list of strange things happening in your store."

"Tell me."

"Okay, Orcus, Pluto, Hades, here goes . . . in another realm, I'm in my fifties and an avid meditator and yogic practitioner. Not long ago, I raised a nine-year-old boy from death, and it has completely altered my life and the life of my partner, Sean."

Orcus remained motionless, staring at me.

"Weeks later, in one of my deep meditative states, I was told by my council of astrological advisors that I needed to learn and experience the kleshas of attachment and aversion. They pulled me back here, to a time in my life when I let people down and broke their hearts. Now, I'm stuck here in this weird convergence of life-path choices and can't get back to my life with my partner."

"You're never stuck," Orcus said, "it's only your perception of your world that ties you to reality. Your perception is the product of the *samskaras*, all the mental imprints your mind collects through past thoughts and actions. You've allowed them to have dominion over your mind."

I sat back and folded my arms.

"You *all* made choices," he said, "you and the people you say you hurt. You perceive it as pain, but what if it was the best thing for all of you?"

"Then why do I have such regret?"

"Because it's how you perceive reality, *and* you're attached to it. Let's be real, regret sucks."

"Yes, it does," I said with a smirk. "But Orcus, why do you suppose I'm in a different time and dimension?"

"Think of yourself as an experiment in quantum physics. Perhaps you're living proof of physicist David Bohm's Implicate Order, where there are multidimensional realities that enfold and unfold into themselves.[2] What we believe determines what we take to be true. What we take to be true is our reality. Perhaps you're learning lessons that are connected to this time, so you can see them and resolve them."

"But I'm stuck," I said.

"Perhaps you need to tune into your inner silence for the answers."

"Nothing's happening in my practices! I try to sit, but—"

"So, you sit with a point of view, and you're attached to a particular outcome."

"No! I know better. It doesn't work that way." I felt the hair on the back of my neck raise.

"Okay," he said. "Well, since your practices aren't yielding what you

---

2   David Peat, "David Bohm, Implicate Order and Holomovement," Sand, https://www.scienceandnonduality.com/article/david-bohm-implicate-order-and-holomovement.

want, perhaps you can gain some insight from the tarot." He slid a deck of cards in front of me.

"You think it will be that easy?" I asked. "I don't think this will help."

His stoic gaze turned to sadness.

"What happened to your deep, unwavering belief in the divine connection?" he asked.

"I'm realizing that connection is fragile," I said. "I work hard to believe in it, but it's so easy to forget."

His eyes were now full of a knowing compassion that roused an inner familiarity with him.

"Have we met before?"

"We've never spoken," he said as he pointed to the deck. "Shuffle and place two cards face up in front of you."

I moved the cards reverently through my hands and then placed the deck on my heart in an effort to regain some connection to the divine.

"I open myself to the guidance I need in this moment," I said. "I open my heart to hear."

I chose two cards and placed them as he instructed.

"What do you see?" he asked.

"The magician and the death card."

"Yes, the images are messages about your connection with the Divine and that times of great sorrow can lead to transformation."

"The death card," I said. "I can't imagine any greater sorrow than what I feel with this separation from Sean."

Orcus nodded.

"What else do you see?" he asked. "What are their numbers?"

"Oh, one and thirteen. One thirteen." I looked up. "Do you know what that means?" I asked.

"More importantly, do you?"

"*Tatra sthitau yatnah abhyāsa*, a very significant Sutra in my life."

"It's also a reminder that at this juncture, you've broken an oath," he said.

"To stay with my practices?" I asked. "But my practices are yielding nothing."

"Steadfastness has no time frame. There is no one who is harboring regret but you. Forgive yourself, Ren."

I sighed.

"Isn't it nice to know," he said, "the Universe reassures and reminds us, as many times as needed, what we are here to learn? Your birthday, Veronica, the Sutra, these cards . . . the reminders just keep coming until you have ears to hear."

"I'm hearing *you*. I need to start again." I stood. "Orcus, what do I owe you?"

"A recommitment to your practices, the openness to listen to your council, and the willingness to feel the love of the feminine that surrounds you—will suffice for payment."

"You're intense," I said. "Plutonian energy pours out of you."

"We speak in our due time," he said as I walked toward the door.

I turned to face him.

"Are you . . . ? Never mind," I said. "It's all what I perceive, correct?"

"Each of us is responsible for our perception of our reality and our spiritual progress. Keep moving forward through transformation."

I gave a slight bow of my head.

"Hold on." He walked over to one of the cases and pulled out a pendant on a chain.

"I'd like you to have this," he said as he placed a silver pentagram around my neck.

"You don't have to do that."

"I want to. In ancient times, it was said, those who wore the pentagram would find their way home again." He fastened the chain around my neck.

"Thank you." Two powerful words.

I turned toward the door. As my foot touched the sidewalk, the fog dissipated. The sun came out. A glimmer of hope that had been missing for far too long was back in my heart.

50

SEAN'S OPPORTUNITY

Sean set out on a new journey—he told himself—to realize his objective, he needed to commit to his practice more than ever. He began to sit for ninety-minute sessions, taking breaks only to eat and nap. Carol kept an eye on both him and Ren, and Sara came in during breaks in the retreat to offer support.

Sean positioned himself on the bed and held Ren's mala beads in his hand. The first five sessions were challenging. His body rebelled through aches and pains. His mind was restless. *What makes you think you can do this? You're letting him die while you sit here.*

There were several times when he almost quit, but another voice counseled him to *breathe and sit*, so he continued. On the sixth round, the timer startled him. That felt like only a few minutes, he thought. I'm making progress. Time is losing its meaning.

Remember to have no attachments to an outcome, he heard a heart whisper.

He readjusted his body, closed his eyes, and deepened his breath.

Something was different as he entered session seven. His lower body felt weighted to the earth, yet he had the sensation of being suspended. His spine elongated toward the sky, and from the crown of his head, he felt a thin stream of light extend into some unknown space far above him. His body had a slight vibration. A sense of peace filled his joints, muscles, and organs. This place was new to him. He was dissolving into no-thingness.

Spontaneously, his fingers glided from one mala bead to the next as he felt guided by the goddess *Saraswati*, to recite the mantra to *Ganesh*, the elephant-headed god, the remover of obstacles.

Om Gam Ganapataye Namah.

He focused on each syllable of the mantra as his fingers continued to move from bead to bead. *I'm dissolving. I'm no longer Sean, male, white, gay* . . . all labels were gone.

Om Gam Ganapataye Namah.

Om Gam Ganapataye Namah.

Stop now before you disappear too, a voice said somewhere inside his head. But he continued his internal chant. The mantra moved him, swayed his body slightly left to right. His breath was long and even. He felt love deep within.

I'm feeling it. I am feeling it for everything, he thought. He slipped further into no-thingness. Time had no meaning as he bathed in this Oneness.

Oh yes, you're doing great. Much better than Ren.

"Ahhhh," he let out with a grunt. "Hello, ego."

He opened his eyes to see Carol and Sara sweetly chanting the Gayatri.

"You okay, Sean?" Carol asked.

"I thought I was going deep, but self-doubt and my ego keep showing up and hooking me," he said. "It's useless."

"Sean, don't get mad, but I'm going to say to you what Ren said to me five years ago when I was ready to give up on meditation: *the mind won*."

"I know, I know," he said, shaking his head. "I'm not going to give up."

"Why don't you take a break?" Sara said. "Go for a walk, stretch, change your scenery."

"Good idea," Sean said, putting Ren's mala around his neck, "if some-thing changes—"

"You'll be the first to know," Sara smiled.

"It's getting dark," Carol said, "I left the lantern on the porch."

Sean walked into the kitchen and out the back door, stopping to admire the early evening sky painted red, orange, and gold, giving an etheric glow to the beech trees and soaring white pines. Rhododendrons as large as Volkswagen Beetles created a carpet beneath the trees.

He grabbed the lantern and walked out beyond the house to where he and Ren saw the earthen mound. This time, he walked up close to the opening.

"Is my man's consciousness somewhere inside you?" Sean asked.

The light in the sky had faded. He turned on the lantern, stepped to the threshold of the entrance, stuck the glowing lamp in, and tried to see. There was nothing but solid blackness.

He took a small step in with one foot but purposefully kept his other foot outside.

Come inside.

He jumped back several feet.

"Who said that?"

Silence.

"Great! My mind's playing tricks on me now," he said aloud, "but if something did say *come inside*, it's not happening, not in this lifetime."

A strong current of cool air then began to funnel out from the hole.

"Okay, that's enough for me," he said, "I'm gonna keep my eye on you from a distance."

Sean set the lit lantern near the entrance and backed up to where he and Ren sat for meditation on the first day of the retreat. He perched himself cross-legged on a rock and stared at the hole.

"I believe in the power of love," he said, taking the mala from around his neck. He rested his left hand on his knee, palm up with his index finger and thumb touching, and recited, "I let go of insecurity and doubt, to the best of my ability, so I can sit in love and let the Universe guide me. Open me to follow my intuition. Provide a breakthrough in my awareness so I can shift my insecurities and deep-seated inferiorities about my connection with the Universal mind. Give me a glimpse into the creative force of all, the Universal heart."

Sean's eyes fluttered closed. His hands spontaneously moved from bead to bead as the mantra of Ganesh passed his lips.

"Om Gam Ganapataye Namah.

Om Gam Ganapataye Namah."

Insecurity entered his consciousness. *Why am I not doing the Gayatri or a specific mantra to the goddess?*

He heard a new voice in his heart:

Ganesh is the gatekeeper to the inner sanctuary of the goddess. He will take you to Her or bring Her to you.

He continued—

"Om Gam Ganapataye Namah.

Om Gam Ganapataye Namah."

His breath was long and even. He felt love deep within and allowed it to flow out to everything. He slipped into no-thingness and communed with Oneness.

Stay centered as you open your eyes.

He did. The light of the lantern and the rising three-quarter moon illuminated ten toga-clad figures forming a V-shape in front of the entrance to the mound.

Sean shifted his breath fully into his heart so as to keep his rational mind subdued.

"Are you Ren's council?" he asked.

"We are *your* council. We are you, and you are *us*," said the female standing at the center.

"I'm listening," Sean said, "how should I proceed?"

"Recognize that *all* beings have the potential to be mystical revolutionaries, including you."

"I'm starting to realize that, but I'd like to know what to do about Ren and our lives."

"Open yourself to experience the least amount of attachment as possible as you journey on."

"I learned that by observing Dottie with her son," he said.

The woman nodded.

It was hard for Sean to make out the council members' specific features in this light, but each of them glowed with an inner luminosity.

"I'm at a loss. Should I be doing something?" Sean asked.

"We invite you to enter the mound with us," she said.

"I had a feeling . . . will I find Ren?"

"Some things cannot be explained but only experienced," the enchanting female said.

"So, you aren't giving me any guarantees?"

"No, but we *are* giving you an opportunity."

The members of Sean's council assumed Abhaya mudra.

"Can I take the lantern?"

"The only light you need is found in your heart."

One by one, the chiton-clad figures turned and slowly walked into the earthen mound.

Sean took a deep breath, assumed Abhaya mudra, and fell in line behind the goddess of ceremonies, whom he now knew he had summoned with his mantra.

As his turn came to cross the threshold into the unknowable, he paused, swallowed, and whispered, "I'm not afraid of my life or what is in my heart."

51

SAYING GOODBYE

Goodbyes are only for those who love with their eyes—
for those who love with their heart and
Soul there is no such thing as separation.

—RUMI

I stood outside the magick store and savored the sun on my face. The encounter with Orcus, who was either Pluto or channeling some strong council energy, brought Sutra 1:13 back home to my heart. I knew I needed to jump back into my practices without a point of view to regain my center and hopefully get back to Sean. I looked at my watch. It was three hours before my lecture, so I headed to campus.

Once in my office, I closed the door, sat upright in my desk chair, and began to breathe. I relaxed my shoulders and the muscles of my face. I visualized breathing in and out through my heart center. I knew if I could return to the depths of practice that accessed the *siddhis* in the first place, I could find my way out of here. I had to rediscover the path back to my heart. I had to start now.

"I dedicate this practice to all the powerful Hindu Goddesses—*Kali, Lakshmi, Parvati, Durga,* and *Saraswati,*" I said as I placed my hands into prayer position.

"There is no past and no future. The present moment is my reality and should be my focus."

Then, I started reciting the Gayatri mantra to clear my energies and let wisdom be my guide.

Immediately, there were challenges. My mind was loud, confident it could grab my focus, but I remained diligent. Finally, I shifted into a space where I heard the subtle sound of my inhale and exhale, and there was a lightness to my whole being. For the first time in three months, there was an internal *let go*.

Nothing's happening.

I continued to breathe deep and worked to stay relaxed. I told myself this would take time, and I needed to access the beginner's mind. I released any delusions of one practice solving my issue. With that, I dropped in even deeper. I felt a thread of light pull my head upward. I savored being home in my practice.

There was a knock on the door. I stayed still and silent.

I heard the door open. Who would just walk right in? I should have locked the door, I thought.

"Oh, you're in here. When there was no answer, I thought I would just put this letter on your desk."

"Oh my god!" I said as I jumped up. "Sean. You're thirty. You're in this life—"

"Uh yeah. What do you mean, I'm in this life?" Sean asked, squinting.

"Come in, come in," I said. "This is unbelievable. I had no idea you were here."

Sean shut the door behind him.

I wanted to wrap myself around this younger version of Sean and tell him I was ready to make a life with him right here, right now.

"Look," Sean said, "I didn't know how else to get a hold of you. I know I'm not supposed to call here or your house and you haven't been to racquetball in months, so this is the only way I could think of to make contact."

"This is perfect," I said.

"So, you're not mad I just showed up?"

"No, I'm thrilled. Sit down." I motioned to the chair on the other side of the desk.

"I'd rather stand, thanks."

He stepped over to the bookshelves.

"Is this your wife and son?" he asked, picking up the photo on the shelf.

"Don't you recognize them? It's Lisa and Josh, of course, they're both much younger than—"

"What?" he asked.

"Sean, we have so much to talk about . . . the last three months have been so intense, I've been trying to—"

"Intense with book deadlines, or is it guilt again?" he asked. "I'm used to you falling off the face of the earth when the guilt sets in, but come on, twelve weeks? For all I knew, you were dead."

"Oh, Sean, I would have called, but I didn't even know you—"

"Didn't know, or didn't care?" Sean asked with a sigh as he replaced the photo on the shelf. "Any doubt I had about what I came here to say is gone after seeing this photo of the happy family. Let's face it; you're in the life you're meant to be in."

"No, I'm not! I am not in the life I chose. I want a life with you."

"Don't!"

"Don't what?" I asked. "Don't tell you what I want and that I plan to move toward?"

Sean walked to the desk and placed a sealed envelope in front of me.

"No! We've been through this before. You're married and raising a kid. I need to move on."

"No! You can't! We have to be together! We have a future. Seeing you now, I know we can be a couple here and now. We can start a life in this time period."

"What's up with you? Here and now?" he asked. "Why didn't you talk like this months ago? You told me then you'd *never* make a move. You said that you couldn't hurt Lisa and Josh and that you would probably lose your job if they found out you're gay."

"I don't care what I said then. I'm not the same person. I'm ready to make a move now!"

"No, you're not. Stop this," he stood tall. "I want someone in my life like you have with Lisa."

"But Lisa and I are only together to raise Josh, not because—"

"It doesn't matter, Ren. You're married. I don't want to be the *other man*. I also don't want to break up a relationship that affects a child. Especially a child who's already lost one set of parents. He needs you."

"But now that I see the plan is for me to stay *here* long term, I'll get a divorce. Josh will get used to it. He loves you."

"What do you mean, *be here long term*? And I've never met Josh."

This Sean is oblivious to us being together in another time, I thought.

"Sean, I've been dreaming of a life with you. In that life, Josh bonds tightly with you."

"Really, but stay here long term? What the hell does that mean?"

"Shit, it's a long story. Lisa knows how I feel about you. This is something we can work out. Please, Sean, please."

"You told her about us without asking me first? Jesus, you're so selfish. Don't you care about the rest of us in this mess? It's time to move on."

"This isn't the way it's supposed to go!" I said, starting to tremble. "This feels like goodbye. It can't be. I just found you again."

"I'm not sure what you're talking about, but this isn't easy for me either. It's hard to let you go."

"Can we get together another time, away from here, so we can discuss this more?" I asked.

"No! It's too hard! I can't keep doing this to myself. It's time to let go."

"Sean, we can figure this out—"

"No, Ren!" he said. "There's nothing to figure out. I'm not breaking up a home. *And* I've met someone."

Number thirteen, the death card—great sorrow leads to transformation.

The devastation I felt shut down my heart center.

"Are you in love?" I asked in a whisper.

"We've only been out a few times. He's coming off a relationship, so we're taking it slow."

I fell back into my chair. The shell of myself sat in silent disbelief.

"Oh my god, I just found you, and I am losing you again," I said with a sense of defeat in both my body and speech.

"What do you mean *again*?" he asked.

"I had a dream last night. We were in our fifties and had been together for thirty years. You and I, at *this* age, in our twenties and thirties, had bonded deeply. We had the most incredible love story. Through our work, we helped lots of people."

I felt a deep sob surfacing.

"It sounds beautiful," Sean said.

"Yes, but in the dream, we end up separated. Then, like now, both of us wanted each other so badly, but it couldn't happen. The circumstances were different, but it's the same."

"It's not that I don't love you, Ren, but I need to do this. We need to make this break so we can live honest lives with no secrets or deception."

"Yes," I said, "so we can be free."

Sean nodded.

"Free from all attachments that do not belong in this place or time," I said. "We need to be free from the chains of the heart. Chains that will only cause pain and agony for one of us, both of us, all of us."

"That's a beautiful way to think of what we are doing," he said, "breaking chains of the heart."

"Once again, you are my greatest teacher," I said. "To live with integrity and to evolve are the most important things to both of us. We need to let go—to face *Raga* and *Dvesha*—RD, Ren Devlin."

I took a deep breath, feeling a small release mixed with a pervasive deep sadness. I wanted to tell him that in a different time and in a different place, we meditate and breathe together every day. In that place, we *are* or *were* together, but instead, I remained silent.

"Okay. I have to go," he said, moving toward the door.

"Can I hug you one last time?" I asked.

"I don't think that's wise. This is already hard enough."

I stood, walked over to him, and put my hand on his forearm.

"Sean—"

"What?"

"I want to beg you not to go, but somehow, I know this goodbye is necessary," I said. "I wish you all the best. Stay true to your beautiful self. Keep loving yourself deeply."

"I will. Make sure you do the same. This is how it's supposed to be. Forgive yourself, nobody's perfect, Ren." He put his hand on my heart. "Make sure to be happy."

Sean turned, opened the door, and walked out. I followed him out into the hallway and watched him descend the stairs until he was out of sight.

One layer of constriction around my heart dissolved while another grew tighter.

The words from the letter at the mound and the key Sean gave me to keep in my heart . . . all rushed through my body—love yourself, forgive yourself, and face R&D. Always and Forever.

I went back to my desk, sat down, and wrapped myself in loneliness. I hoped it would not kill my spirit, but, at this moment, everything I was clinging to for hope was gone.

52

IMPRISONMENT

I stood at the lectern in front of the amphitheater classroom. A hundred or more faces looked at me, waiting. Instead of following my notes, I wanted to tell them to focus on love, the only thing that really matters. I wanted to tell them to work to understand the mystery that underlies their lives and become mystical revolutionaries who spread love, compassion, and kindness. I wanted to scream, *Learn to create everyday miracles in your life!* Instead, I took a deep breath and began the day's curriculum, describing the nineteen-year imprisonment of Mary Stuart, Queen of the Scots, in sixteenth-century England. She went seeking asylum but became a prisoner, held against her will, in a place she did not belong.

I, too, was cut off from my home, from those I loved, and from the places that occupied my heart. Sean, in this realm, no longer wanted to have contact with me. He had let go, severed our bond.

"Paulette," I looked to my teaching assistant sitting next to the stage, "I can't . . ."

I was momentarily speechless as I spiraled deeper into a dark hole.

"Doc, are you all right?"

"No, I need to leave . . ." There were murmurs from the class as Paulette walked toward me. She put her hand over the lectern mic.

"How about you go home and rest?" she asked. "I'll finish class with a review for next week's exam."

I nodded, needing to get out of there before I completely unraveled. I grabbed my things, made a beeline up the long aisle of the classroom, and headed home.

53

REMEMBER YOUR INTENT

Sean's eyes were open, but he saw nothing. He heard nothing as he held the mudra and continued to walk forward into complete darkness. Each time his mind chatter began to surface, he exhaled forcefully to dissipate it.

I am accepting this opportunity. I will follow my intuition. *Om Gam Ganapataye Namah.*

Then, up ahead appeared a dim flicker of light from a candle flame. With each step, it grew brighter until it revealed the silhouettes of the council ahead of him, still in single file but now dressed in jeans, shorts, and T-shirts. One by one, they filed through a double-door entryway. He followed, stopping just inside. He stood at the back of a large, tiered classroom with Formica-topped desk chairs. His council members melded into a crowd of people entering the room from several doorways and taking seats at the desks.

Sean took the first vacant seat and closed his eyes. An image of the luminescent goddess standing at the entrance to the earthen mound appeared in his heart's eye.

Remember your intent, her voice said.

When he opened his eyes, he looked around—*Where am I?* The

teacher's lectern in front of the room had the logo of the University of Cincinnati. *Is this Proctor Hall?* He had taken a few science electives here in the 1980s. *What could this have to do with finding Ren?* He felt his rational mind kicking in.

Remove all doubt, said the goddess. *Know you are worthy.*

He sat up straight. *I am worthy. I can do this.* He took a deep breath.

"Bring it on," he said.

"Excuse me?" said the young woman sitting next to him.

"Oh, nothing."

As more students filtered in, Sean stood and did a three-sixty. Everyone had physics books. He sat down.

I never took physics. He felt a ping of self-doubt.

"Any advice for me?" he whispered to the goddess.

Allow this experience to unfold.

Then the mind voice tapped into Sean's rational mental habits and asked, *How can you be in two places at the same time?*

Another wave of self-doubt washed over him.

Can I do this? He asked himself.

Om Gam Ganapataye Namah, the spontaneous mantra once again filled him.

Compose yourself, she said. *Don't jolt yourself out of this.*

"You're right, you're right!" he whispered, taking a deep breath.

"Excuse me," he now said to the woman next to him, "could I borrow a pen and a piece of paper? I think I might want to take a note."

"Duh," she murmured as she ripped a page from her notebook and retrieved a pen from her book bag.

"Thank you."

He wrote on the page; University of Cincinnati, Physics classroom . . . he stopped with the sound of a man's voice.

"Good morning, class," said a man in his midsixties, who looked like a dark-haired Einstein with wild curly hair and out-of-control, bushy eyebrows as he stood at the lectern. "In reference to the cutting-edge concepts from your homework readings, someone define the process *to morph*."

"To morph is to change from one thing to another," said a male student in the front row.

"Yes! Good," said the teacher. "Somebody else, give me an example. How about somebody from the back of the room."

"A caterpillar to a butterfly," came from somewhere behind Sean.

"Exactly, when we define morphing, it's usually a shift from one thing to another within a *single* organism. It can be a gradual or drastic shift, as in the case of a crawling insect, to something that can fly. But what about Rupert Sheldrake's theory of Morphic Resonance in his book, *A New Science of Life?* What's the big difference?"

The woman next to Sean spoke.

"Dr. Sheldrake says, through inherited memory, when a member of a species learns something new or picks up a skill, it opens the doorway for *other* members of *that* species to do the same."

"Excellent, Mary Beth. What else? Anyone?"

"Sheldrake says there are invisible energetic fields that connect members of a species," another student added.

Sean was never confident enough to participate in classroom exchanges, but suddenly, his hand was up.

"Yes." The professor pointed to Sean.

"Sir, is this scientist proposing a Universal Mind?"

"Universal Mind?" the professor asked, looking puzzled. "Tell me what you're thinking."

"So, if person A lives in close proximity to person B, who has learned something or perfected a technique, then person A might be able to do the same thing as person B? For example, say, Mary Beth," he gestured to the woman next to him, "is an avid meditator who has opened herself to deep levels of consciousness, and we spend years together in an interpersonal, intimate relationship; would Sheldrake propose that I too could be open to such experiences simply out of association?"

"Just for the record," Mary Beth interjected, "I've never met this guy."

The class erupted into laughter.

"I don't recognize you either," said the professor, "and I know everyone. So?"

"Sorry, I crashed your class. I'm a philosophy student who heard you were discussing these concepts."

"These theories have a lot of people thinking. Morphic transference is an interesting topic from many angles," the teacher said. "Right now, scientists are looking at plants. They haven't moved into the human realm, but it's coming. You can see it explains so much about evolution. The first one does it, and it opens the way to possibilities. In the case of your meditation connection. I believe there would have to be *attempts* on your part, *as well* as your connection to your friend."

"Of course," Sean said, "it's like the Yoga Sutras of *Patanjali*. *Practice* worked with consistency and for a long time is also needed. It all works with Sheldrake's Morphic Resonance. It's all about intent, consistent practice, *and* connection. It's the connection we have to each other through being members of the same species."

"Ahhh . . . and, besides philosophy, are you studying world religions?" the professor asked with a laugh.

"Yes," was all Sean could say as his thoughts raced. Ren may have tapped into the Universal Mind and developed yogic superpowers, but they are not only available to him. Under his breath, Sean whispered, "Everything you can do, I can do also."

"Okay, thank you, Mr.?"

"Devlin," he blurted, surprising himself.

"Are you related to Professor Devlin in the history department, young man?"

"I don't believe so," Sean said. Tears welled in his eyes. *I'm close. I know I am.*

"Now, next theory," the professor said, "let's crack open those minds of yours even more."

As the class moved on, Sean closed his eyes and recited the mantra to Ganesh. Eventually, the professor's voice brought him back into the room.

"All right, don't forget, next week's your exam. If you have questions come see me or Claudia during office hours. Have a great day."

"Excuse me, Mary Beth," Sean said, "we're in the science hall at the University of Cincinnati, right?"

"Uh, yeah," she said.

"I know this is an odd question, but what year is it?"

"1986. Are you okay?"

"I think so," he said, reaching up to feel his full head of hair. "Do you know anything about Professor Devlin?"

"I hated history, but he made it interesting," she said.

"Thanks."

"You're odd," she said.

"More than you know," he said with a smile.

"Your comments about meditation freaked me out. I just started studying Buddhism and meditating, so for you to use me as an example—"

"It freaked out your rational, scientific mind," Sean said. "I know the feeling. Start thinking of it as the magnetic radiance of the Universe, which is what I think Sheldrake's tapping into. Those of us on similar paths are pulled toward each other. We're mystical revolutionaries."

"Hmm," she said as she picked up her book bag and started to leave.

"Excuse me," Sean said, folding the piece of paper she had given him and putting it and the pen in his pocket. "One more thing. Where are the history faculty offices?"

"McMicken Hall." She pointed to the door on her left.

Sean brought his hands into prayer position, bowed, and ran out of the classroom.

His heart was pounding as he tore across campus. He tried to stay calm, but his mind was rapid-firing questions: *Would he recognize me? Does he still have his old awareness like I have mine? What will I do once we are together? Are we going to remain here or go back to our other life?*

Breathe. Be present. He heard Her in his heart.

He ran into McMicken Hall and found a directory: Professor Devlin RM 113.

Are you serious? He couldn't get away from that numerical combination no matter where he went.

Sean jumped the steps, two at a time. The plaque on the door read Dr. Reynolds Devlin. He took a few breaths to compose himself.

"Here goes. Please reunite us," he whispered.

54

ATTACHMENT

Once home, I went to my office. All I could think about was Sean and how he was now lost to me in both dimensions. I flipped open my planner, thinking I'd work on next week's classes or the exam. I saw the red *X*. It was like a punch in the stomach.

"Oh my god! I've been here for so long."

Panic rushed through my whole body.

"Are you going to keep me here forever?" I screamed, looking up to the ceiling. "You're holding me here against my will. I don't belong here! Where's my council? Where are the goddesses?"

A dense ball of energy formed just below my rib cage, constricting my breath.

"What do I need to learn so you'll set me free?"

Attachment. Attachment. Attachment.

"Ahhhhh . . ." I grabbed both sides of my head as it felt like it would split open.

Breathe deeper before you lose it all together, I told myself.

It's your meditations that got you here in the first place. You played with fire. Now you're stuck.

"I can't get past this damn mind voice," I yelled. Panic shifted into primal fear. I started to hyperventilate.

I grabbed pillows off the love seat and sat down on the floor. I closed my eyes. Breathe deep, I told myself. You know what to do.

Stop this thing with the breath, the inner saboteur screamed. *All this breathing and letting go has only brought you grief. Now, you lay in a self-induced meditation coma in one life while your consciousness is trapped in this other life, playing Dr. Devlin with Lisa and Josh.*

This voice was not just in my head—it came from the walls, the floor, and the ceiling.

My eyes opened wide. A self-induced meditation coma? Is that what's happening in my real world? I can't believe this voice. It lies. It will say anything to make me afraid, vulnerable, and fragile, I thought. It will take me back to how I lived before I stepped on the path of yoga.

"You're losing it, Ren," I said out loud, "breathe!"

I forced one deep inhale and followed it down into my belly, then followed the long exhale. *You did it. Keep breathing like this.*

Stop this nonsense, the mind voice commanded. *Teach your classes! Your other life is gone. Face it, write your books! Accept this reality! Your NOW is here! You are here forever!*

I took another deep breath.

"*Neti, Neti,* this voice is not me."

You stumbled into something big by raising Mike from the dead. You're the big spiritual celebrity. Look where it got you! You're in limbo land.

"Breathe, breathe into the heart," I instructed myself.

This is where your practices have landed you, the sinister voice berated. *The Yoga Sutras warned you about the* siddhis. *Now you're stuck. Your life is, again, forever changed because you live here. Sean's off with someone else, and you're with Lisa. This is your life now. Live it!*

"Shut up!" I screamed. "Stop it! This is not my reality. This is not where I want to be!" A panic button inside my brain was triggered. My body temperature dropped, yet I began to sweat profusely. My breath was shallow and rapid. Every muscle in my body constricted so intensely I felt my life force was being strangled. Just as I felt I would lose consciousness, the earth quaked, and I was blinded by an intense white flash of light.

The furnishings of my home office dissolved, and I was now standing in my childhood living room with the overstuffed chair, the dark blue area rug, the 1960s color TV, and the picture of Jesus praying in the Garden of Gethsemane.

"No!" I screamed. "I don't want to be here either. I quit! I give up! Saturn, Venus . . . I can't do this! Let me go!"

I paced the three rooms that made up the downstairs of my childhood home like a caged animal. I felt the familiar abandonment, yet now it felt ancient, far older than this lifetime. A nervous tension I used to neutralize with my practices resurfaced.

"NO, NO, NO!" I yelled through my sobs.

"I know I'm a fraud!" I screamed. "I am not an elevated yogi. I am me, an ordinary screwed-up person! I want my partner back. I want my friends back. I want my life back! Do you hear me, council?" My voice cracked. "Enough! Enough!"

The adult me and the nine-year-old that still occupied my body stood shaking uncontrollably.

I dropped to my knees and pounded the floor with my fist. "Ahhhhhhhhh . . ."

Primal, unintelligible sounds came from a deep place inside me that I never knew existed. My heart pounded, and I gasped for breath.

"You are holding me here against my will. Ahhh . . . where is your compassion?" I screamed to the cosmos, arms stretched over my head.

I got to my feet and paced again. The rants and cries continued. I slapped my hands on the wall and then on my head.

"I'm trapped. Alone. Disconnected from everything I've ever known."

I ran to the familiar overstuffed chair in the living room and pulled it out so I could get my adult body behind it. I curled up in a ball and sobbed.

With an involuntary gasp, I felt my consciousness split in two. I *felt* myself in crisis on the floor, but at the same time, I *observed* myself from above. For the first time in months, I sensed the compassionate part of my awareness as it watched the sobbing, snot-nosed me throw a tantrum and experience pain so intense my ego-self thought this was the end.

Let it out, the observer whispered. *Your tears won't fall forever.*

"What the hell?" I screamed.

Let it out. It controls you. It's ancient. You are attached to your pain. Experience it and let it go. Your past and future do not exist. All you have is this moment.

"Mother fucker!" I screamed, "I don't want this moment. I want my old life back. No miracles, no lessons for my soul. Let me go home!"

Then, the hovering me was gone. The only sound was me gasping for breath and sobbing.

"What, you have nothing to say? No words of advice? I don't want to be here! I don't want to learn this lesson. I'm through!"

Fear, anger, and terror rushed through my body and mind.

"Stay silent. I don't care. Fuck you!" I screamed.

I pounded my fists on the floor and continued my primal rampage, allowing what lurks in the shadows and under the surface of desperation and disappointment to drain every ounce of energy out of me.

Between gasps for breath, I heard a voice that was distinctly feminine coming from my heart center:

Let your fears go. You might find that you're not alone. What have you learned? Is it all lost?

"Please forgive me," I said to Her. "Please, please forgive me." As my body rocked of its own volition, I felt I was alternately in the arms of the hazel-eyed goddess and Sean. The rhythm facilitated deep breaths that gradually replaced the gasping, which allowed my solar plexus to relax slightly and eased the gripping around my heart.

Let go of your fears. Her voice again resounded in my heart.

Raise your own little boy from the dead. You might find your way back home.

With one long, audible sigh, the child inside me collapsed into itself. My muscle tension was released. The rage in me subsided. I felt cleansed of something.

I let go of who I thought I was and who I think I am and melted into the floor behind the chair. Exhausted, I lay with my left hand on my heart and my right hand flat on the hardwood floor. My breath continued to slow.

Me and my breath. There is nothing else.

The breath was once again able to make its journey through my whole body. As I lay crumpled, with my tear-stained face and snotty nose, traces of tranquility bubbled up alongside a sense of gratitude for everything, even this breakdown.

If this is where I must stay, I must find happiness, I thought. I must transform my feelings of a trapped ego into being of service to others. I must trust that I am here for a reason. And my beloved, Sean, may he find happiness in all dimensions of his existence.

I heard a sound, a ringing, a phone.

This time is for me to heal. I stayed still, just breathing.

Then I heard it again. This time, there was a voice.

Remain with your acceptance, love, and surrender, I heard Her say from my heart.

I'd been given a glimpse of the beauty of letting go. The world could wait. *I need to be here—right now.*

Gradually, I became more and more conscious of the sound of my long, deep breathing. It was exquisitely comforting.

55

TWO QUARTERS

Sean knocked on the door of office 113.

"Come in."

He was greeted by a petite blond, wearing saucer-size glasses, a pale blue short-sleeve dress with a lace collar, and a beautifully embroidered vest.

"Can I help you?"

"I was hoping to talk with Professor Devlin."

"He left for the day. Do you need help with exam material?"

Sean was thrown off.

"Actually, I'm thinking about changing majors and wanted to ask about the history program." The words just came out.

"I'm Paulette, his teaching assistant. I'd be happy to answer questions from my perspective."

"I think that would be helpful," Sean found himself saying when he really wanted to blurt out that Ren was the love of his life and he needed to see him right now.

"Come in. Sit down. I have a few minutes before my next student meeting."

Sean sat across the desk from her.

"Are you thinking of focusing on any particular time period?"

"Early to Renaissance English history."

"What's your current major?"

"Ahhh," he said, his council putting words in his mouth. "Well, I started in business, and now, it's philosophy with a minor in world religions."

"Philosophy and religion, oh, you need to talk with Dr. Devlin. He's incorporating yoga and Hinduism into the books he's writing."

"Really? Is that a recent development for him?"

"Yes. He's off on a whole new stream of fiction, full of meditation and time travel."

Meditation . . . time travel? "When can I talk with him?"

There was a rap on the door. A slender man in his fifties opened it and stepped halfway in.

"Paulette, has Ren left for the day?"

"Yes, he wasn't feeling well, so he went home."

"Could we talk in the hall for a moment? Excuse us," he said to Sean. "She'll be right back."

As the door closed behind Paulette, Sean heard from his heart, *An opportunity.*

He stood and walked behind Ren's desk. Starring at him from across the room on the bookshelf was the framed photo of Ren, Lisa, and Josh as a small boy.

There's no trace of me in this world, he thought. Tears filled his eyes.

Is he longing for me? Does he even remember me? Help me! What am I supposed to do?

Sean looked down. Under the glass desk protector was a list of phone numbers. Dr. D Home: 431-5381. He pulled the paper and pen out of his pocket, jotted down the number, and then quickly slipped back into the guest chair.

"Sorry about that," Paulette said as she re-entered the room. "I didn't catch your name."

"Sean."

"Well, Sean, my next appointment's here. If you want to talk with either of us, I can put you on Dr. D's calendar."

"Thanks, Paulette," he said, standing, "I'll let you know. Right now, I think I am on the brink of revelation."

Sean walked down the steps, out onto the campus lawn, and began to pace.

Now, what do I do? he thought. Do I call him and say, *Hi bud, this is Sean, your long-term companion from the future? I miss you and want us to be together again—wife or no wife, son or no son.*

Stay centered. Work quickly, said the increasingly familiar female heart voice.

Work quickly, that's right, Sean thought. I don't know how much time I have left in this alternate life. Will I come out of this meditation without seeing him? Then I'd know where Ren was but not be able to help him. Please, no. That would be torture.

Breathe. Listen. Find patience and grace. No fear. No attachment.

Sean took a deep breath and closed his eyes. The *prana* of the breath traveled into the core of his being. As he opened his eyes, the answer was twenty feet in front of him—a phone booth.

I really am in another time and place, he thought. He stepped inside and closed the door. Sitting on the stainless-steel shelf were two quarters.

"Thank you."

He put a quarter into the slot. He dialed. It rang. It rang again. It rang twice more, and then the answering machine picked up. Should I leave a message? *What am I going to say?*

"Hi, you've reached the Devlins'." It was Lisa's voice. "Leave a message, and we'll get back to you."

Sean hung up.

"Guide me."

Call again and leave a message.

"Hi Ren, this is Sean. I hope you know who I am. I need to talk with you. I'm at a phone booth near McMicken. The number's 261-7569. Call me. Please."

Sean felt a huge letdown as he hung up. Why *would* he call me back? *Did he even know who Sean was?*

"I could use an iPhone and the internet right about now," Sean murmured.

Use the phone book.

"Oh, my goddess, yes, if he's listed, it'll give me his address," he said as he opened the huge book. "Devlin . . . Dan Devlin . . . L. Devlin. This matches the number. It's listed under Lisa's name."

He wrote it down, 4323 Ludlow Ave. He took a deep breath. I'm so close, I can run there, he thought.

"Well, my love," he said aloud, "the poor kid from the west side of Newport has moved up in the world. I hope you are not *too* used to your fancy neighborhood, your wife, and your son because I'm here to take you home."

56

THE DOORBELL

I have no idea how long I lay behind the chair in my childhood home; minutes, days . . . it didn't matter. The transformation from lower-mind anger and denial to higher-heart-mind surrender and acceptance could not be rushed. Knowing breakdowns are necessary for breakthroughs, I lay there, healing my heart with deep surrender and waiting for *it* and *me* to return to life. I did not want to return half dead, but rather with a new sense of commitment to the sacred and to my practice, so with my face against the floor, representing Mother Earth, I began to recite the Gayatri.

"*Aum Bhur, Bhuvah, Swaha . . .*"

Ding-dong.

I paused. Was that a bell? Tingsha?

"*Tat Savitur Varenyam . . .*"

"*Bhargo, Devasya . . .*"

Again and again, I heard it.

The doorbell?

I couldn't move.

It rang again. And again.

I opened my eyes and found myself curled up in the middle of the floor of my home office. I was back in an existence I must somehow make peace with.

The doorbell rang again. I got up to my knees, moved slowly to my feet, wiped my nose on my shirt sleeve, my eyes with my hands, and stumbled to the door. I took a deep breath.

"Hi," Sean said as I opened the door. His beautiful blue eyes filled with tears. "I've come to take you home."

"Home?"

He stepped across the threshold and wrapped himself around me.

"You look like you've been through it, Reno."

I buried my face in his neck. *Oh, thank the goddess.* I felt my entire body relax as if the weight of the world had finally come off my shoulders.

"I've been like the walking dead. I'm coming out of a complete breakdown. I'd finally given up. I abandoned every attachment and just decided to make the best of this existence . . . without you." I held him tighter.

"Why don't you invite me in and tell me everything about the last three days?"

"Three days?" I said, leading him into my office. "According to *my* calendar, I've been here three months."

"Ahh, bud, no wonder you're freaking out."

"My council's been completely silent, I can't meditate, *and* I'm married to Lisa and raising Josh as our son."

"I know," he said.

"How?"

"I stopped by your office, looking for you. I saw the photo and put it all together. I was hoping you hadn't forgotten me."

"Oh, Sean. I've been desperate to get back to you."

We sat close together on the love seat.

"There *is* a Sean here, but he has no inkling of the future us. We're attracted to each other, but . . . he cut me loose earlier today. He told me he's moving on."

"Whoa, I'm not sure how I could compete with a younger man, even . . . if it was *me*." He smiled.

"Seriously, Sean, how *did you* get here and find me?"

"Sara was fairly sure you were in a recapitulation coma, dealing with some heavy stuff. I was afraid you'd never come back, so with Sara's guidance and encouragement, I went deep in my meditation. *Everything I can do*—came to life for me. I went back to the mound and ended up face-to-face with *my* council. With their coaxing, I followed them into the earth, which took me to a physics class, where I learned you were a professor. Then I found your office and met Paulette, saw your phone number on the desk, stepped outside, made a call, left a message, then found your address in the phone book."

"Wow, wow," I said, sitting up and moving to the edge of the seat. "Your breakthroughs led you here, just at the right moment."

I took a deep breath and took his hand in mine, but I could not meet his eyes.

"Sean, this has been about my attachment to you but also my attachment to guilt."

"Guilt?"

"I've been riddled with guilt over abandoning Josh and Lisa *and* never telling you about it."

"Wait a minute, abandoning them?"

"Yeah, right before we met, Josh wanted to come live with me after the accident. I said no. Lisa offered to help, I said no. I didn't tell you because I had a hard time facing myself. And I didn't want you to think I was shallow and unfeeling."

"Ren, you know better. We all have our stuff. Shallow and unfeeling aren't words I've ever used to describe you."

"Well, I just lived three months of what that life could be like, *and* because of my attachments, I *was* shallow and unfeeling toward Josh and Lisa, and I made their lives pure hell."

"That's why the key in the waiting room was *love yourself, forgive yourself, and face attachment,*" he said.

"To say I'm attached to you is a huge understatement."

"You'd be fine without me," Sean said. "We can't give over our life to anyone else. Not even each other."

"I came to that realization fifteen minutes ago as I screamed and cried behind my childhood chair. I knew I couldn't stay lost in you. A voice finally made its way through the darkness into my heart. I realized no matter where we are, all we have is the moment."

"Promise me . . . wait, let's promise each other," Sean said, "that if one of us wakes up from whatever this is . . . without the other . . . we'll live our life to the fullest."

"I promise, especially after today, but . . . I know I will never forget you or let you go in my heart."

"That's part of the problem," he said, pulling me close. "We have to learn to love without attachment. Otherwise, it wrings the life out of life."

"Not an easy lesson for someone whose initials match *Raga* and *Dvesha*," I said.

"And your office is 1-13?" Sean smiled. "There's no escape, Ren Devlin, for you or any of us from our connection to the Universe."

The levity in his voice felt good.

I stood and pulled him to his feet.

"I want to kiss you," I said, standing face-to-face, "but . . ." I placed my hand on his chest.

"But what . . . ?"

"I'm afraid if I close my eyes, you'll be gone when I open them."

"What if instead," he said, moving my hand from his chest, "we kiss, it breaks the spell and brings us back to our other life?"

"Let's forget about my fear *and your* fairy tale endings," I said, "and savor *one* kiss in this *one* moment."

We merged our lips and arms.

"Why do I feel I am barging in on some romantic reunion?"

Sean and I stepped back to see Lisa in the doorway.

"Shit!" she said, walking closer to us. "This is all real somehow, isn't it? Let me guess," she said, turning to Sean, "you're actually from the other dimension and have come to take him back."

"How do you know that?" Sean asked.

"Call it air sign intuition. Besides, Ren's told me everything." She shook her head and then pointed at me. "He's not easy to deal with," she said with a deep sigh and an exasperated shrug of her shoulders.

"Now what?" she asked curtly. "Do you two vanish back through a hole in the earth, and I get *my* Ren back?"

"I don't know. I hope so," I said.

"You know," she said, "for being such an advanced yogi, you leave a lot to be desired."

"Thanks," I said with a chuckle.

"Touché, Lisa," Sean said with a laugh.

"Seriously, where is *my* Ren? Will he remember any of this? Honestly, I'm okay with waking up from this, realizing it's all been a dream." She looked at me with an eyebrow lifted. "Can you or your council arrange that?"

"Lis, I have no idea where the other Ren is. I don't know if Sean and I go back or we stay here and move on from this point."

"Shit, shit, shit." She paced the office with one hand on her forehead. "I want my old life back. It may not have been complete bliss, but I liked it. You and I, he and I, whoever, we had an unspoken agreement about what we were doing. We had similar goals and mutual respect for each other. It was *really* good."

She stopped, now standing between Sean and me.

"I want you to be happy," she said, looking at me. "I know you have something with him that we could never have. What we have is beautiful, but it's *not* this. I feel it."

She shifted her gaze to the floor.

"The last three months, I felt I was losing you, but right now, it feels like a death. I could burst into tears if I let myself, but we all know I won't. At least, I hope not." There were tears in her eyes, but her voice was strong. "Ren, you and I have always been best friends, but we're not ultimate soul mates, I know that. I've been with the two of you for no more than five minutes, and I *know* you belong together. My head doesn't want it to be so, but my heart knows true love."

"Lis—"

"Ren, let me do this *and* listen closely. Love overrides attachment. Do you hear me?"

I nodded.

"Maybe I am being overly objective, but I don't think so. I think we're on some transformational precipice together. I already told you I forgive you for whatever it is you think you've done, but can you forgive yourself for being human and having emotions and desires? You aren't superhuman. None of us are. Relax. Figure out what makes you happy in your life and go for it."

I felt the death she mentioned, but I also felt a rebirth of hope in my heart for all of us.

"I love you deeply, Lis."

"I know you do. I love you, too, and I *always will*, but it's time for me to let go. It doesn't mean I don't care about you, but I have to let go of wanting something that doesn't exist. You say there's love between the three of us in your other life, so I'll trust *that* love is enough. It's okay, Ren. Love, forgive, and detach."

"I feel the nurturing of the Moon, the love of Venus, and the strength of Athena come through your words," I said. "You really are a goddess."

"I told you I was months ago," she said with a hint of a smile.

"I should have believed you."

She winked.

"Okay," I said, "I'd like to recognize the sacredness of this moment between the three of us. My suggestion may sound odd—"

"Odder than you two being here from an alternative life?" Lisa snickered.

"You're right," I said.

"Of course, I'm right," she said, now with a full smile.

"Some things are exactly the same over time and space," Sean said.

"I believe you're acknowledging my humility." She raised an eyebrow. "Ren tells me we're all friends off in the future." She shook her head at the absurdity of her words. "I bet I'm just as understanding and incredible."

"Oh, more than you know," Sean said with a grin.

"You're *definitely* growing on me." She gave him a playful wink. "Ren, back to your odd suggestion."

"Yes, let's form a tight circle and place your left hand on your heart. Then, Lisa, place your right hand on Sean's back. Sean, place your hand on my back, and I'll put mine on Lisa. This represents a ring of fearlessness between us." We formed a human Abhaya mudra.

"Close your eyes, take a few deep breaths, and feel our connection from the heart."

"Whoa," Lisa said softly. "I feel love, acceptance, and . . . forgiveness, already."

I felt the presence of the goddesses come through Lisa.

I opened my eyes. There were silver threads streaming from our crown centers, traveling up, then joining together as they moved through the ceiling of the room. I closed my eyes.

"I wish you both happiness," Lisa said.

"You too, my love," I said. "Your unconditional love is a great teacher for me."

"For all of us," Sean added.

Sean began to recite *The Prayer for All Beings*. I joined him.

"May all beings have happiness and the causes of happiness.

May all beings be free from suffering and the causes of suffering.

May all beings know the sacred place that lies beyond suffering.

May we all have equanimity beyond hatred, anger, attachment, and fear, and

May we know the equality of all that lives."

"Please join me in an *om*," I said.

The sound of our combined voices went straight to my heart. Our united, silver cord extended higher and higher, out beyond the planet, even beyond the boundaries of our sky.

"Open your eyes, and let's join our hands," I said.

We stood silently gazing at the silver threads in complete equanimity.

Then we heard the front door open and close.

"Lis, I'm home," said a voice that sounded exactly like mine.

"Holy shit!" Lisa said with eyes wide open. "He's back!"

I took a deep breath and closed my eyes.

"Welcome home!" I opened my eyes to see Carol's tear-stained face and Sara standing next to her.

"Sean!" Carol screamed and ran from the room. I heard the back door slam. "Sean, Sean," she yelled in the distance. "He's home!"

"As soon as you started to recite the prayer," Sara said, "we knew you were coming home."

"Oh, my goddess, Sara."

"Take it easy." She placed her hand on mine and smiled.

"Where's Sean?"

"He went to the woods last night to find you," she said.

"He found me all right," I said, reaching for the pentagram around my neck. "And he brought me home."

57

A CHAT WITH LOVE

Sean rushed into the room and into my arms.

"Oh, my goddess," Sean said, "we did it; you're home."

"I'm thrilled to be back in my *real life*," I said, hugging him tight. "I'm so looking forward to hearing your take on this whole experience—do you remember your process of finding me?"

"Ah-yeah, meeting *my* council, following them into a hole, and ending up on a college campus in the 1980s—it's burned into my soul," Sean said. "It was the kick in the butt I needed to get over my attachment to *not* believing in myself."

"I love you, I love you, I love you," I said, squeezing him even tighter.

The entire rest of the day I felt a heightened sense of emotion that was a strange mixture of euphoria and sadness. I also felt an urgent need to dive back into the deep inner practices I had abandoned, so I went out to the earthen mound to meditate. I sat near the entrance and began my *samyama* process.

Immediately, I was in front of my council.

"This opportunity was difficult, Ren," Venus said.

"Yes, it was difficult *and* downright scary."

"As you know, *Raga* and *Dvesha* were your constant companions. Do you see how attachment equals death?" she asked.

"My attachments to Sean are abyssal. I felt I was dying without him."

"Everyone has to battle their attachments and aversions that are burrowed deep in the human psyche," Venus said. "The lesson is to enjoy and savor the beauty of your life without clinging."

She stood, emanating an inner radiance.

"I love you," she said.

I bowed my head as tears formed.

"We all love you." She gestured to both sides of the table. "We know how hard you've worked to understand your life and be a good person. We, as your council, guide you through the kleshas by providing opportunities to grow and expand in conscious awareness. That's the cosmic game of existence. As your co-chair, I want to encourage you. You're exactly where you need to be on your journey. Your belief in the power of love and the feminine is an intricate part of life. Show by example what's possible. Keep your heart open and continue to demonstrate to the world how love creates miracles. Dismiss any feelings of martyrdom as you face the last of the kleshas."

She smiled. "Remember, as yoga teaches, life is always a mixture of light and dark. Do you understand?"

"I do. This last roll of the dice with *Raga* and *Dvesha* made me well aware of what martyrdom and self-pity feel like."

"Imperfection is the beauty of being human," she said. "What you continue to learn from Saturn and all the references to 1:13 of the Sutras is that consistent inner reflection leads to deeper self-love, which fosters universal compassion for yourself and all beings, even when you or they are imperfect. Then you can enter the ecstatic realm of being able to give love for the sake of giving with no expectations."

"That's you, Venus in Pisces," I said.

"Yes, and *every* human has the potential to access this level of love no matter where I reside in their chart. For you, this lesson of selfless love is part of your karmic evolution. So I, along with Pluto, the deity of transformation, will be orchestrating the next phase of your journey."

"The last klesha?" I asked and then looked to Pluto, the only one of the ten not in white. His black Roman wrap was draped over one shoulder, his stare penetrating. "I believe I met an incarnation of you in the magick store . . . Orcus?"

He gave a slight, tilted nod.

"Pluto is a quintessential master of manifestation, as you'll see," said Venus.

"Should I do anything to prepare?" I asked, returning my attention to her.

"Yes, listen to me through your heart," Venus said, "and continue to practice, breathe, and acknowledge the power of the feminine."

"And surrender," said Pluto in a deep, baritone voice.

My eyes opened. I was staring at the mound. Surprisingly, I felt gratitude rather than anxiety. I stood, brought my hands into *Anjali* mudra at my heart, and bowed.

"I thought I might find you here."

I turned to see Sara.

"I'm getting ready to head home," she said. "Let me know how else I can help. A recapitulation meditation like what you've just been through usually means you're ready for some big breakthroughs."

"Big breakthroughs . . . yes," I said. "I just learned Venus and Pluto will lead the next phase of my journey with the kleshas."

"Quite the combo," she said, nodding. "The god of the underworld is perfect to lead you through the klesha of fear, *Abhinivesha*."

"And Venus is always there to guide me with love," I said.

"*All* the goddesses are surrounding you," she said, moving in to hug me.

"Yes, they are," I said, holding her tight. I stepped back, held her by the shoulders, and looked into her clear, blue eyes. "And *you*, my dear teacher, will always be part of my goddess brigade."

"Always," she said with a hint of a smile.

58

THE DRIVE HOME

The next morning, Sean, Carol, and I loaded the car in silence. A unique reverence for what this time had provided permeated our movements. I climbed into the back seat, Sean drove, and Carol claimed shotgun.

"This retreat turned out completely different than I anticipated," Carol said as we pulled away from the cabin.

"Welcome to our world." Sean said.

We all laughed.

"As soon as we get phone service, I'll go over any messages that came in while we were unplugged," she said.

We drove for about fifteen minutes through the peaceful, rolling hills of Kentucky before we merged onto the interstate.

"We have internet!" Carol said, turning to look at me. "What are you working on all spread out back there?"

"Just writing in my journal," I said. "There's so much to process between the last three days and a chat I had with Venus earlier about approaching the fifth klesha."

"Oh, jeez," Sean said.

"I guess I'm gonna have to sign up for the next yoga teacher training, so I'll know all this," Carol said. "But for now, fill me in on number five."

"*Abhinivesha*," Sean said. "It's the culmination of the journey through the kleshas because you come face-to-face with all the unconscious fears the other four create. The anecdote is to remember you are eternal and more than your physical body." Sean looked up at me in the rearview mirror. "How'd I do, Mr. Yoga?"

"A-plus," I said. "*Abhinivesha* translates to the *will to live*, so it's specifically the ultimate attachment to your body and the aversion from separating from it."

"Death?" Carol asked.

"Yep."

"Okay, can we take a break?" she asked, shaking her head. "My brain's still reeling from comas and alternate lives."

Carol settled into her seat like a kid with a video game and began to review our phone messages and texts. I closed my eyes and breathed in a deep sense of gratitude for being exactly where I was in the moment. I savored the friendship, love, and normalcy. Sean steered the car toward home.

"I want to admit something to you guys," Carol said, breaking the silence. "I'm *attached* to going through your social media and correspondence. I never know what'll be in there."

"So, what did you find this time?" Sean asked.

"Okay," she said, turning in her seat to look at both of us. "Here's today's briefing on your lives. I am happy to report that things *are* settling down for you. There's less than half of the stuff you've been getting."

I let out a sigh.

"On your personal list—Dottie Gant's assistant texted and asked if you could do Dottie's massage earlier than Friday."

"Sure, tomorrow afternoon?" Sean asked.

"I'll confirm that," Carol said.

"Next, Kate wants to know if you could do a follow-up class on the Yoga Sutras for the teacher trainees. She said it's not open to the public, so it'll be low key, and asked if Friday late afternoon would work."

"Now that we've moved Dottie's massage," I said, "that'll be perfect. The Universe is again at work."

"That class is going to bombard you with questions about what you've been through," Sean said, glancing back at me.

I nodded, "But I can't wait to be with them, more normality."

"Lastly *and* most importantly, Josh and Whitney want you to come to Harry's birthday party Saturday."

"Yes, yes, yes," Sean said, gripping the steering wheel. "Oh my goddess, we're headed back to our regular life."

"Let's all take a deep breath," Sean said, anticipating chaos as we turned onto our street.

"Wow, it's midday, and there's no one here," Carol said, "except that guy in the car across the way."

"He's not getting out," Sean said as he pulled in front of the house. "Maybe he's not here for us . . . imagine that."

I let out a deep sigh, feeling my physical, mental, and emotional body decompress.

"Aren't you just a little disappointed that your celebrity status has faded so quickly?" Carol asked as we unpacked the car.

"I'm grateful to be nobody again," said Sean.

"Anonymity is bliss," I said.

"So, you had a talk with Venus about *Abhinivesha*," Sean said over dinner. "Anything I should know?"

"Basically, Venus and Pluto are orchestrating this next experience, and I should listen to the feminine through my heart."

"Pluto, the god of the underworld, is finally getting *his* time in the spotlight," Sean said. "He's intense. Are you nervous?"

"Right now, I'm not. I'm just thrilled to be with you, in full attachment." I smiled.

59

HEAL HER

The next afternoon, as we headed to Dottie's, a midwestern thunderstorm was brewing. The nimbus clouds were dark gray, almost black. The wind plummeted heavy rain onto the windshield of the car. Brilliant flashes of lightning were quickly followed by angry claps of thunder as we pulled into the garage of Dottie's building.

Susan, Dottie's assistant, greeted us at the condominium door.

"Guys, Dottie is not feeling well this week," she said softly. "That trip to Cleveland really took it out of her."

We heard coughing in the next room.

"The doctors say it's pneumonia."

A clap of thunder shook the windows.

"Pneumonia? Does Walt know?" I asked.

"Yes, he's still in Cleveland, but they've been able to video chat."

"Should we come back another day?" Sean asked.

"No. She's adamant about getting a massage. I'm not sure if it's the massage she wants or just to be with the two of you."

"Well, today she's going to get both," Sean said.

The coughs from the other room sounded like gasps for survival. I spontaneously placed my hand on my heart. I *felt* her discomfort. I took a deep breath.

We stepped into Dottie's sitting room to find her propped up in bed. Her skin was translucent. She had deep, dark circles under her eyes and looked frail and vulnerable, very different from the commander-in-chief persona we saw less than a week ago in Cleveland. I felt Yama, the god of death, close.

"Get me on that massage table, boys," she said when she saw us. "You have your work cut out for you today."

She tried to push herself up but collapsed back into her bed.

"Relax, Dottie," Sean said as he scooped up all one hundred pounds of her and carried her to the table.

We elevated her back and head to an almost upright position. The coughing persisted. There was none of the usual chitchat. She was deep inside trying to maintain.

We stood on either side of her and began to gently massage her shoulders and arms. Her breathing remained labored, but gradually, her cough subsided as her body relaxed with our soft, reverent touch.

Within minutes, she had another coughing fit. She tried to sit up. Sean handed her tissues. She eventually relaxed and quieted.

"How can we make this easier for you?" I asked.

"I'm not sure this is worth the fight, boys. I may not ride this one out." She was interrupted by another coughing fit that consumed her body. When she was done, she looked at me and then over at Sean, who had tears rolling down his cheeks.

"Oh, sweet boy, are you crying for me?" she asked Sean.

His lips quivered as he shook his head.

"Don't," she said in little more than a whisper. "I said I'd trade places with Walt, and I meant it. I'm not afraid. Actually, I'm excited to see what's next."

Again, the coughing, sitting up, the tissues, and then she relaxed back into the cushion. After several moments of silence, she asked, "What do you think heaven's like?"

"I think whatever you want in your heart will be there when you open your eyes after your last breath," I said.

"So, I'll see my husband and my daughters?"

"If that's what you want."

"That would be wonderful," she said with a sigh. "But I must admit, I have my doubts."

"About what?" I asked.

"I've been so privileged. Haven't I been living in heaven? What more can there be?"

"There's so much more, Dottie. The spiritual sages say death is just a doorway we pass through. Once we surrender and release ourselves from the confines of our bodies, we'll feel the bliss and contentment of Oneness."

"You make me want to be there right now," she said, closing her eyes. "You know, boys, I can't imagine a better way to go than to drift off on this table with you two by my side. Doesn't that sound lovely?"

Sean and I glanced at each other.

Eyes still closed, she said, "It might not be great for you." She opened her eyes, smiled, then broke off in another coughing fit.

As her coughing subsided, she said, "You know I'm starting to have my doubts about you."

"Really?" I asked.

"You've been here close to an hour, and I don't feel any better. Jeez." She winked.

"Oh, I see. You wanted me to heal what ails you today?" I said with a chuckle.

"Of course. I'm a busy woman with no time for this little cough," she mused.

"Remember, I'm not in control—"

"I remember," she said as she reached for my hand. "I'll always be grateful for what you did . . . what *we* did for Walt." Now, she squeezed my hand tight. "Don't waste a miracle on me. Give it to someone younger, someone with a growing family, or better yet, save another child who might change the course of history for the better. I'm ready for a new adventure. I'm not afraid at all."

No fear. What a beautiful example of facing *Abhinivesha*. Perhaps it wasn't Yama I'd felt, but rather Pluto, the god of transformation.

I felt a slight tingle in my right arm as we held hands. It grew into an undeniable electrical sensation extending from my shoulder to my fingertips.

She took a full, deep breath—the first one of the day. Her wheezing subsided, as did her cough.

"She's breathing better," Sean whispered. "You did it."

"*Love yourself, forgive everyone, and let go.*" Venus's words came through me.

Her muscles released, her body went limp, and her chest ceased to move. A sacred presence filled the room.

I felt a light caress on my right cheek and heard a whisper that echoed through the entire room: *Thank you.*

I looked at Sean.

"I heard her," Sean said, sobbing.

Kneeling next to my friend Dottie, I placed her hand on my cheek and cried. "Let yourself be carried on the wings of the angels and be protected by the arms of the mother, Holy Mary, Mother of God," I said.

A brilliant flash of lightning, followed by the roaring sound of thunder, filled the room.

60

ON THE WINGS OF THE ANGELS

That clap of thunder and lightning plunged the whole city into blackness. Sean, Susan, and I sat with Dottie in her candlelit sitting room until the emergency crew arrived. By the time we started our journey home, the storm had passed.

"For the next thirteen days, I'd like to set time aside to recite the *Maha Mrityunjaya*," I said to Sean as we turned onto Columbia Parkway, "and dedicate it to Dottie for a pleasant transition."

Sean gave my leg a soft squeeze. "I still can't believe she died right in front of us," he said, shaking his head. "But it's the way she wanted it, and if anyone could direct their final exit, it would be her."

I nodded. "It was a beautiful experience, right down to the thunderbolt and taking out the lights of the city with her last breath."

"And what a way to watch someone face the final klesha. She wasn't afraid," Sean said. "In fact, she seemed excited."

"I'd want to face that transition like Dottie," I said. "What a gift to experience someone hold both life and death in their heart and face the inevitable with such grace and hope."

I recited the Gayatri mantra silently as we passed through the intersection where my encounter with Mike had brought Dottie into our lives.

We noticed shards of glass on our porch and then the broken window as we walked toward the front door.

"Storm damage, I guess," Sean said, carefully walking over the glass that covered the library floor, "but there's no tree limb or—"

"But there is this," I said, picking up a brick that was halfway across the room. "It has *liar* painted on one side and *fake* on the other."

"Carol and I've seen those words on our social media."

"Hhhmmm," I murmured, looking at the shattered window.

"Ren—"

"I'm good, Sean." I took a deep breath.

"What's going through your head?"

"Dottie was just the beginning," I said, nodding and looking at the words painted on the brick. "Our journey with *Abhinivesha*, klesha number five . . . it's just getting started."

The next morning, nestled into our library, we recited one hundred and eight rounds of the *Maha Mrityunjaya*. I held an image of Dottie in my mind's eye, breathed deep into my heart center, and thanked her for her consummate example of fearlessness. We finished the last round and sat in silence. My energetic body floated in bliss like an autumn leaf slowly wafting in the air. After several breaths, I was standing in front of the open council doors.

I stepped in. They were all present, sitting with their hands folded in front of them.

"Your timing's perfect," I said, taking my usual seat. "I have some questions about—"

"Not today," Saturn said, looking pensive, "we've work to do."

"Yes, we need you to review with us your understanding of the five kleshas," Venus added in a somber tone I had never heard from her.

"Are we having role reversal?" I asked. "I feel calm and relaxed, and you all seem uptight."

My comment was met with only their concentrated stares.

"Okay, but we've been through this already," I said, "the kleshas are the five poisons that cause suffering because we identify with our ego instead of our divine nature. You've walked me through ignorance, ego, attachment, aversion—"

Pluto cleared his throat and stood. He now wore a black hooded robe that draped the floor. His thick, black hair framed his high, almost bony cheekbones. His eyelids were heavy, making it hard to see his green eyes, but I knew he was looking at *me*. I followed his movement as he walked around the long table, stopping six feet in front of me.

"And now," he said, "there's *Abhinivesha*, the intense attachment to life itself."

"Yes, sir, I know."

"To *know* is a mental supposition. My question regarding this next step through the kleshas goes beyond the mind. Are you afraid of death?"

"Does this have something to do with being with Dottie during her transition?" I asked. "That didn't scare me. It was a perfect example of human surrender into the unknown."

"So, your answer is?"

Our eyes were locked into a hypnotic stare. I swallowed hard. "I hope I'm not afraid, but until I face it, I'll never know."

"Do you believe you are more than your body and that your consciousness is eternal?" asked the god of transformation. He stepped closer.

"I believe our consciousness is energy and, like physics tells us, energy can neither be created nor destroyed, it only changes form. In theory it makes sense."

"If this *theory* makes sense, why are so many humans afraid to let go of their physicality when faced with death?"

"Because we forget our divine nature at birth when our spark squeezes into our body. We spend years learning to talk, walk, and take care of ourselves. We fall into a spiritual amnesia that has us identify only with our body and ego. Yoga helps us wake up and remember our divine nature has *only* changed forms and we are more than the physical, we *are* eternal and like Dottie, see death as a new adventure."

"Where are you in this process of waking up?"

"Every day, I move into more trust and surrender. Being with Dottie yesterday was a huge spiritual gift, and after my experience with the earthen mound, I'm back to my practices with a renewed commitment."

In my peripheral vision, I saw Saturn nod.

The eleven of us took a deep breath. Pluto stepped back from me.

"I know I'm not supposed to ask any questions in this session, but is there more to my *Abhinivesha* journey than saying goodbye to my dear friend?"

Venus stood. "Love unselfishly, with no expectation," she said.

"That wasn't an answer to my—"

"Be diligent," Saturn said as he rose to stand tall beside the goddess of love. "And know when to surrender."

"Let yourself be carried on the wings of the angels and be protected by the arms of the mother," Venus said in a whisper.

"Carried on the wings of the angels? Arms of the mother? What's going on?" I asked.

"Keep her words, these grains of truth, forefront, Ren," Pluto said as he assumed Abhaya mudra. "*Believe* in your heart rather than *think* with your mind."

Sean sounded the tingsha, which brought me back into our library and sent my council into the deep part of me where they live.

I wrote the details of my council conversation in my journal, underscoring *the wings of the angels* and *arms of the mother*, and then worked on materials for my private session with the twelve teacher trainees, who I knew would be full of questions about Pada Three and the journey I'd been on since we last gathered together.

"I'm thrilled you're going to be with me today to finally meet these exceptional women," I said to Sean as we drove to the studio.

"I wouldn't miss it. What's on the agenda?"

"I'm going to start with a meditation, then move into a discussion of Pada Three. I know they're champing to discuss it."

The phone rang.

"It's the glass installer," I said to Sean. "He's at the house already to replace the window."

"Darn, I thought they were coming tomorrow."

"Sir, can you hang out for about twenty minutes?" I asked the guy on the other end of the call. "Great. Thank you."

"Just drop me off. It'll be fine."

"This shouldn't take long," Sean said. "I'll be back as soon as I can."

"Great. Remember, Kate had a security system installed, so she'll buzz you in."

I walked into class and was smothered with hugs and kisses and tons of questions that I promised to answer. It was a beautiful homecoming. I went to the front of the room to get myself set up. On the wall behind the teacher's mat were hand-painted small and large starbursts ranging from deep crimson at the bottom to violet at the top. It was a gorgeous depiction of the chakra-energy centers. I put my notes and a statue of *Saraswati* at the top of my mat.

"It feels so good having you back in the studio," Kate said, giving me a big hug.

"You have no idea how grateful I am to be here," I said, squeezing her back. "Sean had to take care of something at the house. I told him to ring the buzzer."

"No worries," she said.

Once everyone was situated on their mats, I brought my hands into prayer position and met each of their eyes with a bow.

"Come to a comfortable seat," I said with a long sigh. "Let your eyes softly close and allow your breath to deepen. Imagine the breath coming in from the top of the head. Follow it down toward the tailbone. As you exhale, focus on the breath moving up and out through the crown chakra, *Sahasrara*. As you breathe in and out through this crown center, open yourself to release any fear or anxiety that blocks you from knowing your true inner-self."

I heard the buzzer and Kate's movement from her mat to the office and back again. Sean's back already? I thought.

"Now, find a pause at the top and bottom of your breath," I continued. "The pause is slight. There's no need to hold the breath in either place, simply note the pause."

I heard the door to the studio open and close.

"Relax," I said, "go to a place in your heart where there's no fear."

The group breathed as a synchronized unit.

"Access the place of deep inner calm where you know you are always fine," I said, "where even the most intense experiences of your life have a home. Acknowledge *all* your life experiences as necessary."

I took a deep breath.

Open your eyes slightly and scan the room, whispered a female voice inside my heart. I did as instructed. Everyone was sitting serenely with eyes closed, experiencing the rhythm of their breath. Then I spotted someone standing behind the opaque, sheer drapes in the back corner near the door. I opened my eyes a little more. A man in his early thirties, six-foot-two, muscular, with thick black hair and a heavy brow, stared at me with the same intense gaze I had experienced with Pluto earlier.

"Continue to breathe deep to tap into your inner guides," I instructed the class.

I closed my eyes and sent a line of unswerving heart energy in that man's direction. It boomeranged so quickly that I gasped. His voice was loud and clear inside my heart, *This is bullshit!*

I felt his pain. Thick, unyielding tentacles of anger and hate constricted his heart. Rage consumed his whole being.

Stay calm in your center, my heart voice advised.

I took a deep breath. *My* consciousness moved into *his* mind, which was dark like a violent cloudy wind squall, forming an erratic cyclone. I did not want to be there, but I could not let it go. I worked to keep my breath smooth.

"Open yourself to the possibility of a life without fear," the words flowed through me from my goddess guides, "a life without fear of even death—"

"This is bullshit!" the man screamed. Everyone jumped and turned.

"You liar!" he continued, slowly moving toward me across the classroom. "You can't raise the dead or heal anyone! You're a fake."

"Stay on your mats, everyone. It's okay," I said calmly.

I caught eyes with Kate, who looked ready to get up. I shook my head.

"Everything's *not* okay, you fake mother fucker!" He reached me, grabbed me by my T-shirt, and yanked me up to eye level.

"Now what, Mr. Miracle?" He threw me against the back wall, cracking the drywall. "Are you still calm and centered?"

With one hand around my neck and the other pressed on the wall, he held me tight against the now-crumbling chakra symbols.

I felt the angst of the students on their mats. Some of them began to stir.

"Don't move!" he barked. "Do what miracle man asked. Get rid of your fear." His almost-black eyes bore into me, his face within inches of mine. I smelled alcohol seeping from his pores. "How about you, liar? Are you afraid now? You should be! You're the one who needs a miracle. *Save yourself! Save yourself!*"

Someone started crying.

"*Shut up! Shut up!*" he shouted over his shoulder. "You don't have anything to cry about. You all sit here breathing and listening to his bullshit."

He tightened his grip around my neck.

"They're afraid," I gasped. "Let them go."

"*NO!* If anyone opens that door, I'll snap your neck. I will."

The students sat still.

Send love to his heart, send love to his heart, send love to his heart.

I kept the internal chant going in my own heart and managed to bring my hands into Abhaya mudra. Over his shoulder, I saw the students follow suit.

Relax into yourself, a soothing female voice whispered to me. *Let go of fear and surrender.* I was beginning to feel lightheaded. *Was this voice inside or outside me?*

I let go of the tension in my body and now silently recited the Abhaya mudra mantra: *I am not afraid of my life or what's in my heart*, I added, *or death.* I felt as if I was melting into the wall behind me.

The man's eyes narrowed as he felt me let go.

"Let them leave," I gasped through his grip on my neck.

"Why should I do anything for you? You've done nothing for me but raise my hopes and crush me!"

Tell Gabe to let the students go. I recognized Her voice inside my heart.

"Let them go, Gabe, please."

Flames ignited in the man's widened eyes. "How do you know my name?" He grabbed my shirt tighter around my neck and, using both hands, smacked my body off the back wall again and again.

I began to feel delirious. *Was I losing consciousness, or was my spirit separating from my body?*

"Tell me how you know." His face was now so close I could feel his breath.

"You were named for an angel, el arcángel Gabriel," I said in little more than a whisper.

"What? How do you—?"

"Let the students go," I gasped.

"Get out! Get out!" he screamed to the class as he pressed his face even closer.

No one moved off their mats. They held Abhaya mudra.

I heard the buzzer.

"If a cop walks in, you're dead."

Again, the buzzer.

"Why did you let him die?" he screamed. "Why couldn't you help him?"

"I don't know, Gabe."

"Stop calling me by my name!" he said.

I felt his anger shift as he began to cry. "Why did *my* son die? My wife brought him here . . . to you. You held him. He still died. You cured all those other people. But not my boy!" He intensified his hold on my throat. "You let him die! He was my whole life . . ." He paused and then choked out the final words, "And *you* let him die."

From every direction, a gentle, warm, sweet, loving embrace entered my heart and flowed out to Gabe.

"May your son be carried on the wings of the angels and protected by the arms of the mother," I whispered.

"No, no . . . oh, Tita . . . you can't know that . . ." Gabe shook his head as his grip lessened, but he still held me against the wall.

Then, from the hearts of all the students and Kate, silver light threads flowed into Gabe. He released his grip. I slid down the wall to the floor with my legs outstretched. My body labored to regain strength.

Gabe dropped to his knees and buried his head in his hands until his sobs became a deep wailing of pain.

"Forgive me. Please, forgive me," he pleaded. "I had no one else to blame."

"Forgive *me*. I'm sorry I couldn't save him."

The large, grief-consumed man crawled closer to me.

"To be carried on the wings of the angels," he said, "was my grandmother's blessing."

With all the strength I could muster, I pulled him onto my lap. I placed one arm around his neck, the other under his legs, and assumed the position of love I'd received from Sean and the beautiful hazel-eyed woman.

I heard sirens drawing near.

"Gabe, we are more than our bodies. Our essence lives on eternally." I closed my eyes and saw an image of him in the arms of a motherly, gray-haired woman.

"Because your son will be carried on the wings of the angels and be protected by the arms of the mother, he will never be forgotten."

The student angels in front of us continued their vigil, holding Abhaya mudra.

The mantra lullaby from that special Sunday with Mike welled in my heart, so I sang to him, and the students joined me.

"*Aum Bhur, Bhuvah Swaha, Tat Savitur Varenyam . . .*"

61

FOR THE LOVE
OF DOG

"It was only a matter of time until something like this happened," Sean said, shaking his head. "I should've been with you."

"There was no way to know," I said, sitting across from him in our library.

"Maybe that brick through the front window was a clue," he said, raising both eyebrows and pointing to the new window.

"It needed to happen just the way it did, bud."

"When no one answered on the second buzz," Sean said, "I climbed onto the air conditioning unit and looked in the window." His eyes filled with tears. "When I saw you pinned against the wall . . . I . . . was shaking so bad, I could hardly dial 911." He swallowed and took a deep breath. "We still need to be careful."

"We have nothing to worry about from Gabe," I said.

"Maybe not, but there are a lot of other . . ." He paused and took another deep breath. "Listen, I know you're on this *klesha* path, but I thought Dottie dying was the last of it."

"She was a beautiful part of it, but I needed to experience the fifth klesha personally. Gabe was the next step."

"And the last step? I mean, you had a near-death experience," he said, shaking his head again. "You handled it like a champ. So, it's over, right?"

"Yes, it's over," I said with a smile.

"Good." He leaned back in his chair. "Tomorrow's birthday party is going to be a true taste of normal life. I've never looked so forward to a kid's birthday party, not even when I was a kid."

We laughed.

"I told Josh we'd be out early to help set up," Sean said. "He and Whitney want to play games in the yard. I think it'll be safe, but if—"

"It'll be fine," I said with a sigh.

"I know, but we need to keep our eyes peeled."

I nodded.

"I'm going up to my studio to reflect on this whole Dottie and Gabe thing. The council's definitely put *Abhinivesha* in my face."

Once upstairs, I cleared my mind and sat for the sheer enjoyment of meditating. There was no council, no talking statues . . . just a deep immersion into internal bliss.

That evening, after dinner, we sat in the Adirondack chairs in the backyard and watched day fade into twilight, then into a night filled with lightning bugs and the sounds of crickets. It was deliciously uneventful.

Shortly past midnight, we made our way to bed. "Goodnight, lovely man," I said.

"Goodnight, buddy. Sweet dreams . . . or in your case, *no* dreams might be better."

I breathed in this moment of ordinariness with a gratitude that filled my whole being.

"I'm having cake *and* ice cream today," Sean said as he rang the doorbell at Josh and Whitney's. "I might even play games if the kids let me."

"Hi, Uncle Ren and Uncle Sean!" Harry said, opening the door with an ear-to-ear smile. His reddish hair and freckles matched his dad's, but he took his green eyes from his mom. At four and a half feet, he was tall for his age.

"Happy birthday, big guy." I stooped down to hug him.

"How does it feel to be seven?" Sean asked, taking his turn to hug.

"No different than six; I still can't drive myself to the library."

Sean chuckled. "That'll come soon enough."

Harry had always been precocious. As a baby, he was ahead of the curve with his movements and use of sound. I noticed early on how *present* he was when spoken to.

"Hey guys, come on in." Whitney, Josh's wife, greeted us with a big smile. As we crossed the threshold, she gave us hugs and kisses. Her long, dark hair hung loosely over her shoulders. Her vibrant eyes were a dark forest green, and her cheeks were flushed with color. Over her fitted white capri pants and short-sleeved powder-blue T-shirt, she wore an apron that read *Queen of the House*. "Thanks for coming early. We have our hands full already, and soon we'll be surrounded by nine seven-year-old neighbor kids—plus Chaz, our very energetic four-year-old."

"Put us to work," Sean said.

"We want to set everything up in the front yard. Josh is in the garage pulling out tables and—"

"Great," Sean said. "I'll go help him."

"Uncle Ren?" Harry said, now standing on the bottom step of the staircase.

"Yeah, bud?"

"Will you come up to my room?"

Whitney smiled. "Go ahead. We have at least an hour before the party begins."

I followed Harry up the stairs. As we crossed the threshold into his little-boy world, I smiled at his Indy-500 race car–shaped bed and was in awe of the meticulously organized shelves of puzzles, board games, and books. His desk was neatly arranged with a miniature microscope and a world globe. I walked toward the window where a child's yoga mat was rolled out.

"Are you doing yoga?" I asked as Harry shut the door.

"I do it with Mommy."

"Do you like it?"

"I like the animal poses."

"Ahh . . . cat-cow?"

"Yep," he said as he walked toward me. "Uncle Ren, I have something to show you. Will you lie down on the mat, please?"

I did as requested.

"Close your eyes," he whispered.

I sensed him kneel next to me. Then I felt his hand on the middle of my chest.

"Ohhhhmmmm," he chanted.

I squinted and watched him place his other hand on his chest. His breath was slow and steady. I was pulled to match it. My eyes closed, and I felt a deep relaxation spread through my body.

"You can open your eyes now. You're all better," Harry said.

"Thank you." I was disoriented. *How long did I lie there?*

"That's how you did it, right? That's how you helped the little boy?" he asked, nodding.

I sat up so we were eye to eye. "Yes, Harry, that's where my hands were, but it wasn't just me, the other people also helped."

"I know," he said, looking me directly in the eyes with a slight grin.

He *does* know, I thought.

"Harry," Whitney called up the stairs, "your guests are here."

Was I lying there for an hour?

Harry rushed toward the door, stopped, then turned to me and said, "Thank you." I had a flash of another boy, Mike, saying those same words on the Parkway. Harry then looked to the ceiling, "And *thank you*, beautiful lady." He ran out and down the steps.

A bit dazed, I got up, knowing I needed to pay attention, but to what, I didn't have a clue. I walked downstairs and out onto the front porch to be instantly surrounded by kids, dogs, and neighbors—the party was in full swing. Whitney orchestrated games on the lawn as Josh, Sean, and I sat in folding chairs and watched from our perch. Harry was having the time of his seven-year-old life.

"Sorry I didn't help with setup," I said to Josh. "Harry had something to share with me."

"That boy is something else. I hope he didn't bombard you with questions."

"Oh no, nothing like that. But he had me lie down, and he placed his hands—"

There was the high-pitched screech of car tires and a *thump*, immediately followed by screams.

Harry!

I stood and turned.

A girl, no more than sixteen, was hysterical in the driver's seat of her hot-pink Volkswagen Beetle. Pinned under the front tires of her car was the neighbor's dog.

"Back up," someone yelled to the girl.

Gigi, the next-door neighbor's seven-year-old daughter, and Harry ran into the street. They knelt on either side of the dog.

"No, no . . . Pluto," Gigi wailed.

Harry lovingly guided Gigi's hand to the dog's side and her other hand to her heart—he did the same. They bowed their heads. The crowd fell silent.

"Oh, my goddess," I whispered as my jaw dropped open.

Silver threads of light began to float from the bystanders, then more lights came from beyond the scene, all going toward the lifeless animal lying on the asphalt. The children remained still with their heads bowed. Then, the dog's chest expanded into Gigi and Harry's hands, its limbs began to move, and its tail began to wag. Within seconds, the golden lab jumped up, licked Gigi, and then Harry.

The kids stood and then hugged. The reverent silence of the crowd was broken by a collective exhale, that soon turned to cheers, then into cries of *Miracle!*

"Harry!" Whitney screamed. She ran into the street and grabbed him and Gigi. She nudged the little girl toward her parents who were standing nearby, then she ran full force into the house with Harry in her arms. Josh snatched up their youngest.

I was caught in the euphoria of the mesmerizing moment.

"Come on," Sean said, pushing me toward the door, "all hell's about to break loose . . . again."

Josh and Sean pulled the blinds on the windows and locked the doors. Whitney had taken Harry to his room. She now paced the length of the kitchen.

"I should've stopped him," Whitney said, desperation coming through her voice, "but I couldn't. I literally *could not* move. Harry was so calm—how could he be so focused? He's seven." She turned to me. "Now what, Ren? *You've* been hounded, *we've* been hounded because of our relationship to you, but . . ." She covered her face with her hands.

"Whitney . . . I . . ."

She looked up, wide-eyed.

"You said your meditations were some kind of *opening* for *your* miracle to happen. Harry's a kid. Yeah, I see him sitting quietly, but is he *really* meditating? He says when he sits like that, a beautiful lady sits with him. What's that, Ren?"

Is Harry sitting with a goddess? I wondered.

"Is he going to do more miracles? Oh my god," she shook her head and looked at Josh, "we might have to move."

"Slow down," Josh said, putting his arm around her, "I know this is traumatic, but let's stay calm."

"As crazy as *our* lives were," Sean said, "the paparazzi eventually backed off and lost interest."

"He's right," I said, holding onto the back of the kitchen chair for support as chaos swirled.

"So, do you think the kids saved the dog?" Josh asked.

I shrugged, but I knew—*death, transformation, a dog named Pluto* . . .

"The silver lights were pretty," Harry said, now standing at the bottom of the stairs.

"Oh buddy, I'm sorry I just tossed you in your room. Are you okay?" Whitney asked. She walked over and wrapped her arms around him.

"I didn't mean to upset you, Mommy, but Pluto needed us," he said. "He wasn't ready to die. He pulled me over, and the beautiful lady told me to do it." His big green eyes filled with tears.

"It's okay, honey, we just want what's best for you," Whitney said. "What you did was a big surprise."

"I've been practicing," Harry said, staring at me over his mom's shoulder.

Sean and I exchanged glances.

"Josh, you and Whitney should get out of here now! Take the kids to her grandparents' farm. Sean and I will talk to the media *if* they show up."

"*When* they show up," Sean said.

"This will settle down, I promise," I said to Josh, Whitney, and their oldest son, Harry, the new miracle worker.

The family was on the road within minutes.

"Carol texted," Sean said, looking at the phone as we stood in Josh's living room. "It's all over social media already. Jeez, I guess people have their phones glued to their foreheads."

"Here they come!" I said, peeking out the closed blinds on the front window. "The first news crew just pulled up."

The doorbell rang.

"I've got it." Sean opened the front door and greeted a man with a microphone. "Hi, do me a favor and set up on the sidewalk. We'll be out in a few minutes. Ren will give a statement. Thanks." He closed the door.

"I'm giving a press conference?" I asked, half joking.

"Call in your muse and get busy. I just bought you time to write a statement."

Fifteen minutes later, Sean and I walked out the front door to where four local news crews, three radio stations, and a large group of neighbors had gathered.

"I know you have questions," I said, "but honestly, we have no idea what just happened or how."

"Is this miracle thing genetic?" one reporter asked.

"Did my great-nephew save the dog because he's related to me? Perhaps, but doesn't our entire human race share a gene pool? Aren't we *all* related? *Yes*, we are," I said, holding up my hand to stop the next question. "Which brings me to what I have repeated all along: everything I can do, *you* can do also."

"But how do you explain—?" another reporter asked.

"Let me finish. There's a growing mystical revolution of beautiful, feminine power—a swirling undercurrent of radical love working to pull humanity out of fear and anger where the world is dark. The feminine speaks in whispers, but just because her voice is more subtle than hate and aggression, don't downplay her power.

"Deep down, *everyone* wants to believe in Love. We *want* to see people pull together and send love to an injured boy on a bike or a young girl's dying dog. We all want to feel supported by a humanity that cares for each of its members."

"Ren?" I looked to my right to see Haley Smithers, a comforting, familiar face. "Do you think that kind of utopia is possible?" she asked.

"I do, Haley," I said, placing my hands on my heart. "When we drop our individual desires and open ourselves to goodwill for US, our United Souls, love creeps in one miracle at a time. And as our US grows larger, love grows, it spreads, because it's contagious."

Sean stepped between me and the microphones. "That will be all for now," he said to the crowd. "Ren will be doing a national morning show *very* soon. Watch for it. Thank you."

He pulled me away as the reporters shouted questions.

"What are you talking about?" I asked Sean as he dragged me back to the house. "A national morning show?"

"Trust me, what you just said out there about United Souls, the US, is going to get *a lot* of attention on both sides of the fence."

"Okay . . . but a *national* morning show? What the hell was that about?"

"Do you remember that dream you had right before all this started, about being interviewed by Katie Couric in New York?"

"Yeah . . . ?"

"Well, I have a strong intuitive feeling it's about to come true."

62

UNITED SOULS

Sean pulled our car into Josh's garage. I curled up in a ball and lay in the back of the Subaru.

"Good thing you do yoga," Sean said as he pulled the cargo cover over me.

"This is crazy."

"Trust me, they'll leave us alone if they think you're still in Josh's house."

I heard the garage door open and felt the movement of the car.

"Here they come," Sean said.

I heard the window go down. "It's just me, folks. Have a good day." I heard the window again and felt the car move.

"Good thing no one's interested in me."

"*I'm* interested in you, buddy," I said, getting used to the fetal position I was in. "Always."

"Forever, Ren, forever."

"We're pulling up to the house now," Sean said to me from the driver's seat. "Wow, the street's packed. I'll back into the driveway so you can sneak in the side gate."

I slipped out of the back of the car and darted to the kitchen door. The phone rang as we walked in.

"It's Carol," Sean said, putting her on speaker. "Hi, sweetness. Are you calling with an update?"

"I'm happy to report Harry and Gigi's miracle is being broadcast worldwide! You guys are trending again."

"Oh, goddess." I shook my head.

"Hey, it's job security for me," Carol said with a laugh. "Tell Josh and Whitney I'm happy to help monitor any social media for them."

"We're going to keep the kids as far away from this as possible," Sean said. "Ren will be the public face."

"He already is," Carol said. "Witnesses describe Ren watching from the porch at Josh's, and the news reports are featuring footage from *both* miracles."

"Both miracles," I said, again shaking my head.

"Ren, honey," Carol said, "everyone wants to know more about the power of love through United Souls."

"I told you," Sean whispered, nodding with wide eyes.

"You hit a chord with the lovers of the world," Carol continued, "but there's also pushback from the haters."

There was a silence for several moments.

"Ren?" Carol finally said.

"Yeah?"

"People are hungry for it. We all need to be reminded about love because there doesn't seem to be much of it in our world right now."

"I know," I said, "but love's always with us. We just have to get quiet to hear it."

"Are you ready for this?" she asked. "I think the hoopla is gonna be the same as it was after Mike and the Parkway."

"Thankfully, Sean and I are different now," I said. "We're much calmer. Everything we've been through—the miracles, the media, the council opportunities—it's changed us. This round will be easier to handle."

I heard Carol take a deep breath. "I believe you," she said, "and I believe in US. I know how powerful the love is between the three of us, so multiply that by a million or billion, and things will change."

Sean winked at me as he nodded. I bowed my head.

"Thanks for all you do for us, Carol," I said. "I'm going to head upstairs."

I went to my studio and peeked out the window to see the growing crowd. I took my meditation seat with a sense of gratitude for life, for connection, even for the people gathered out front. I closed my eyes, tapped into my breath, and began a mantra that encompassed all goddesses:

Om, Aim, Hreem, Shreem, Kleem.

After several rounds of this mantra, my inner eyes opened, and I was standing in front of the ever-familiar doors. They slowly opened of their own volition. Seated at the center of the conference table was the feminine contingency of my council—Venus, the Moon, and Athena. Next to Athena was a veiled woman dressed in black. I took my usual seat.

"Welcome, Ren," said Venus in her smooth, beguiling way. "We see your transformation. Do you?"

I smiled. "I *feel* it. I'm finally experiencing inner peace after all these years."

The goddess of love smiled back. "Raising your consciousness to awaken the mystic has been the focus all along."

"It's the journey from human animal to human being," Athena added. "Breaking your addiction to the lower emotions has taken an incredible amount of energy. Now you can experience the bliss of love and compassion."

"That's yoga," I nodded.

"You're now moving into the world from the heart of the feminine," said Venus. "Congratulations."

"Don't commend me too loudly," I said, "my ego's waiting to be fed."

The three of them smiled.

"Continue to talk about love while you hold fear at bay," the Moon said.

Athena placed her hands over her heart. "*Her* love will help you face all that frightens and limits you. Make e*verything I can do, you can do also* your battle cry."

Venus looked deeply into my eyes. "Remember, your evolution is a spiral. There's *always* another level."

I sighed and gestured to the woman veiled in black. "Does my next level have anything to do with our visitor?"

The unknown female stood, walked behind the goddesses, and pulled aside a black drape, revealing a movie screen. Images of all the veiled women who had encouraged me on this journey were projected one by one onto it: Veronica, the goddess in the park, Mary Magdalene, Clare, and the nuns in Assisi.

Never forget US, I heard in my heart. The screen went black.

Venus, the Moon, and Athena placed their hands in Abhaya mudra.

"She is he, and he is She, and all the lessons flow back to *their* powers of transformation," Venus said, gesturing to the figure standing behind them. An image of Times Square slowly emerged on the screen as Venus, the Moon, and Athena recited:

"I'm not afraid of my life or what is in my heart."

My eyes opened. I was once again sitting on my cushion. The strange yet familiar image of New York lingered.

It all leads back to the powers of transformation, I thought, and transformation leads to awakening love.

Deep breath in, deep breath out.

63

AN OFFER YOU CAN'T REFUSE

"Ren! Ren!" Sean called up from the bottom of the stairs.

"What is it?" I asked, hurrying down.

"My intuition was right on," he said and shook his fist in a sign of victory. "I just finished talking to William Miller, the guy from NBC who set up the interview you did with Haley Smithers."

"Yeah—?"

"They want you to be on *The Today Show* Monday morning." He grabbed me by the shoulders. "And . . . they're working to get Katie Couric to do the interview. Can you believe it? Just like in your dream."

"Wow," I said in a monotone, as a mixture of shock and disbelief flashed through my body.

"They want you to talk about United Souls, Abhaya mudra . . . they're going to fly us to New York tomorrow and—"

"It's happening too fast," I said, shaking my head.

"What? They're getting Katie Couric."

I continued to shake my head as I looked to the floor.

"Ren, I thought you'd be all over this." He lifted my chin to look into my eyes. "This is what your council's been preparing you for through this whole *klesha* thing."

I walked into the library and glanced out the front window. More than fifty people were gathered in the street. My heart filled with compassion for them.

"This is your opportunity to reach huge numbers of people with this message of love," Sean said, following me into the library.

I sat on the floor in front of the fireplace, rested my elbows on my knees and my head on my interlaced hands, and sighed, trying to release a tightness I felt rising in my chest.

"We both believe love's the glue that holds everything together," he said as he walked behind me and began massaging my neck and shoulders, "but with our world riddled with war, ego-obsessed politicians, and greed, it's hard to hold on to a belief in love. I lose *my* grip on it." He came around and sat cross-legged in front of me. "We need hope, bud. We need a miracle of the heart to join more of us together as United Souls." He reached over and took my hand. "This is your chance to do something big! You thought it was the church, but *this* is what the goddesses have been talking about all along."

"I know," I said, looking at him. "All the stars have aligned."

I stood and walked over to the bookshelf, retrieved my journal, opened it to my entry of the Times Square dream from four weeks ago, and handed it to him.

He glanced over it.

"Yep, this is the one, flying over Times Square, the interview with Katie, thousands of people doing Abhaya mudra—"

"And a shrouded female in black, the jumbotron going dark and me being pulled up and away from Earth, through the stars, and losing myself in . . ." I sighed.

Sean stared at me.

"Earlier today in meditation, the goddesses of my council introduced me to the tall figure in black from my dream. I'm fairly certain she's Pluto in his female form. She showed me an image of Times Square on a large-scale movie screen."

"Now I understand your hesitation," Sean said, slowly nodding his head, "and to be honest, Carol and I are seeing an increase in negative posts online. Maybe we need to rethink this."

I took a deep breath.

"Maybe we should postpone *or* even cancel it," Sean said as he stood.

"But ... if we don't do this, fear wins," I said, now shaking my head. "Something's shifted in both of us, and this is our opportunity to face fear head-on with love as our guide."

"I feel like a rope in a tug-of-war," Sean said.

"We can't shy away from this," I said, "but we can rethink it like you suggested. Let's bring in free will."

Sean's eyes narrowed. "What?"

"Let's alter the dream so it's not a premonition. Tell NBC we will do the interview, but we want Haley Smithers instead of Katie, *and* . . . you'll be on stage with me."

"Wait, wait, wait . . . I might be able to handle the disappointment about Katie, but me on national TV?"

I tilted my head and gave him a hint of a smile.

"Okay," Sean said, "but do I have to talk?"

"I have your back, buddy. It'll be fine. And I'll be so much more comfortable with you by my side."

"I'll make the call."

64

KILLING LOVE

Chaos disorients and brings up fear
until we sense something new will soon be birthed into our life.
Swirl freely in the dance of chaos . . .
feel that which from inside you—craves a birth.
—**Ren Devlin; Journal entry March 20**

Sean was perusing email when I walked into the kitchen the next morning.

"So much came in overnight," he said, looking up from his computer. "Everything's confirmed with NBC. Haley flew up this morning, and we're scheduled to fly out of Lunken airport tonight."

"Lunken? There aren't any commercial flights out of there."

"We're flying on a private jet again," he said, raising his eyebrows and then returning his gaze to the computer screen.

I shook my head. "We sure do travel in style these days."

"The network also arranged for a car to pick us up here, one to take us to the hotel in New York, and we'll have security the whole time."

"Security?"

"They're being careful. I think it's a good thing. Some people are really riled up," he said, shaking his head. "Who knew talking about love could be so dangerous?"

"Come on, you said there's been negative stuff but dangerous?"

"Along with the thousands who are *inspired* by United Souls, there've been some threats."

"Threats," I said, shaking my head. "Why is there so much hate for those who love?"

"They crucified Jesus," Sean said, still looking at his computer.

"Sean!"

"Look," he said, placing his elbows on the kitchen table and resting his head in his hands, "it's not too late to rethink this interview."

I raised my left eyebrow.

"There've been threats since this whole thing started," he said, "but after yesterday, there are specific ones from organized hate groups. The *anti-everythings* are coming out of the woodwork. Carol's sent a couple of the threats to the police, who've notified the FBI as a precaution."

I put my hand up. "Death threats?"

"I didn't say *death* threats!"

"But if the FBI's involved—"

"You're considered a public figure now, so . . ."

I closed my eyes but quickly opened them when the mysterious figure in black appeared in my mind's eye.

"Harry and Gigi raising her dog Pluto—by the way, can you believe that name?" he asked, shaking his head and widening his eyes. "Anyway, that's brought you right back into the limelight. You'd think another miracle and your talk of love and United Souls would inspire everyone, but . . . there are those who . . . want to kill love."

Tears welled in my eyes. "Sean, no one can kill love."

"I know, Reno," he reached over and held my hands, "but right now, things don't seem to be moving in the right direction."

"That's why we have to do this," I said with a big exhale and squeezing his hands.

Later, as we sat waiting for takeoff, I wrote in my journal.

> As sure as I am of the existence of my own soul, I know love cannot be killed. Love is the glue of the Universe that holds US together. It cannot be diminished. It's an invisible bond that is always present. Love's the nectar that transforms the bitter taste of poison. It's the flame that illuminates the darkness. Darkness is not the absence of Love, for love holds all things—even darkness.

I leaned back in my seat. Silently called on the goddess in all Her forms: *Om, Aim, Hreem, Shreem, Kleem.*

"You're *really* quiet," Sean said.

"I'm trying to keep my mind focused on the moment rather than jump ahead to tomorrow. I keep repeating the goddess mantra."

"Tomorrow's *all* I can think about," Sean said. "It's driving me crazy. I'm gonna take your lead with the mantra."

"One journey ends as another begins," I said, remembering Caroline's words from her hospice bed, which now seemed like an eternity ago. I closed my eyes.

"Enjoy takeoff, bud," he said, squeezing my hand. Sean knows how much I love meditating on planes. The g-force at takeoff and the sensation of climbing take me deep inside. As the plane leveled off, my body bounced forward slightly. I slid into the depths of my being. I was standing in front of the council chamber doors.

I pushed one door slightly open and slid in. The members were all present, sitting in their usual seats—hands folded in front of them, wearing their mythical garb. I walked to my chair but remained standing. There was one glaring difference from all the other encounters—each of them had a single piece of silver duct tape placed over their mouth.

"Why am I here if you're not going to talk?" I asked.

Silence.

"Are we going to do this telepathically?"

Silence.

"Is your silence its own message?"

Silence.

"Tomorrow will be what it will be," I said. "I'm definitely going to lead with my heart full of love rather than fear. There's a struggle between the two right now. I feel it in me *and* see it in the world."

Silence.

"I want you to know I'm different from when this journey began," I said, nodding, "and I have deep gratitude for all your intensity." I smiled. "The fires you made me walk through *were* opportunities. They've made me more dedicated to my practices, and more than ever, I know *every* moment's sacred."

They sat still in their taped silence. I took a deep breath.

"Thank you." I placed my hands into prayer mudra at my third eye and bowed to each of them one by one. "Namaste."

I turned, took a few steps toward the doors, then stopped and turned back. Their hands were now in Abhaya mudra. I joined them and said, "I'm not afraid of my life or what is in my heart." I swallowed. "This feels like goodbye." There was a tightening in my throat. "You're not going to disappear again for another thirty years, are you?"

Venus, the Moon, and Athena stood. They pulled the tape from their lips and, in unison, said, "May you be blessed by the holy waters of love."

Tears streamed down my face.

"There are no endings, only new beginnings," Venus said.

"I know." I wiped the tears from my cheeks.

"You did *not* forget us," she said with just a trace of a grin, "nor will we *ever* forget you—because we are you, and you are us."

I sighed.

A familiar love squeeze on my forearm brought me back to myself.

"We're about to land," Sean whispered.

"That was fast." My eyes were still closed.

"You doing okay?"

"Oh, yeah. The goddesses of love are surrounding us for sure."

"I feel them, too."

We were escorted to the Sheraton at 52nd and 7th Avenue, blocks from Rockefeller Center. After we settled into a spacious two-room luxury suite on the forty-fifth floor, we stood at the floor-to-ceiling windows and looked down the Times Square canyon to the jumbotron.

"Do you think you'll be able to sleep?" Sean asked.

"I think so."

"You seem weirdly calm, Ren. I'm not sure what I am expecting, but—"

"I feel some fear, bud," I said, reaching for his hand, "but the goddesses from my council gave me a blessing, so I've been repeating it for the world: *May we all be blessed by the holy waters of love.*"

He turned toward me, put his hands on my shoulders, and guided me so we were face-to-face.

"Ren, we're in this together."

"I know. I've never felt closer to you."

"I keep hearing a comforting female voice inside," Sean said, "telling me everything will be fine."

"With as much as you've fine-tuned your intuition over the last month, I'd listen to her," I said with a slight smile.

"I keep wondering if she's part of *my* council and if they're ever going to show up again."

"They will. Trust me."

"I wish I could see her."

"Close your eyes." I placed my hand on his heart as he took a deep breath.

"I see her now," he said. "She has hazel eyes." He let out a long sigh. "And her energy feels so nurturing."

"I know, she's universal," I said. "She holds and blesses us all with the holy waters of love."

"Yes," he said, "and along with all the other goddesses and angels, she's protecting us too."

65

THE NIGHT BEFORE

To the Divine Dark I pass again.
As a horse shakes free its mane,
I have Shaken off evil. Freeing myself
From bonds of birth and death . . .
—THE CHANDOGYA UPANISHAD, VERSE 13.1

I took my seat in front of the makeshift altar we created on a coffee table in our hotel room and lit three candles. As I do in times of deep self-reflection, I put my pen to the journal page and let it flow.

As I contemplate tomorrow, I feel apprehension and doubt. I would be lying to say I did not, but with all that has transpired in these last weeks—the reemergence of my council, the guidance of goddesses and veiled women, the hypnotic allure of a mantra, a mudra of fearlessness, and the unexplained miracles—I know I am different! I'm moving more freely in the yogic heart that gives meaning to each breath and senses beauty in anything to which I bring my focus, even this intense moment of uncertainty.

I believe I've untangled myself from the kleshas and the ego side of the siddhis and have gained clarity about the indubitable truth behind all I've learned—

Everything I can do, you can do also.

I took a deep breath, looked at the burning wicks of the candles, and admired the beauty of the ever-moving and changeable flames. The pen resumed its journey on the page.

There is a recurring question in my heart—as a collective, is it possible to learn to heal with our touch by giving of ourselves without ego or attachment? To develop the gifts of the siddhis of yoga in this way, with full awareness of a pure heart, would be such a gift to humanity.

I am resolute to do what we are going to do tomorrow, regardless of those who would kill love. This is a decision Sean and I have made together. This is about both of us and, just as importantly, about the collective—United Souls. We must all confront our fears, increase hope, and believe fully that love never dies.

I closed my journal, placed my hands in Abhaya mudra, and sang the Gayatri softly. "I bow to you, my inner teachers. May you illuminate my mind and heart with true wisdom. Namaste."

"Namaste," Sean said from the edge of the bed.

I turned. "Have you been there long?" I asked.

"Longer than you'll ever know. Tomorrow's a big day, how about we try to get some sleep?"

He reached out and helped me up. I crawled into bed and into his arms. As we spooned our bodies, I made a silent request:

Let any remnants of doubt burn away, and the wisdom I need at this moment come through loud and clear.

I closed my eyes and quickly drifted off.

As my body lay asleep in the arms of my beloved, my internal eyes opened to see the familiar doors.

Do not go in. Once you cross that threshold, there's no going back. I recognized the ego voice I knew all too well. I exhaled forcibly to clear my head.

"I'm going in!" I pushed the stainless-steel doors open.

"Step inside." A breathy female voice surrounded me from all sides.

Hesitantly, I took a step forward as the doors disappeared into blackness. There was no conference table, no council of ten. Columns of white-gray smoke spiraled up, twisting from myriad smoldering piles of dirt, creating a gauzy fog. There was a putrid stench.

Is this a cemetery or a cremation site?

My vision was limited, but I sensed a presence.

"Feel me." The voice was omnipresent.

"I feel you. Who are you?"

"Come nearer. It's time." Now, the voice came from directly in front of me.

I froze.

"Closer!" Her voice was more demanding.

Cautiously, I took three small steps. Then I heard a whispered chorus coming from above me, *we are you, and you are us.* It was my council. I took a deep breath and two more reluctant steps as I exhaled.

Instantly, I felt surrounded by energies I could not see. Indistinguishable, hushed mutterings moved around my feet, and currents of air brushed my skin.

"Nearer," she beckoned.

My heart pounded as fear pulsated through me.

Breathe deeper, the council counseled in their united undertone, *calm the inner fire.*

In a blinding flash, hundreds of eight-foot columns of cherry red, bright orange, yellow, and blue flames erupted into the air from the smoldering earthen tombs, illuminating grotesque, disfigured beings standing amid the blazing infernos. The fire creatures let out a chorus of deafening howls that sent me to my knees. I covered my ears.

"*AAAAAAAAAAHHHHHHHHHHHHHHHHHHHH!!!!!!!*"

I'll make myself invisible to the human eye, I thought as I huddled close to the ground.

"Do not squander your energy. Mine are not human eyes. I will see you."

"Who are you?" I screamed, just as the screeching stopped and the flames receded.

Now, in the eerie silence, I heard my rapid heartbeat and the sound of my quick, shallow breath. I forced a deep inhale. My body relaxed ever so slightly.

"You who have eyes to see, see." The voice was closer.

The veil of smoke began to thin.

Ten feet in front of me stood the six-foot-tall shrouded female figure in black from last night's goddess meeting. She inched closer and closer. Through her diaphanous veil of mourning, I saw her hooked-crooked nose, wrinkled, splotchy skin, close-set eyes, and thin, pale, cracked lips.

She now stood just beyond arm's reach.

"I am he, and he is me, and all the lessons flow back to our powers of transformation."

"All the clues flow to Pluto," I said.

There was a hint of a smile on her paper-thin lips.

"Like humans, each celestial member of the council has their feminine and masculine energies, and although Pluto and I are one and the same, I predate the myths of Greece and Rome before men obnubilated me in the trappings of their sex to mask the fierceness of the feminine. I terrify men because they cannot control me."

She inched closer.

"I am the dark goddess, *Ereshkigal, Kali, Chinnamasta*. I am the womb from which you came, *and* I am the tomb to which you will return." She made a sweeping motion with her right arm. "These charnel grounds are my domain. I am the witch you project your fears onto. I'm the garbage you push away, the desperation you hope will vanish from your soul. I am the rage of humanity's injustice."

She pulled taut the bottom corners of her veil, as she came one minute step closer.

"To live in joy, *all* humans must reconcile their existential grief through my deep powers of transformation." She slowly lifted her sheer facial shroud.

I swallowed.

"I bring change, one way or another." As she folded back her veil, her features transmogrified into the countenance of a perfectly proportioned sculpture of a mythological goddess.

"Remove the veil," she said, "and bring what you fear into the light, and it will transform."

I let out an involuntary, audible sigh.

"Tonight, through acceptance and surrender, we will transform *your* fear into love," she said.

She pulled the veil from her head and held it out with her index finger and thumb. Releasing it, it wafted to my feet.

"Am I to wear the widow's veil?"

"Not yet," she said as she reached for my hand. Silently, we walked through the cremation grounds until we came to a fifteen-foot round hole. Three feet below the rim, I saw dark, tumultuous waters. Something beneath the surface was stirring it up.

"Surrender, Ren," she said as we stood next to each other, gazing into the abyss.

"It's hard to let go," I said, transfixed on the churning movements of the turbulent water.

"What guides you?" she asked. "Fear or love?"

Actions speak louder than any words, I heard in my heart.

I clutched her hand. "Join me, won't you?" I said and jumped.

I woke before the alarm, staring at the ceiling. Through the early morning darkness, the lights of Times Square reflected on the ceiling and walls of our room. I watched the brilliant dance of color. Everything is relevant. Everything is significant.

I slid my hand under Sean's.

"I'm awake; I have been," he said. "How about you?"

"I met the female form of Pluto, the dark goddess, last night."

I heard him take a deep breath. "And?"

"We met in a cemetery, where she guided me to the edge of a massive hole filled with dark, churning water. We held hands and jumped."

"She *made* you go in?"

"Actually, I jumped first and pulled her with me."

"And then you traveled to some underworld . . . or?"

"All I remember is the jump. Initiating the leap was what I needed to do. And now I feel calm and peaceful and ready for national television."

"Oh my, *I* just got really nervous," Sean said.

"Let go, surrender," I said, turning to him. "All you have to do is sit next to me and be your beautiful self."

"That's all," he said, "in front of twenty thousand people."

He turned so we were lying face to face.

"To prepare ourselves for today," I said, scooting even closer to him, "let's combine our energies and become one through an ancient alchemical ritual."

"Really? And how do we do that?"

"Dearest Universe," I said, looking into Sean's eyes, "we two separate beings now become one through our mutual creation."

I placed my lips on his.

"Forever."

"Always."

66

THANK YOU

If the only prayer you ever say in your entire life is—
Thank You—it will be enough.

—MEISTER ECKHART

"Raphael called. He's our contact at NBC," Sean said with his hand on the handle of the hotel door. "He wanted us to know there's been security outside our room all night."

"Security outside *our* door?"

"Raphael said the network isn't taking any chances with all the negative pushback, *and* they're also pretty sure there's an internal leak at the studio because *somehow* the protesters found out we're staying here. They're out front."

I nodded. "I wish the goddess would P.U.T.P. on changing the world."

We both smiled.

Sean opened the door.

"The name's Foster," said a massive man, at least 6'7" and 250 pounds, dressed in a black suit, shirt, and tie. "I'm part of your security team."

The three of us stepped into the elevator.

"Hey, this may be a stretch, but you said the NBC guy is named Raphael," I said, holding Sean's hand. "In my NYC flying dream, I was escorted inside the studio by an angel. Raphael is the archangel of healing. Interesting, if nothing else."

"It's *all* interesting," Sean said, giving my hand a light squeeze.

Foster led us through the lobby and the revolving door. Across the street, a group of twenty held signs with the same word they chanted.

"Antichrist! Antichrist! Antichrist!"

"That's him!" one of the protesters shouted as the group started to cross 7th Avenue.

Out of nowhere, two more enormous security guards dressed in black surrounded us as we bolted to the car. When Foster opened the car door, I saw a gun in a vertical shoulder holster under his jacket. I exhaled and jumped into the back. Sean climbed in behind me, and Foster took the front passenger seat.

The sedan quickly pulled away from the curb and turned onto 50th Street only to be blocked by several garbage trucks. I sensed the undistinguishable hushed mutterings that moved around my feet in last night's encounter, but now, I felt them coming from behind. The protesters had caught up with us. They rocked the stopped car and pounded on the windows.

"Don't make eye contact," Foster yelled.

Sean closed his eyes, leaned back, and began softly singing Jane Siberry's "Calling All Angels."

Once again, we heard them chanting, "Antichrist! Antichrist!"

One man, dressed in a dark sweatshirt and ski cap that covered his face, was right up against my window. I scooted closer. Our eyes locked.

With less than an inch of bullet-resistant glass separating our faces, I said, "You can't kill love."

The rage of his fist pounding on the window intensified. "I'll kill love," he screamed.

"May love melt your heart," I said. "May you be carried on the wings of the angels."

"Do *not* engage them," Foster barked.

"I'm not afraid," I said. "No matter what they do or say, I want them to see love."

The driver finally maneuvered around the trucks. Within minutes, we pulled up to a nondescript gray metal door.

I looked around. "No protesters."

"There are plenty at the official studio entrance," Foster said.

Just as quickly as we had entered the car, Foster hurried us through the metal door.

"Don't let this rattle you, Ren." Sean placed his hand on my shoulder. "Your council, the goddesses, saints, archangels, *and* I have your back."

"I feel you all," I said.

"As we left the hotel, I put a big protective energetic bubble around you."

"Put one around yourself," I said, "and while you're at it, cover everyone around us."

"Even the protesters?"

"Especially the protesters. That kind of hate blinds us to love." The image of the angry man's hate-filled eyes on the other side of the car window was seared into my mind.

"Gentlemen," Foster said, holding open a second security door. Sean gestured me in.

Another threshold, I thought.

We were greeted by a thirty-something tall, handsome Latino man.

"Good morning, I'm Raphael," he said and placed his hands into Abhaya mudra and bowed.

Sean and I returned his gesture.

"Raphael," I said, "is one of the archangels. It's comforting to be greeted by you this morning."

"I would have worn my wings, but I didn't want to draw attention," he said with a smile. "Like everyone here, I am so excited to meet you. What you've done is absolutely amazing. I can only hope—"

"Remember," I said, "everything I've done, you can do too."

"Of course." Raphael smiled. "Let me take you to makeup so they can get you prepped." He led the way down a long marble hallway.

"This is already different from the dream," I said to Sean, taking his hand. "I was in this hallway, but I had no idea where you were."

"Here you go, gentlemen," Raphael gestured to an open door. "Have a seat. Patrick will be right with you."

"Another difference," I whispered to Sean, "in the dream, it was a woman named Kelly."

The makeup room was exactly the same—two barber chairs faced oversized vanity mirrors, surrounded by softball-sized bright lights.

"Patrick will also escort you out to the stage," Raphael said. "I'll see you afterward."

"Sit here, Sean," I said, pointing to the first chair. "That's where I sat in the dream."

"This is so strange," Sean said as we looked at each other in the mirrors.

"Strange? Which part—sitting in a makeup room at NBC, reliving a dream from weeks ago, our escort named Raphael, or being interviewed on national TV?"

Sean shook his head. "Right, could it get any weirder?"

In the reflection, I saw a man and woman stop in front of the open door. I recognized her.

"Cosmically weird," I whispered to myself.

"Come on, Patrick, let me do their makeup," the woman said. "I *really* want to meet him. Please . . . ?"

"Oh boy, here comes Kelly," I said to Sean.

"Do you want to ask for Patrick?"

"So much is already different just by having you with me," I said, "it'll be fine."

A woman in her midforties with shoulder-length blond, curly hair, mint green eyeshadow, and bright red lipstick walked into the room. "Hi, guys. I'm Kelly."

Sean looked at me in the mirror with a slight shake of his head.

"I'll be getting you ready. I'm so excited to meet you . . . I'm a love child from way back."

The familiarity of her voice summoned a memory from my dream— her commenting on the word *Abhinivesha* tattooed on my forearm. I looked down. *No tattoo!*

She worked first on Sean and then on me.

"Okay, miracle man," she said, squeezing my shoulders and smiling into the mirror, "let's get you on the set so you can inspire the 20,000 people here at Rockefeller Center and who knows how many watching it live on the jumbotron in Times Square."

"Whoa," Sean said, putting his hand up, "that was a reality check I did *not* need."

We all laughed.

"I'm so glad the network didn't cancel your segment with all the fallout and threats," Kelly said, undoing the barber's cape from around my neck.

Sean and I glanced at each other. "We saw some protesters—"

"Are you nervous?" she asked.

"Not really. I'm ready. I'm supported from a lot of different angles," I said.

"Angles or angels?" Sean asked as we stood and walked toward the makeup room door.

"Both." I gave him a nudge.

"You're so calm," she said, stepping into the familiar hallway.

"It's my Leo rising and Sagittarius Moon you're seeing right now and *not* my Capricorn Sun."

She stopped and turned to me slack-jawed.

"Oh . . . my . . . god, I'm Leo, with Sagittarius rising and Capricorn Moon."

"We have a lot in common," I said with a wink.

Her face lit up with a broad, bright smile. "May I hug you?"

"Of course," I said, opening my arms.

We resumed our walk, stopping short of a door that I *knew* was the only thing separating us from Rockefeller Center.

"Kelly, can we take a moment before we go out to the stage?"

"Sure. We have time."

"Will you join me in a blessing for today?" I reached my hands to her and Sean.

"Absolutely," she said, accepting my gesture.

"May the world know love," I said. "Let all beings live fully from the heart. May we remember the loving essence of the feminine, which will bring love back into our world. *Swaha.*"

"Amen, *and* thank you," she said.

She placed her hands on the pressure bar, paused, turned slightly, and said, "Ready?"

Sean and I nodded.

She pushed the door open. Whoosh . . . the air was electric with energy. We stepped out and stood at the bottom of a set of black metal stairs that led to the stage. To our left were thousands of people.

"Oh my goddess," Sean said, taking a deep breath.

"This is exactly what I remember in the premoni—"

"*Dream*, remember, we're changing it," Sean said.

"Break a leg. Brady will take care of you from here," Kelly said, pointing to a slender young woman wearing a sleek, black wireless headset, an NBC T-shirt, and a huge smile. She motioned us up the stairs.

I waved to the crowd as we stepped onto the stage, and they returned the salutation with cheers and waving of handmade posters with love, peace, and hope written on them.

"I'm Brady. Let's get you in place," she said, leading us to the center of the stage where two director's chairs sat to the left of a small table, and a third stood alone on the right. "You guys will be next to each other. Sean on the outside, Ren in the middle, and Haley will be over there." She pointed to the lone chair.

I experienced a strange mixture of déjà vu and vivid recollection as Brady placed a mic pack on me. I took a deep breath and asked the collective group of the feminine, the *Mahadevis*, who had orchestrated my journey thus far, to guide me in thought, word, and action. Under my breath, I repeated, "*Om, Aim, Hreem, Shreem, Kleem.*"

I looked at Sean and took his hand.

"Brady, can we have the audience OM?" I asked as she finished placing Sean's mic. I'd done this before, too, I thought.

"Let me check." Brady walked over to a tall, middle-aged man with salt and pepper hair at the edge of the stage who was engaged with the audience. The man turned to me.

"Your mic's live," he said, "get us started."

"Hello, everyone," I said. Even though the moment was enwreathed in a feeling of déjà vu, the roar from the crowd took my breath. "Let's build a sense of peace." I stood and assumed Abhaya mudra. "Close your eyes and take a deep breath." The power in our unified inhale and exhale was palpable. "Let go of fear so our lives can be filled with hope *and* love."

Twenty thousand people followed my lead and recited with me.

"I am not afraid of my life or what's in my heart."

"Please join me for three oms—take a deep breath in . . ."

In the few seconds of silence after the oms, my sense of self dissolved, and I experienced a connection to everything, the same feeling I had on the Parkway.

"Thank you." I bowed my head. As I took my seat, Haley was taking hers. While the production crew clipped on her mic, I said in a whisper, "May we be of service to all living things, past, present, and future."

"We have plenty of time today," Haley said. "There will be several commercial breaks where we'll have opportunities to chat." She reached over and touched my knee lightly. "Thank you for being here *and* for requesting me. I'm honored." She placed her hand on an ear pod. "It's show time."

"From NBC News this is *Today* with guest host Haley Smithers, live from Rockefeller Plaza."

The thunderous applause and cheering felt like an energetic avalanche.

"Thank you for joining us," Haley said to the camera. "My special guests are Ren Devlin, who the world has nicknamed The Miracle Man, and his partner, Sean Carson."

After recapping for the viewers how our private lives had recently become public with miracles and widespread healing, Haley turned to us.

"I'm thrilled you're here today," she said with a genuine, warm smile. "Ren, specific to you and Michael Cuberry, did practicing yoga and meditation for the last thirty years enable you to resurrect him?"

"I'll never know for sure, Haley. The Yoga Sutras do enumerate a list of superpowers anyone can develop with enough concentrated practice, but—"

"Yes," she said, "it also lists physical invisibility, comprehending foreign languages with no prior study, and even predicting the time of your own death."

"Well . . . ," I said, taking a deep breath, "you've done your homework."

"Do *you* think anyone who practices and meditates enough can do what you've done?" she asked.

I shrugged. "Actually, the Sutras caution that these abilities only distract us from what yoga's really about," I said, "which is to develop a personal relationship with the divine and stop waiting for some outside savior to solve our problems. What we seek is in here." I placed my hand on my heart. "Yoga helps us step back from the rational fact-addicted mind to learn to trust the feminine, nurturing voice inside—our intuition."

"Intuition—like telepathy, clairvoyance, precognition?" she asked.

I nodded.

"So, there's no place for science?"

"When science works in tandem with intuition, it's a great partner," I said, "but when we make science into a god, it imprisons us in our mind, and there's no room for its higher powers of elevated empathy, self-awareness, and compassion. If you want miracles . . ." I took a deep breath, ". . . find your heart and lose your mind."

"Find your heart, lose your mind," Haley said, smiling and turning to the camera. "Stay with us. We'll be back to continue our fascinating conversation with Ren Devlin and introduce his partner, Sean Carson."

The *On Air* light went dark.

"This is going so well," she said, beaming. "In the next segment, I'll focus a little on Sean's perspective and move into your concept of United Souls." She glanced out to the audience and back to me. "We're all looking to be inspired."

I nodded and turned to Sean.

"This is wonderful," he said, smiling ear to ear.

I felt the familiar swell in my heart. *I'm feeling it!* I then extended it out to the mass of humanity gathered for this love fest. An image of the hate-filled eyes of the angry man from this morning flashed across my mind's eye. I took a breath. Love will prevail, I thought, no matter how dark the night may seem. That's when I saw *them*, clad in their celestial regalia, lined up exactly as they always were, sitting in the front row: my council. I blinked and shook my head. *Could anyone else see these ten beings wearing togas?*

"We have ten seconds," Haley said.

The *On Air* light illuminated.

"Welcome back." She turned on her television charisma for the live camera. "This morning, we've been talking with Ren Devlin. His partner, Sean Carson, is also with us today. Welcome," she said, directing her attention to Sean.

"Good morning, Haley."

"Tell us, is your routine of yoga and meditation the same as Ren's?"

"They're similar," he said, "and many times we practice together."

"Do you also perform miracles?"

"Well," he chuckled, "while my practices *have* shifted my life in miraculous ways, I've not yet walked on water." He patted me on the shoulder.

Haley turned to me wide-eyed. "Oh, have you—?"

"No," I said, shaking my head and smiling.

She laughed. "So Sean, what kind of miraculous shifts have *you* experienced?"

"I'm referring to personal shifts of the mind and spirit—the light bulbs that go on when we raise our consciousness. When someone elevates their way of thinking, through educating themselves and diving deep into self-contemplation, that's just as much a miracle as walking on water."

"Then, the goal of yoga is to raise one's consciousness?" Haley asked.

"Yoga's a never-ending process, so *goal* is not the way to think about it, *but* yoga does work to elevate our conscious awareness, so we come to know the commonality of humanity," Sean said. "That's how the planet can eventually be unified, and we can ultimately experience one big love fest."

There was applause.

"Unification and love fest," Haley said, looking into the camera.

"Please stay with us. When we return, we'll discuss United Souls with Ren Devlin and Sean Carson."

The *On Air* light went dark.

"This is the kind of inspiration we need right now," Haley said to us. Then, a production assistant walked up to her, and she shifted her attention away.

"You seem relaxed," I said, turning to Sean, "and so eloquent."

"I meant what I said. I've experienced some big shifts in my life. Yoga has come alive for me, especially in the last few weeks. This stuff really works," he smiled. "And buddy, I feel so good being up here with you and knowing we're in this together."

"Yes, we are," I said, giving his knee a squeeze.

"And as far as your dream goes," he said, "this is *so* different. It was definitely not a premonition."

"Having the council in the front row also adds to the difference," I said.

"What? Where?" Sean turned toward the audience.

As I pointed to the front row, Pluto stood and walked toward the black metal stairs. I watched him pass behind a massive speaker at the corner of the stage. When he emerged on the other side, he was *HER*, once again dressed in a full-length black robe and veil. The comfort I felt from her presence, rather than angst, assured me our leap last night had successfully transformed my fear into love.

"Do you see her?" I asked Sean, pointing to the dark goddess at the bottom of the stage stairs.

"I don't see—"

"She's right—"

The *On Air* light once again illuminated.

"Welcome back," Haley said to the camera, then turned to me.

"Ren, on Saturday, after your great-nephew and his friend reanimated the dog, you made some inspiring comments about United Souls and the ever-present power of love coming from the feminine that will pull humanity together. How do you see that happening?"

"By letting our individual love be unconditional," I said. "By spreading goodwill, by seeing beyond differences and seeing all we have in common. There's a slow but steady increase of mystical revolutionaries in the world, all doing the work of love by refusing to succumb to the fear we're constantly fed."

Haley nodded.

"Remember," I said, "there's *always* struggle with growth, and we have to travel the dark night of the soul to find the comfort and ecstasy of the sunrise. But United Souls is a tangible possibility because deep inside, we all want to believe in love."

"Ren, we only have a minute left. Do you have final words to inspire us?"

I looked to the dark goddess who was now standing on the top step. I remembered her question to me as we stood at the abyss looking down. I turned in my seat to face the audience directly.

"Ask yourself in times of doubt," I said, "what guides you—fear or love? If you find fear has invaded your heart, transform it by reminding yourself that nothing can kill love because love is eternal—it's where you came from and where you will return. Be part of the mystical revolution, awaken the mystic inside you, choose love, and let love unite US."

"Beautiful," Haley said. "Thank you so much for being with us."

The veiled goddess slowly walked across the stage.

I looked to the front row where the council held Abhaya mudra.

I glanced at Sean and back to the council, who were now slowly nodding. Pluto, as the dark goddess, now stood directly in front of me. I was the only one who could see her. I knew it. Like last night, she removed her widow's veil, but instead of dropping it at my feet, she handed it to me.

Am I now to wear her veil? I wondered.

A man in a black sweatshirt and ski cap jumped up behind Saturn. Our eyes met . . . again.

"I can kill love," he shouted, just as he had through the car window. "I'll kill *your* love."

Sean.

"He has a gun!" several people shouted.

As confusion ensued, an acceptance of the reality of the moment spread out from my heart into every cell of my being as the journey of the kleshas came to its climax.

"Get off the set," echoed from every direction.

It happened in a matter of seconds, yet for me it was all slow motion. I stood, turned, and moved directly in front of Sean. We looked into each other's eyes with a knowing that our connection was more complete than ever. I placed the veil . . . over *Sean's* head. I heard the firework-pop just like in the dream. I felt a deep relaxation—the inner peace I had sought my entire life. My body was propelled forward. I went limp on top of Sean and heard a faint *Thank you.*

Then, the details from the dream unfolded in the same way: I was hovering above Rockefeller Center and then pulled high enough to also see Times Square. I watched as the people stared at the stage we occupied and at the black screen of the jumbotron, where only moments before, the interview with Haley was being broadcast. Everyone stood silently, holding Abhaya mudra.

I was then pulled upward, moving faster and faster, losing sight of the crowd, then losing sight of the Earth and the stars and finding myself in total blackness. Not being able to see anything, I had become an essence of myself, hearing only a hum.

Was this OM the sound of the Universe?

Then, all thought was gone. What was left?

Peace, bliss, euphoria, Ananda, love, kindness, compassion . . . and a comforting blackness.

67

THE COSMIC PLAN—
THROUGH SEAN'S EYES

There was so much chaotic movement and noise surrounding us, yet without hesitation, Ren stood and turned to face me. There was a telepathic exchange between us: everything was happening exactly as it was designed, according to a cosmic plan, decided upon between this life and the last. Then there was the blast, and Ren was propelled forward onto me, his body covering me like a shroud. I lifted him and carefully placed him on the floor of the stage. My actions were reverent, without thought or fear. *She* was guiding me. A quiet descended upon the scene; everything was completely still except me . . . except US.

Instinctively, I knelt along Ren's right side. I placed my right hand on Ren's heart center and my left hand on my own. I felt a stirring of air and a slight sound of electricity.

One by one, then hundreds by hundreds, the threads of light streamed from the crowns of the thousands. The lights were not just coming from the crowd but from the surrounding buildings and beyond. They traveled individually and then met in the Heart Chakra of my fallen lover.

Time had no meaning. The Universe was paused.

Somewhere in my awareness, I heard the soft chant of many . . .

I am not afraid of my life or what is in my heart.

68

. . . a comforting blackness

. . . love, kindness, compassion . . . and a comforting blackness.

Into my euphoria crept an incredible surge of pain. They existed together as bliss was replaced by pain, replaced by *Ananda*, replaced by pain, replaced by Love.

In the silence, I sensed the fluttering of bird wings around me. Then a thought crept in: *Angels*.

I remained in the blackness, experiencing everything and yet the no-thingness of the ultimate void. In that space, I felt the presence of my council. We communicated without words through a sensory awareness in the *Hridaya* of my soul.

The kleshas are complete.

Yes.

The platform was used for love.

Yes.

The feminine is returning through miracles.

Yes.

And now I hear the sound of angel wings. Have they been sent by the Mother to take me back to the source, to the Oneness of All?

I heard the council answer in unison . . .

"*Not yet.*"

. . . one journey ends as another begins.

ACKNOWLEDGMENTS

The initial spark for this story was an unanticipated "inspired vision" I had while driving one Sunday morning on Columbia Parkway. I wrote about the vision for three months before telling anyone. By the time I decided it was a novel, two years later, I had written 220,000 words. I want to thank the Universe for trusting me to write this story, and I'd also like to thank the beautiful souls who encouraged, cajoled, and loved me deeply as this story unfolded.

It was my partner, Steve Bolia, who instantly saw the potential in what I was writing and encouraged me to publish it. I do not exaggerate when I say there would not be a book without him. He was an editor, a cocreator when I needed him, and the most vocal and excited cheerleader helping me through any self-doubt. The intimacy we continue to share working together on every stage of this creative project is life changing and will forever be part of my soul. My deepest gratitude and love to you—Steve. Forever and Always.

I give a deep bow of love and gratitude to Carol Sherman-Jones, who, for three years, came over for once-a-month, mini-retreat sleepovers, during which I read "stories" to her and Steve long into the night. Your child-like, Gemini enthusiasm was just what I needed at times to keep moving forward.

I extend heartfelt thank-yous to all my teachers who materialized exactly when I needed you. A special hand-to-heart to Linda Goodman, who taught me much about astrology but also the difference between a teacher and a guru. Alan Oken, thank you for being an influential, strong male energy, exquisitely infused with the feminine. And deep, deep heart chakra appreciation to Sally Kempton, who, from my first flash of inspiration, continually encouraged me to tell this story. I keep your words—"How gorgeous. I suspect it will be guided every step of the way. Saraswati seems to flow"—on my desk and etched in my heart.

To my friends who listened, read, guided, encouraged, and loved: Eileen and Mark Bolia, Stephanie Vietor, Bobbi Carson, Mary Ann Meyer, Kathie Morbitzer, Michele Mascari, Leslie Korbee, Bonnie Mill, David Orr, Sheila Williams, Meredith Hogan, and Tanner Hines—thank you so much.

To Greg Seibert, Lisa and Don Busam, David Wilson, Cindy Sellars, Dave and Connie Dorgan, Mark and Debbie Schmidt, Quincy Bissic, Fernando Martinez, Heather Schmidt, John Crow—your friendship over all the decades of my life is a heart treasure.

Prayer hands to third eye to all the students in our Tuesday night yoga class, who have been showing up on their mats for the past twenty years, and to all our students from classes and retreats, who encouraged and patiently awaited the birth of this story.

A special namaste to Kate Noble, for providing the opportunities and encouragement to expand myself through teaching. I am forever grateful.

In gratitude to all the real goddesses in my life: my mom, Dottie; Bobbie Corbean; Alice Loving . . . and Saraswati, who is as real to me as anyone I know.

I give a special love nudge of appreciation to the three furies of editing:

To Carrie Herzner, for her gentle look at the story and her early encouragement.

To Dr. Alexandra Rego, who dropped out of the sky via my reconnect with her parents. Thank you.

To Erin Brown, whose professionalism, kindness, and constant encouragement will never be forgotten. I knew the moment I met you that you were meant to be a midwife for this story.

To everyone at Greenleaf who helped with the birth of the book, thank you for understanding the uniqueness of this story and my concerns with retrogrades, void-of-course Moon, and numerology.

Thank you, thank you to Kayla Spelling, our web designer, social media advisor, and friend. for all her patience with us and sharing her expertise, and Michaela Ruebel, for her loving guidance in areas way beyond us, in the IT world of SEO and beyond. We are grateful the Universe brought you both into our lives.

Steve and I are surrounded by an incredibly strong circle of love that sustains us on so many levels—that includes those of you who faithfully follow our "Two-Minute Tuesday" meditations on social media and the astrology students and clients who trust us with your heart and souls—thank you all, and may you have hope and happiness—always.

GLOSSARY

Abhaya mudra: The "gesture of fearlessness" is a *mudra* gesture using the hands that represents reassurance and safety, which dispels fear and accords divine protection and bliss in many Indian religions. The right hand is held upright, the palm is facing outward, and the left hand is placed on the heart center This is one of the earliest mudras found depicted in a number of Hindu, Buddhist, Jain, and Sikh images.

Abhyāsa: The Sanskrit word meaning "practice" and refers to a practice that aims at achieving a tranquil state of mind.

Ajna chakra: Ajna, the brow or third eye chakra, is the sixth primary chakra in the body according to Hindu tradition. It is a part of the brain that can be made more powerful through meditation, yoga, and other spiritual practices.

Ananda: Sanskrit word for "joy" or "bliss."

Asana: Sanskrit word originally meaning "a sitting posture." Today, it refers to all postures in Hatha Yoga.

Bhakti: Sanskrit word often translated to mean "devotion." It is a spiritual path focused on loving devotion and cultivating unconditional love. Bhakti Yoga is one of the three classical paths leading to spiritual liberation.

Bija sounds: "Seed Sounds" that essentially vibrate at the frequency of each of the seven chakras. From the 1st to the 6th chakra, they are Lam, Vam, Ram, Yam, Ham, and Om. The 7th chakra bija is Silence.

Chakra: The chakras are organizational centers that receive, assimilate, store, and transmit life force energy at each of their respective levels: earth, water, fire, air, sound, light, and thought. Together, the seven chakras provide a profound formula for wholeness, one that bridges mind, body, and spirit.

Charnel grounds: An above-ground site for the putrefaction of bodies, generally human, where formerly living tissue is left to decompose uncovered.

Chinnamasta: The headless Dark Goddess of Transformation. She demands that we look for the sacred in the forbidden and terrifying. Her name means "head (chinna) cut off."

Chonyid Bardo: The second after-death state described in *The Tibetan Book of the Dead*. It corresponds to feelings of intense tranquility and perfect knowledge.

Dharana: The sixth limb or level of the eight-step yoga practice set down by Patanjali. In Sanskrit, it means a state of mental concentration on an object without wavering.

Dhyana: The seventh limb or level of the eight-step yoga practice set down by Patanjali. In Sanskrit, it means absorption into meditation, implying a state of abiding calm.

Durga: See Shakti.

Ereshkigal: Sumerian Queen of Death and the Underworld. Her name translates as "Queen of the Great Below." Her male counterpart in modern mythology is Pluto.

Everything I can do, you can do also: Reference to a quote attributed to Jesus Christ in John 14:12 of the New Testament.

Ganesh: A God in the Hindu pantheon, readily identified by his elephant head. He is widely revered as the remover of obstacles and the lord of beginnings.

Gayatri mantra: A Sanskrit prayer and a mantra found in the *Rig Veda*. The Gayatri mantra comprises twenty-four syllables organized inside a triplet of eight syllables. *Gayatri* also means "she who protects the singer" (from *gai*—"to sing," and *trai*—"to protect"). Gayatri is also a name for the Divine Mother—she who protects her children and leads them toward self-realization. Esoterically, it is said to awaken the subtle body to give knowledge of Oneness—that of the individual with the supreme.

Hridaya: "Spiritual Heart." It translates from its root words as *hri*, which means "to give," *da*, which means "to take," and *ya* from *yam*, which means "balance." *Hridaya* is "that which gives and takes in perfect balance." In the same way, as the physical heart does this with blood flow, *Hridaya* is the center for giving and taking on a spiritual level and is therefore associated with the heart center.

Kaivalya: Refers to the ultimate liberation from the cycle of rebirth. It is the ultimate freedom.

Kali: Fierce Goddess of Transformation.

Karma: The law of cause and effect: for every action, there is a reaction. In the theory of reincarnation, the sum of a person's actions in this and previous states of existence decides their fate in future existences.

Kleshas: Enumerated in Patanjali's Yoga Sutras as the five mental states that cloud the mind and cause suffering. 1) *Avidya*—Ignorance; 2) *Asmita*—Ego; 3) *Raga*—Attachment; 4) *Dvesha*—Aversion; and 5) *Adhinivesha*—Fear of Death.

Lakshmi: Most commonly known as the goddess of good fortune, wealth, and boons. She is more than wealth. Lakshmi provides the inner essence for cultivating and experiencing a good life.

Mahadevi: The supreme force that creates, preserves, and destroys the Universe. She is the highest intelligence, referred to as *Brahma-vidya*. *Mahadevi* is the soul of the Universe and the Universe itself. She is the source of wealth, knowledge, forgiveness, peace, faith, fortitude, fame, modesty, and mercy.

Maha Mrityunjaya: A mantra that bestows longevity, wards off calamities, and prevents untimely death. It also removes fears and heals holistically. It is a verse from the Rig Veda and is considered to be the most powerful Shiva mantra. Known as the great death-conquering mantra, it is used to focus on health and happiness and to help facilitate a peaceful death. It helps to overcome obstacles and is a healing force that dives deep into the body and mind.

Mantra: Translates to "tool of the mind." A word, a series of words or sounds, repeated to aid concentration in meditation.

Maya: Conceals the true character of spiritual reality. It is known as the veil of illusion. It is said to be that which blinds us from knowing our true Self and presenting the illusion of separation between all things.

Moira: A Greek concept of fate or destiny represented in mythology by the goddesses *Klotho (Clotho)*, the spinner; *Lkhesis (Lachesis)*, the apportioner; *Atropos,* the cutter.

Muladhara: The first or Root Chakra said to be housed in the perineum of the body. It is known as the root and basis of existence. *Mula* means "root," and *adhara* means "basis." It is symbolized by a lotus with four petals and the color pink or red.

Mysticism: The experience of mystical union or direct communion with an ultimate reality reported by mystics. It is the belief that direct knowledge of God, spiritual truth, or ultimate reality can be attained through subjective experience, such as intuition or insight.

Namaste: Sanskrit word meaning "the divine light within me recognizes the divine light within you." It is a salutation recognizing the divine spark in each being.

Neptune: The eighth planet in our Solar System. In astrology, it represents mysticism, dreams, imagination, and all things spiritual. It is also said to represent unconditional love, that gives for the sake of giving. In astrology, Neptune represents yoga and, therefore, is aligned with the yoga concept of "Oneness."

Neti: Sanskrit word meaning "not me," "not this," or "not that." As a meditation, Neti negates every identification of the mind until we return to our true essence.

Nine: In numerology, 9 relates to wisdom and responsibility. The ultimate goal of the number 9 is to serve humanity. The vibration of 9 has come to serve the world through selflessness and compassion and make it a better place for all to live.

OM: Technically pronounced AUM. It is thought to be the primordial sound of the Universe, a mystical Sanskrit syllable considered the most sacred mantra in Hinduism and Tibetan Buddhism. It appears at the beginning and end of most Sanskrit recitations, prayers, and texts.

The Four Stages of Consciousness found in OM: There are three main states of consciousness that you reliably cycle through every twenty-four hours: *waking state, dreamless sleep,* and *dream state.* Each of these states is characterized by a distinctive electrical brain activity. Long before we could study brain waves, yogis knew about these states. They postulated that all states of consciousness are reflected in the symbol and sound of *aum.* The three letters A-U-M are then followed by silence. The fourth state is found in silence and is called *Turiya,* which means fourth. This fourth state is the absence of thought. This is *Pure Consciousness* itself, which we learn to experience through meditation.

Pada Three: Book three of Patanjali's Yoga Sutras. It elaborates on the *Siddhis,* or super abilities a Yogi may attain through consistent practice. (Padas is the plural of Pada.)

Parama Suksma: The process of moving into the highest yet most subtle form of your practice.

Parvati: See Shakti.

Pluto: The ninth planet in our solar system. In astrology, Pluto represents transformation, regeneration, and rebirth. Pluto asks us to transcend that which we know, redeem ourselves in the process, and come out stronger as a result.

Prana: Sanskrit word for "breath," "life force," or "vital principle." It permeates reality on all levels, including inanimate objects.

Pranam: Sanskrit word meaning "bowing forward" or prostrating in front of something or someone out of reverence.

Pranayama: The fourth limb or level of the eight-step yoga practice set down by Patanjali. It is the art of mastering or controlling the timing, duration, and frequency of the vital breath. The focus of *Pranayama* is to connect your body and mind.

Pratyayasya paracitta jnanam: Sutra 19 from Pada Three. This describes the ability to enter other people's consciousness. It is a gift (siddhi) that a yogi can attain through intense practice.

Sadhana: Sanskrit word meaning "methodical discipline or practice to attain desired knowledge or goal." Everything and anything can be a *Sadhana*, i.e., the way you eat, walk, stand, or the way you live your life—use everything as a tool to enhance your well-being. Pada Two of Patanjali's Yoga Sutras outlines spiritual practices to bring you closer to god.

Sahasrara: The final of the seven chakras, located at the top of the head. It is also called the *Crown Chakra* or the "Thousand Petaled Lotus." It creates a strong connection with the supreme Self. The awakening of the Crown Chakra allows a universal flow of energy and spiritual enlightenment to enter the body. It is represented by pure white or violet light.

Samadhi: The eighth limb or level of the eight-step yoga practice set down by Patanjali. It is a state of intense concentration achieved through meditation (*Dharana* and *Dhyana*). In yoga, this is regarded as the final stage, at which union with the divine is reached.

Samskaras: Sanskrit word meaning *sam* (complete or joined together) and *kara* (action, cause, or doing). According to yogic philosophy, we're born with a karmic inheritance of mental and emotional patterns, known as *samskaras*, through which we cycle over and over again during our lives. Through our spiritual practices, we are given the opportunity to clear out samskaras with each lifetime.

Samyama: It is the combined simultaneous practice of *Dharana* (concentration), *Dhyana* (meditation), and *Samadhi* (union) that brings together all the parts of the human being.

Saraswati: The Hindu Goddess of Creativity through Language, Speech, and Sound; Wisdom and Inspiration.

Saturn: The sixth planet in our Solar System. In astrology, Saturn is the

"Ruler" of the sun sign Capricorn. It is considered to be the ultimate father in the zodiac and rules discipline, hard work, responsibility, maturity, time, and Karma.

Saturn Return: In Astrology, Saturn takes twenty-eight to thirty years to travel once around an individual's horoscope. A person can have up to three Saturn Returns in one lifetime. Upon its first return to the place it was at the moment of your birth, it is considered to be the first "adult" transit. It is a time of major events and challenges in one's life. These events can include—getting a new job, getting married/divorced, having your first child . . . anything that can and will shape your life for the next twenty-eight to thirty years when it once again comes back to the place it was at the moment of your birth. Each Return signals major life shifts.

Shakti: She is the personification of creative and sustaining energy, as well as destructive energy. She is the divine cosmic energy that represents the feminine and creation. She is the compliment to Shiva's masculinity. She can take many forms and is also referred to as The Mother Goddess and the Dark Goddess, Parvati, Durga, and Kali. She is energy, ability, strength, effort, power, and capability.

Shiva: The primal Atman (soul, self) of the Universe. In Hinduism, he is one of three gods—Brahma, the creator god; Vishnu, the sustainer; and Shiva, the destroyer. Shiva is known to have untamed passion, which leads him to extremes in behavior. Sometimes, he is an ascetic, abstaining from all worldly pleasures. At others, he is a hedonist. His powers of destruction and recreation are used to destroy the illusions and imperfections of this world, paving the way for beneficial change. His destruction is not arbitrary but constructive. Shiva is one who combines many contradictory elements.

Siddhis: Specific to this book—this term pertains to the spiritual or seemingly supernatural accomplishments attained by a yogic practitioner described in Pada Three of *The Yoga Sutras of Patanjali*.

Sthitau: Steadfastness or stability. The pursuit of an equanimity or balance of self that can always remain with you.

Sushumna Nadi: *Nadis* are energy pathways found throughout the body. The *Sushumna Nadi*, meaning "very gracious," is the main energy pathway that corresponds to the spinal cord. Running from the Root to the Crown Chakra, it's the path of the kundalini when it is released through spiritual practice.

Sutra: Sanskrit word meaning "string or thread." *The Yoga Sutras of Patanjali* are a collection of ancient Indian texts discussing the aims and practice of yoga. They are a practical guide for a spiritual journey of remembering who you really are.

Swaha: Sanskrit word meaning "so be it." It is often said to mark the end of a mantra and urges god to accept whatever you are offering.

Synchronicity: The simultaneous occurrence of events that appear significantly related but have no discernible causal connection.

Tantra: A yogic philosophy that enumerates practices in which the student engages the life force (*kundalini*) for the purpose of self-realization. This tantric path emphasizes enjoying the fruits of your everyday life without attachment. Everyday life is seen as a spiritual path unto itself.

Transits: In the context of this book, this refers to the mathematical relationships (Conjunctions, Squares, Sextiles, Trines, and Oppositions) made by the current position of "the planets" (Sun, Moon, Mercury, Venus, Mars, Jupiter, Saturn, Uranus, Neptune, and Pluto), to the position of "the planets" in a person's Natal Chart. Their continual movement creates energy within the chart on a daily/weekly/monthly basis.

Trident: A three-pronged spear usually associated with Poseidon or Neptune. It signifies the domination of the seas in mythologies. Each prong represents one of the three Gunas (Tamas-earthy/grounded, Rajas-fiery/movement, and Sattva-balance/brightness).

Vandana: Meaning "worship, reverence, adoration, or praise." In this practice, the student lightly touches the feet or the ground in front of a deity or teacher out of respect.

Vedas: The most ancient Hindu scriptures, written in early Sanskrit and containing hymns, philosophy, and guidance on ritual for the priests of Vedic religion. Believed to have been directly revealed to seers among the early Aryans in India and preserved by oral tradition, the four chief collections are the Rig Veda, Sama Veda, Yajur Veda, and Atharva Veda.

Veritas vos Liberabit: Latin, meaning "the truth will set you free."

Vibhuti Pada: The third Pada (or book) of *The Yoga Sutras of Patanjali*. It means negating and transcending earth-based consciousness. It is here that Patanjali further explains the meaning of *Dharana* (concentration), *Dhyana* (meditation), and *Samadhi* (supreme bliss). He also enumerates the *siddhis* a practitioner may attain through steady, focused discipline.

QUESTIONS AND TOPICS FOR DISCUSSION

1. From the beginning of the novel, Ren is seeking inner peace. What does inner peace look like for him? Does Ren find inner peace by the end of the novel? What would inner peace look like for you?

2. How do Ren and Sean each transform from the beginning of the novel to the end? Are there similarities in their individual transformations?

3. How does the practical nature of the phrase "Everything I can do, you can do also" complement or contrast with the concept of Mystical Revolutionaries?

4. Ren, a dedicated student of yoga, who follows the path outlined in Patanjali's Yoga Sutras, is taken on a journey by his astrological council through the kleshas—the five mental afflictions responsible for pain and suffering, which block the path to inner peace. In chapter 10, "Return of the Council," Ren is told that through study and diligent meditation practice, he has already faced the first of the kleshas: *Avidya* or ignorance. The journey through the remaining four kleshas forms three arcs in the book.

- In arc one, chapters 15–36, Ren is challenged by the second klesha: *Asmita*, or ego, which comes at him like a freight train. How does the expression of ego in chapter 17, "Wake Up," when he ends up on stage with the band, differ from the ego that almost has him succumb to the invitation of the Catholic Church?

- In arc two, chapters 37–56, Ren and Sean both face the kleshas of *Raga* (attachment) and *Dvesha* (aversion). What attachments and aversions did Ren face in his travel back in time through the meditation coma? What does Sean learn about himself through this same experience?

- In arc three, chapters 57–68, Ren and Sean face the last klesha: *Abhinivesha*, or the fear of death. How did Ren's experience with the intruder Gabe in the yoga studio prepare him for what was to come?

5. There is a feminist theme that runs throughout the novel. Who makes up the "legion of the feminine" throughout the book? What do these women teach Ren about love? How do Dottie and Athena impact Ren's journey? Are there similarities between these two characters? Lisa, Ren's former girlfriend and wife in the reverse time travel, says in chapter 47, "I'm not channeling the goddesses, I am one." In chapter 49, Lisa tells Ren to "Watch out . . . They're all in here," and then lightly pounds her chest with a closed fist. "Venus, Athena, Saraswati, Durga, and even a little Kali," she clarifies. Is Lisa speaking figuratively or literally?

6. There are brief descriptions throughout the novel of what each planetary council member represents as an archetype.

Sun = Will; Moon = Emotions; Mercury = Communication

Venus = Love/Personal Magnetism; Mars = Personal Drive

Jupiter = Expansion/Higher Learning; Saturn = Consolidation/Manifesting

Uranus = Intuition/Higher Mind; Neptune =
Illumination/Higher Love

Pluto = Transformation/Regeneration

7. Ren had Saturn and Venus as co-chairs. Who might be Sean's chairperson(s)? Which of these would be the chairperson(s) of your council?

8. Free will is mentioned seven times: several times by the council and by Ren and Sean during the last interview in New York. Do you see the effects of free will in the story, or is it fate?

9. Were you surprised that Harry and Gigi raised the dog from the dead in the cul-de-sac? How did that event add to the theme of "Everything I can do, you can do also"?

10. Because the Yoga Sutras describe everything Ren does throughout the novel as real and attainable with enough diligent spiritual practice, does that eliminate any magical realism from the story?

11. Were you surprised by the ending? How might the final scene relate back to the last line of the author's note: *Stay open to possibilities*?

ABOUT THE AUTHOR

ROB DORGAN has an MA in European History from the University of Cincinnati. He began writing fiction at the age of seven with his first short story, "Murder at the La Brea Tar Pits," followed by "Murder at the Art Museum." Since second grade, his interests and content have changed, but his love for telling a good story has remained.

While working on his doctorate, the trajectory of Dorgan's life path was drastically altered when he was introduced to the mystical arts of astrology and yoga. He left academia and, along with his partner, Steve Bolia, moved to Colorado to study and work with Linda Goodman, the author of *Linda Goodman's Sun Signs, Love Signs, Star Signs,* and *Gooberz*. He then spent many years mentoring with master astrologer and teacher of the Ancient Wisdom, Alan Oken.

Dorgan began studying yoga in the 1980s when most people in the West thought it was a cult. He studied with many yoga teachers, including Sianna Sherman, John Friend, and the preeminent Sally Kempton, in meditation.

Yoga, along with astrology, changed his life. While Dorgan's debut, *Awakening the Mystic*, is fiction, it is full of real possibilities for the future of our human species and Mother Earth.

Dorgan is a certified yoga educator, international retreat facilitator, meditation teacher/devotee, and practicing astrologer. He is currently working on a sequel to *Awakening the Mystic*, along with a memoir about his time as Linda Goodman's personal assistant and a collection of short stories based on his unique childhood with his mom, Dottie.

Dorgan welcomes the opportunity for live chats with reading groups about *Awakening the Mystic*. He is also available to speak on the benefits of yoga and meditation, as well as teach group and corporate classes. He also offers one-on-one meditation and astrology counseling sessions, which focus on using those tools to better understand and love yourself and to uncover your inner council, for a fuller life.

Visit www.awakeningthemystic.net for more information.

www.ingramcontent.com/pod-product-compliance
Lightning Source LLC
Chambersburg PA
CBHW020523110726
47899CB00004B/1223